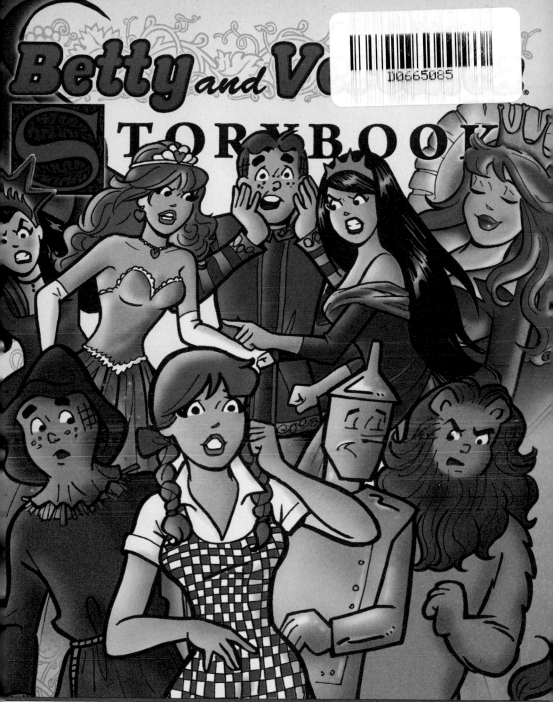

STORY ADAPTATIONS & PENCILS BY DAN PARENT

INKING BY RICH KOSLOWSKI & JIM AMASH
ETTERING BY JACK MORELLI, JANICE CHIANG & TERESA DAVIDSON
COLORING BY BARRY GROSSMAN & DIGIKORE STUDIOS

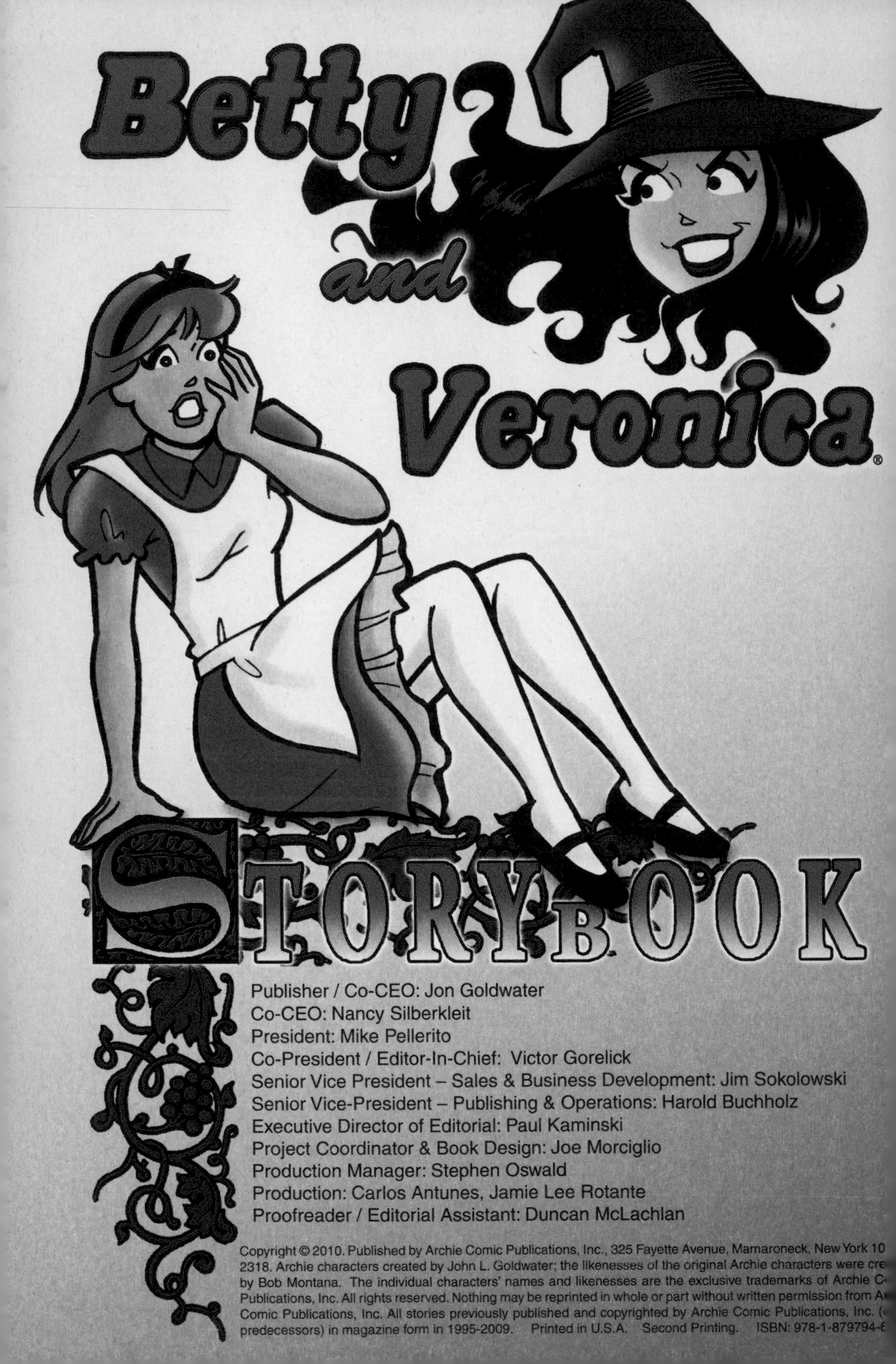

Betty and Veronica® Storybook

Publisher / Co-CEO: Jon Goldwater
Co-CEO: Nancy Silberkleit
President: Mike Pellerito
Co-President / Editor-In-Chief: Victor Gorelick
Senior Vice President – Sales & Business Development: Jim Sokolowski
Senior Vice-President – Publishing & Operations: Harold Buchholz
Executive Director of Editorial: Paul Kaminski
Project Coordinator & Book Design: Joe Morciglio
Production Manager: Stephen Oswald
Production: Carlos Antunes, Jamie Lee Rotante
Proofreader / Editorial Assistant: Duncan McLachlan

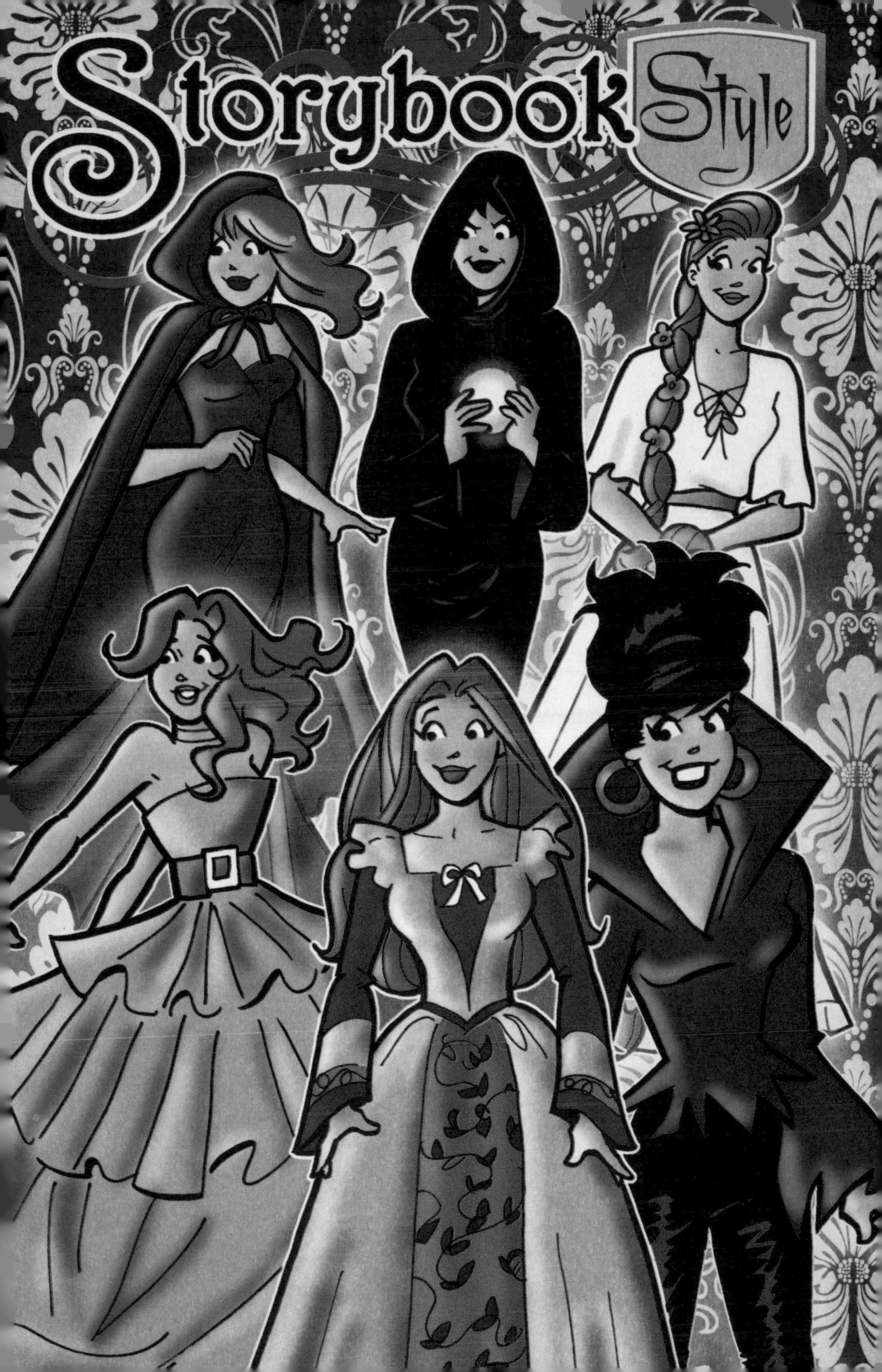
Storybook Style

Betty in Wonderland

In 1865, English author Lewis Carroll wrote the novel "Alice's Adventures in Wonderland." It tells the story of a girl named Alice who falls down a rabbit hole into the fantasy world known as "Wonderland." This world is populated by strange creatures. The story's nonsense logic has kept it popular with adults and children for many years.

Riverdale meets Wonderland when Betty goes through the looking glass! In this modern twist on a classic fairy tale, everyone's favorite girl-next-door, Betty, takes on the role of Alice. While chasing after the ever-late Archie, Betty lands in a strange and remarkable place known as Wonderland. The adventure unfolds as Betty encounters some interesting and rather familiar characters, including a bookish worm, Tweedle-Dee and Tweedle-Dum and a Cheshire…dog? With the help of some "special" products from Pop Tate's, Betty must find her way home, and away from the menacing yet beautiful Queen of Hearts, Veronica! It's an adventure Betty won't soon forget!

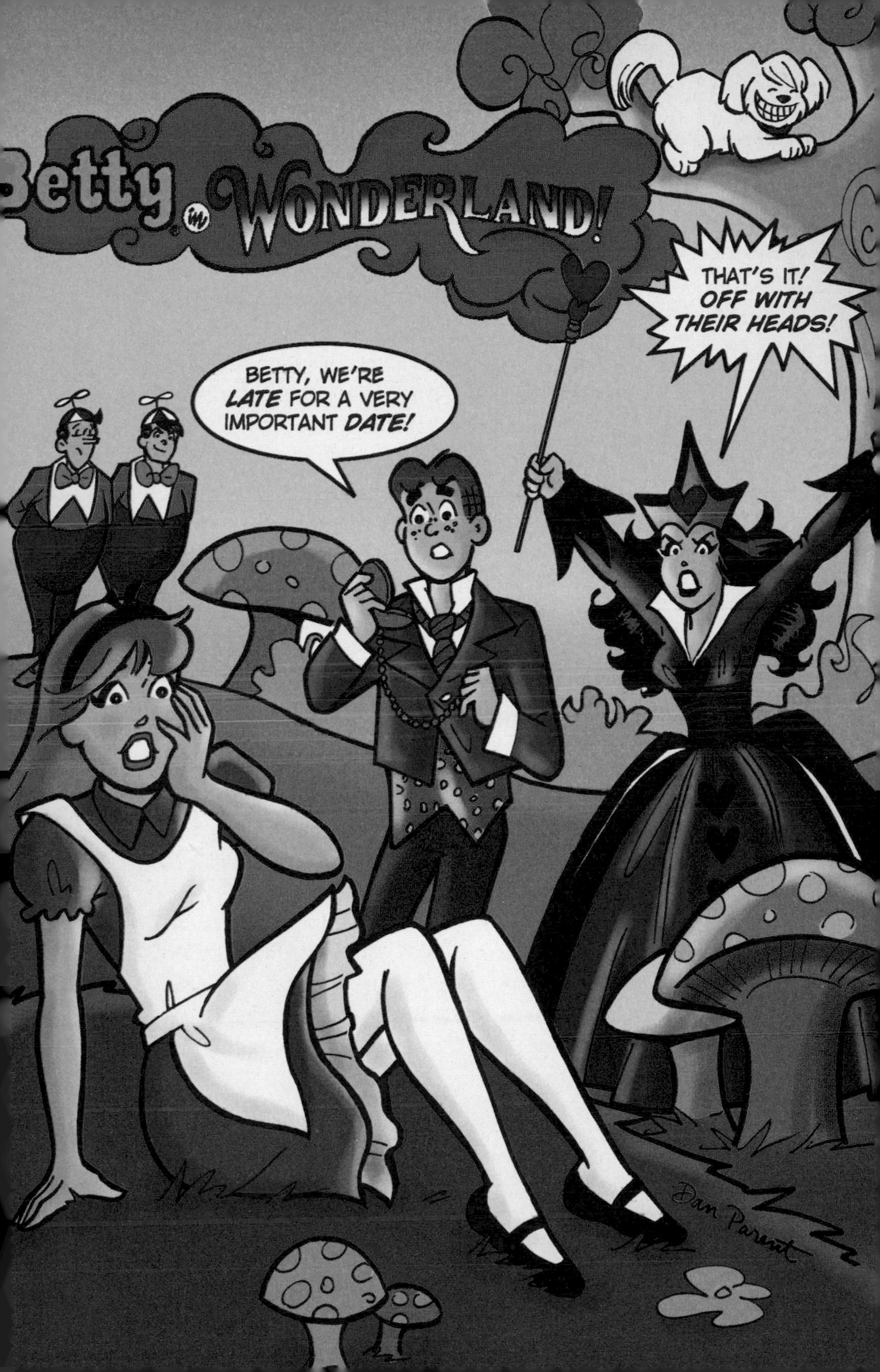
Betty in WONDERLAND!
BETTY, WE'RE LATE FOR A VERY IMPORTANT DATE!
THAT'S IT! OFF WITH THEIR HEADS!
Dan Parent

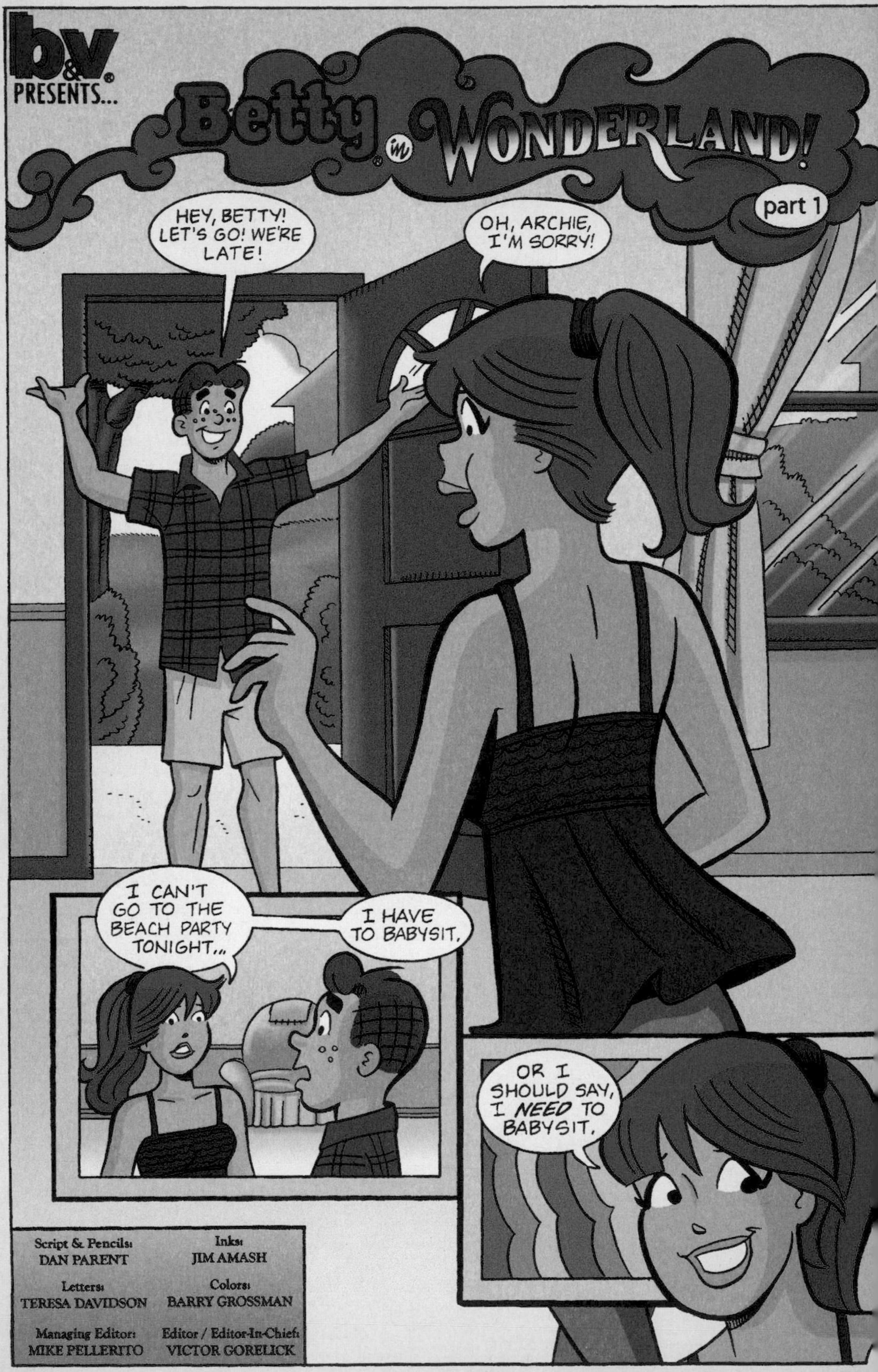

b&v PRESENTS...
Betty in WONDERLAND!
part 1
HEY, BETTY! LET'S GO! WE'RE LATE!
OH, ARCHIE, I'M SORRY!
I CAN'T GO TO THE BEACH PARTY TONIGHT...
I HAVE TO BABYSIT.
OR I SHOULD SAY, I NEED TO BABYSIT.
Script & Pencils: DAN PARENT
Inks: JIM AMASH
Letters: TERESA DAVIDSON
Colors: BARRY GROSSMAN
Managing Editor: MIKE PELLERITO
Editor / Editor-In-Chief: VICTOR GORELICK

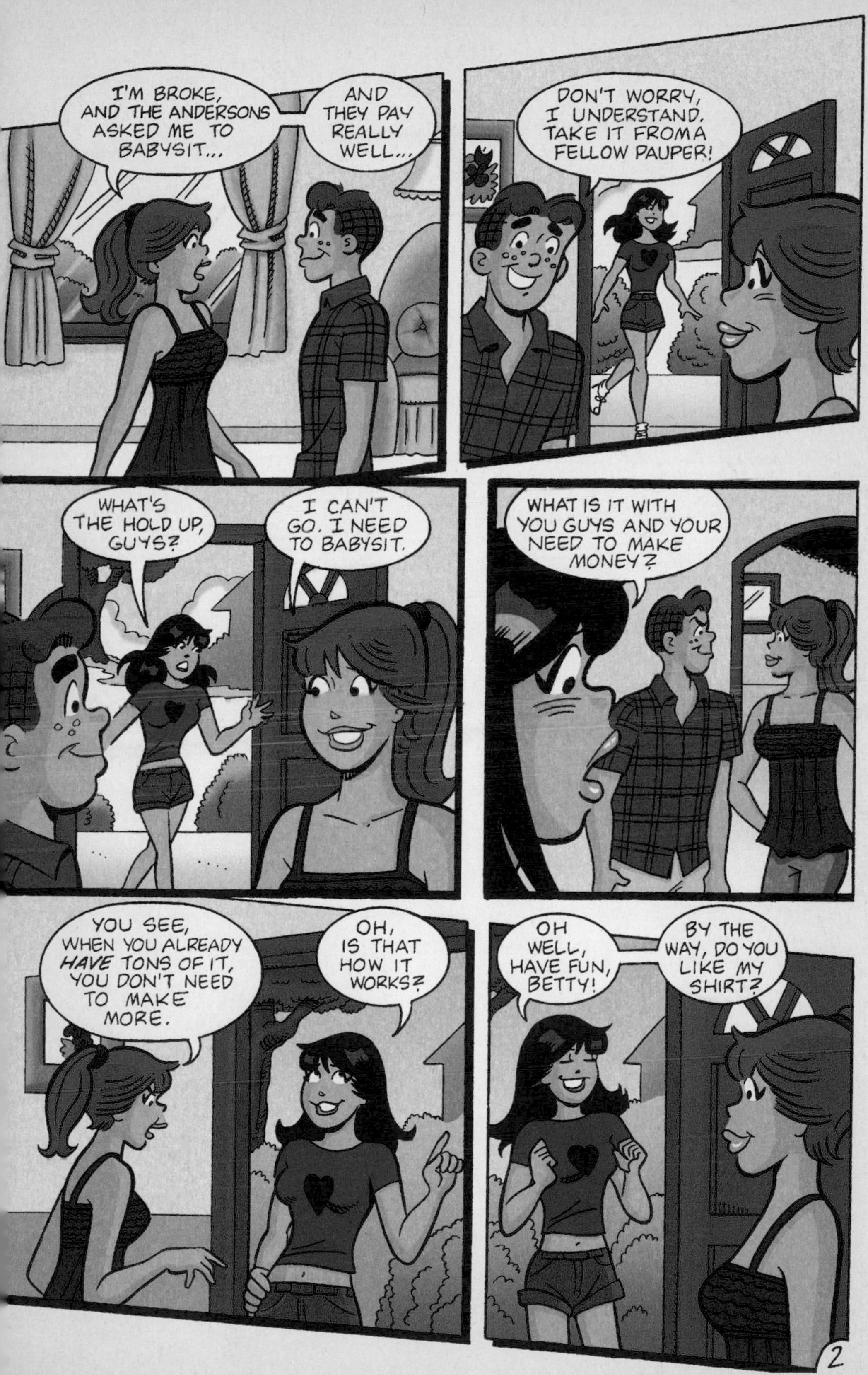
I'M BROKE, AND THE ANDERSONS ASKED ME TO BABYSIT...
AND THEY PAY REALLY WELL...
DON'T WORRY, I UNDERSTAND. TAKE IT FROM A FELLOW PAUPER!
WHAT'S THE HOLD UP, GUYS?
I CAN'T GO. I NEED TO BABYSIT.
WHAT IS IT WITH YOU GUYS AND YOUR NEED TO MAKE MONEY?
YOU SEE, WHEN YOU ALREADY *HAVE* TONS OF IT, YOU DON'T NEED TO MAKE MORE.
OH, IS THAT HOW IT WORKS?
OH WELL, HAVE FUN, BETTY!
BY THE WAY, DO YOU LIKE MY SHIRT?

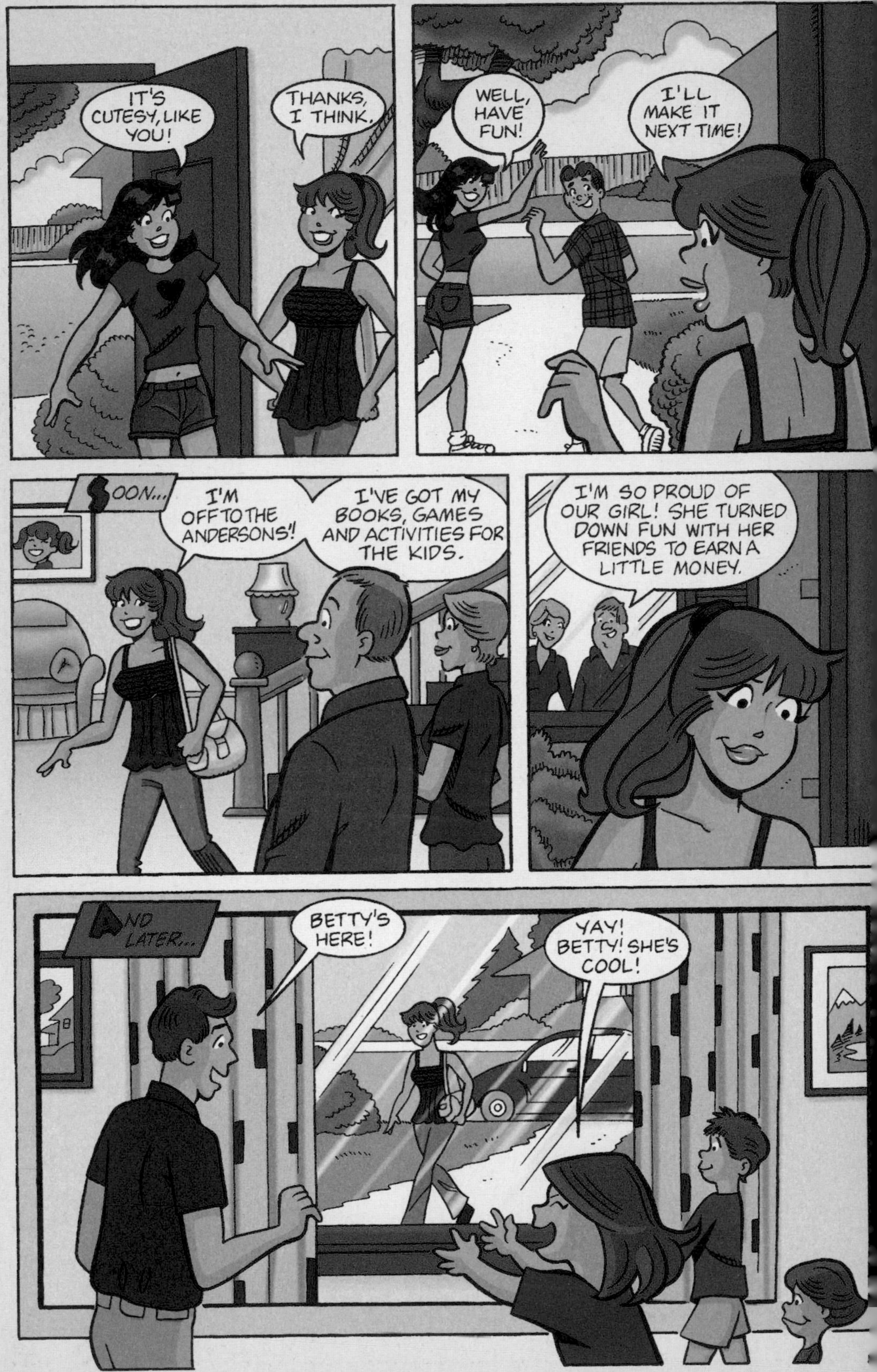
IT'S CUTESY, LIKE YOU!
THANKS, I THINK.
WELL, HAVE FUN!
I'LL MAKE IT NEXT TIME!
SOON...
I'M OFF TO THE ANDERSONS'!
I'VE GOT MY BOOKS, GAMES AND ACTIVITIES FOR THE KIDS.
I'M SO PROUD OF OUR GIRL! SHE TURNED DOWN FUN WITH HER FRIENDS TO EARN A LITTLE MONEY.
AND LATER...
BETTY'S HERE!
YAY! BETTY! SHE'S COOL!

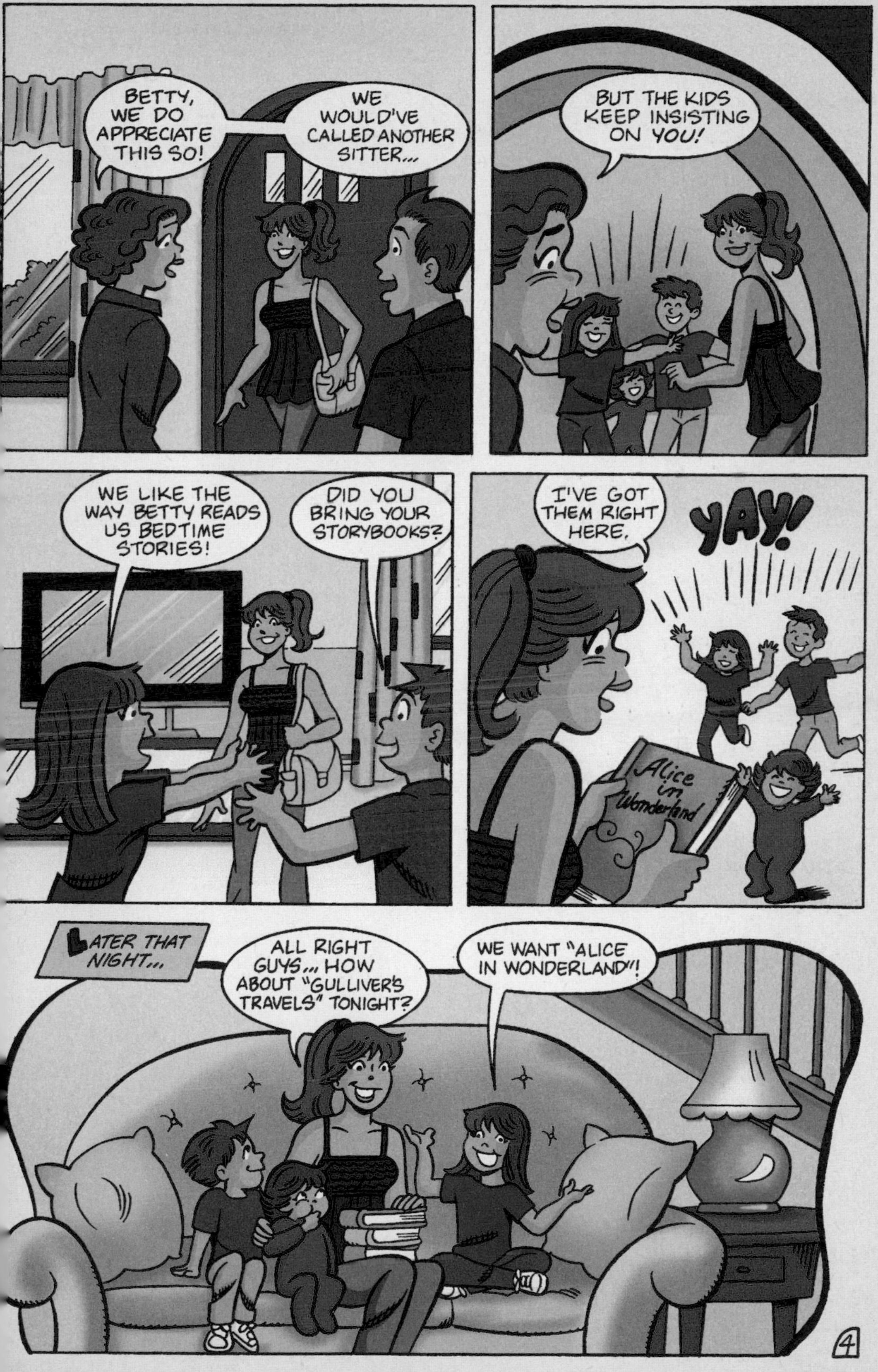
BETTY, WE DO APPRECIATE THIS SO!
WE WOULD'VE CALLED ANOTHER SITTER...
BUT THE KIDS KEEP INSISTING ON YOU!
WE LIKE THE WAY BETTY READS US BEDTIME STORIES!
DID YOU BRING YOUR STORYBOOKS?
I'VE GOT THEM RIGHT HERE.
YAY!
Alice in Wonderland
LATER THAT NIGHT...
ALL RIGHT GUYS... HOW ABOUT "GULLIVER'S TRAVELS" TONIGHT?
WE WANT "ALICE IN WONDERLAND"!
4

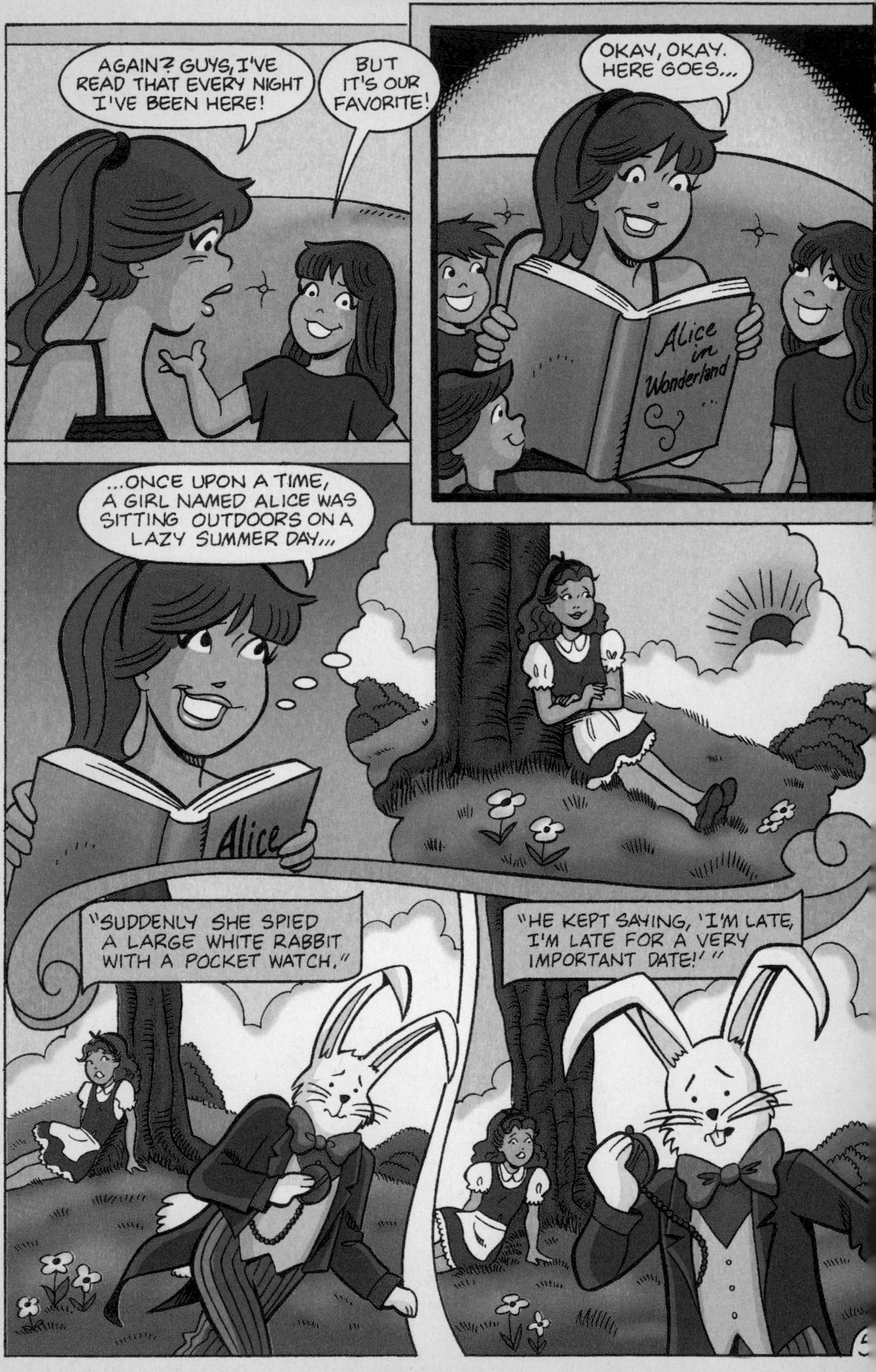
AGAIN? GUYS, I'VE READ THAT EVERY NIGHT I'VE BEEN HERE!
BUT IT'S OUR FAVORITE!
OKAY, OKAY. HERE GOES...
Alice in Wonderland
...ONCE UPON A TIME, A GIRL NAMED ALICE WAS SITTING OUTDOORS ON A LAZY SUMMER DAY...
Alice
"SUDDENLY SHE SPIED A LARGE WHITE RABBIT WITH A POCKET WATCH."
"HE KEPT SAYING, 'I'M LATE, I'M LATE FOR A VERY IMPORTANT DATE!'"

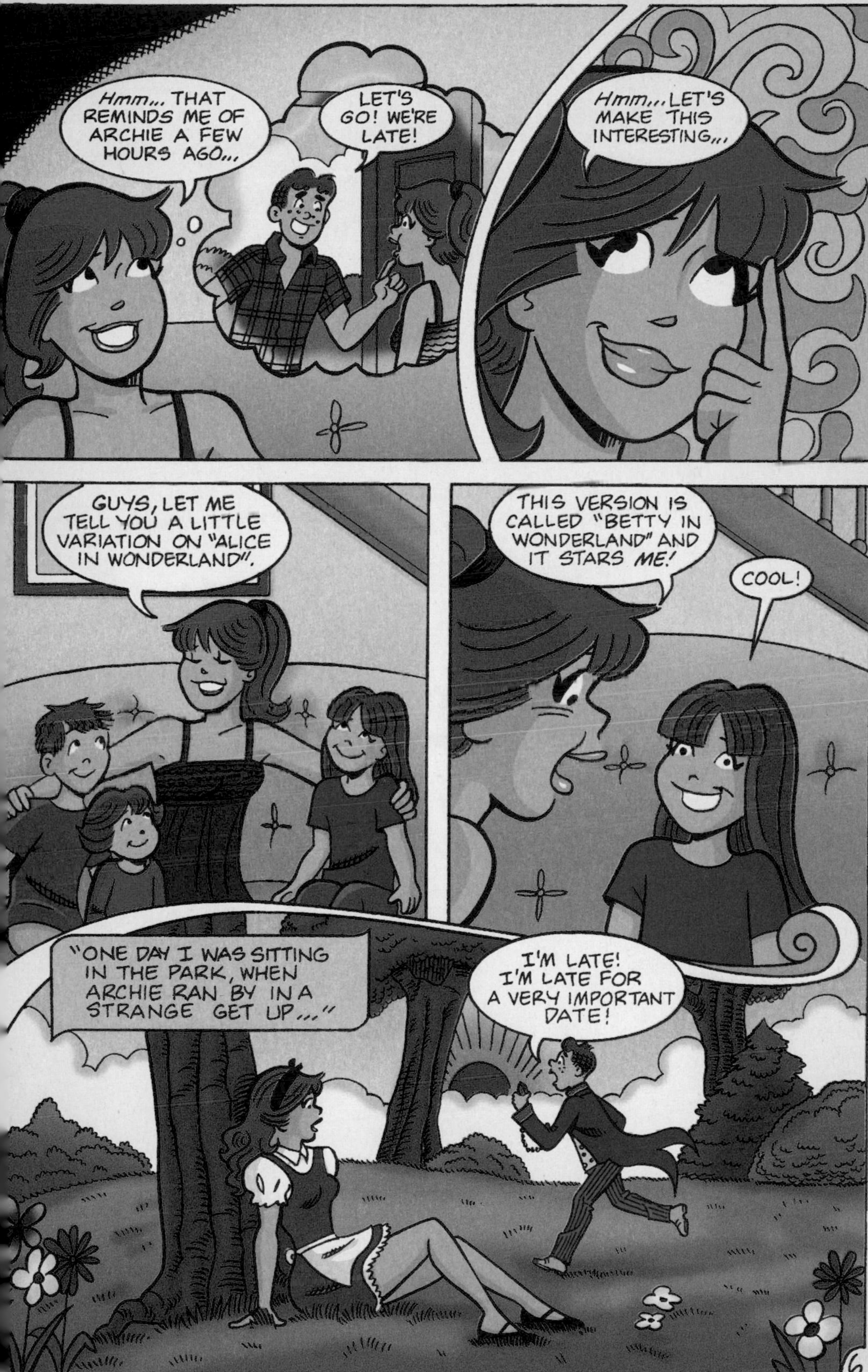
Hmm... THAT REMINDS ME OF ARCHIE A FEW HOURS AGO...
LET'S GO! WE'RE LATE!
Hmm... LET'S MAKE THIS INTERESTING...
GUYS, LET ME TELL YOU A LITTLE VARIATION ON "ALICE IN WONDERLAND".
THIS VERSION IS CALLED "BETTY IN WONDERLAND" AND IT STARS ME!
COOL!
"ONE DAY I WAS SITTING IN THE PARK, WHEN ARCHIE RAN BY IN A STRANGE GET UP..."
I'M LATE! I'M LATE FOR A VERY IMPORTANT DATE!

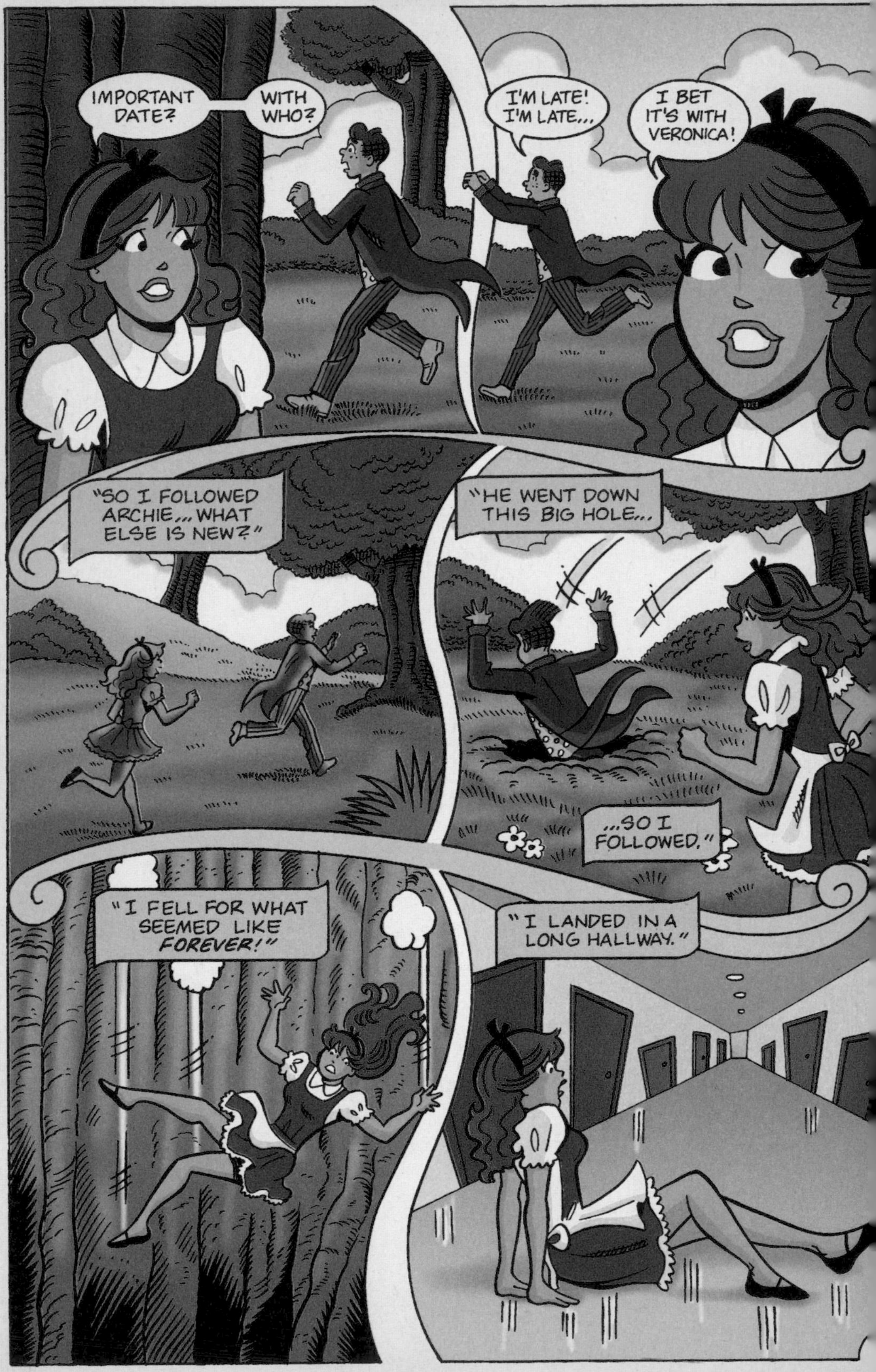
IMPORTANT DATE?
WITH WHO?
I'M LATE! I'M LATE...
I BET IT'S WITH VERONICA!
"SO I FOLLOWED ARCHIE... WHAT ELSE IS NEW?"
"HE WENT DOWN THIS BIG HOLE...
...SO I FOLLOWED."
"I FELL FOR WHAT SEEMED LIKE FOREVER!"
"I LANDED IN A LONG HALLWAY."

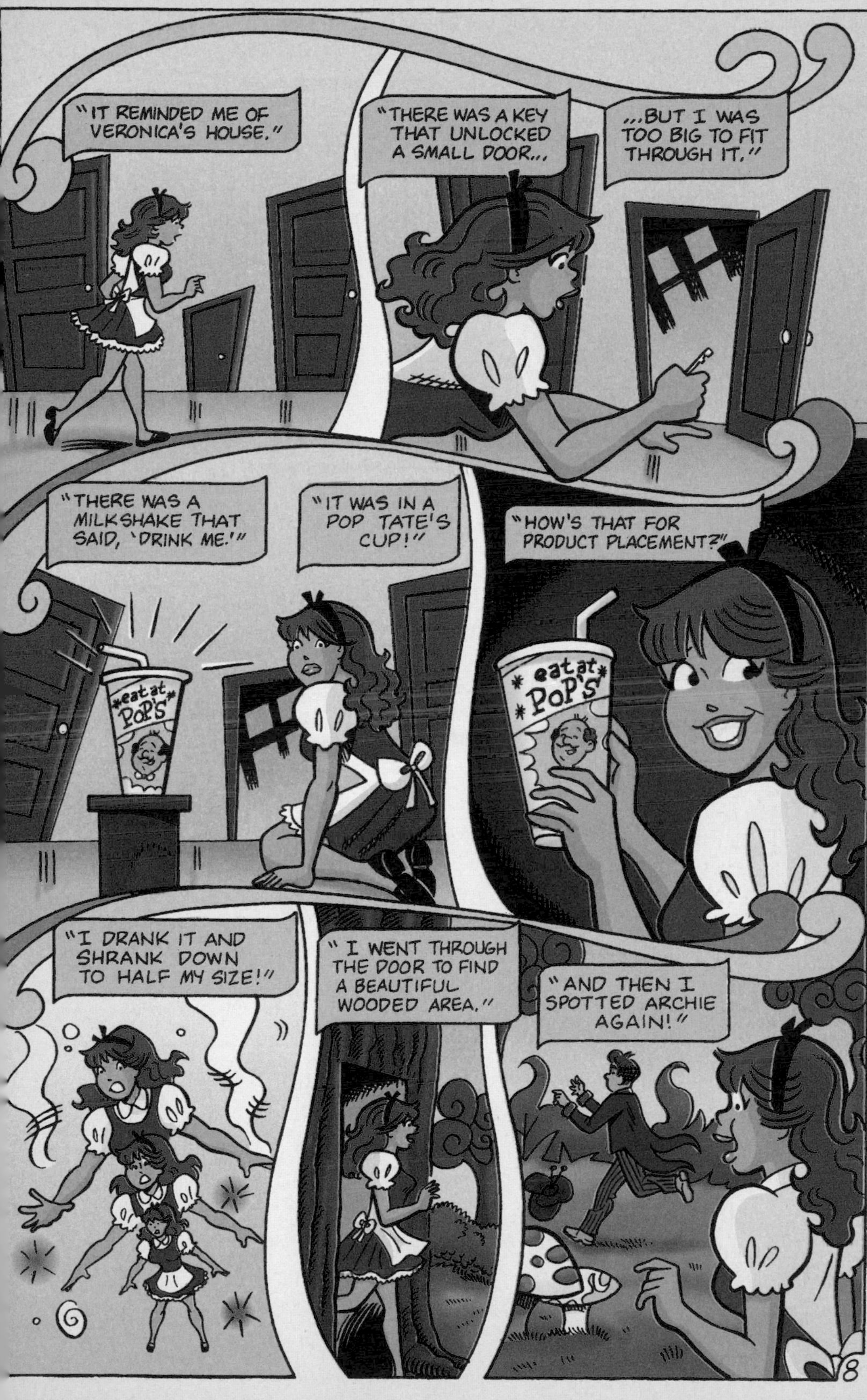
"IT REMINDED ME OF VERONICA'S HOUSE."
"THERE WAS A KEY THAT UNLOCKED A SMALL DOOR...
...BUT I WAS TOO BIG TO FIT THROUGH IT."
"THERE WAS A MILKSHAKE THAT SAID, 'DRINK ME.'"
"IT WAS IN A POP TATE'S CUP!"
eat at POP'S
"HOW'S THAT FOR PRODUCT PLACEMENT?"
eat at POP'S
"I DRANK IT AND SHRANK DOWN TO HALF MY SIZE!"
"I WENT THROUGH THE DOOR TO FIND A BEAUTIFUL WOODED AREA."
"AND THEN I SPOTTED ARCHIE AGAIN!"

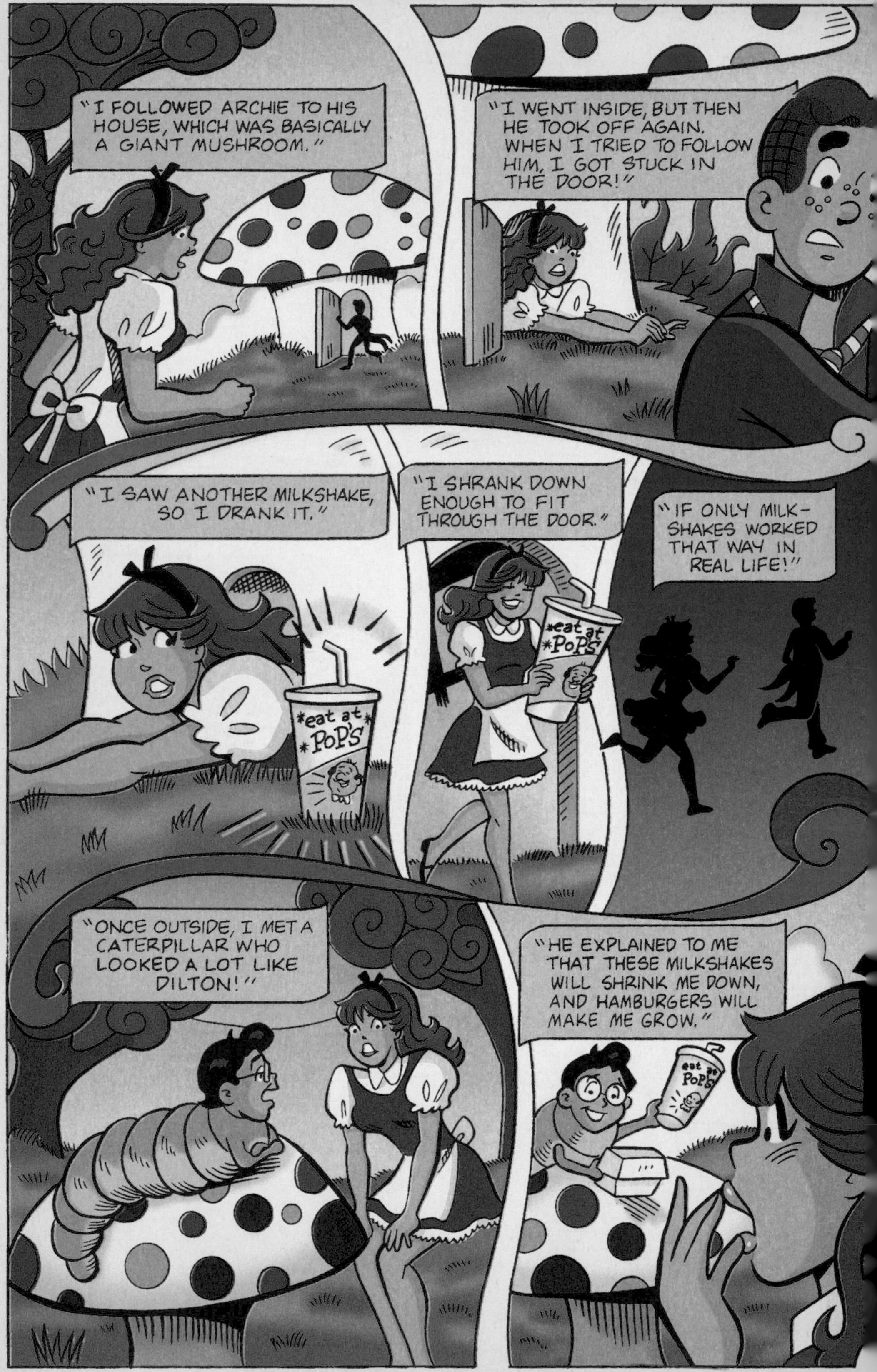
"I FOLLOWED ARCHIE TO HIS HOUSE, WHICH WAS BASICALLY A GIANT MUSHROOM."
"I WENT INSIDE, BUT THEN HE TOOK OFF AGAIN. WHEN I TRIED TO FOLLOW HIM, I GOT STUCK IN THE DOOR!"
"I SAW ANOTHER MILKSHAKE, SO I DRANK IT."
eat at POP'S
"I SHRANK DOWN ENOUGH TO FIT THROUGH THE DOOR."
eat at POP'S
"IF ONLY MILK-SHAKES WORKED THAT WAY IN REAL LIFE!"
"ONCE OUTSIDE, I MET A CATERPILLAR WHO LOOKED A LOT LIKE DILTON!"
"HE EXPLAINED TO ME THAT THESE MILKSHAKES WILL SHRINK ME DOWN, AND HAMBURGERS WILL MAKE ME GROW."
eat at POP'S

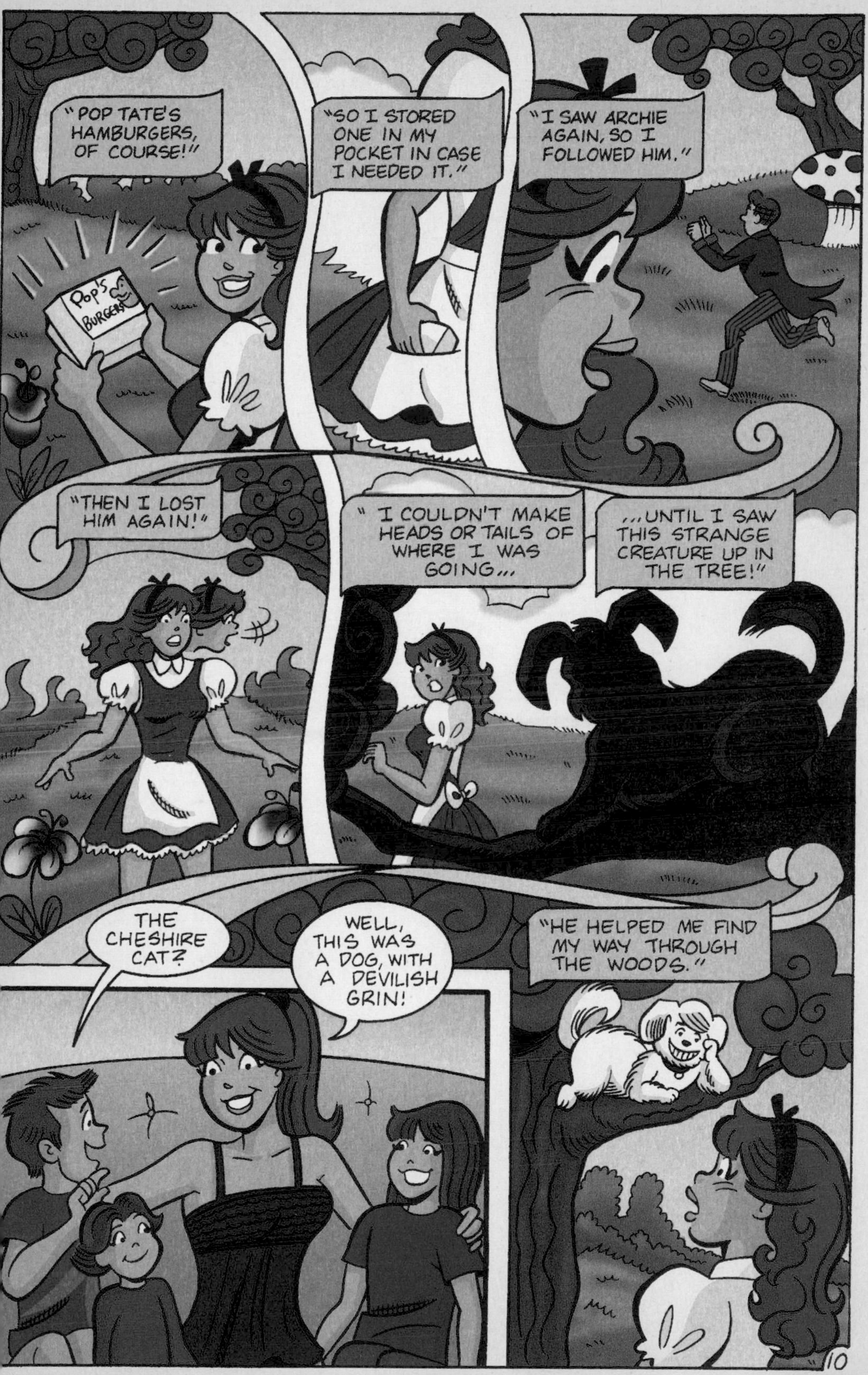
"POP TATE'S HAMBURGERS, OF COURSE!"
POP'S BURGERS
"SO I STORED ONE IN MY POCKET IN CASE I NEEDED IT."
"I SAW ARCHIE AGAIN, SO I FOLLOWED HIM."
"THEN I LOST HIM AGAIN!"
" I COULDN'T MAKE HEADS OR TAILS OF WHERE I WAS GOING...
...UNTIL I SAW THIS STRANGE CREATURE UP IN THE TREE!"
THE CHESHIRE CAT?
WELL, THIS WAS A DOG, WITH A DEVILISH GRIN!
"HE HELPED ME FIND MY WAY THROUGH THE WOODS."

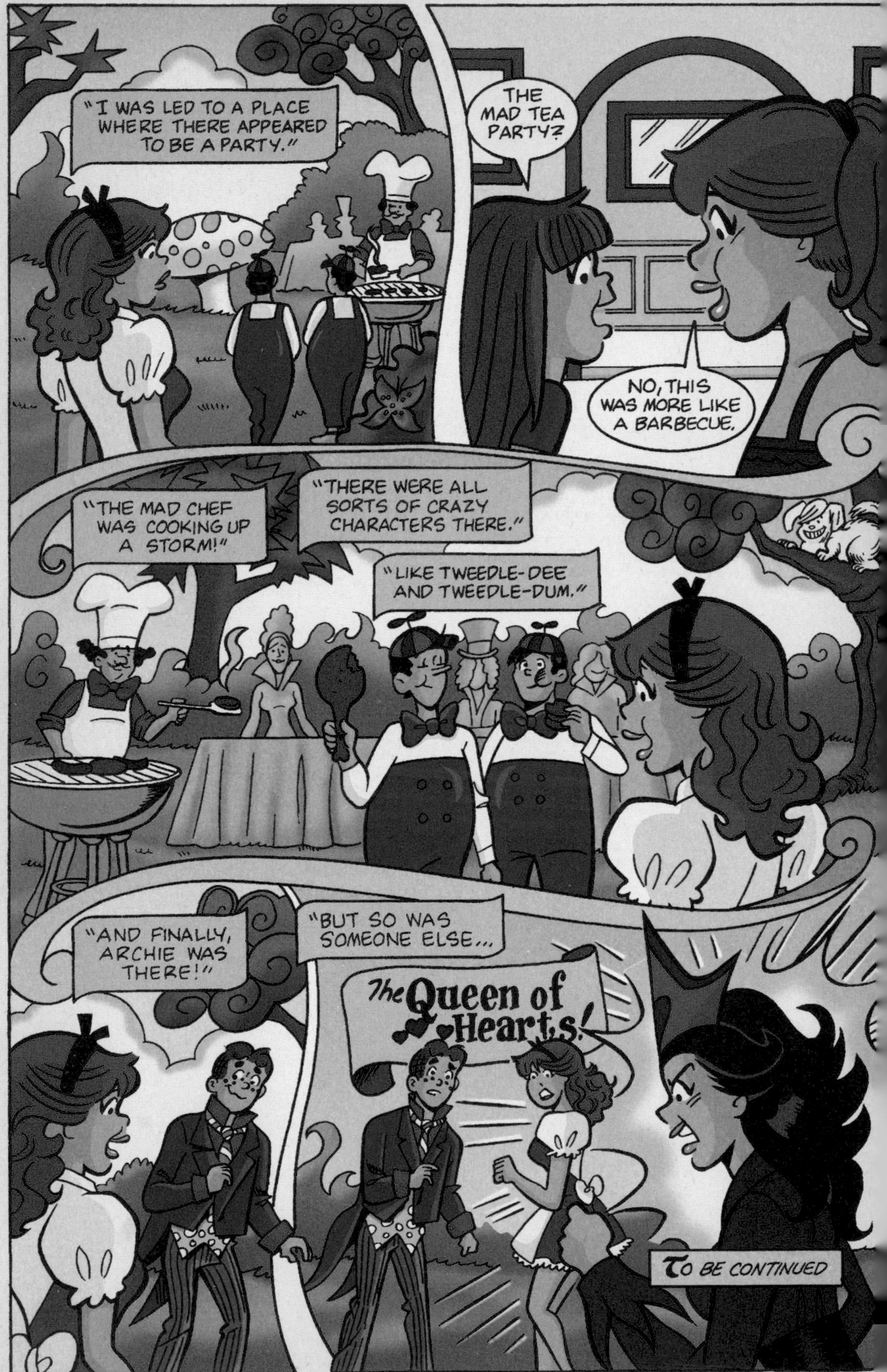
"I WAS LED TO A PLACE WHERE THERE APPEARED TO BE A PARTY."
THE MAD TEA PARTY?
NO, THIS WAS MORE LIKE A BARBECUE.
"THE MAD CHEF WAS COOKING UP A STORM!"
"THERE WERE ALL SORTS OF CRAZY CHARACTERS THERE."
"LIKE TWEEDLE-DEE AND TWEEDLE-DUM."
"AND FINALLY, ARCHIE WAS THERE!"
"BUT SO WAS SOMEONE ELSE...
The Queen of Hearts!
TO BE CONTINUED

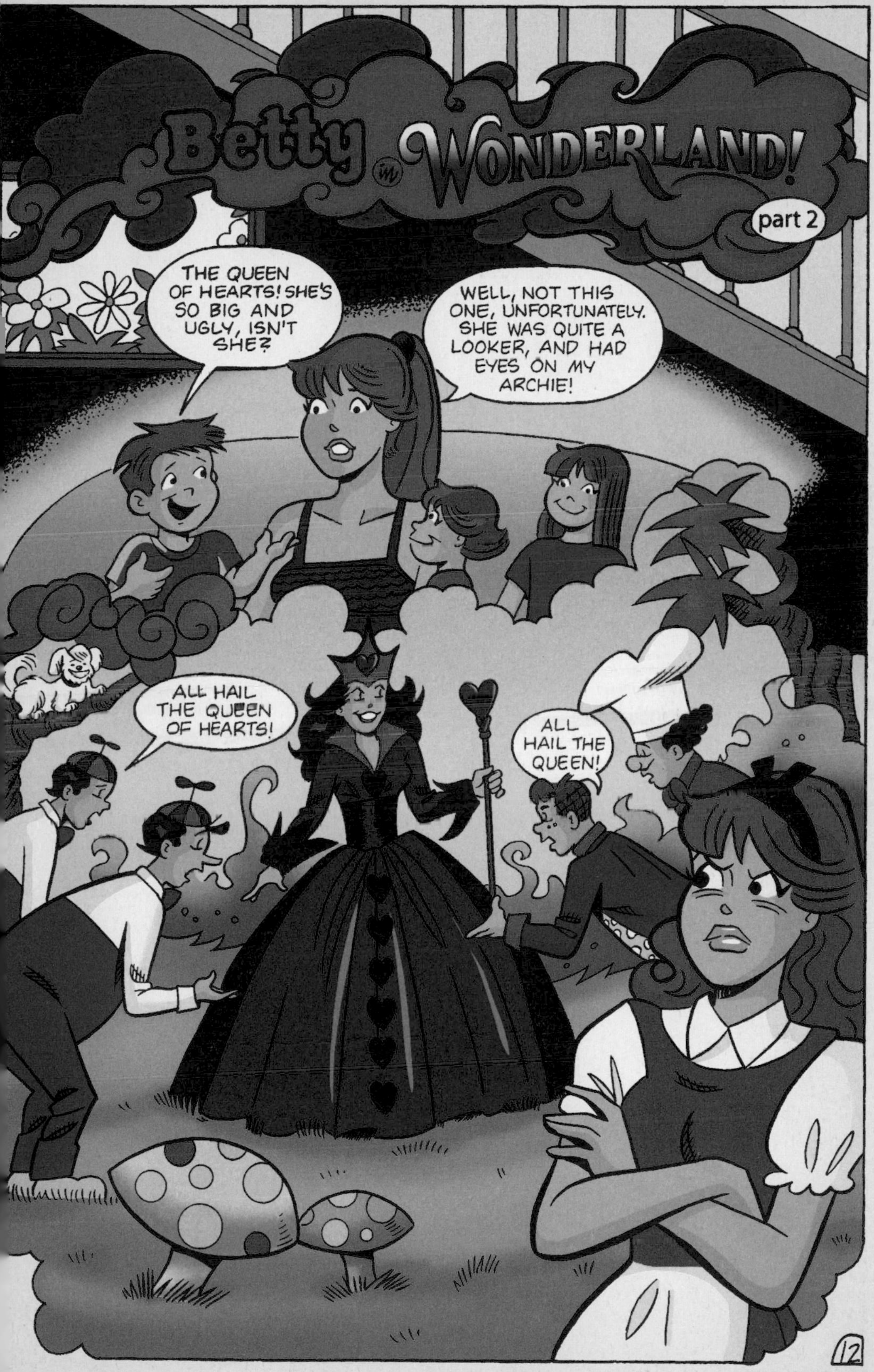
Betty in WONDERLAND!
part 2
THE QUEEN OF HEARTS! SHE'S SO BIG AND UGLY, ISN'T SHE?
WELL, NOT THIS ONE, UNFORTUNATELY. SHE WAS QUITE A LOOKER, AND HAD EYES ON MY ARCHIE!
ALL HAIL THE QUEEN OF HEARTS!
ALL HAIL THE QUEEN!

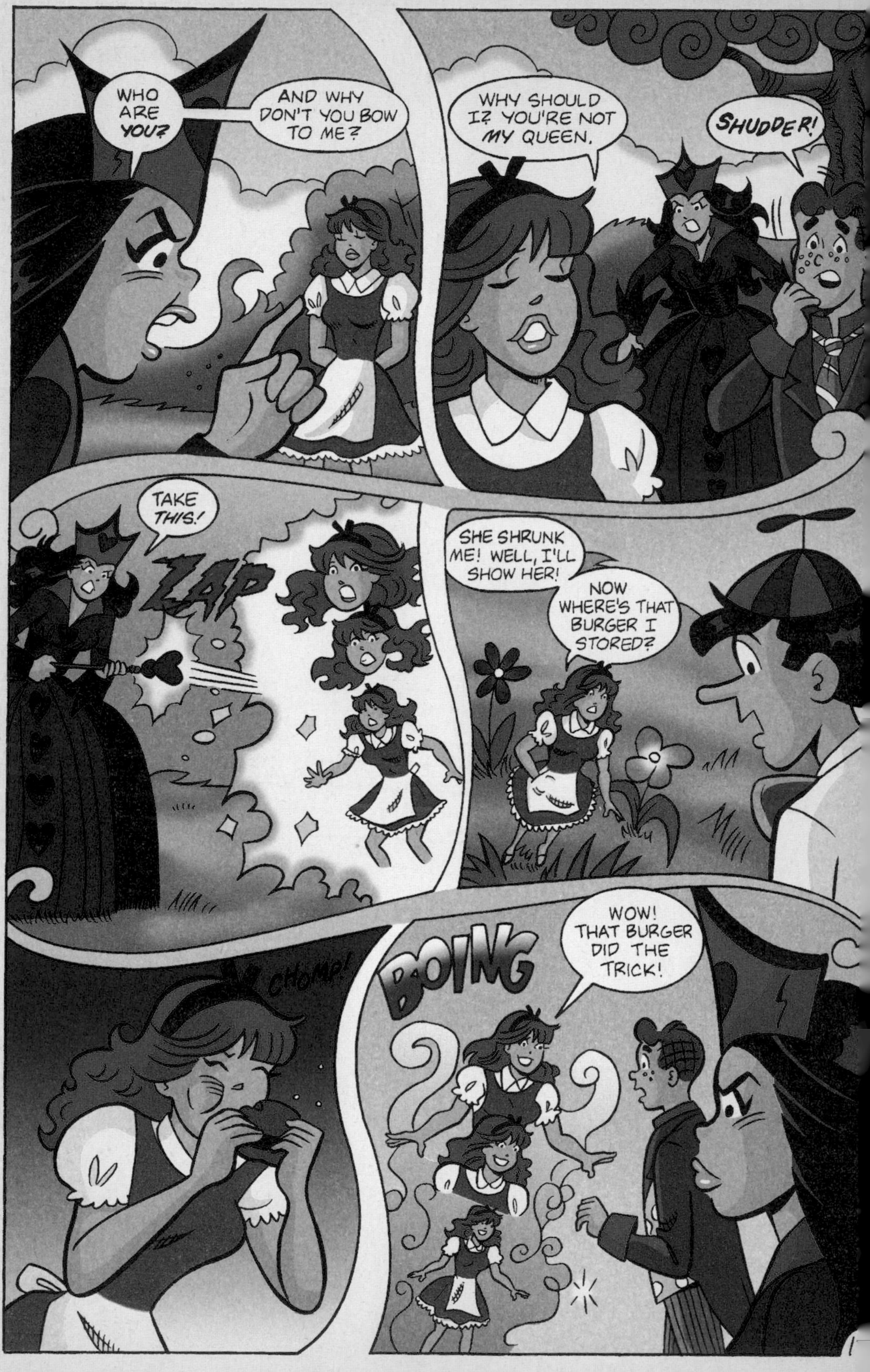
WHO ARE YOU?
AND WHY DON'T YOU BOW TO ME?
WHY SHOULD I? YOU'RE NOT MY QUEEN.
SHUDDER!
TAKE THIS!
ZAP
SHE SHRUNK ME! WELL, I'LL SHOW HER!
NOW WHERE'S THAT BURGER I STORED?
CHOMP!
BOING
WOW! THAT BURGER DID THE TRICK!

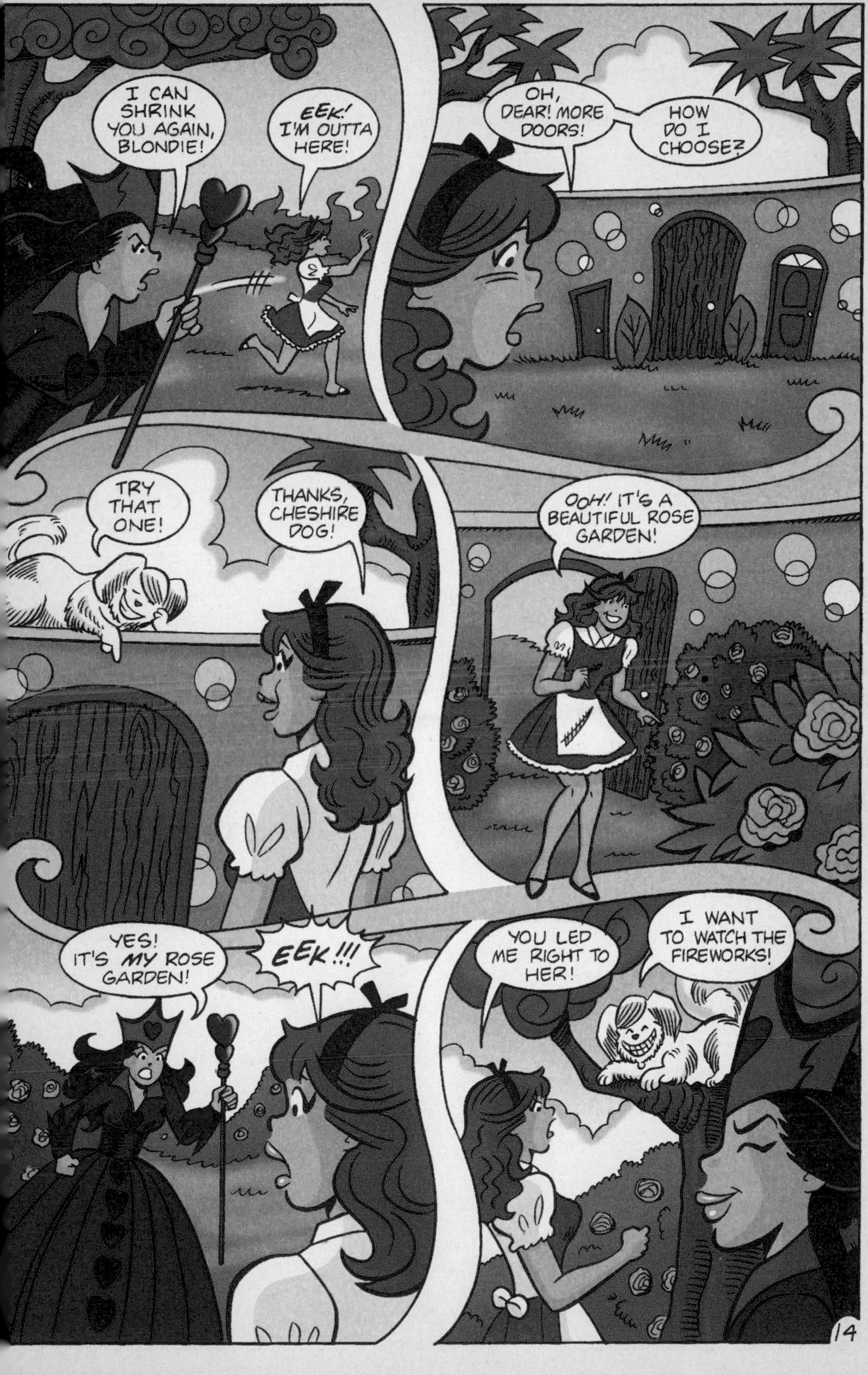
I CAN SHRINK YOU AGAIN, BLONDIE!
EEK! I'M OUTTA HERE!
OH, DEAR! MORE DOORS!
HOW DO I CHOOSE?
TRY THAT ONE!
THANKS, CHESHIRE DOG!
OOH! IT'S A BEAUTIFUL ROSE GARDEN!
YES! IT'S MY ROSE GARDEN!
EEK!!!
YOU LED ME RIGHT TO HER!
I WANT TO WATCH THE FIREWORKS!

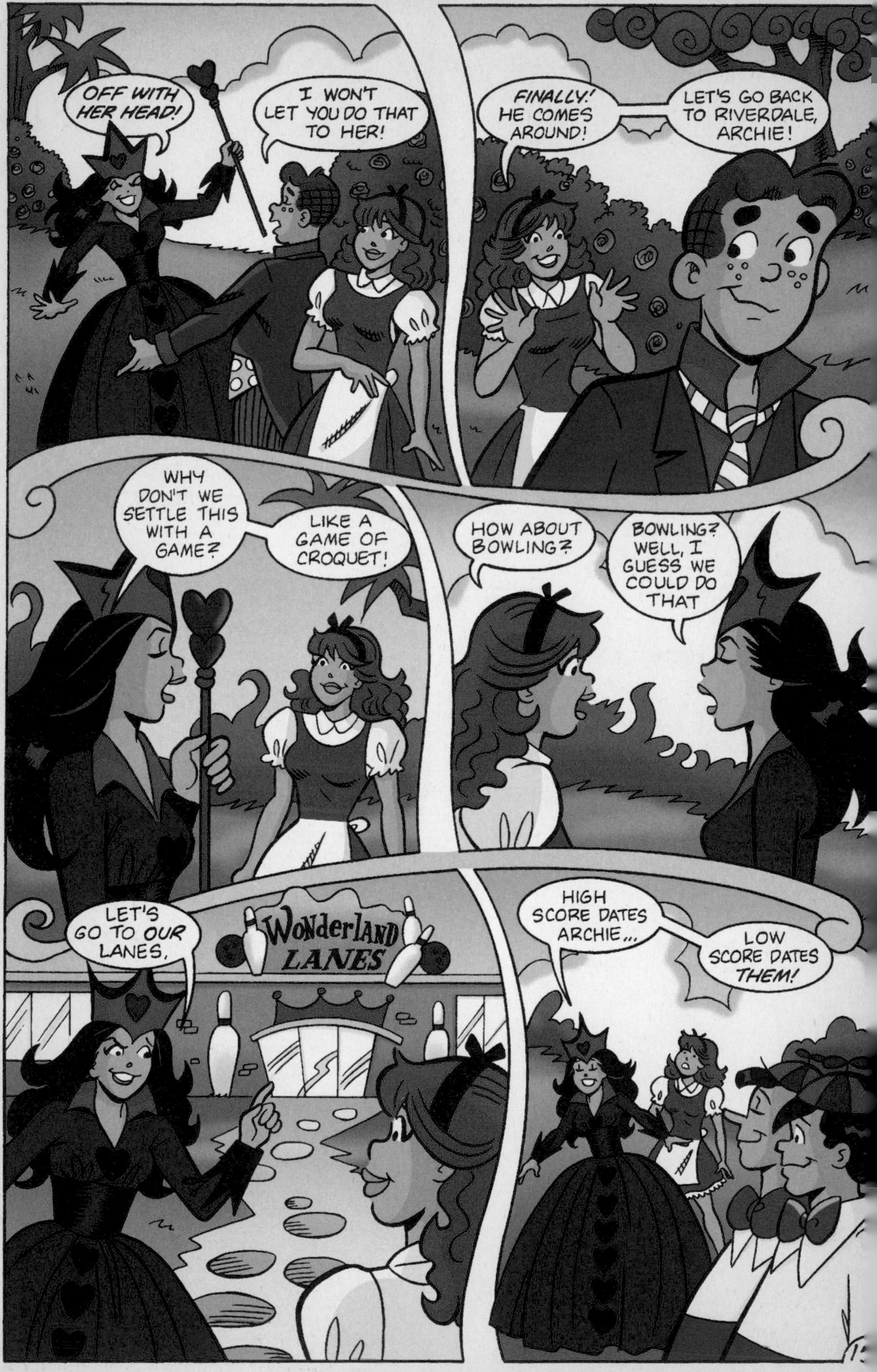

OFF WITH HER HEAD!
I WON'T LET YOU DO THAT TO HER!
FINALLY! HE COMES AROUND!
LET'S GO BACK TO RIVERDALE, ARCHIE!
WHY DON'T WE SETTLE THIS WITH A GAME?
LIKE A GAME OF CROQUET!
HOW ABOUT BOWLING?
BOWLING? WELL, I GUESS WE COULD DO THAT
LET'S GO TO OUR LANES.
WONDERLAND LANES
HIGH SCORE DATES ARCHIE...
LOW SCORE DATES THEM!

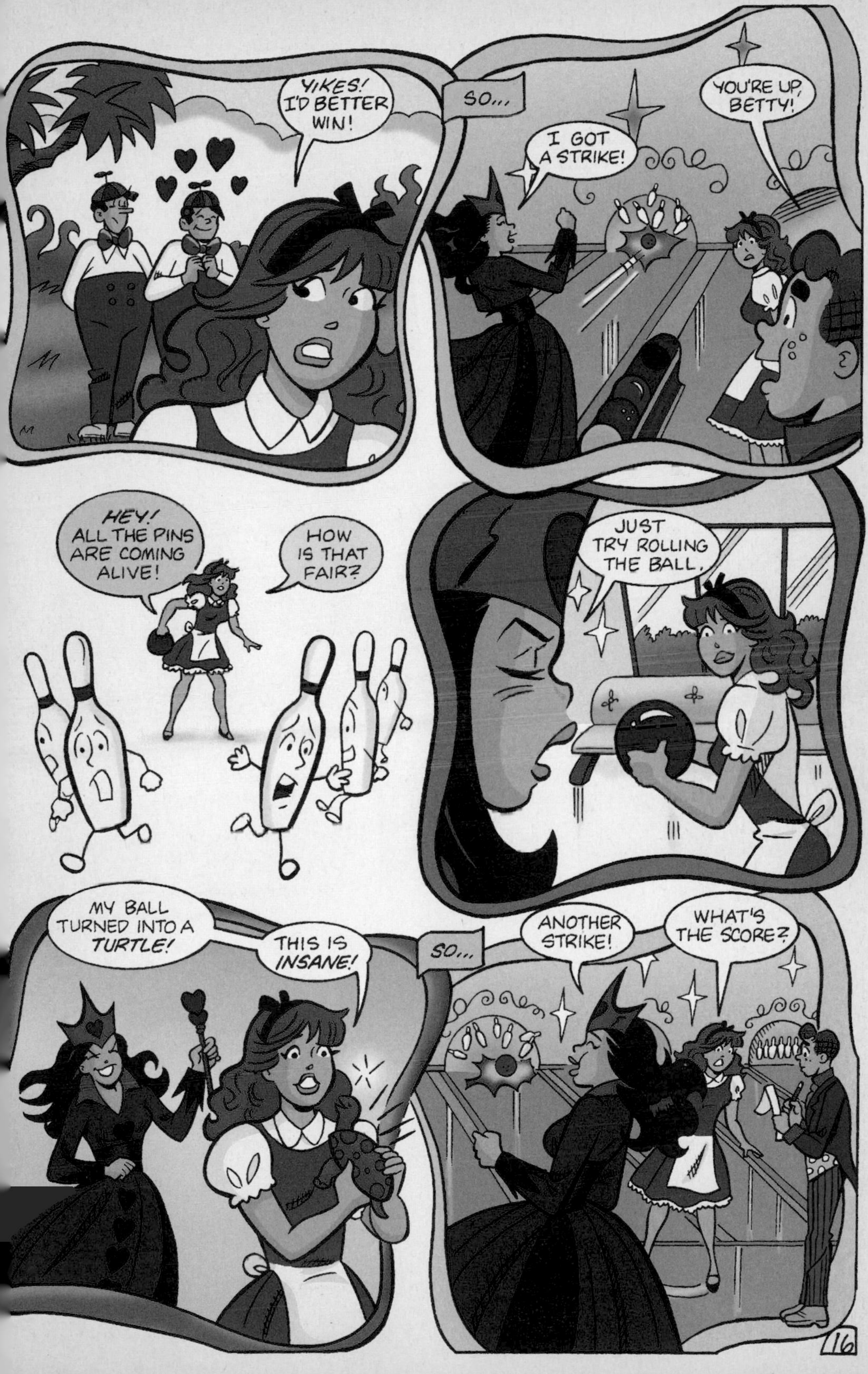

YIKES! I'D BETTER WIN!
SO...
I GOT A STRIKE!
YOU'RE UP, BETTY!
HEY! ALL THE PINS ARE COMING ALIVE!
HOW IS THAT FAIR?
JUST TRY ROLLING THE BALL.
MY BALL TURNED INTO A TURTLE!
THIS IS INSANE!
SO...
ANOTHER STRIKE!
WHAT'S THE SCORE?

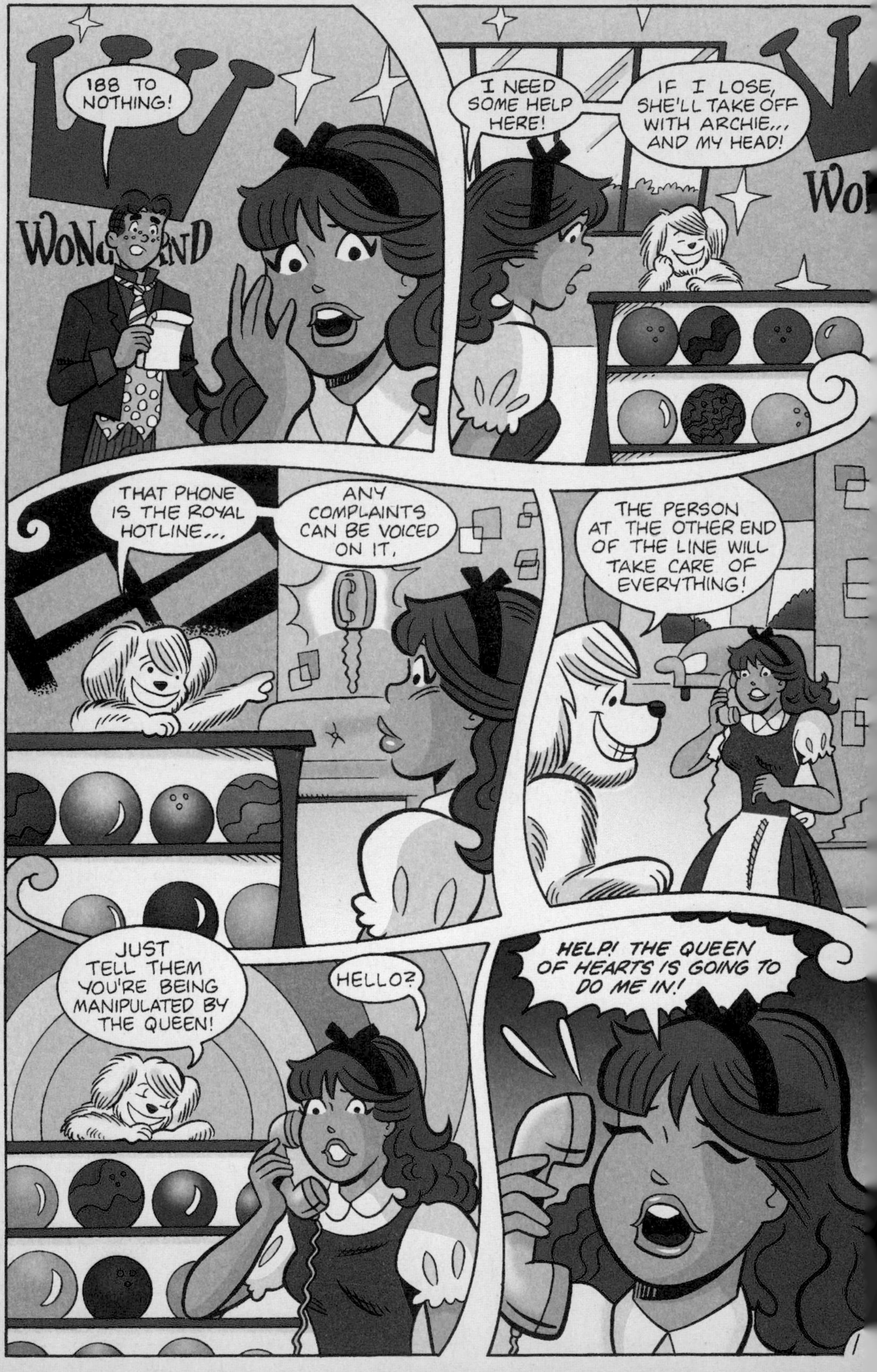
188 TO NOTHING!
WONDERLAND
I NEED SOME HELP HERE!
IF I LOSE, SHE'LL TAKE OFF WITH ARCHIE... AND MY HEAD!
THAT PHONE IS THE ROYAL HOTLINE...
ANY COMPLAINTS CAN BE VOICED ON IT.
THE PERSON AT THE OTHER END OF THE LINE WILL TAKE CARE OF EVERYTHING!
JUST TELL THEM YOU'RE BEING MANIPULATED BY THE QUEEN!
HELLO?
HELP! THE QUEEN OF HEARTS IS GOING TO DO ME IN!

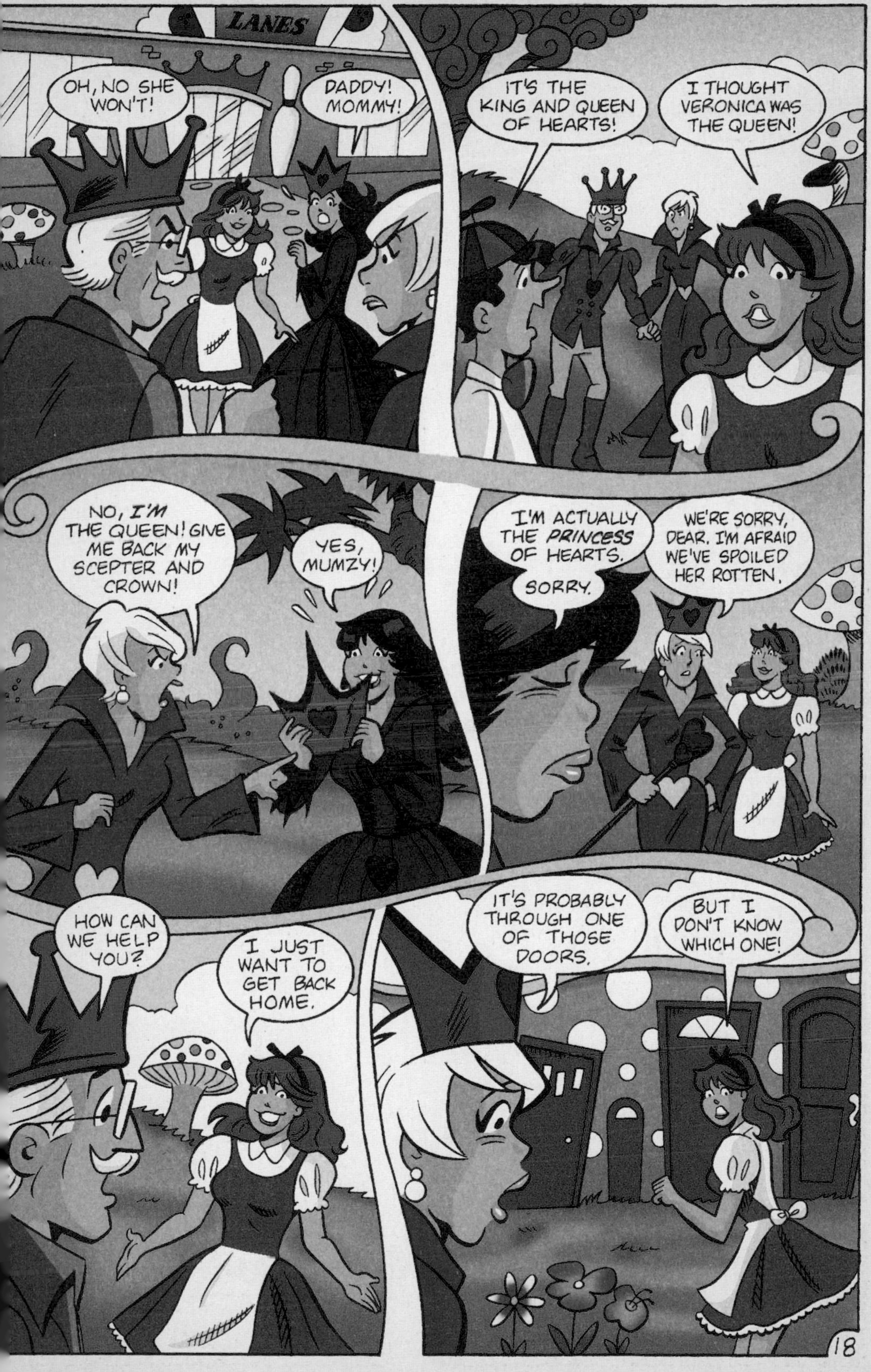

LANES
OH, NO SHE WON'T!
DADDY! MOMMY!
IT'S THE KING AND QUEEN OF HEARTS!
I THOUGHT VERONICA WAS THE QUEEN!
NO, *I'M* THE QUEEN! GIVE ME BACK MY SCEPTER AND CROWN!
YES, MUMZY!
I'M ACTUALLY THE *PRINCESS* OF HEARTS.
SORRY.
WE'RE SORRY, DEAR. I'M AFRAID WE'VE SPOILED HER ROTTEN.
HOW CAN WE HELP YOU?
I JUST WANT TO GET BACK HOME.
IT'S PROBABLY THROUGH ONE OF THOSE DOORS.
BUT I DON'T KNOW WHICH ONE!

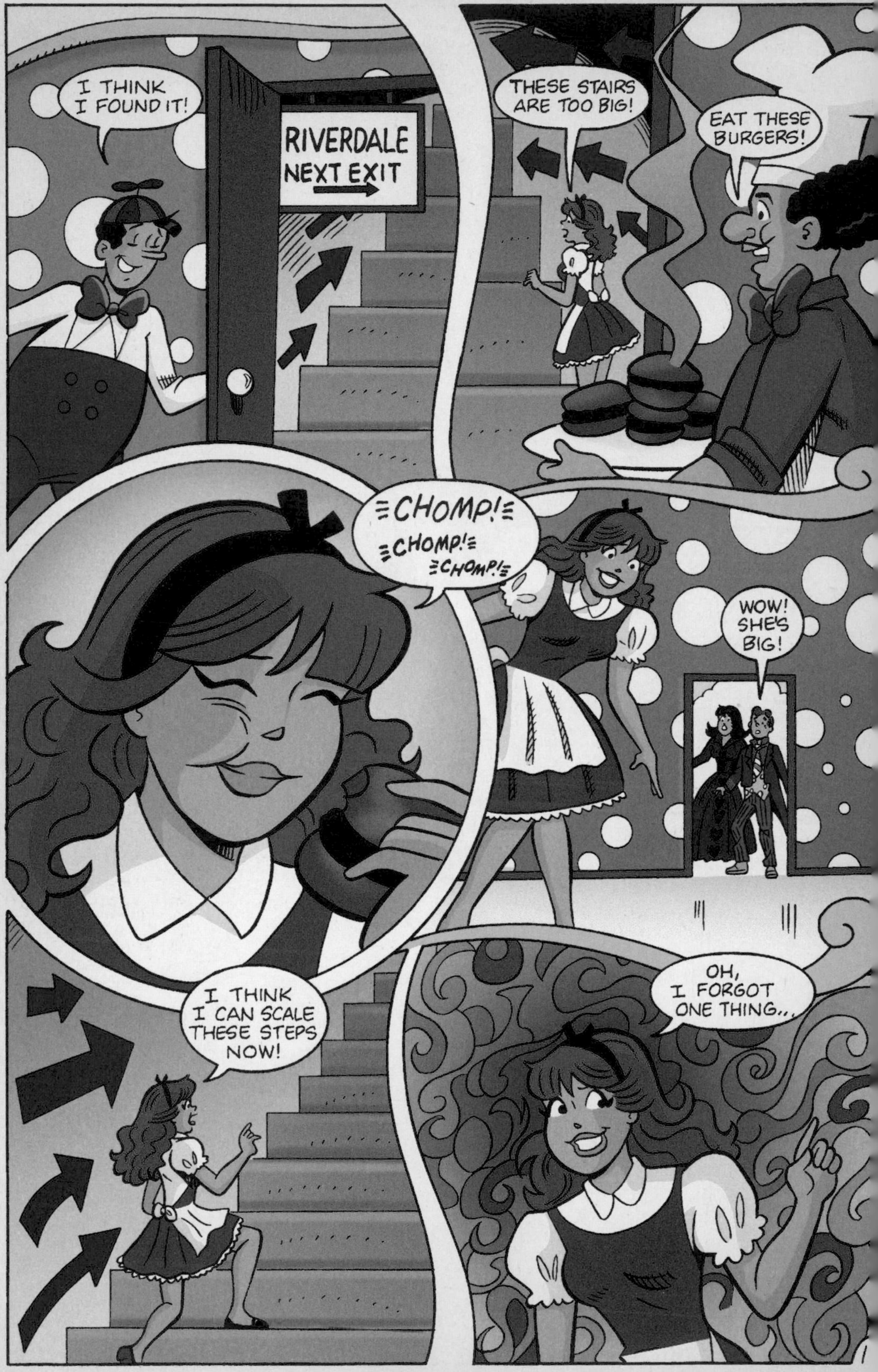
I THINK I FOUND IT!
RIVERDALE NEXT EXIT
THESE STAIRS ARE TOO BIG!
EAT THESE BURGERS!
CHOMP! CHOMP! CHOMP!
WOW! SHE'S BIG!
I THINK I CAN SCALE THESE STEPS NOW!
OH, I FORGOT ONE THING...

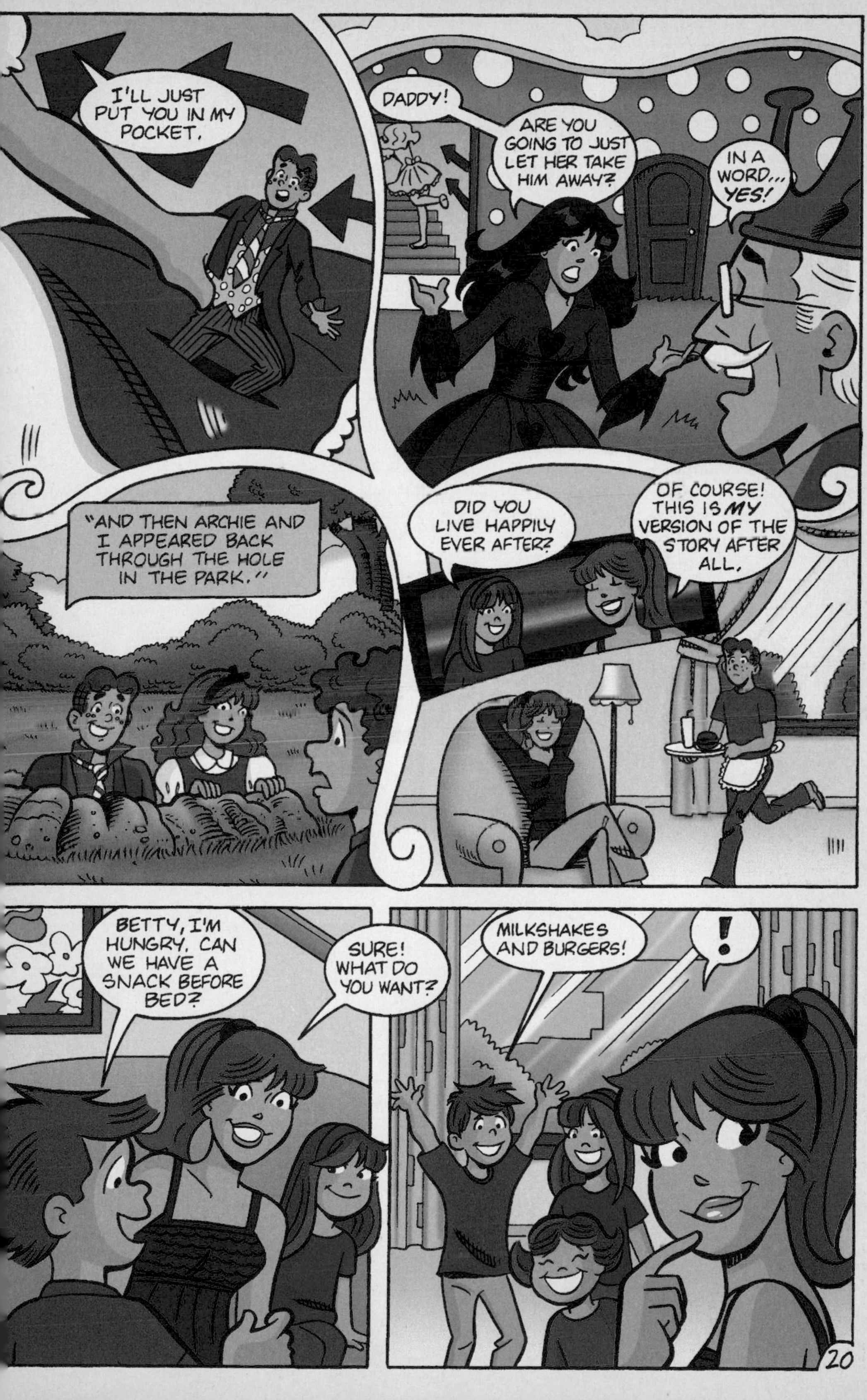
I'LL JUST PUT YOU IN MY POCKET.
DADDY!
ARE YOU GOING TO JUST LET HER TAKE HIM AWAY?
IN A WORD... YES!
"AND THEN ARCHIE AND I APPEARED BACK THROUGH THE HOLE IN THE PARK."
DID YOU LIVE HAPPILY EVER AFTER?
OF COURSE! THIS IS MY VERSION OF THE STORY AFTER ALL.
BETTY, I'M HUNGRY. CAN WE HAVE A SNACK BEFORE BED?
SURE! WHAT DO YOU WANT?
MILKSHAKES AND BURGERS!
!

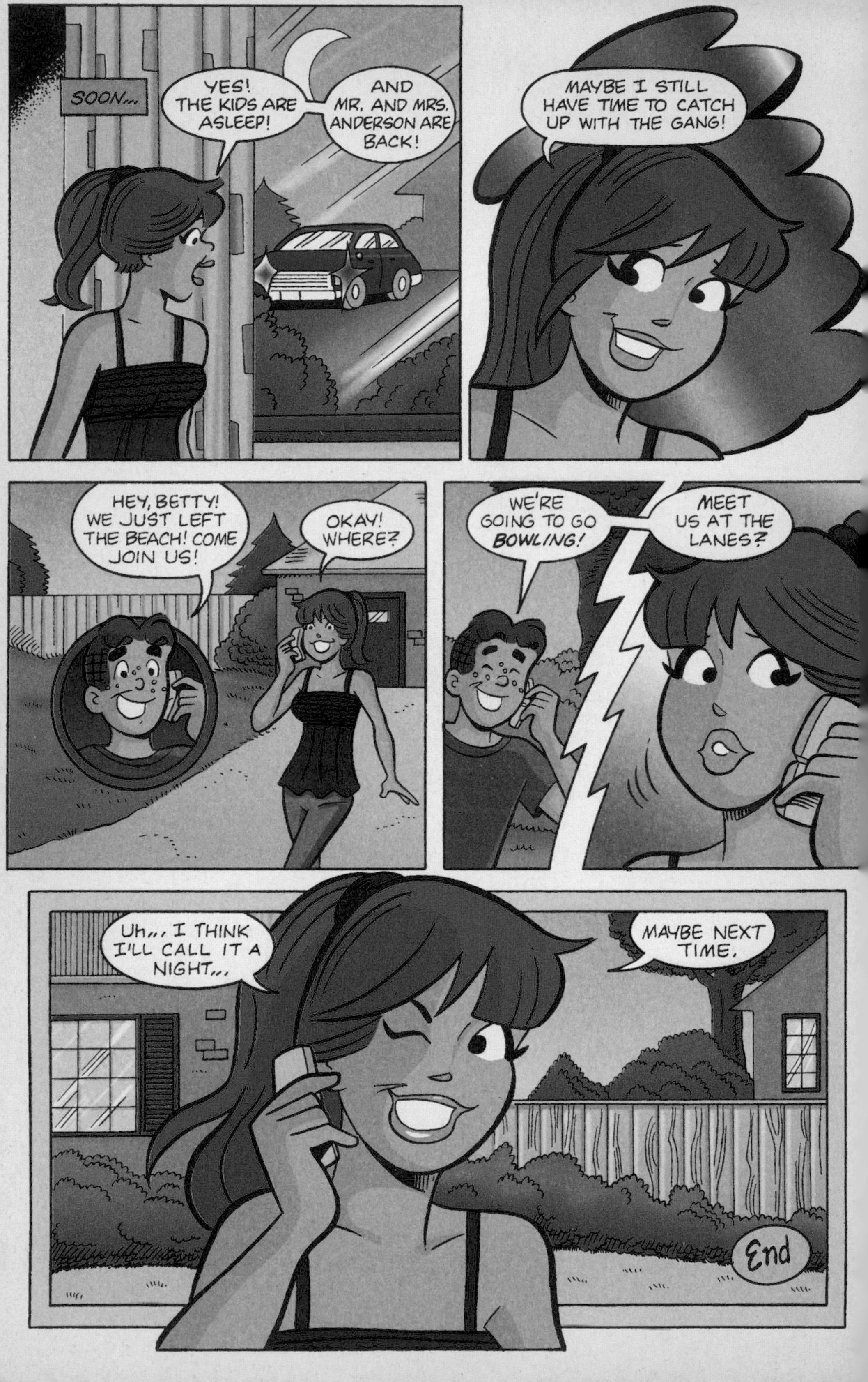
SOON...
YES! THE KIDS ARE ASLEEP!
AND MR. AND MRS. ANDERSON ARE BACK!
MAYBE I STILL HAVE TIME TO CATCH UP WITH THE GANG!
HEY, BETTY! WE JUST LEFT THE BEACH! COME JOIN US!
OKAY! WHERE?
WE'RE GOING TO GO BOWLING!
MEET US AT THE LANES?
Uh... I THINK I'LL CALL IT A NIGHT...
MAYBE NEXT TIME.
End

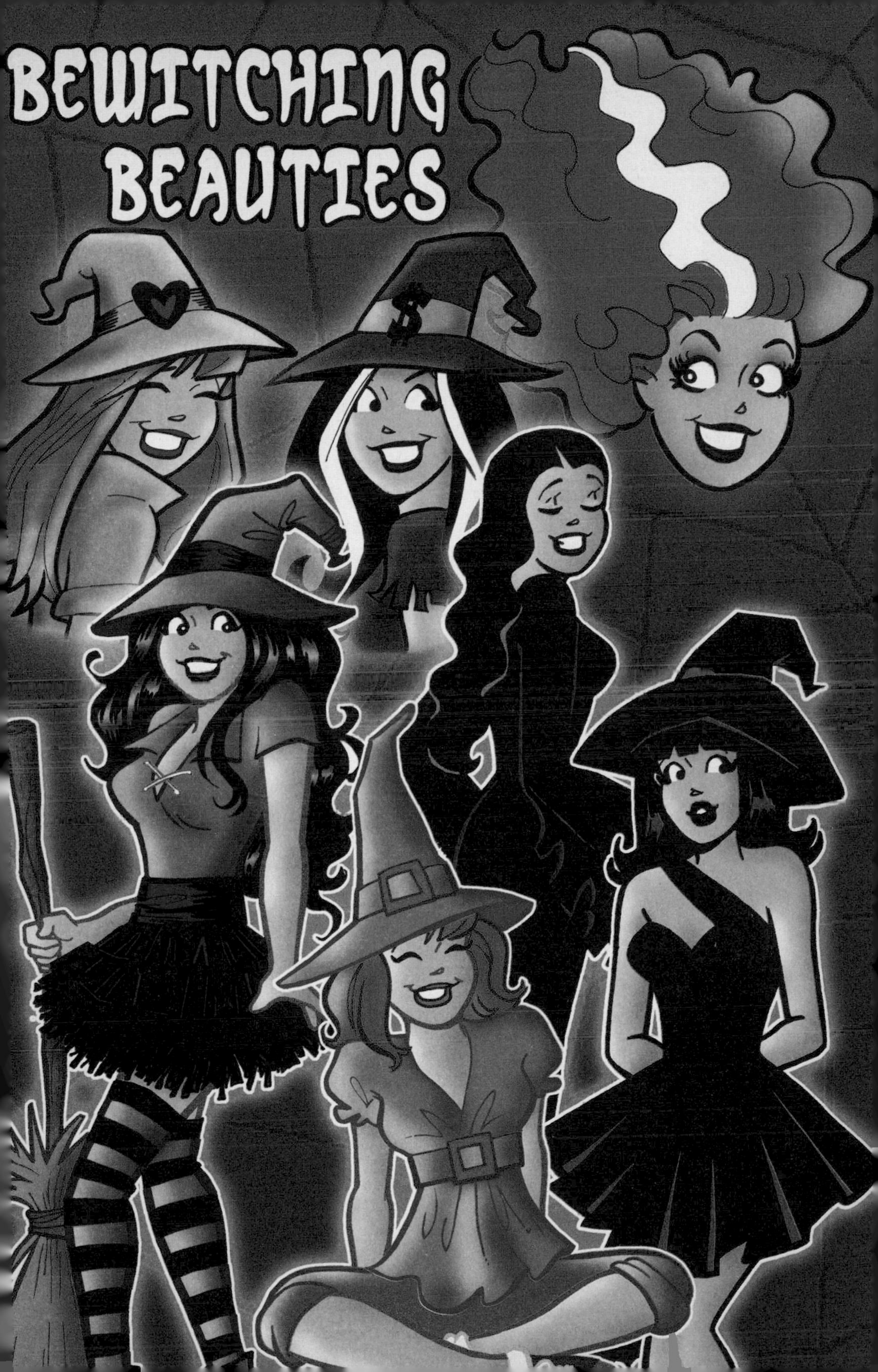
BEWITCHING BEAUTIES

Sleeping Betty

Sleeping Beauty is a classic fairy tale that involves a beautiful princess, a handsome prince, magic and destiny. It was first published in 1697 in "Tales of Mother Goose" by Charles Perrault. In 1890 it was made into a ballet by Tchaikovsky, whose music was adapted in the version of the story most familiar to English speakers, the 1959 Walt Disney animated film. In this adaptation, the new-born Princess Aurora is cursed by the evil witch Maleficent, who declares that before Aurora reaches her sixteenth birthday she will die by a poisoned spinning-wheel. To try to prevent this, the king places her into hiding in the care of three good-natured – but not too bright – fairies, Flora, Fauna and Merryweather.

In "Sleeping Betty," King and Queen Cooper are celebrating the birth of their daughter, Princess Betty! She receives enchanted gifts from three magical sisters: Ethel, Ginger and Nancy. The evil Veronica appears and casts a wicked spell of sleep on Betty! Doomed to fall into a deep sleep on her sixteenth birthday, Ethel, Ginger and Nancy hide her. Things are going great until she finds out that soon she will be married to the neighboring family's son – a prince! Now Betty has to avoid the curse, embrace her new life of royalty and prepare for her marriage – even though she's in love with someone else! What's a girl to do?!

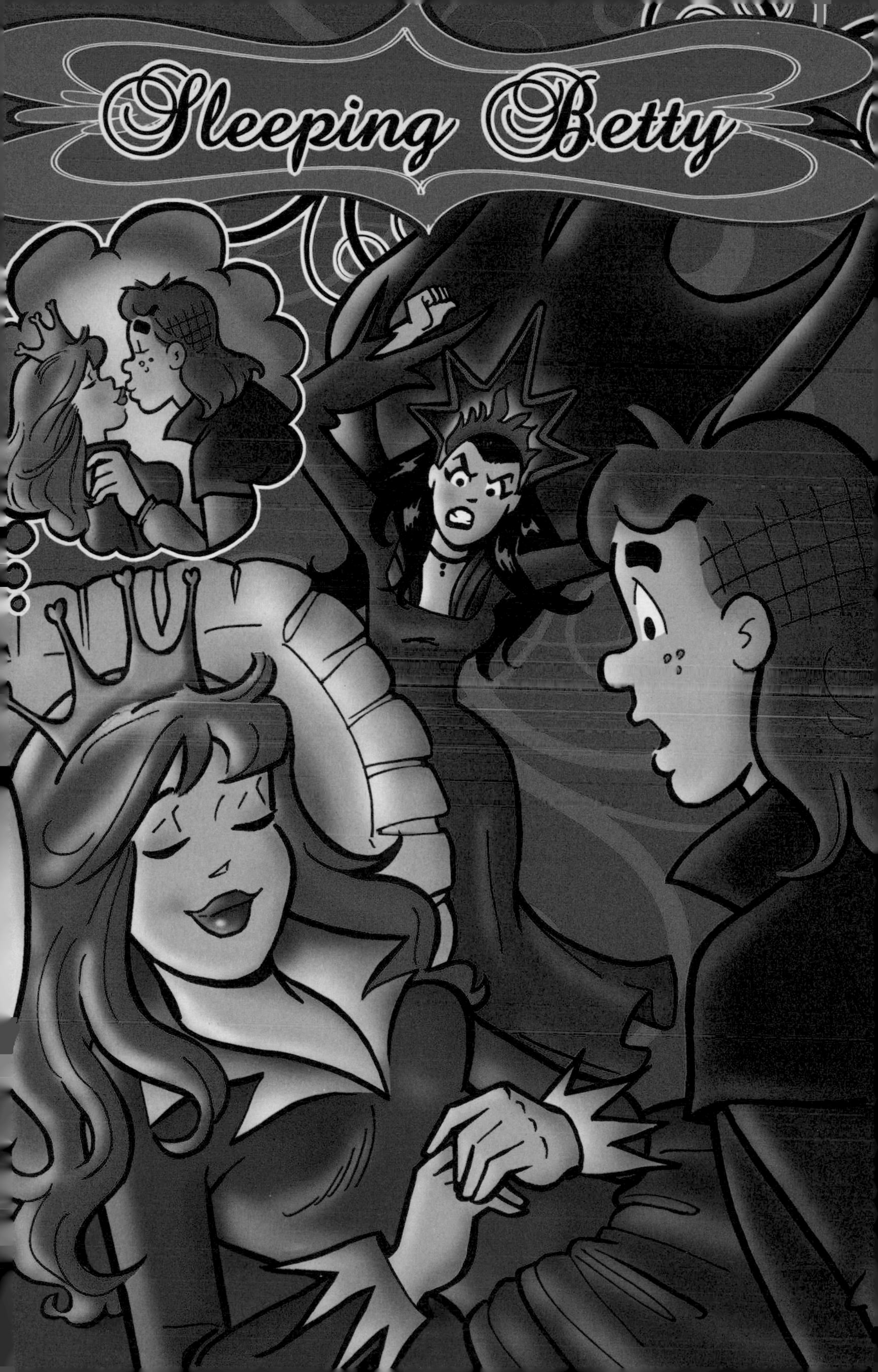
Sleeping Betty

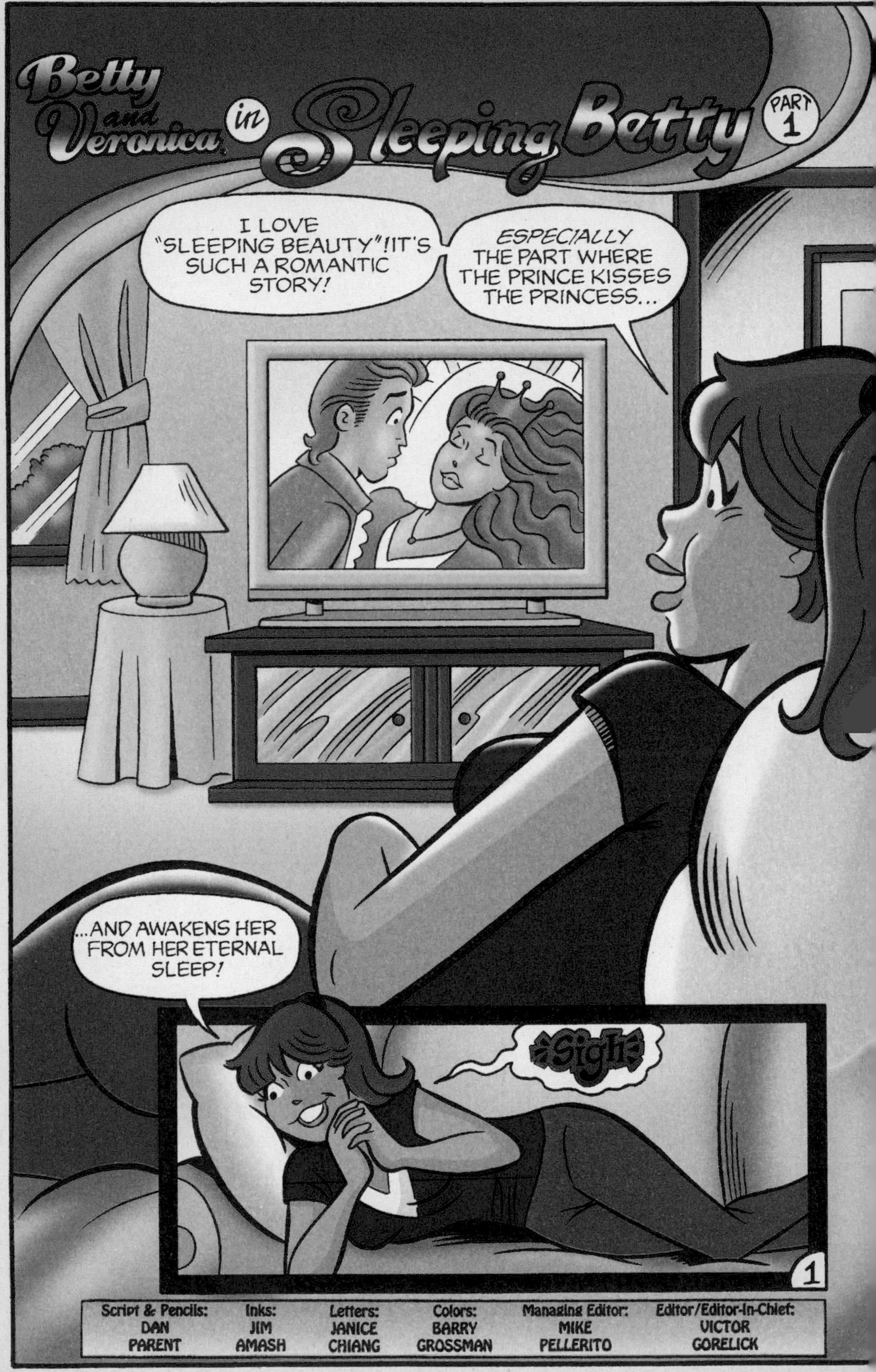
Betty and Veronica in Sleeping Betty PART 1
I LOVE "SLEEPING BEAUTY"! IT'S SUCH A ROMANTIC STORY!
ESPECIALLY THE PART WHERE THE PRINCE KISSES THE PRINCESS...
...AND AWAKENS HER FROM HER ETERNAL SLEEP!
Sigh
1

Script & Pencils: DAN PARENT | Inks: JIM AMASH | Letters: JANICE CHIANG | Colors: BARRY GROSSMAN | Managing Editor: MIKE PELLERITO | Editor/Editor-In-Chief: VICTOR GORELICK

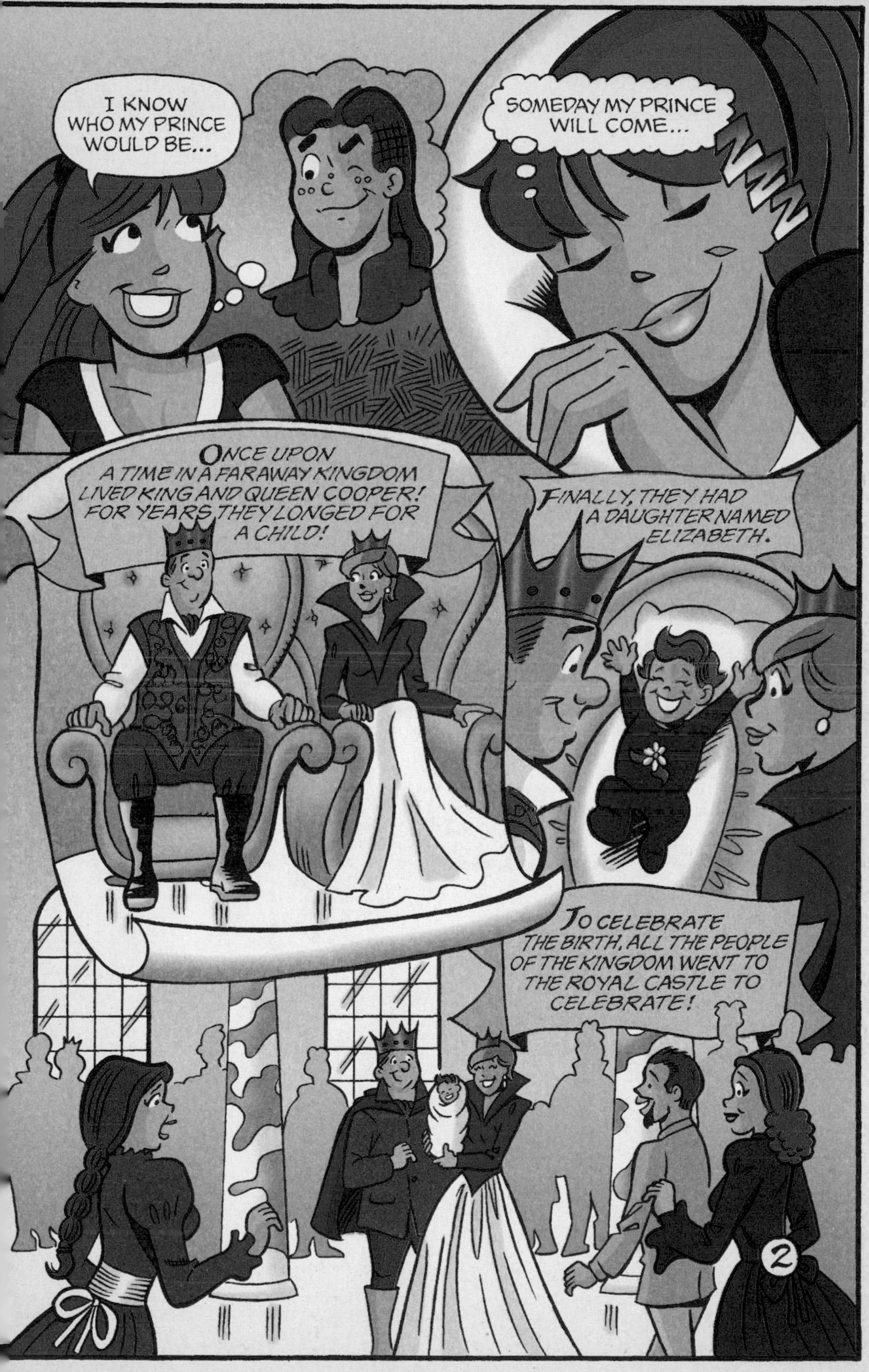
I KNOW WHO MY PRINCE WOULD BE...
SOMEDAY MY PRINCE WILL COME...
ONCE UPON A TIME IN A FARAWAY KINGDOM LIVED KING AND QUEEN COOPER! FOR YEARS THEY LONGED FOR A CHILD!
FINALLY, THEY HAD A DAUGHTER NAMED ELIZABETH.
TO CELEBRATE THE BIRTH, ALL THE PEOPLE OF THE KINGDOM WENT TO THE ROYAL CASTLE TO CELEBRATE!
2

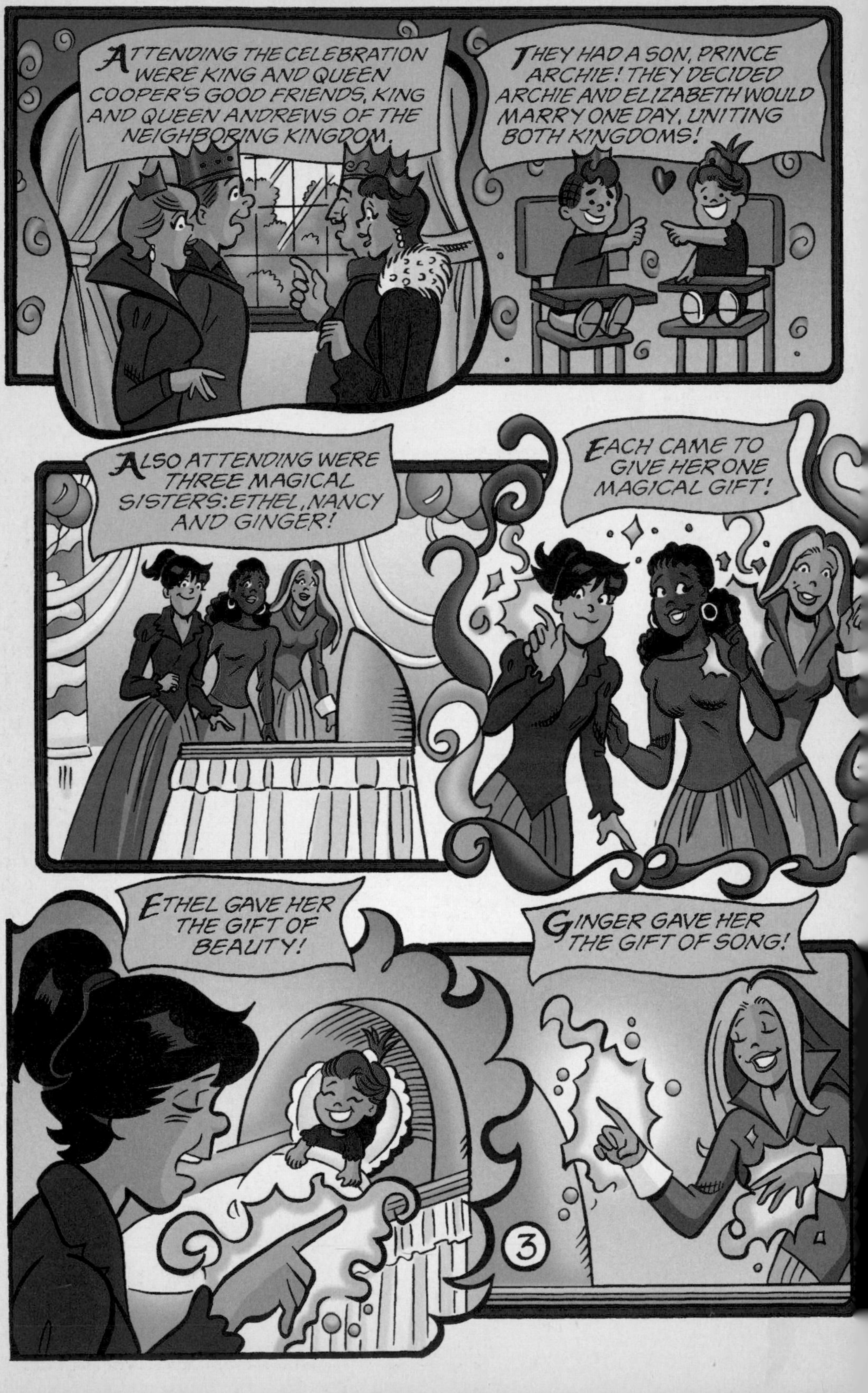
ATTENDING THE CELEBRATION WERE KING AND QUEEN COOPER'S GOOD FRIENDS, KING AND QUEEN ANDREWS OF THE NEIGHBORING KINGDOM.
THEY HAD A SON, PRINCE ARCHIE! THEY DECIDED ARCHIE AND ELIZABETH WOULD MARRY ONE DAY, UNITING BOTH KINGDOMS!
ALSO ATTENDING WERE THREE MAGICAL SISTERS: ETHEL, NANCY AND GINGER!
EACH CAME TO GIVE HER ONE MAGICAL GIFT!
ETHEL GAVE HER THE GIFT OF BEAUTY!
GINGER GAVE HER THE GIFT OF SONG!
3

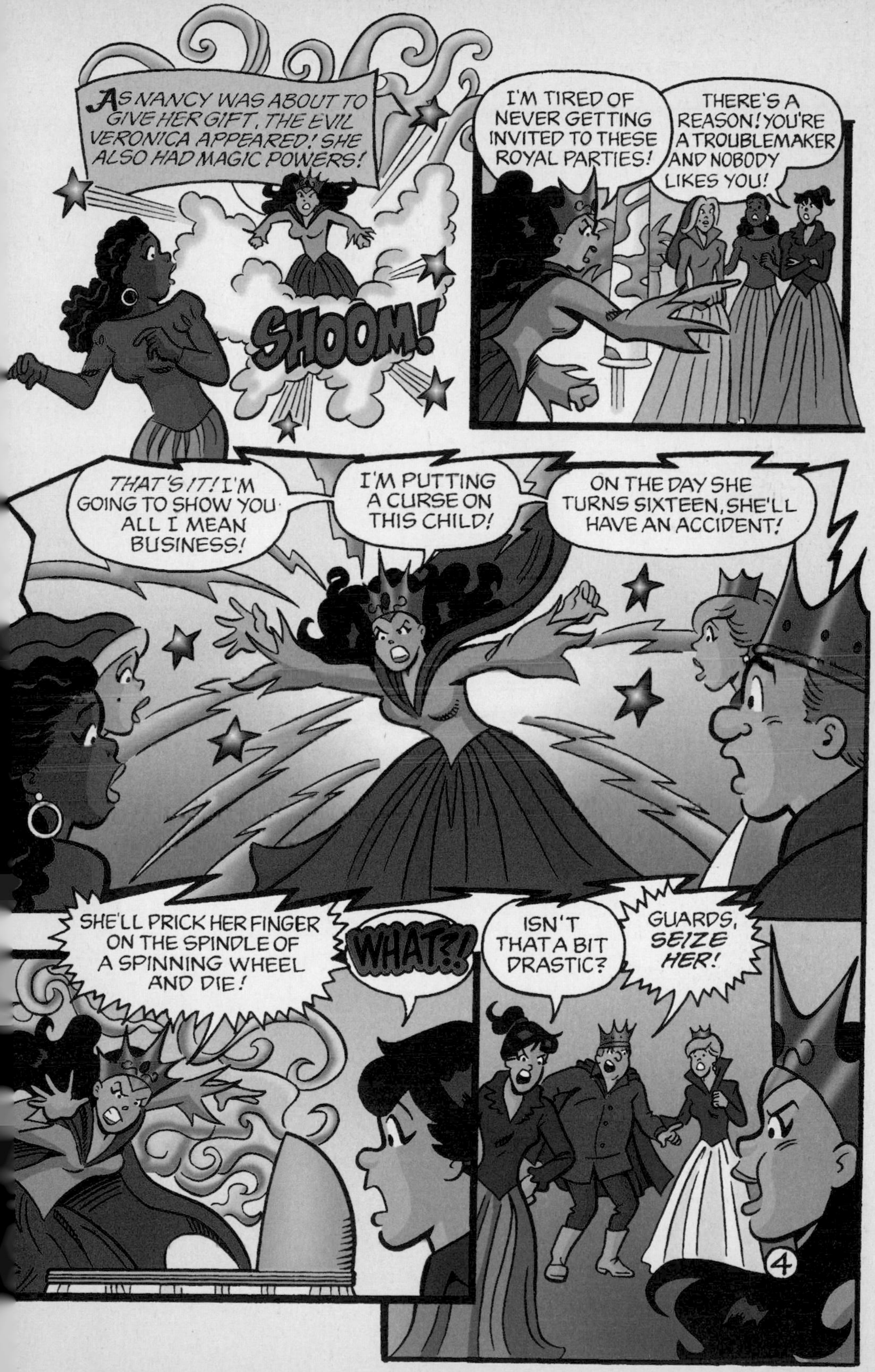
AS NANCY WAS ABOUT TO GIVE HER GIFT, THE EVIL VERONICA APPEARED! SHE ALSO HAD MAGIC POWERS!
SHOOM!
I'M TIRED OF NEVER GETTING INVITED TO THESE ROYAL PARTIES!
THERE'S A REASON! YOU'RE A TROUBLEMAKER AND NOBODY LIKES YOU!
THAT'S IT! I'M GOING TO SHOW YOU ALL I MEAN BUSINESS!
I'M PUTTING A CURSE ON THIS CHILD!
ON THE DAY SHE TURNS SIXTEEN, SHE'LL HAVE AN ACCIDENT!
SHE'LL PRICK HER FINGER ON THE SPINDLE OF A SPINNING WHEEL AND DIE!
WHAT?!
ISN'T THAT A BIT DRASTIC?
GUARDS, SEIZE HER!
4

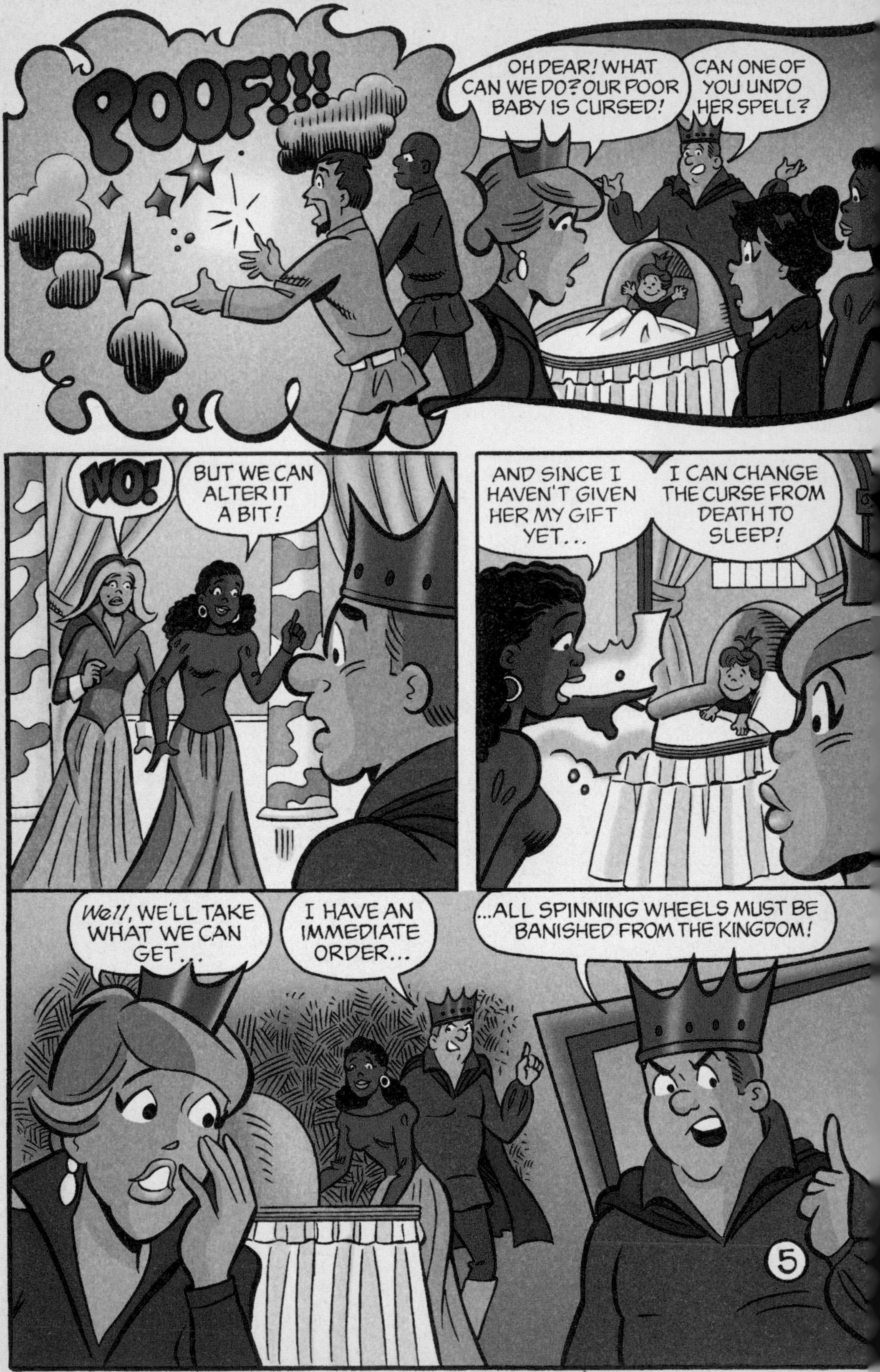
POOF!!!
OH DEAR! WHAT CAN WE DO? OUR POOR BABY IS CURSED!
CAN ONE OF YOU UNDO HER SPELL?
NO!
BUT WE CAN ALTER IT A BIT!
AND SINCE I HAVEN'T GIVEN HER MY GIFT YET...
I CAN CHANGE THE CURSE FROM DEATH TO SLEEP!
Well, WE'LL TAKE WHAT WE CAN GET...
I HAVE AN IMMEDIATE ORDER...
...ALL SPINNING WHEELS MUST BE BANISHED FROM THE KINGDOM!
5

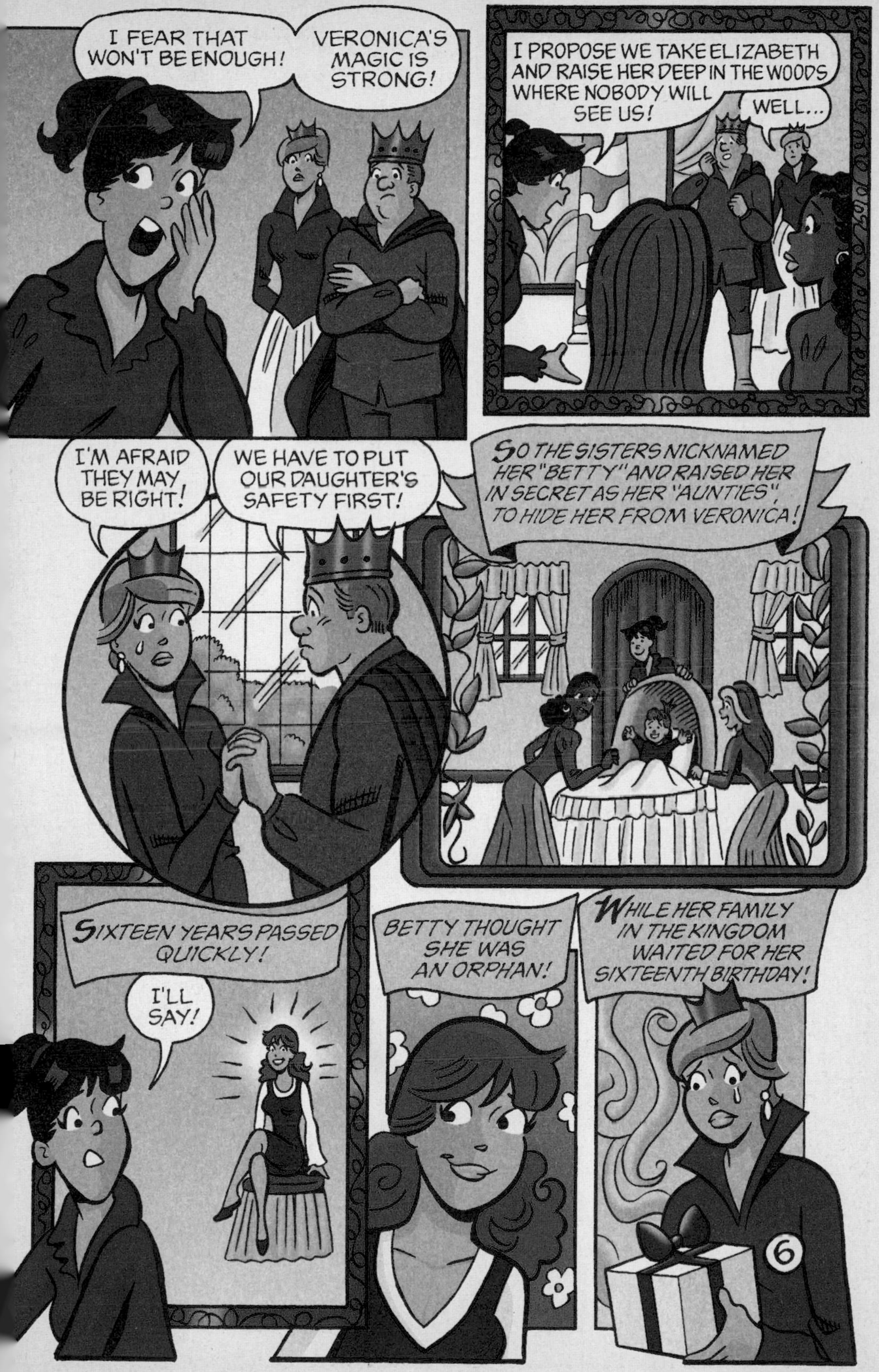
I FEAR THAT WON'T BE ENOUGH!
VERONICA'S MAGIC IS STRONG!
I PROPOSE WE TAKE ELIZABETH AND RAISE HER DEEP IN THE WOODS WHERE NOBODY WILL SEE US!
WELL...
I'M AFRAID THEY MAY BE RIGHT!
WE HAVE TO PUT OUR DAUGHTER'S SAFETY FIRST!
SO THE SISTERS NICKNAMED HER "BETTY" AND RAISED HER IN SECRET AS HER "AUNTIES", TO HIDE HER FROM VERONICA!
SIXTEEN YEARS PASSED QUICKLY!
I'LL SAY!
BETTY THOUGHT SHE WAS AN ORPHAN!
WHILE HER FAMILY IN THE KINGDOM WAITED FOR HER SIXTEENTH BIRTHDAY!
6

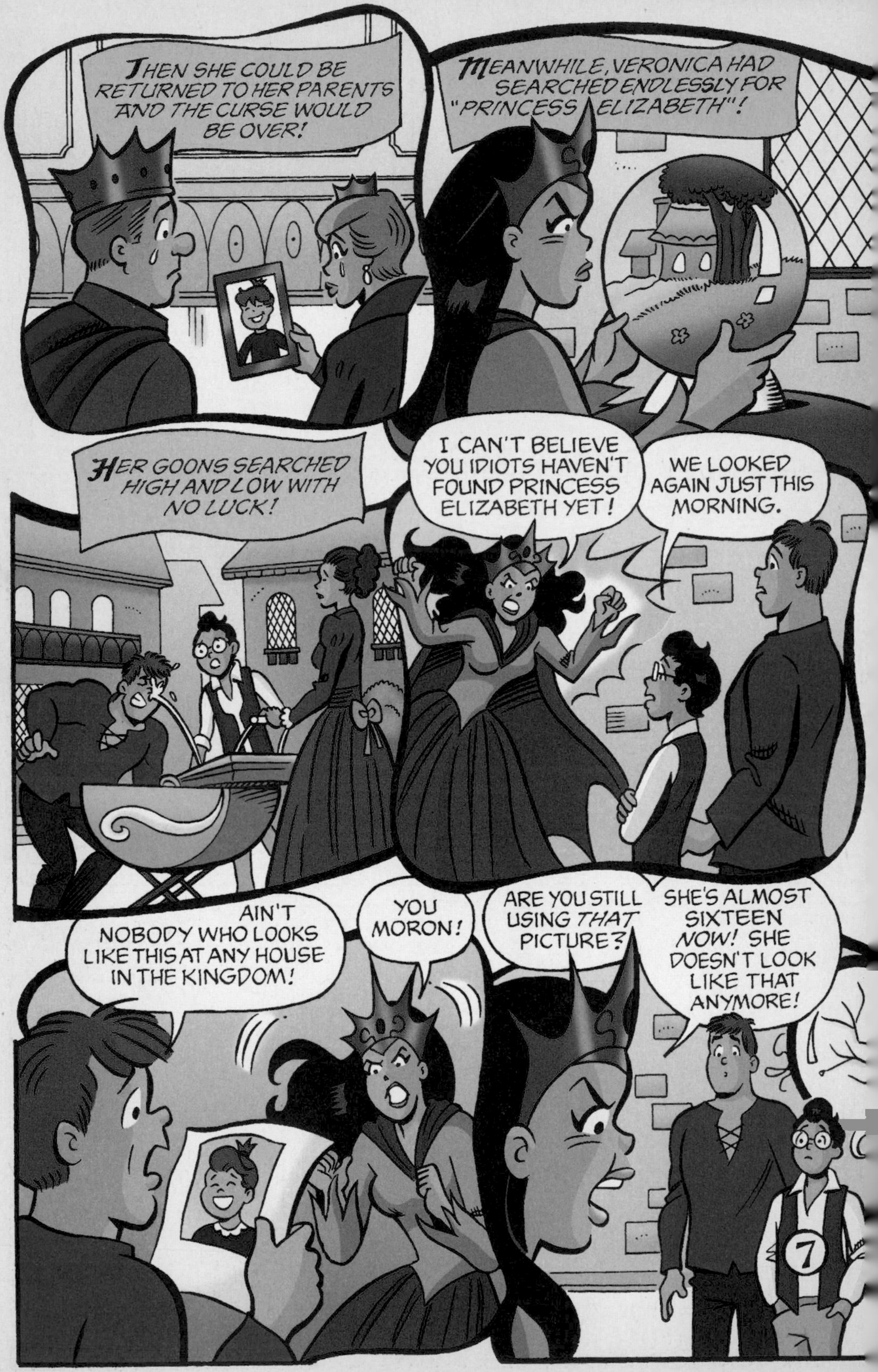
THEN SHE COULD BE RETURNED TO HER PARENTS AND THE CURSE WOULD BE OVER!
MEANWHILE, VERONICA HAD SEARCHED ENDLESSLY FOR "PRINCESS ELIZABETH"!
HER GOONS SEARCHED HIGH AND LOW WITH NO LUCK!
I CAN'T BELIEVE YOU IDIOTS HAVEN'T FOUND PRINCESS ELIZABETH YET!
WE LOOKED AGAIN JUST THIS MORNING.
AIN'T NOBODY WHO LOOKS LIKE THIS AT ANY HOUSE IN THE KINGDOM!
YOU MORON!
ARE YOU STILL USING THAT PICTURE?
SHE'S ALMOST SIXTEEN NOW! SHE DOESN'T LOOK LIKE THAT ANYMORE!
7

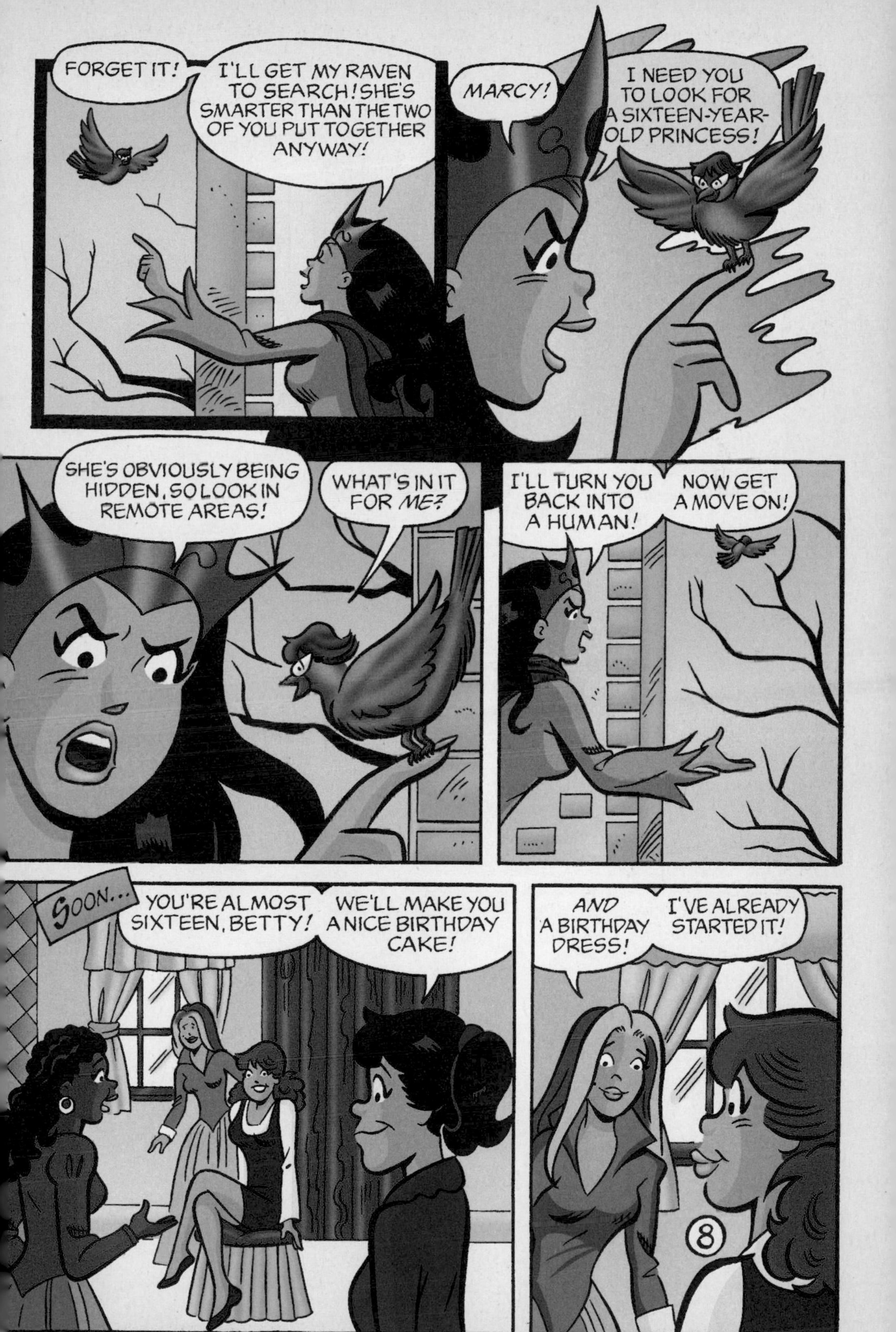
FORGET IT!
I'LL GET MY RAVEN TO SEARCH! SHE'S SMARTER THAN THE TWO OF YOU PUT TOGETHER ANYWAY!
MARCY!
I NEED YOU TO LOOK FOR A SIXTEEN-YEAR-OLD PRINCESS!
SHE'S OBVIOUSLY BEING HIDDEN, SO LOOK IN REMOTE AREAS!
WHAT'S IN IT FOR *ME?*
I'LL TURN YOU BACK INTO A HUMAN!
NOW GET A MOVE ON!
SOON...
YOU'RE ALMOST SIXTEEN, BETTY!
WE'LL MAKE YOU A NICE BIRTHDAY CAKE!
AND A BIRTHDAY DRESS!
I'VE ALREADY STARTED IT!
8

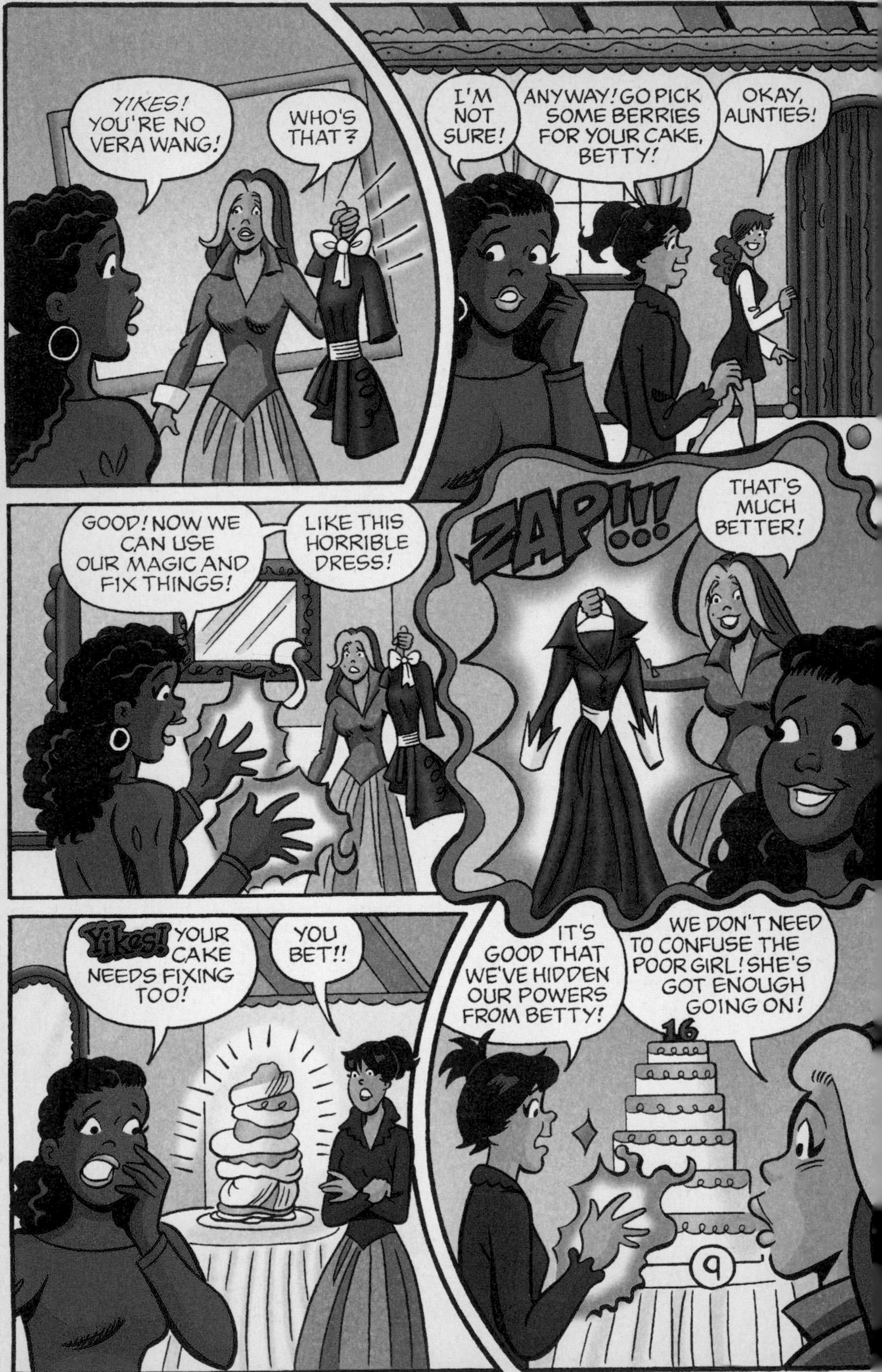
YIKES! YOU'RE NO VERA WANG!
WHO'S THAT?
I'M NOT SURE!
ANYWAY! GO PICK SOME BERRIES FOR YOUR CAKE, BETTY!
OKAY, AUNTIES!
GOOD! NOW WE CAN USE OUR MAGIC AND FIX THINGS!
LIKE THIS HORRIBLE DRESS!
ZAP!!!
THAT'S MUCH BETTER!
YIKES! YOUR CAKE NEEDS FIXING TOO!
YOU BET!!
IT'S GOOD THAT WE'VE HIDDEN OUR POWERS FROM BETTY!
WE DON'T NEED TO CONFUSE THE POOR GIRL! SHE'S GOT ENOUGH GOING ON!
16
9

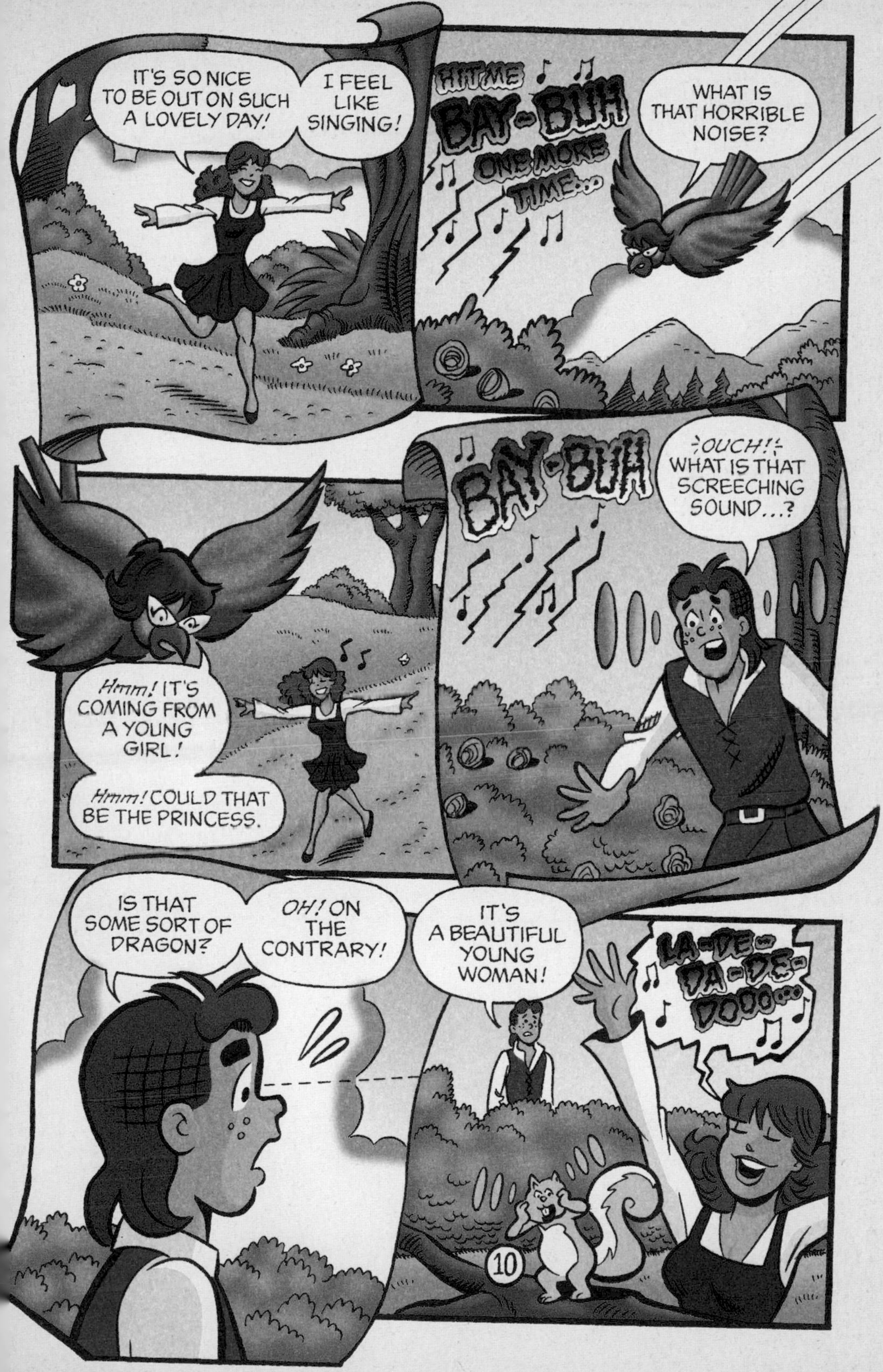

IT'S SO NICE TO BE OUT ON SUCH A LOVELY DAY!
I FEEL LIKE SINGING!
HIT ME BAY-BUH ONE MORE TIME...
WHAT IS THAT HORRIBLE NOISE?
Hmm! IT'S COMING FROM A YOUNG GIRL!
Hmm! COULD THAT BE THE PRINCESS.
BAY-BUH
OUCH! WHAT IS THAT SCREECHING SOUND...?
IS THAT SOME SORT OF DRAGON?
OH! ON THE CONTRARY!
IT'S A BEAUTIFUL YOUNG WOMAN!
LA-DE-DA-DE-DOOO...

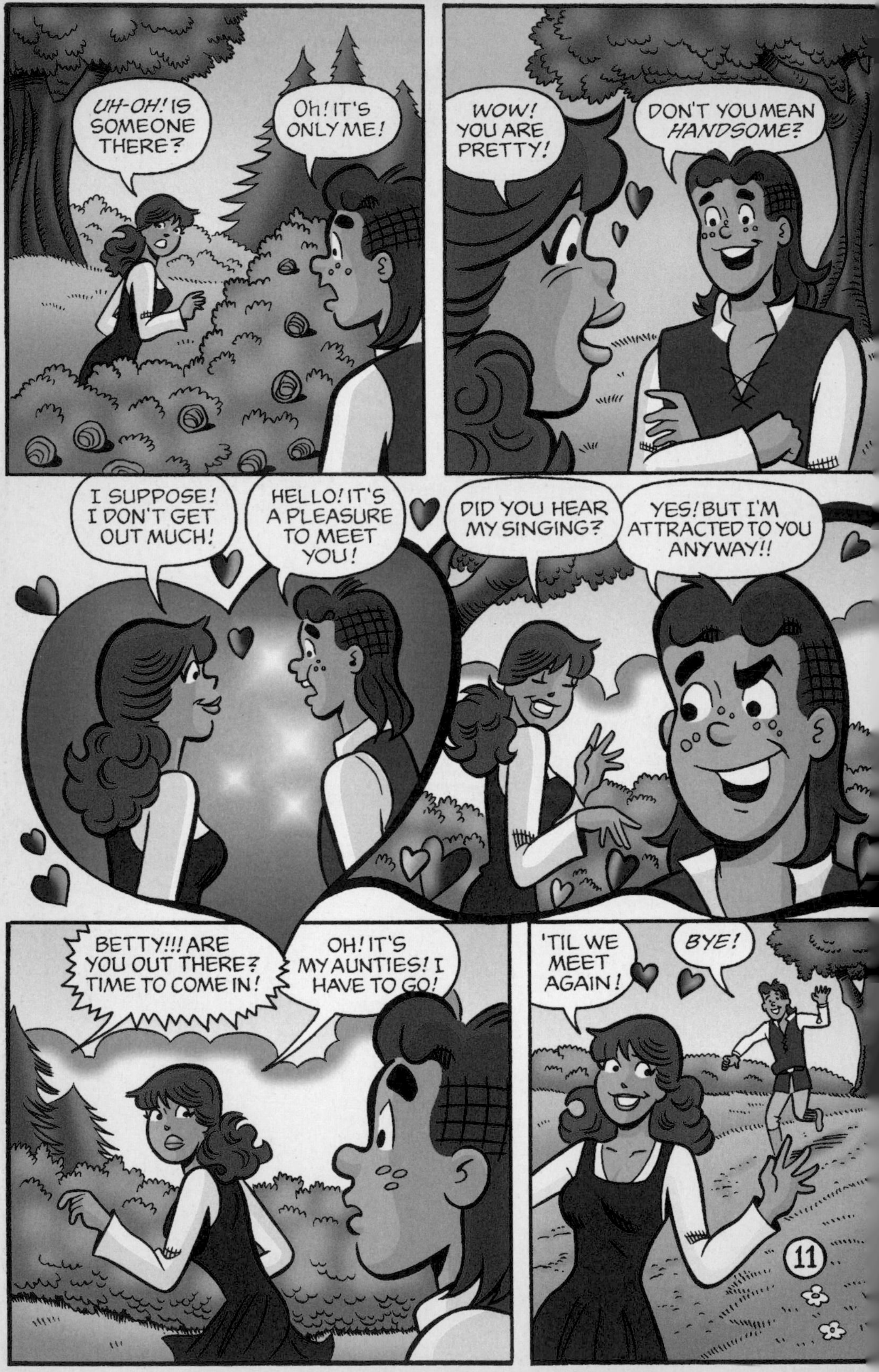
UH-OH! IS SOMEONE THERE?
Oh! IT'S ONLY ME!
WOW! YOU ARE PRETTY!
DON'T YOU MEAN HANDSOME?
I SUPPOSE! I DON'T GET OUT MUCH!
HELLO! IT'S A PLEASURE TO MEET YOU!
DID YOU HEAR MY SINGING?
YES! BUT I'M ATTRACTED TO YOU ANYWAY!!
BETTY!!! ARE YOU OUT THERE? TIME TO COME IN!
OH! IT'S MY AUNTIES! I HAVE TO GO!
'TIL WE MEET AGAIN!
BYE!
11

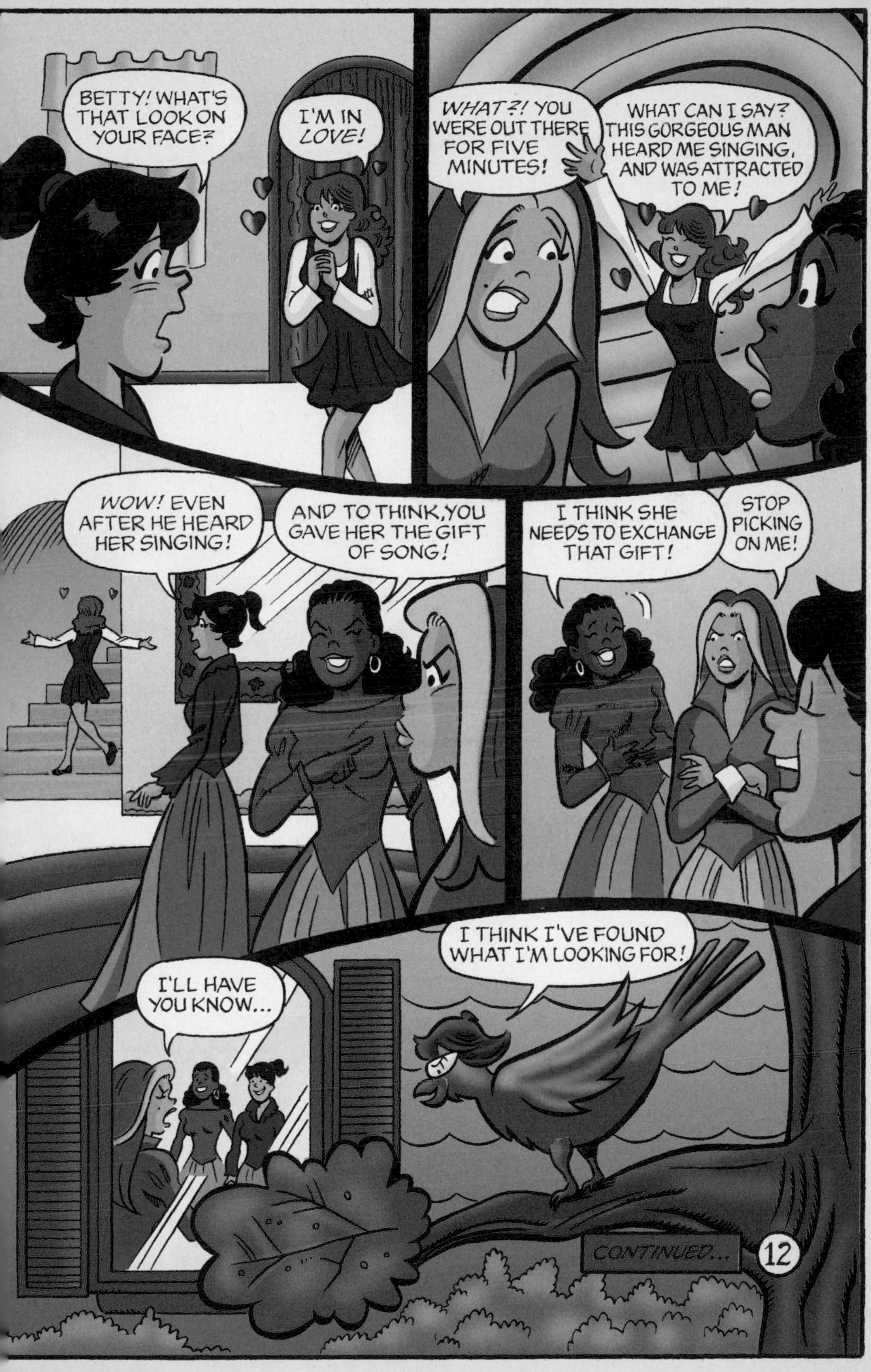
BETTY! WHAT'S THAT LOOK ON YOUR FACE?
I'M IN *LOVE*!
WHAT?! YOU WERE OUT THERE FOR FIVE MINUTES!
WHAT CAN I SAY? THIS GORGEOUS MAN HEARD ME SINGING, AND WAS ATTRACTED TO ME!
WOW! EVEN AFTER HE HEARD HER SINGING!
AND TO THINK, YOU GAVE HER THE GIFT OF SONG!
I THINK SHE NEEDS TO EXCHANGE THAT GIFT!
STOP PICKING ON ME!
I'LL HAVE YOU KNOW...
I THINK I'VE FOUND WHAT I'M LOOKING FOR!
CONTINUED...

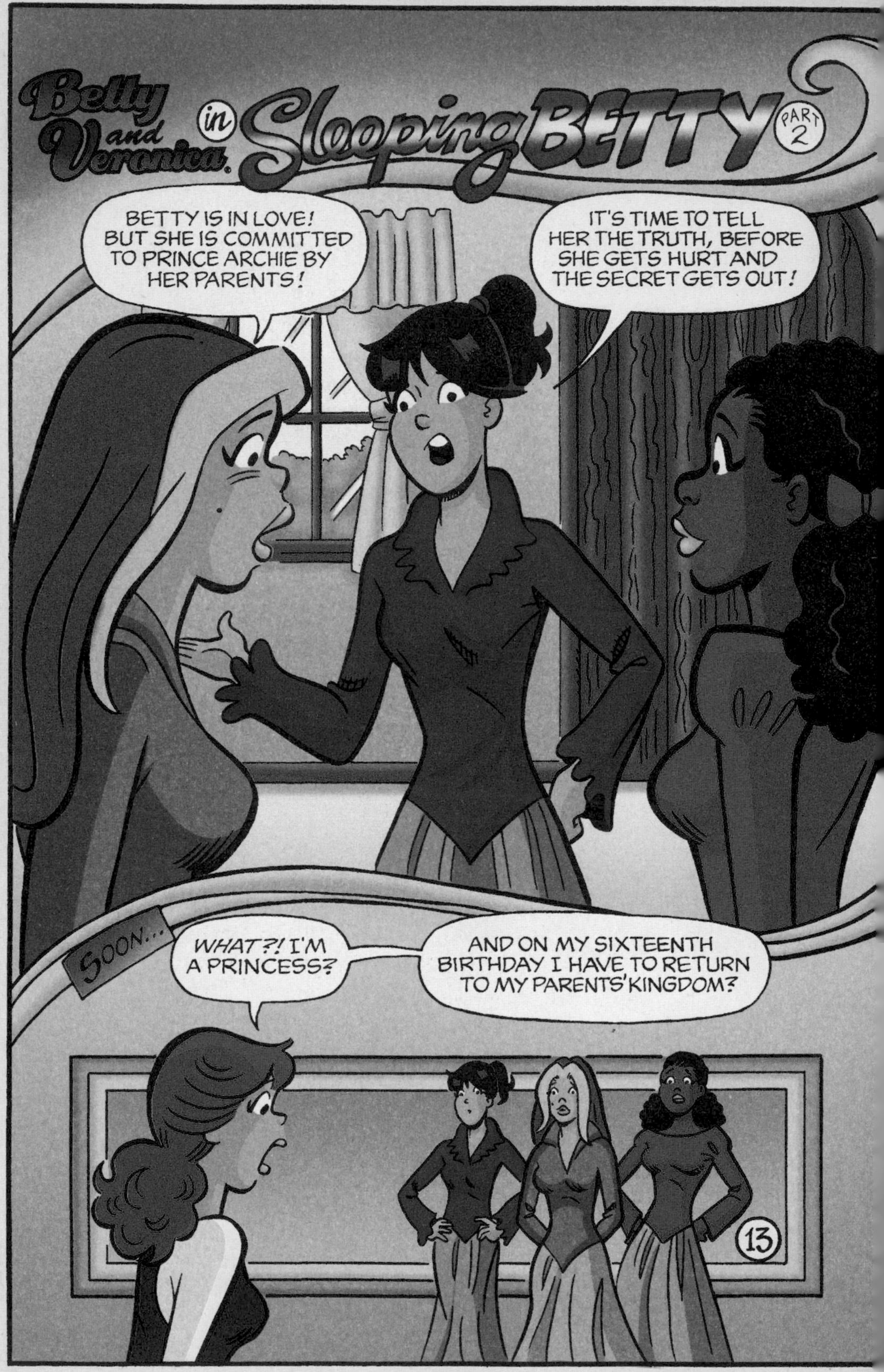
Betty and Veronica in Sleeping BETTY PART 2
BETTY IS IN LOVE! BUT SHE IS COMMITTED TO PRINCE ARCHIE BY HER PARENTS!
IT'S TIME TO TELL HER THE TRUTH, BEFORE SHE GETS HURT AND THE SECRET GETS OUT!
SOON...
WHAT?! I'M A PRINCESS?
AND ON MY SIXTEENTH BIRTHDAY I HAVE TO RETURN TO MY PARENTS' KINGDOM?
13

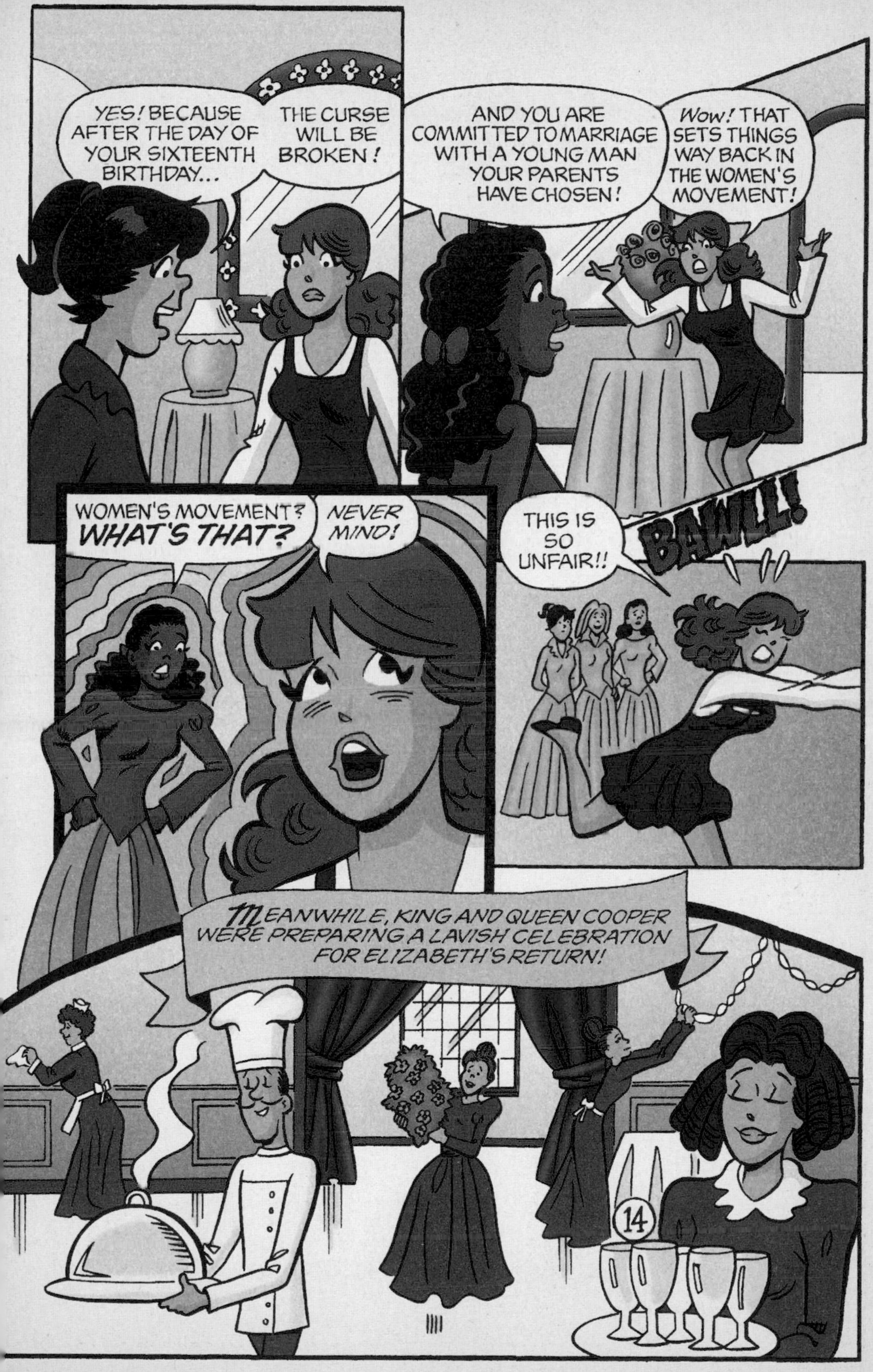
YES! BECAUSE AFTER THE DAY OF YOUR SIXTEENTH BIRTHDAY...
THE CURSE WILL BE BROKEN!
AND YOU ARE COMMITTED TO MARRIAGE WITH A YOUNG MAN YOUR PARENTS HAVE CHOSEN!
Wow! THAT SETS THINGS WAY BACK IN THE WOMEN'S MOVEMENT!
WOMEN'S MOVEMENT? WHAT'S THAT?
NEVER MIND!
THIS IS SO UNFAIR!!
BAWL!!
MEANWHILE, KING AND QUEEN COOPER WERE PREPARING A LAVISH CELEBRATION FOR ELIZABETH'S RETURN!
14

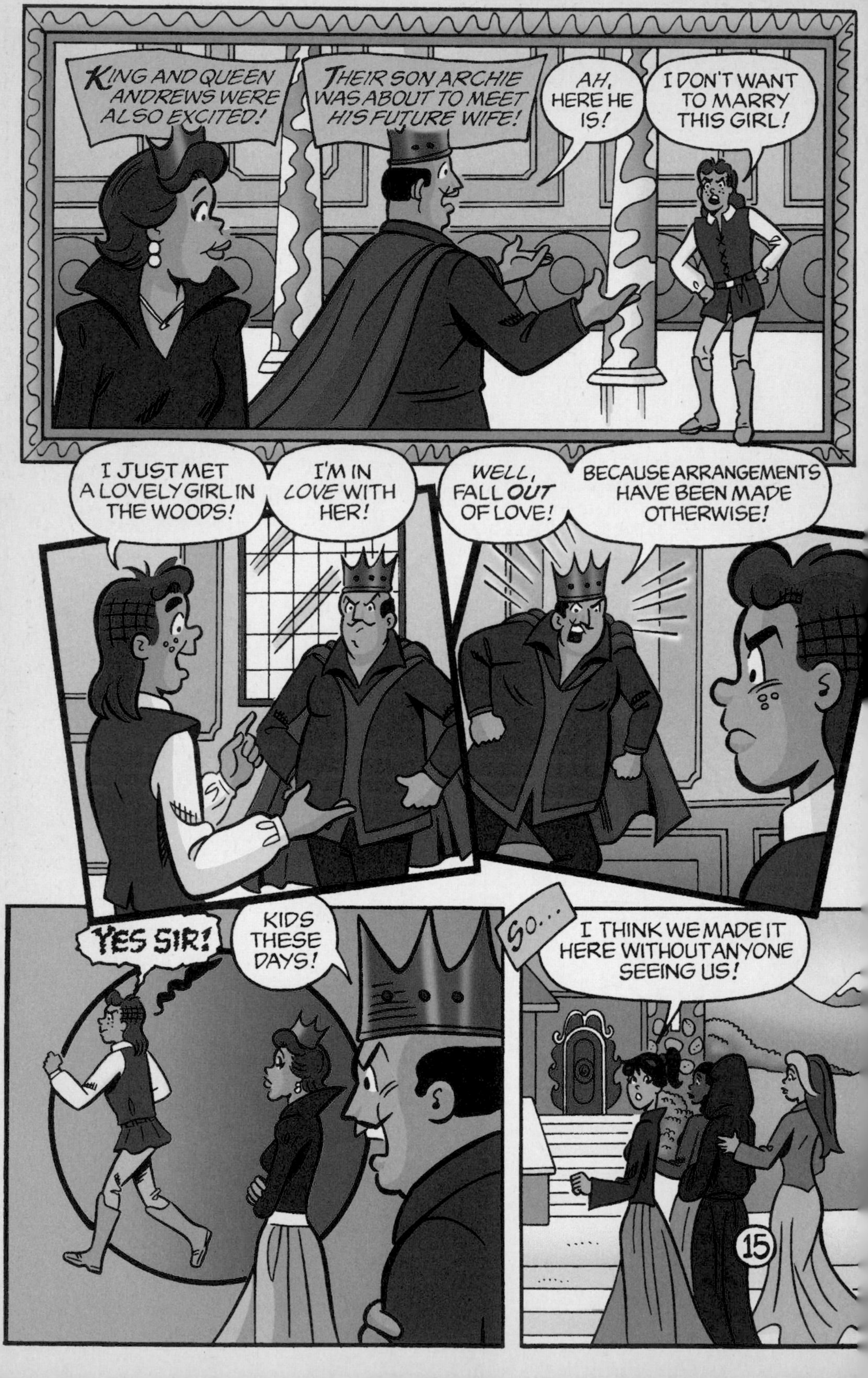

KING AND QUEEN ANDREWS WERE ALSO EXCITED!
THEIR SON ARCHIE WAS ABOUT TO MEET HIS FUTURE WIFE!
AH, HERE HE IS!
I DON'T WANT TO MARRY THIS GIRL!
I JUST MET A LOVELY GIRL IN THE WOODS!
I'M IN LOVE WITH HER!
WELL, FALL OUT OF LOVE!
BECAUSE ARRANGEMENTS HAVE BEEN MADE OTHERWISE!
YES SIR!
KIDS THESE DAYS!
SO...
I THINK WE MADE IT HERE WITHOUT ANYONE SEEING US!
15

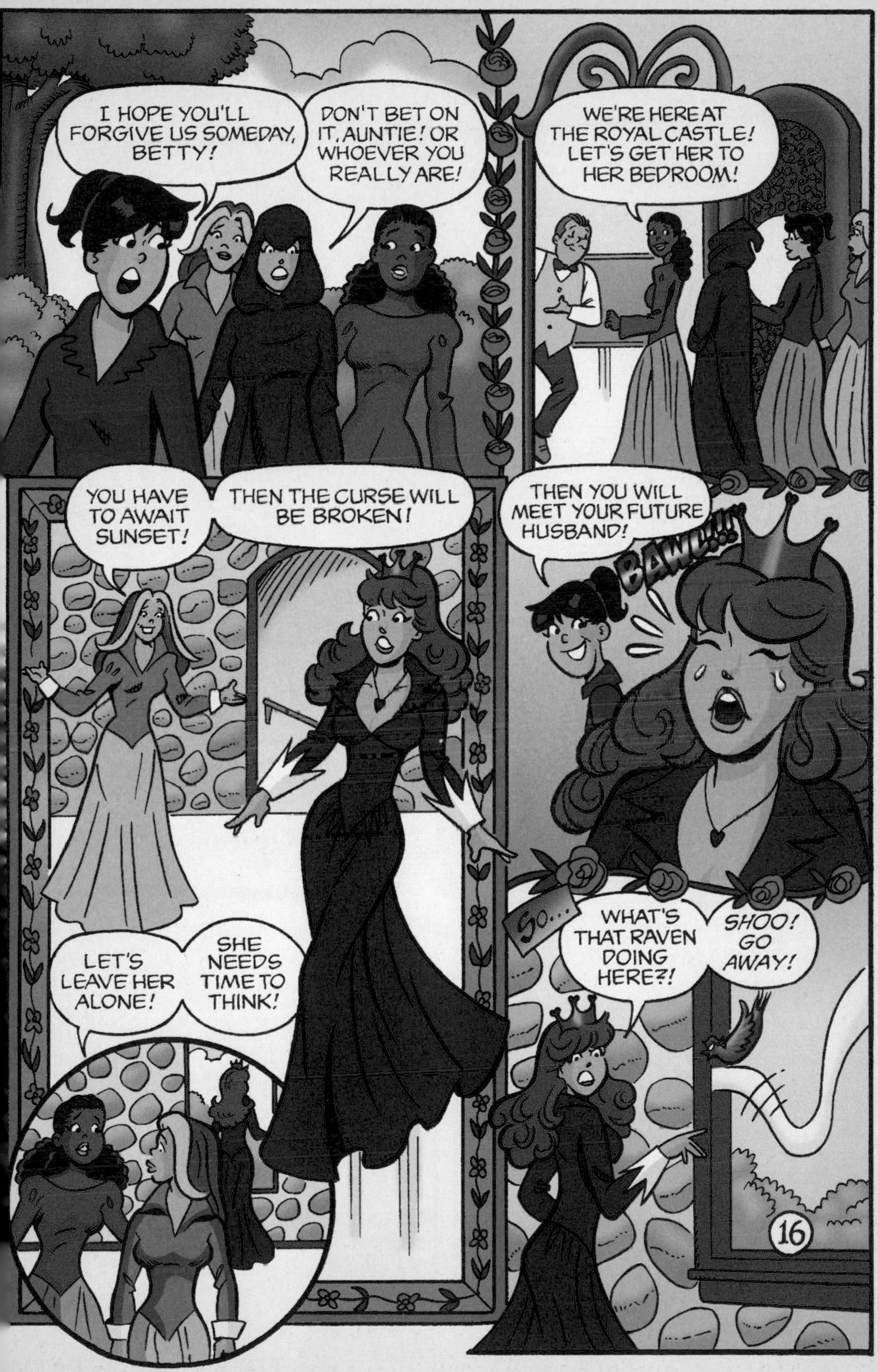
I HOPE YOU'LL FORGIVE US SOMEDAY, BETTY!
DON'T BET ON IT, AUNTIE! OR WHOEVER YOU REALLY ARE!
WE'RE HERE AT THE ROYAL CASTLE! LET'S GET HER TO HER BEDROOM!
YOU HAVE TO AWAIT SUNSET!
THEN THE CURSE WILL BE BROKEN!
THEN YOU WILL MEET YOUR FUTURE HUSBAND!
BAWL!!!
LET'S LEAVE HER ALONE!
SHE NEEDS TIME TO THINK!
SO...
WHAT'S THAT RAVEN DOING HERE?!
SHOO! GO AWAY!
16

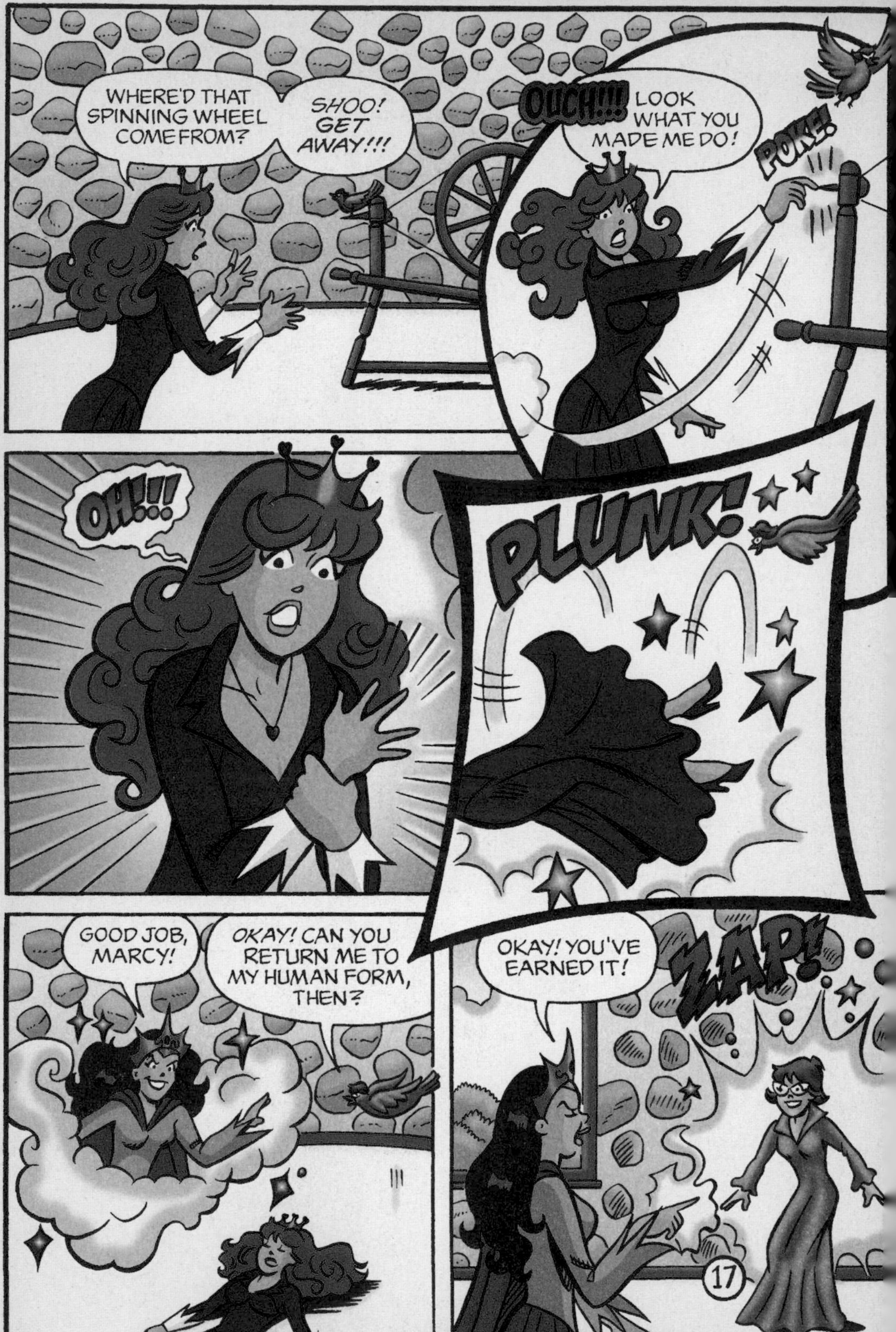
WHERE'D THAT SPINNING WHEEL COME FROM?
SHOO! GET AWAY!!!
OUCH!!!
LOOK WHAT YOU MADE ME DO!
POKE!
OH!!!
PLUNK!
GOOD JOB, MARCY!
OKAY! CAN YOU RETURN ME TO MY HUMAN FORM, THEN?
OKAY! YOU'VE EARNED IT!
ZAP!

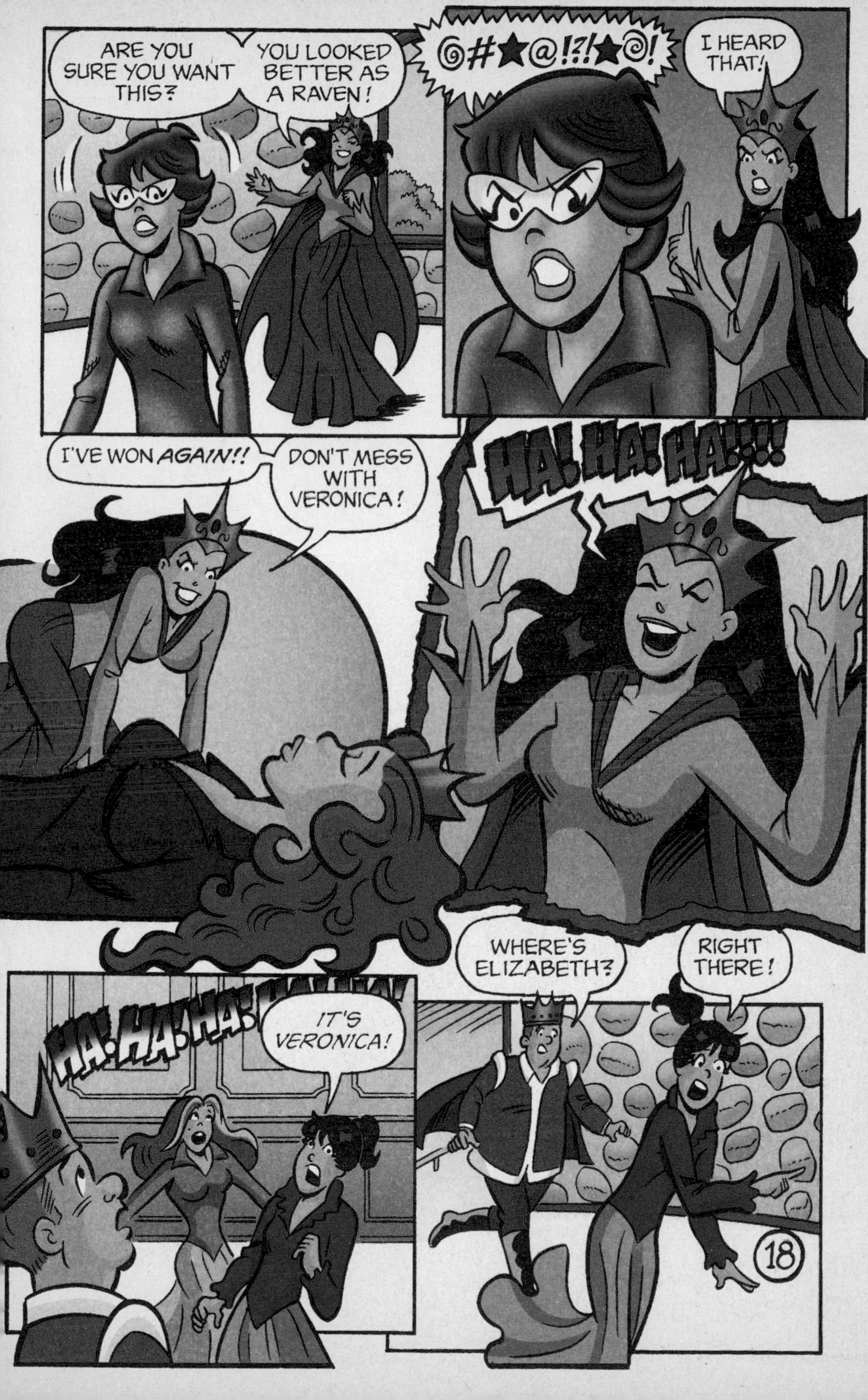
ARE YOU SURE YOU WANT THIS?
YOU LOOKED BETTER AS A RAVEN!
@#★@!?!★@!
I HEARD THAT!
I'VE WON AGAIN!!
DON'T MESS WITH VERONICA!
HA! HA! HA!!!!
HA! HA! HA!
IT'S VERONICA!
WHERE'S ELIZABETH?
RIGHT THERE!
18

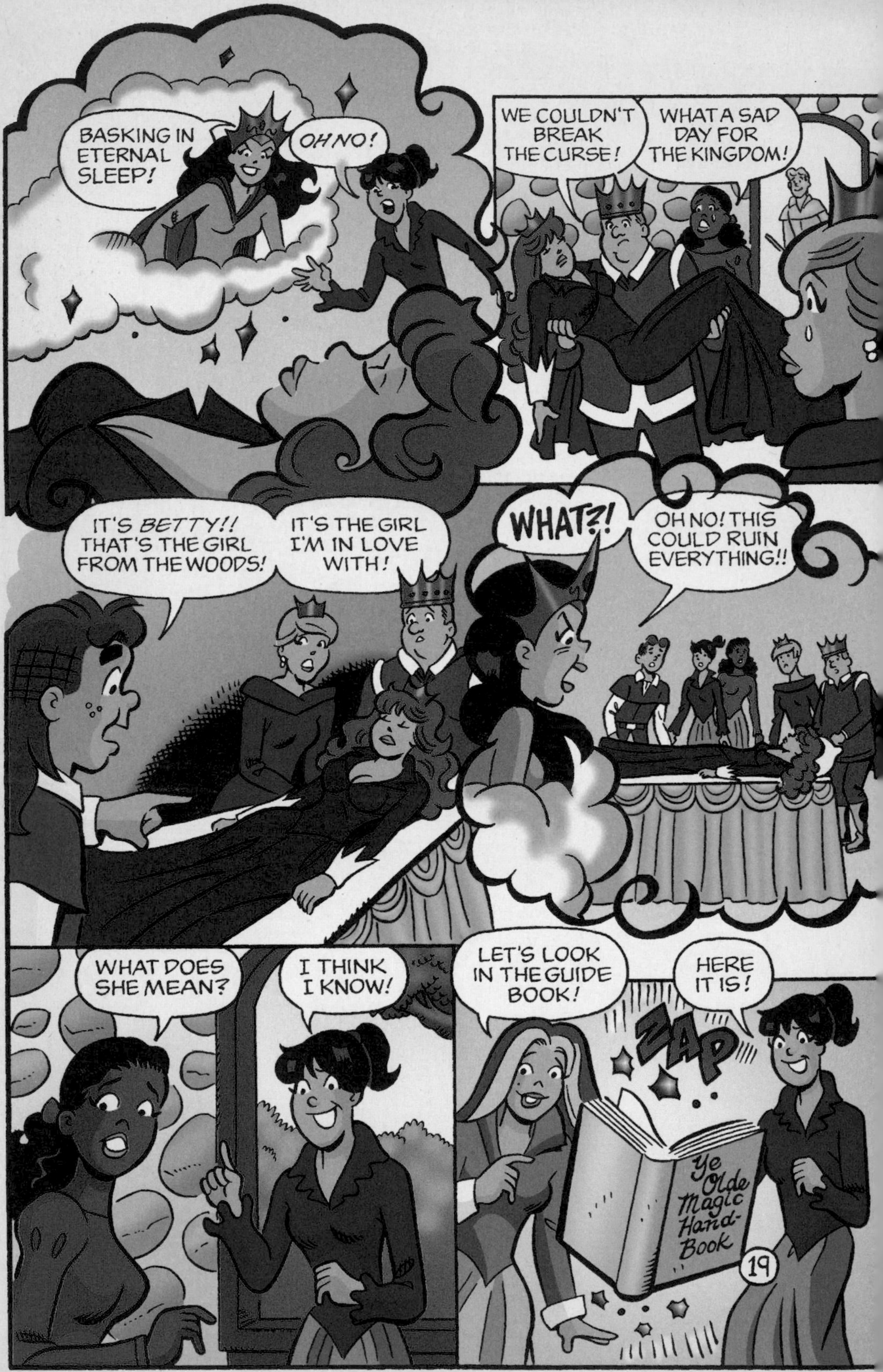
BASKING IN ETERNAL SLEEP!
OH NO!
WE COULDN'T BREAK THE CURSE!
WHAT A SAD DAY FOR THE KINGDOM!
IT'S *BETTY!!* THAT'S THE GIRL FROM THE WOODS!
IT'S THE GIRL I'M IN LOVE WITH!
WHAT?!
OH NO! THIS COULD RUIN EVERYTHING!!
WHAT DOES SHE MEAN?
I THINK I KNOW!
LET'S LOOK IN THE GUIDE BOOK!
HERE IT IS!
ZAP
Ye Olde Magic Hand-Book

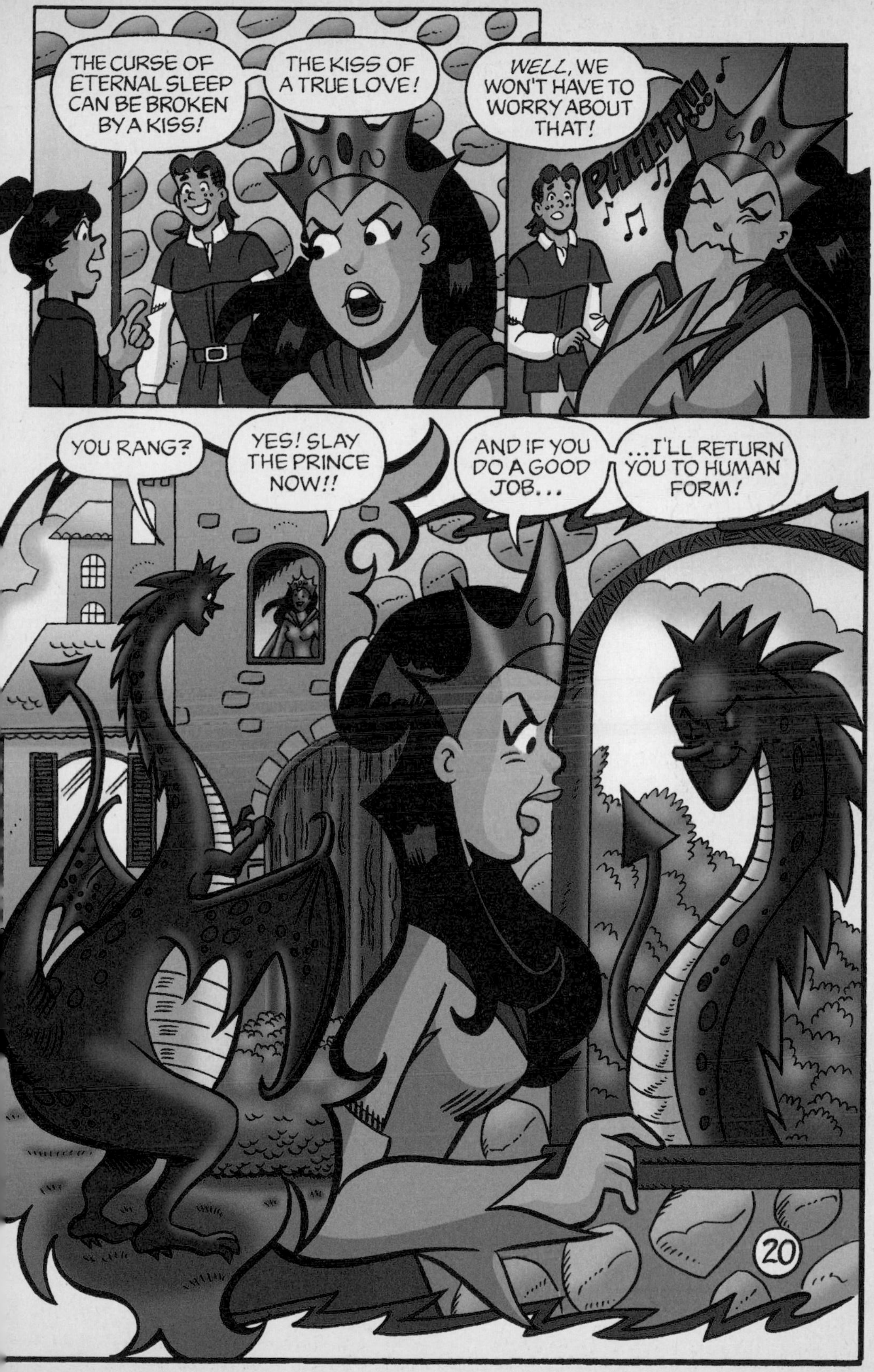
THE CURSE OF ETERNAL SLEEP CAN BE BROKEN BY A KISS!
THE KISS OF A TRUE LOVE!
WELL, WE WON'T HAVE TO WORRY ABOUT THAT!
PHHHT!!!
YOU RANG?
YES! SLAY THE PRINCE NOW!!
AND IF YOU DO A GOOD JOB...
...I'LL RETURN YOU TO HUMAN FORM!

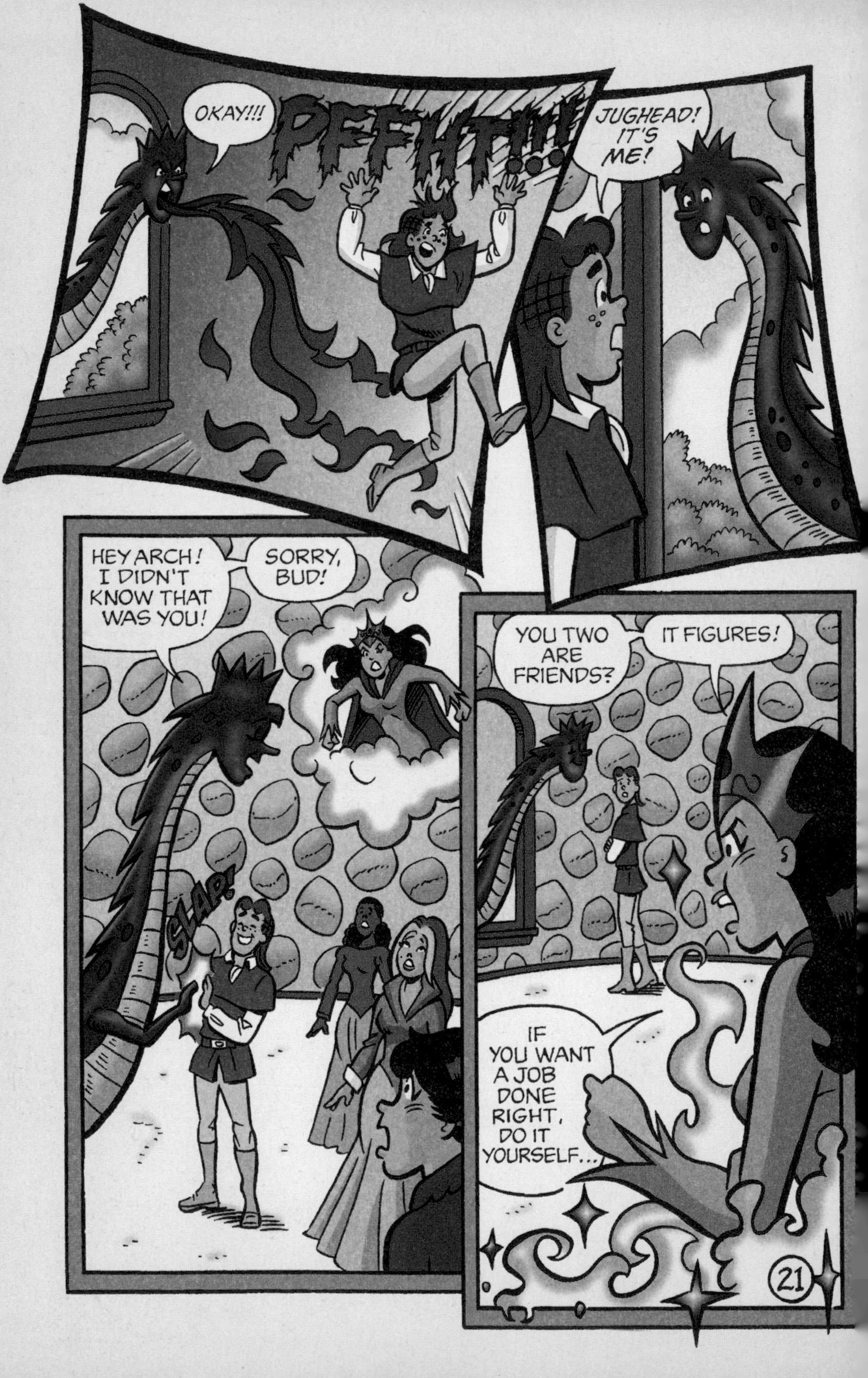

OKAY!!!
PFFHT!!!
JUGHEAD! IT'S ME!
HEY ARCH! I DIDN'T KNOW THAT WAS YOU!
SORRY, BUD!
SLAP!
YOU TWO ARE FRIENDS?
IT FIGURES!
IF YOU WANT A JOB DONE RIGHT, DO IT YOURSELF...

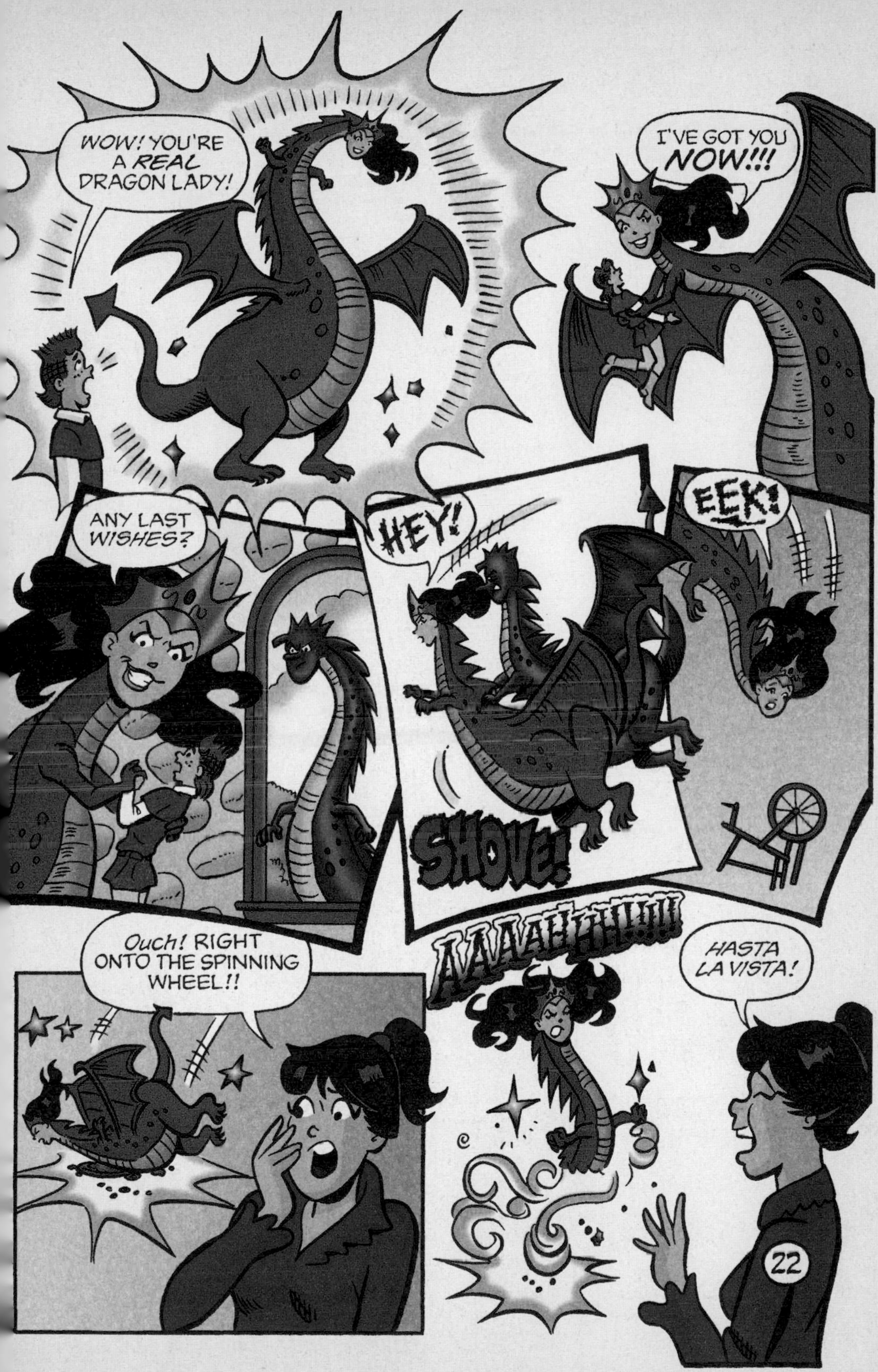

WOW! YOU'RE A REAL DRAGON LADY!
I'VE GOT YOU NOW!!!
ANY LAST WISHES?
HEY!
SHOVE!
EEK!
AAAAHHH!!!!
Ouch! RIGHT ONTO THE SPINNING WHEEL!!
HASTA LA VISTA!

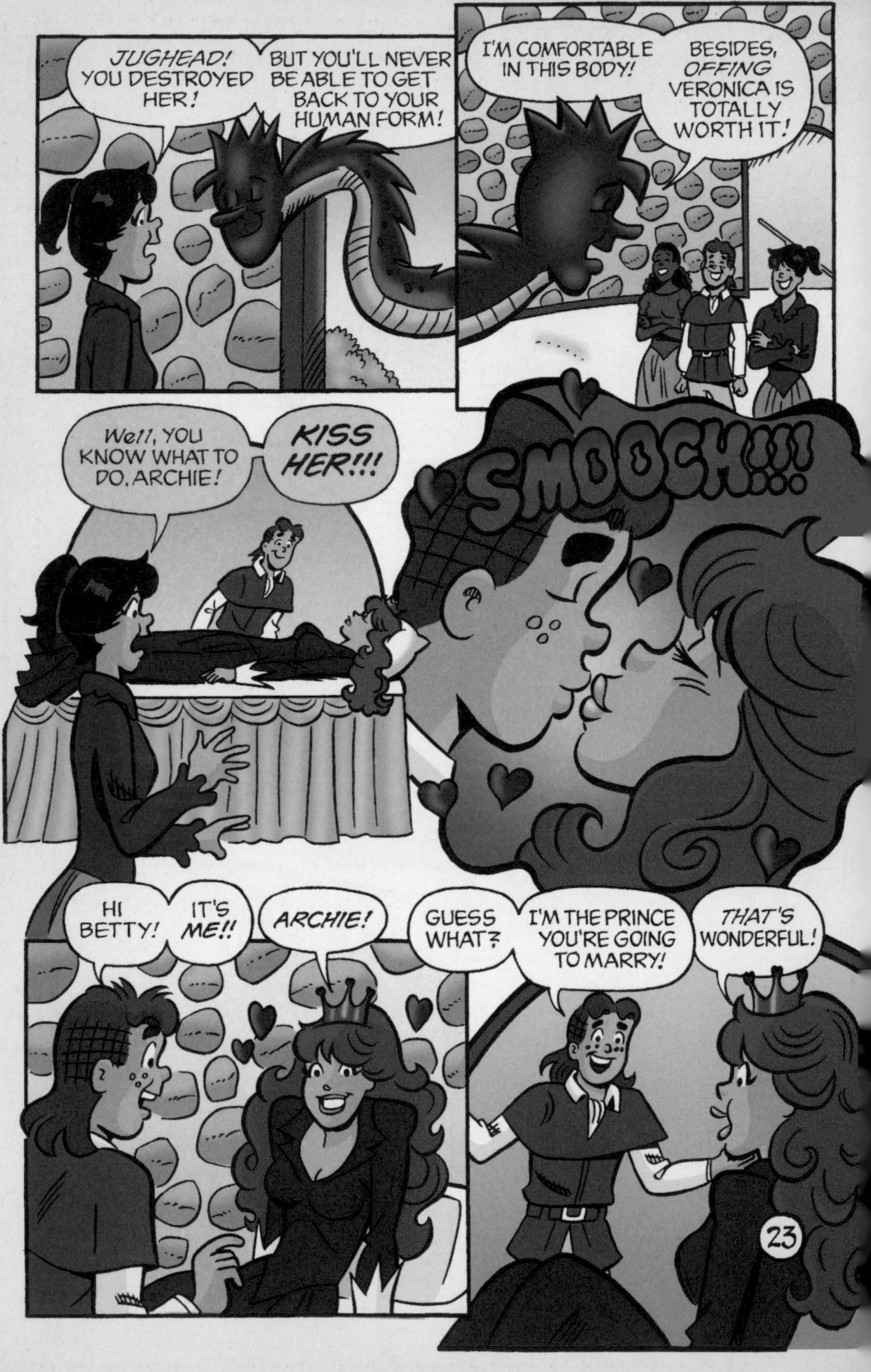
JUGHEAD! YOU DESTROYED HER!
BUT YOU'LL NEVER BE ABLE TO GET BACK TO YOUR HUMAN FORM!
I'M COMFORTABLE IN THIS BODY!
BESIDES, OFFING VERONICA IS TOTALLY WORTH IT!
Well, YOU KNOW WHAT TO DO, ARCHIE!
KISS HER!!!
SMOOCH!!!
HI BETTY!
IT'S ME!!
ARCHIE!
GUESS WHAT?
I'M THE PRINCE YOU'RE GOING TO MARRY!
THAT'S WONDERFUL!
23

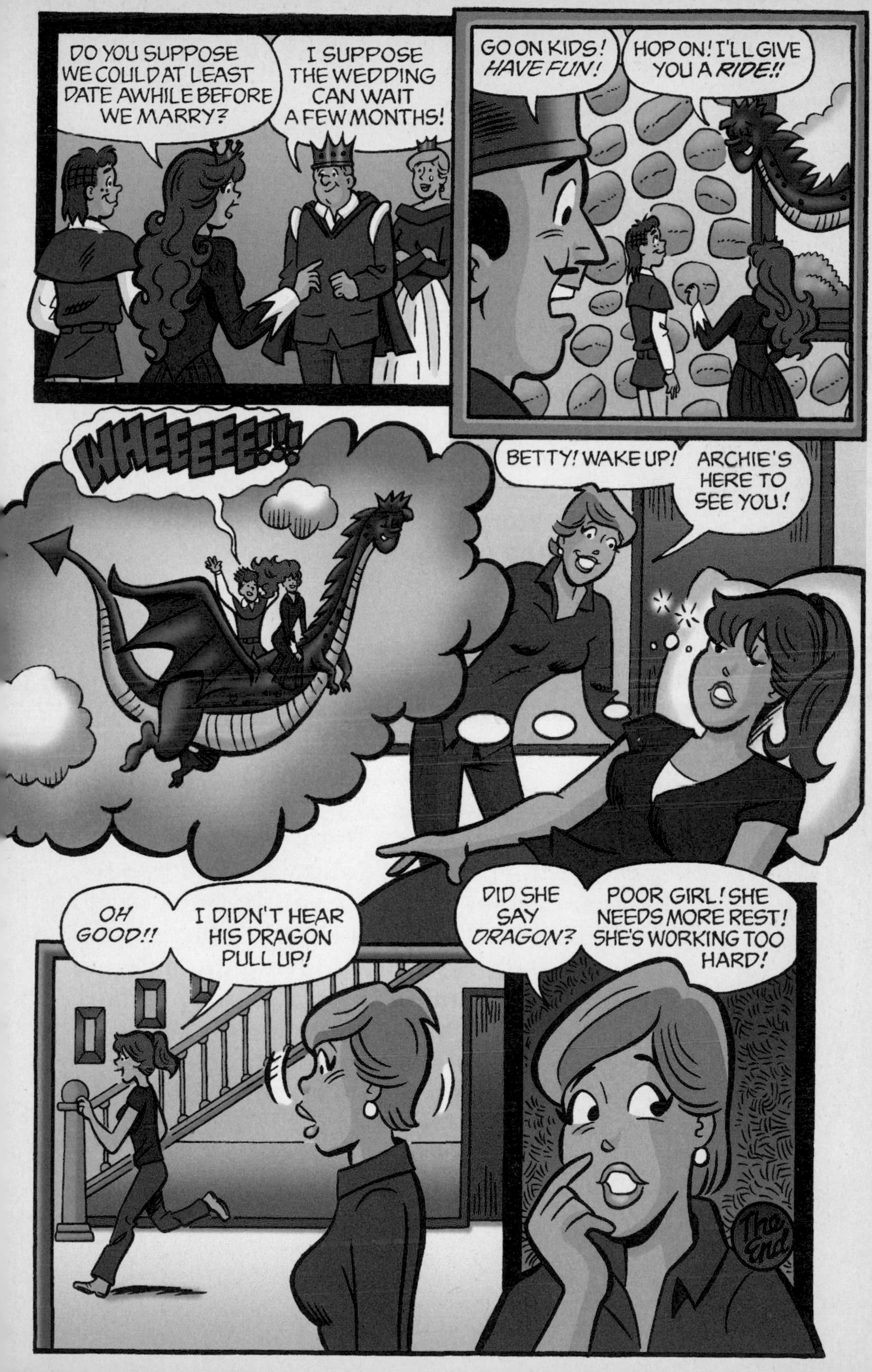

DO YOU SUPPOSE WE COULD AT LEAST DATE AWHILE BEFORE WE MARRY?
I SUPPOSE THE WEDDING CAN WAIT A FEW MONTHS!
GO ON KIDS! HAVE FUN!
HOP ON! I'LL GIVE YOU A RIDE!!
WHEEEEE!!!
BETTY! WAKE UP!
ARCHIE'S HERE TO SEE YOU!
OH GOOD!!
I DIDN'T HEAR HIS DRAGON PULL UP!
DID SHE SAY DRAGON?
POOR GIRL! SHE NEEDS MORE REST! SHE'S WORKING TOO HARD!
The End

There's No Place Like Riverdale

The Wonderful World of Oz **was a children's book written by L. Frank Baum and illustrated by W.W. Denslow. It was originally published in 1900 and has been continually reprinted ever since. The story tells of Dorothy's adventures in the strange and fantastical Land of Oz. The book was adapted into a well-known 1902 stage play and later the classic 1939 film version. The film's popularity has helped make** *The Wonderful World of Oz* **one of the most well-known stories in the world, having been translated into many different languages.**

In "There's No Place Like Riverdale," a bump on the head sends Betty into a whirlwind of excitement – literally! Follow Betty and her faithful cat Carmel down the yellow-brick road as she encounters a munchkin (yes, just one), a brainless scarecrow, a pizza-loving tin man and a vain lion as she embarks on a journey to find the wizard and find her way home. She must help out her new pals while also dodging the Wicked Witch of East, Veronica. Will Betty find her way home from Oz?

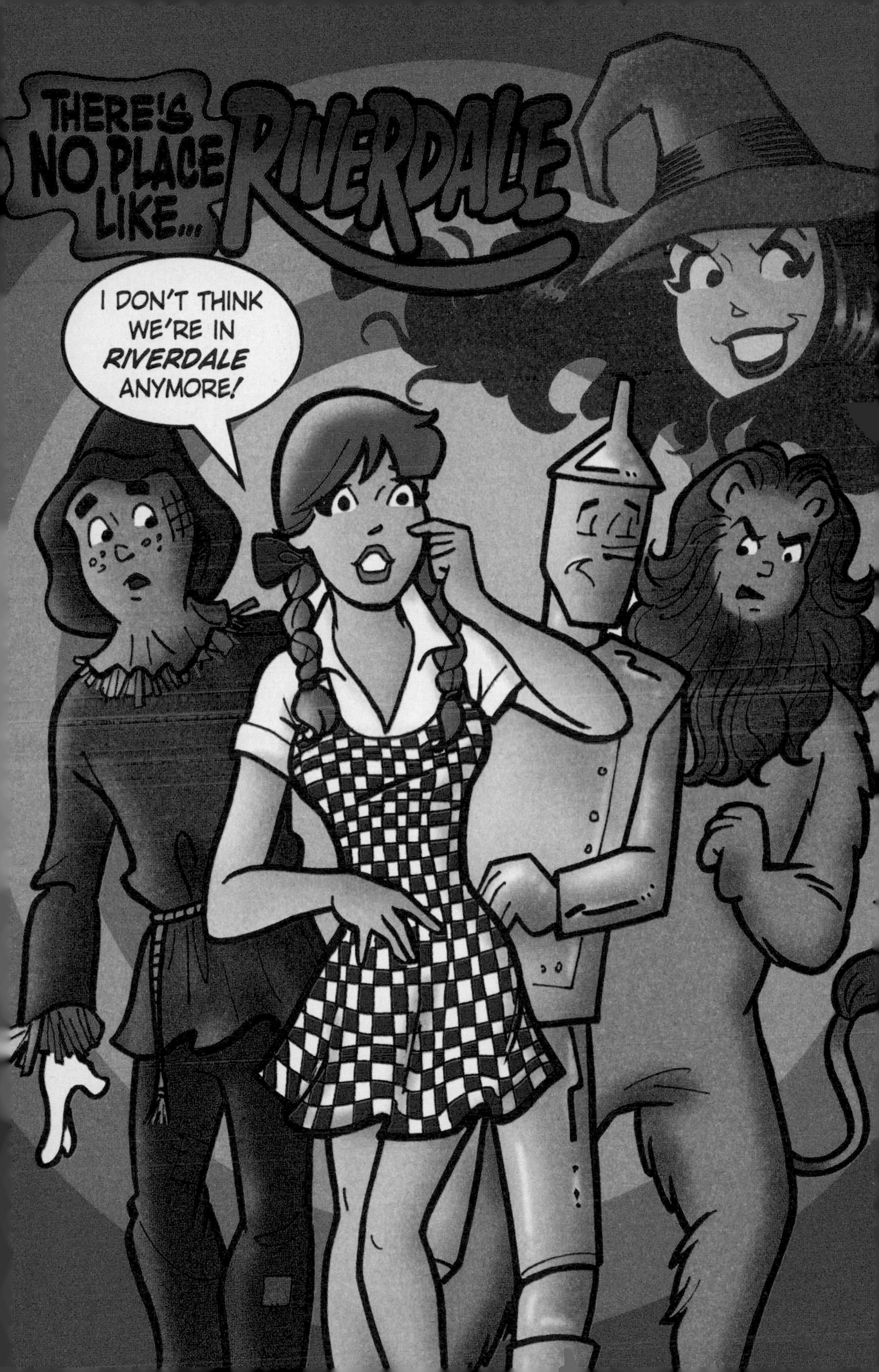
THERE'S NO PLACE LIKE... RIVERDALE
I DON'T THINK WE'RE IN *RIVERDALE* ANYMORE!

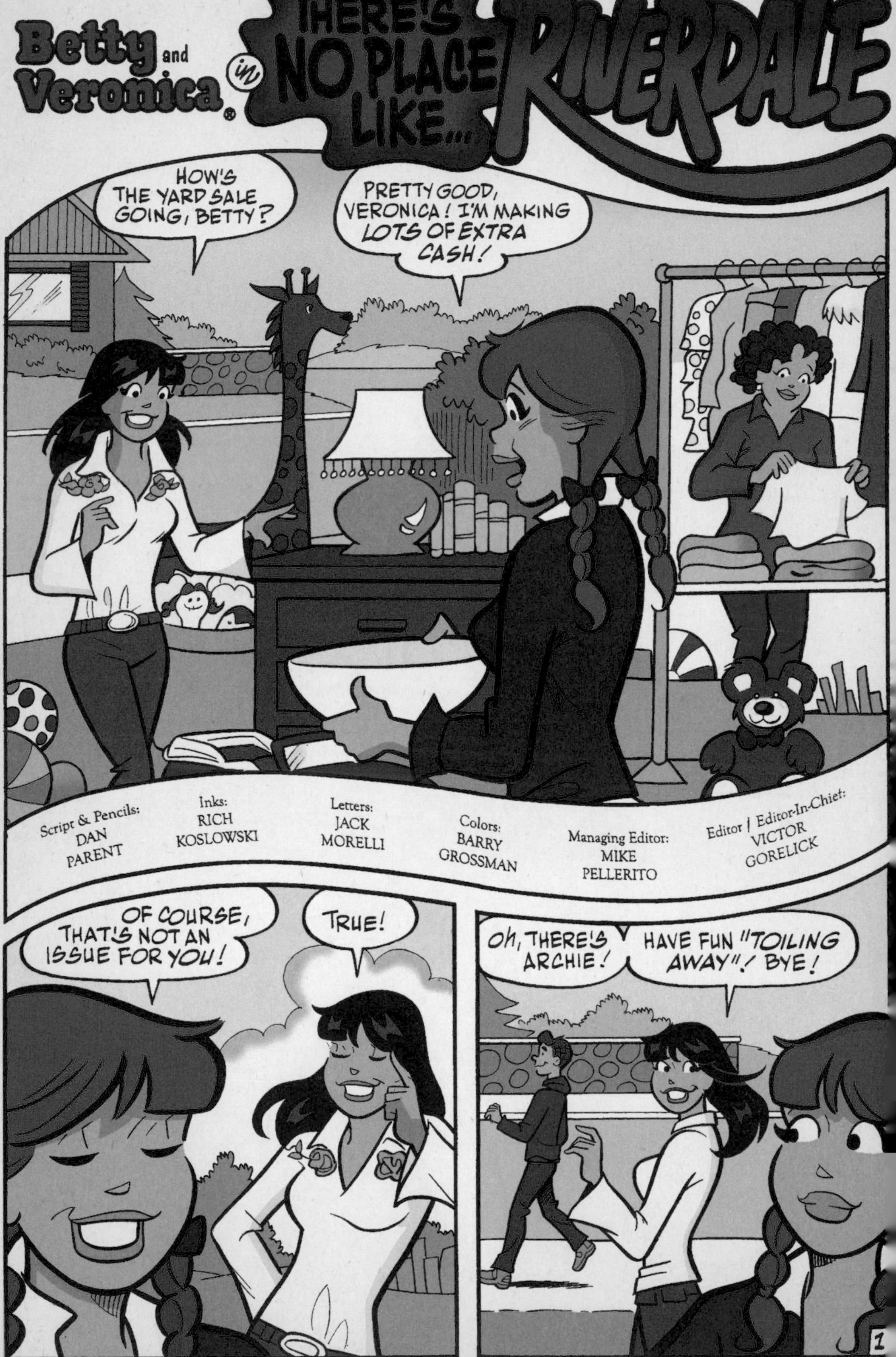
Betty and Veronica® in
THERE'S NO PLACE LIKE... RIVERDALE
HOW'S THE YARD SALE GOING, BETTY?
PRETTY GOOD, VERONICA! I'M MAKING LOTS OF EXTRA CASH!
Script & Pencils: DAN PARENT
Inks: RICH KOSLOWSKI
Letters: JACK MORELLI
Colors: BARRY GROSSMAN
Managing Editor: MIKE PELLERITO
Editor / Editor-In-Chief: VICTOR GORELICK
OF COURSE, THAT'S NOT AN ISSUE FOR YOU!
TRUE!
Oh, THERE'S ARCHIE!
HAVE FUN "TOILING AWAY"! BYE!
1

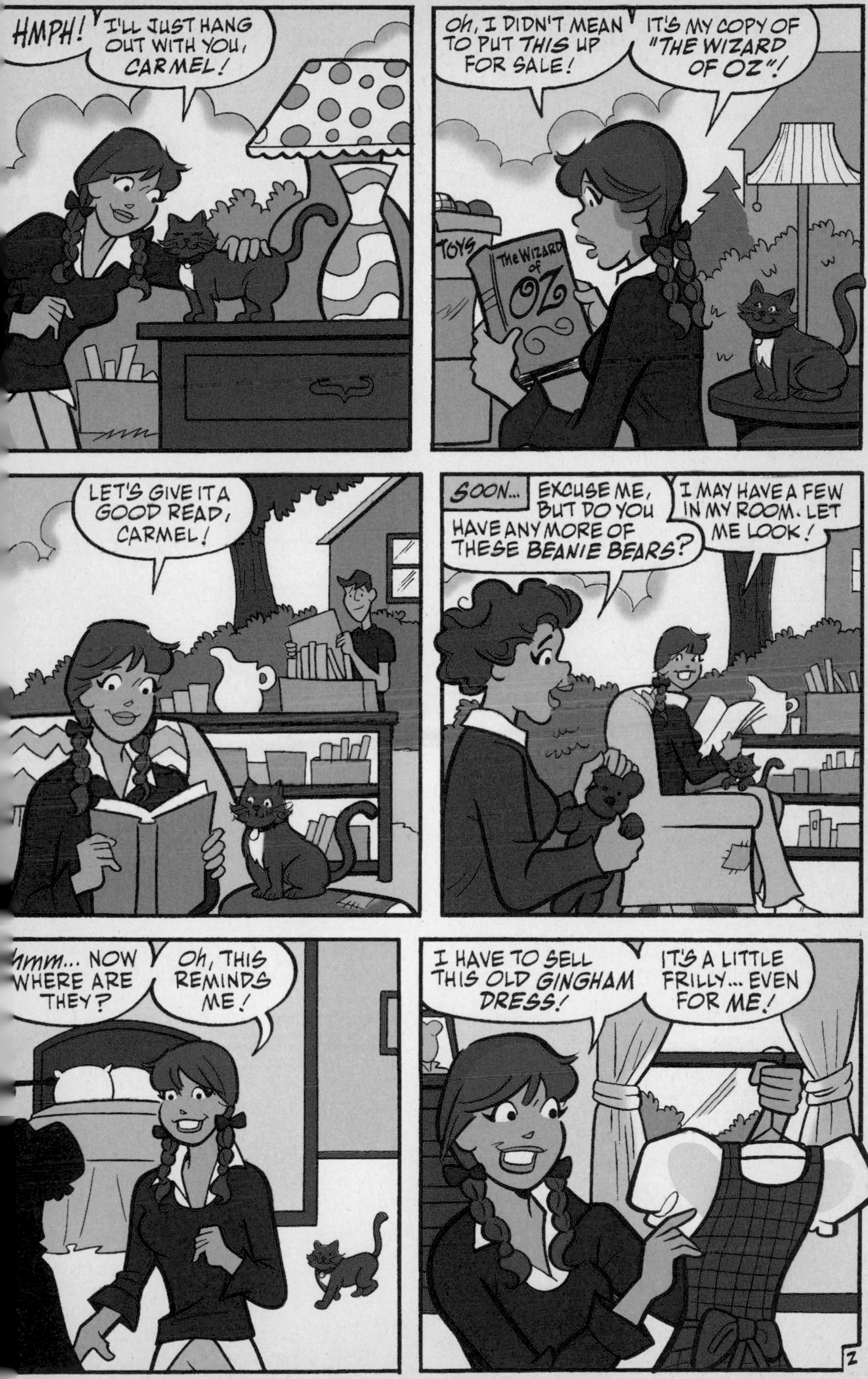

HMPH!
I'LL JUST HANG OUT WITH YOU, CARMEL!
Oh, I DIDN'T MEAN TO PUT THIS UP FOR SALE!
IT'S MY COPY OF "THE WIZARD OF OZ"!
TOYS
The WIZARD of OZ
LET'S GIVE IT A GOOD READ, CARMEL!
SOON...
EXCUSE ME, BUT DO YOU HAVE ANY MORE OF THESE BEANIE BEARS?
I MAY HAVE A FEW IN MY ROOM. LET ME LOOK!
mm... NOW WHERE ARE THEY?
Oh, THIS REMINDS ME!
I HAVE TO SELL THIS OLD GINGHAM DRESS!
IT'S A LITTLE FRILLY... EVEN FOR ME!

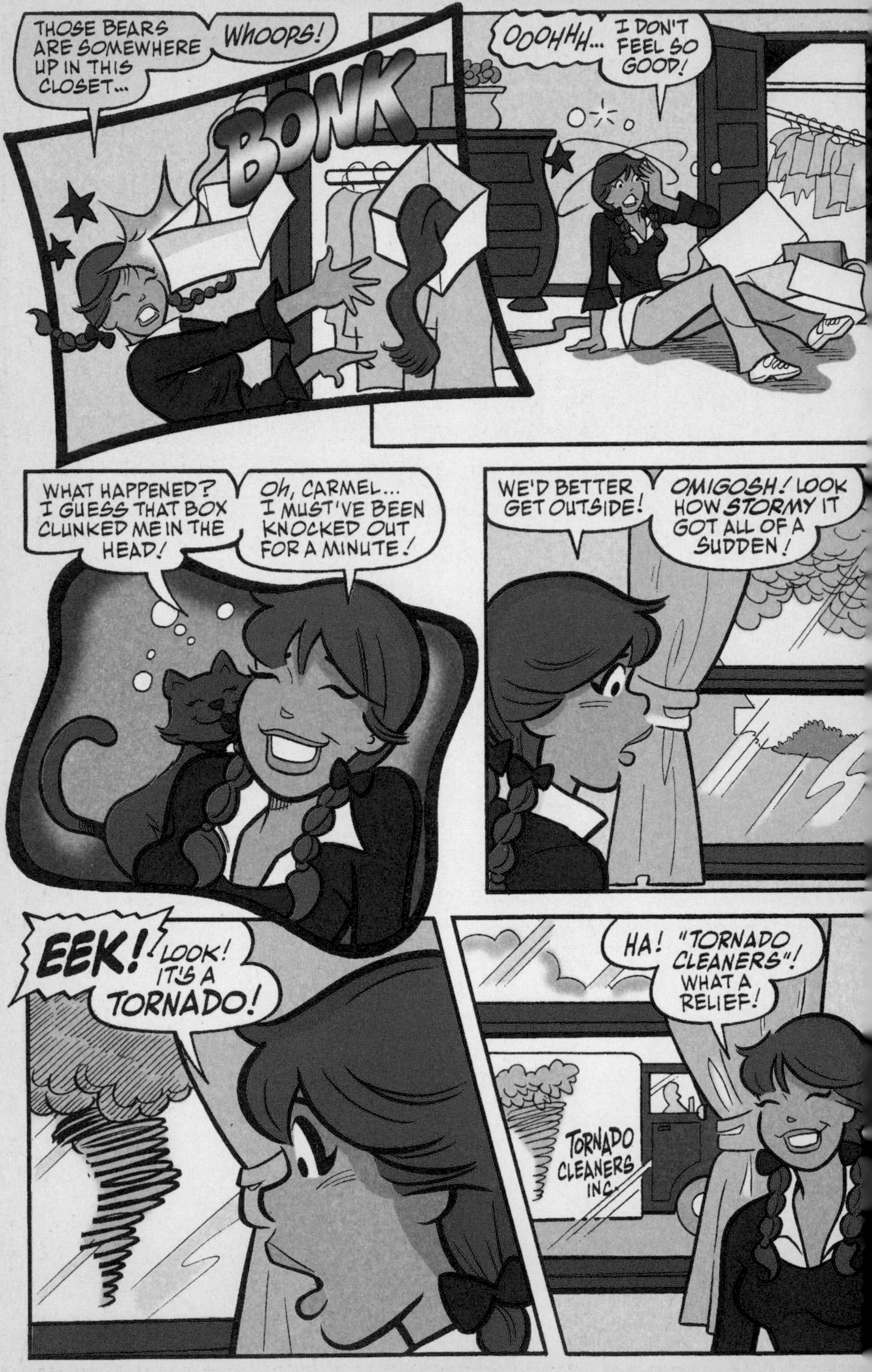
THOSE BEARS ARE SOMEWHERE UP IN THIS CLOSET...
WHOOPS!
BONK
OOOHHH... I DON'T FEEL SO GOOD!
WHAT HAPPENED? I GUESS THAT BOX CLUNKED ME IN THE HEAD!
Oh, CARMEL... I MUST'VE BEEN KNOCKED OUT FOR A MINUTE!
WE'D BETTER GET OUTSIDE!
OMIGOSH! LOOK HOW STORMY IT GOT ALL OF A SUDDEN!
EEK! LOOK! IT'S A TORNADO!
HA! "TORNADO CLEANERS"! WHAT A RELIEF!
TORNADO CLEANERS INC.

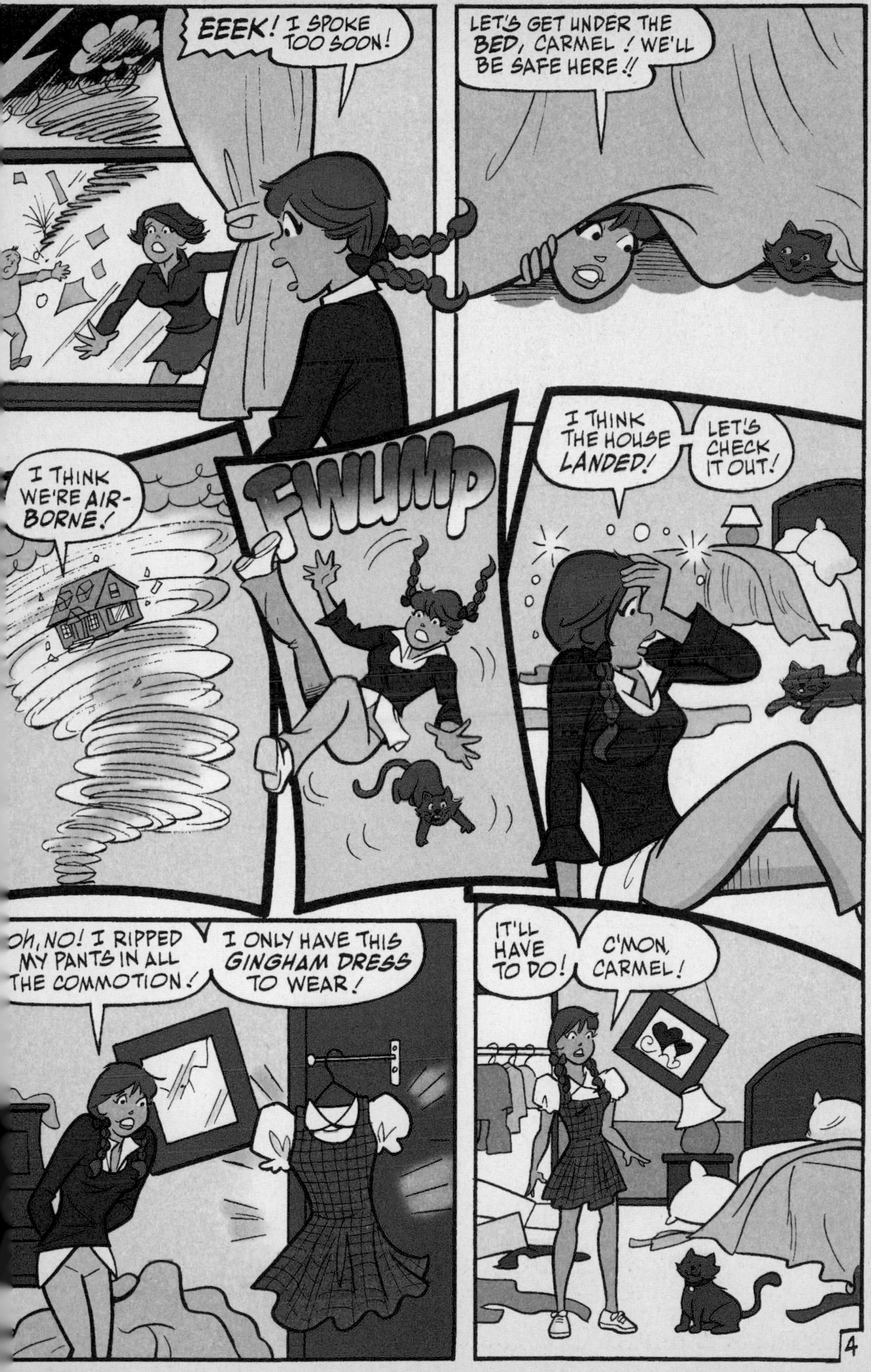
EEEK! I SPOKE TOO SOON!
LET'S GET UNDER THE BED, CARMEL! WE'LL BE SAFE HERE!!
I THINK WE'RE AIR-BORNE!
FWUMP
I THINK THE HOUSE LANDED!
LET'S CHECK IT OUT!
OH, NO! I RIPPED MY PANTS IN ALL THE COMMOTION!
I ONLY HAVE THIS GINGHAM DRESS TO WEAR!
IT'LL HAVE TO DO!
C'MON, CARMEL!
4

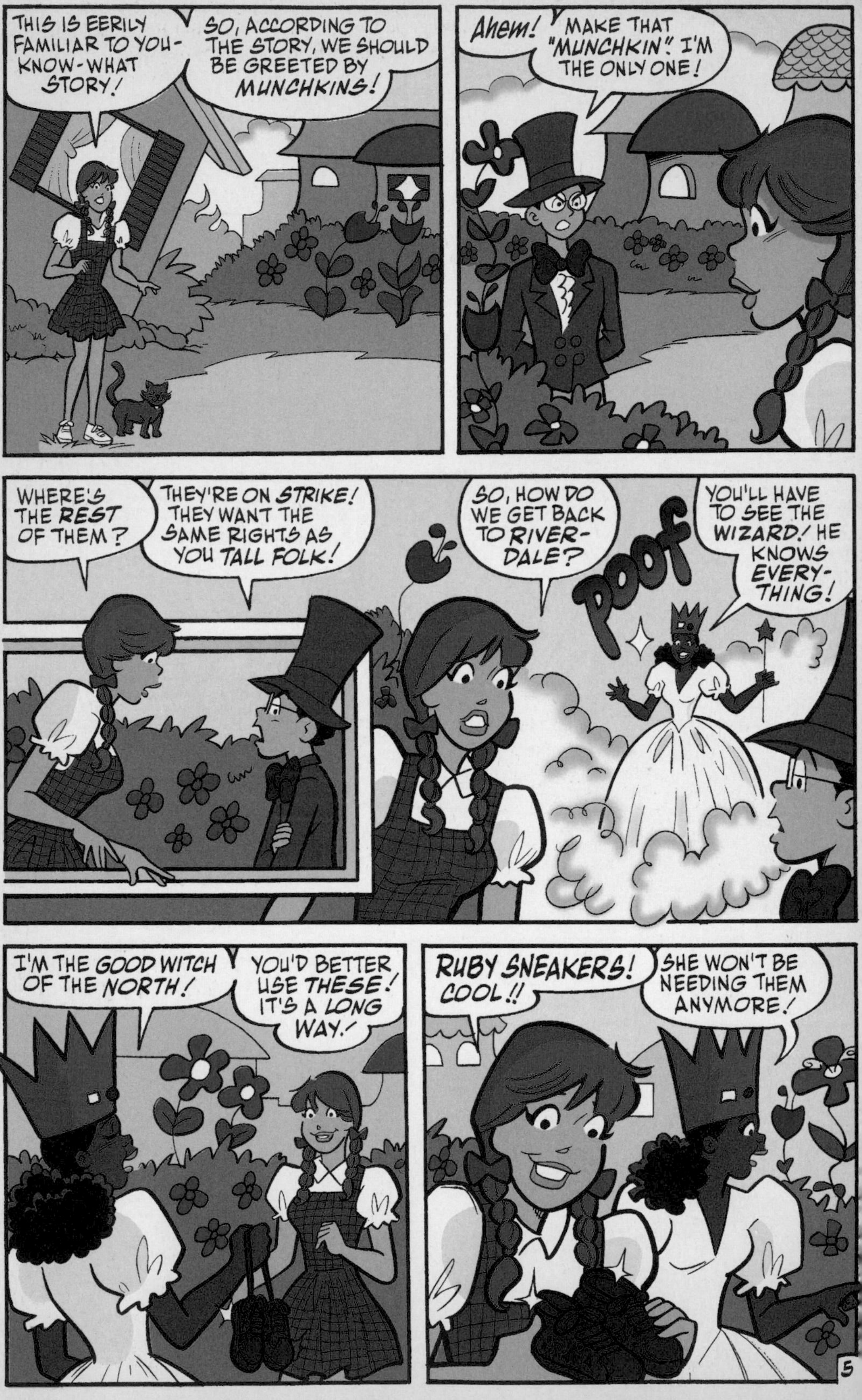
THIS IS EERILY FAMILIAR TO YOU-KNOW-WHAT STORY!
SO, ACCORDING TO THE STORY, WE SHOULD BE GREETED BY MUNCHKINS!
Ahem!
MAKE THAT "MUNCHKIN"! I'M THE ONLY ONE!
WHERE'S THE REST OF THEM?
THEY'RE ON STRIKE! THEY WANT THE SAME RIGHTS AS YOU TALL FOLK!
SO, HOW DO WE GET BACK TO RIVER-DALE?
POOF
YOU'LL HAVE TO SEE THE WIZARD! HE KNOWS EVERY-THING!
I'M THE GOOD WITCH OF THE NORTH!
YOU'D BETTER USE THESE! IT'S A LONG WAY!
RUBY SNEAKERS! COOL!!
SHE WON'T BE NEEDING THEM ANYMORE!

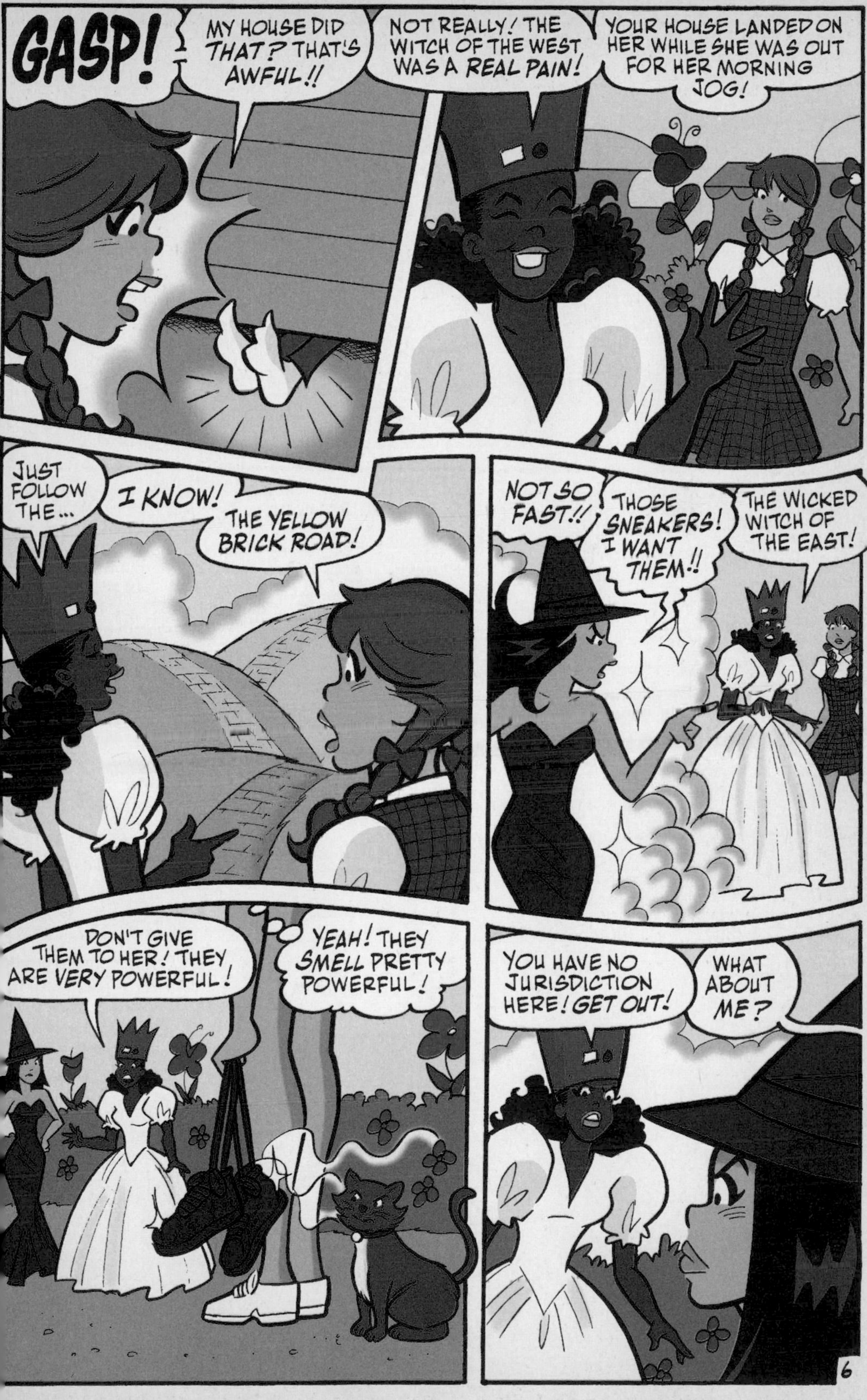
GASP!
MY HOUSE DID THAT? THAT'S AWFUL!!
NOT REALLY! THE WITCH OF THE WEST WAS A REAL PAIN!
YOUR HOUSE LANDED ON HER WHILE SHE WAS OUT FOR HER MORNING JOG!
JUST FOLLOW THE...
I KNOW!
THE YELLOW BRICK ROAD!
NOT SO FAST!!
THOSE SNEAKERS! I WANT THEM!!
THE WICKED WITCH OF THE EAST!
DON'T GIVE THEM TO HER! THEY ARE VERY POWERFUL!
YEAH! THEY SMELL PRETTY POWERFUL!
YOU HAVE NO JURISDICTION HERE! GET OUT!
WHAT ABOUT ME?
6

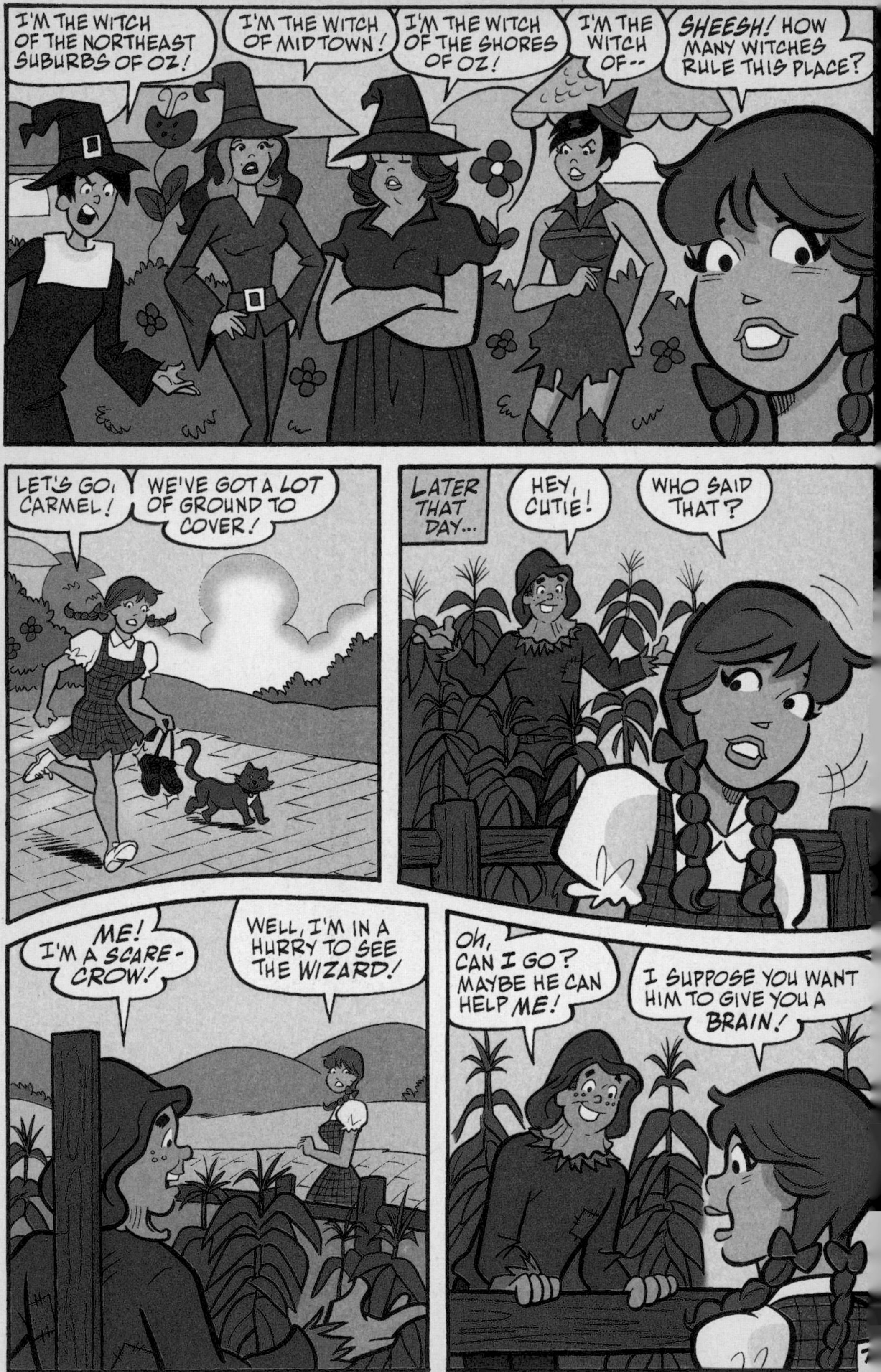

I'M THE WITCH OF THE NORTHEAST SUBURBS OF OZ!
I'M THE WITCH OF MIDTOWN!
I'M THE WITCH OF THE SHORES OF OZ!
I'M THE WITCH OF--
SHEESH! HOW MANY WITCHES RULE THIS PLACE?
LET'S GO, CARMEL!
WE'VE GOT A LOT OF GROUND TO COVER!
LATER THAT DAY...
HEY, CUTIE!
WHO SAID THAT?
ME! I'M A SCARE-CROW!
WELL, I'M IN A HURRY TO SEE THE WIZARD!
OH, CAN I GO? MAYBE HE CAN HELP ME!
I SUPPOSE YOU WANT HIM TO GIVE YOU A BRAIN!

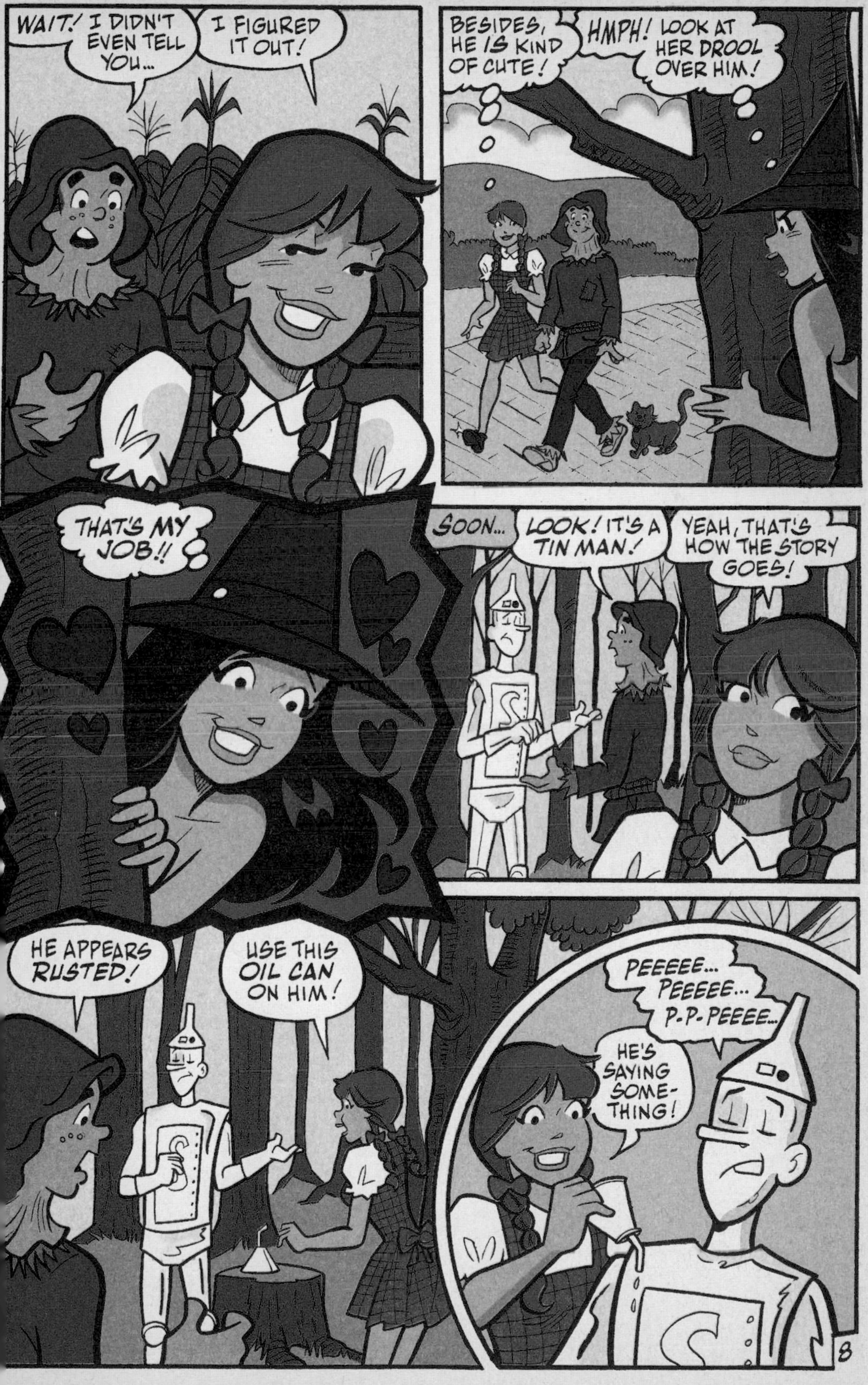
WAIT! I DIDN'T EVEN TELL YOU...
I FIGURED IT OUT!
BESIDES, HE IS KIND OF CUTE!
HMPH! LOOK AT HER DROOL OVER HIM!
THAT'S MY JOB!!
SOON...
LOOK! IT'S A TIN MAN!
YEAH, THAT'S HOW THE STORY GOES!
HE APPEARS RUSTED!
USE THIS OIL CAN ON HIM!
PEEEEE... PEEEEE... P-P-PEEEE...
HE'S SAYING SOME-THING!

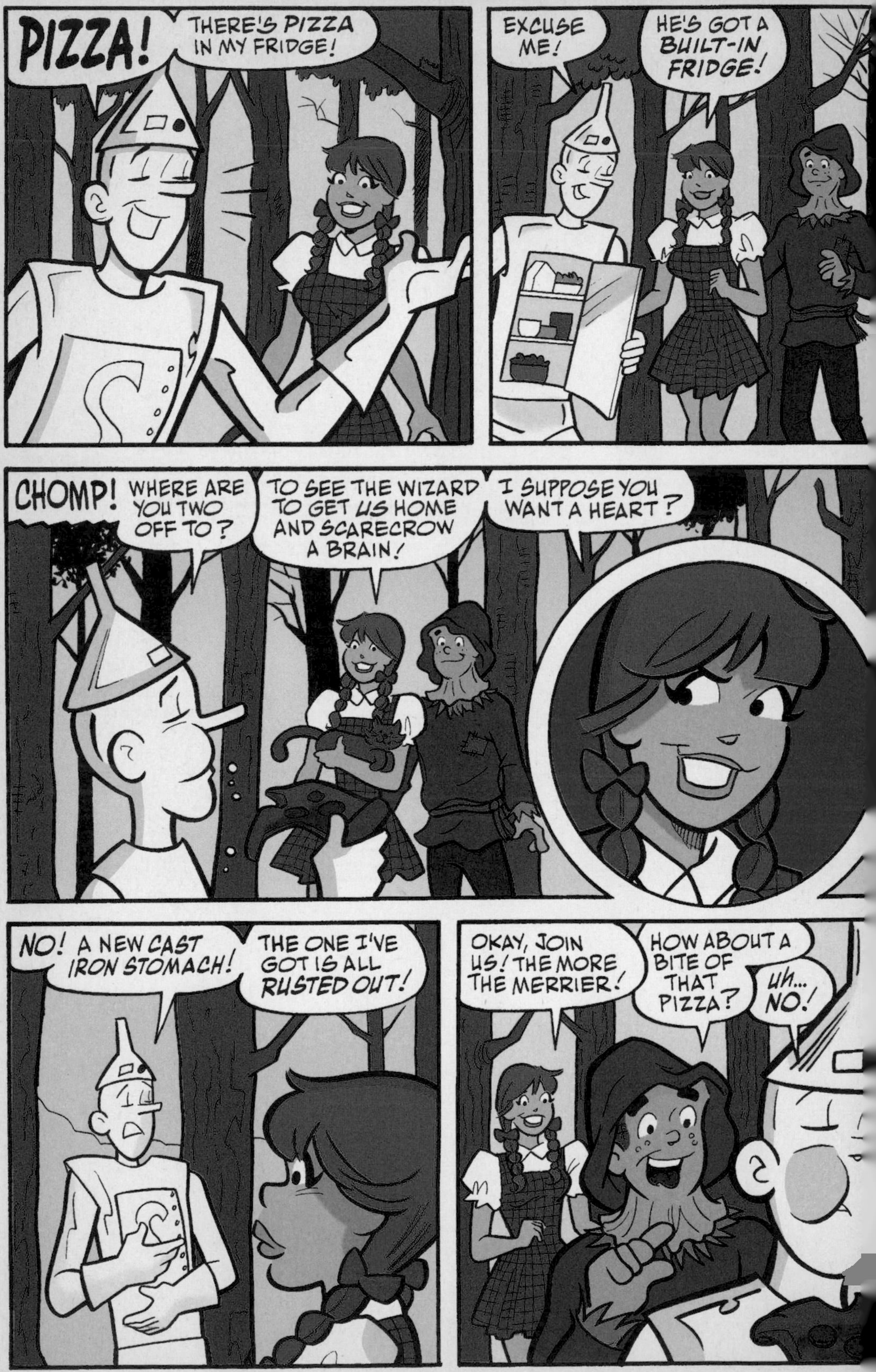
PIZZA!
THERE'S PIZZA IN MY FRIDGE!
EXCUSE ME!
HE'S GOT A BUILT-IN FRIDGE!
CHOMP!
WHERE ARE YOU TWO OFF TO?
TO SEE THE WIZARD TO GET US HOME AND SCARECROW A BRAIN!
I SUPPOSE YOU WANT A HEART?
NO! A NEW CAST IRON STOMACH!
THE ONE I'VE GOT IS ALL RUSTED OUT!
OKAY, JOIN US! THE MORE THE MERRIER!
HOW ABOUT A BITE OF THAT PIZZA?
UH... NO!

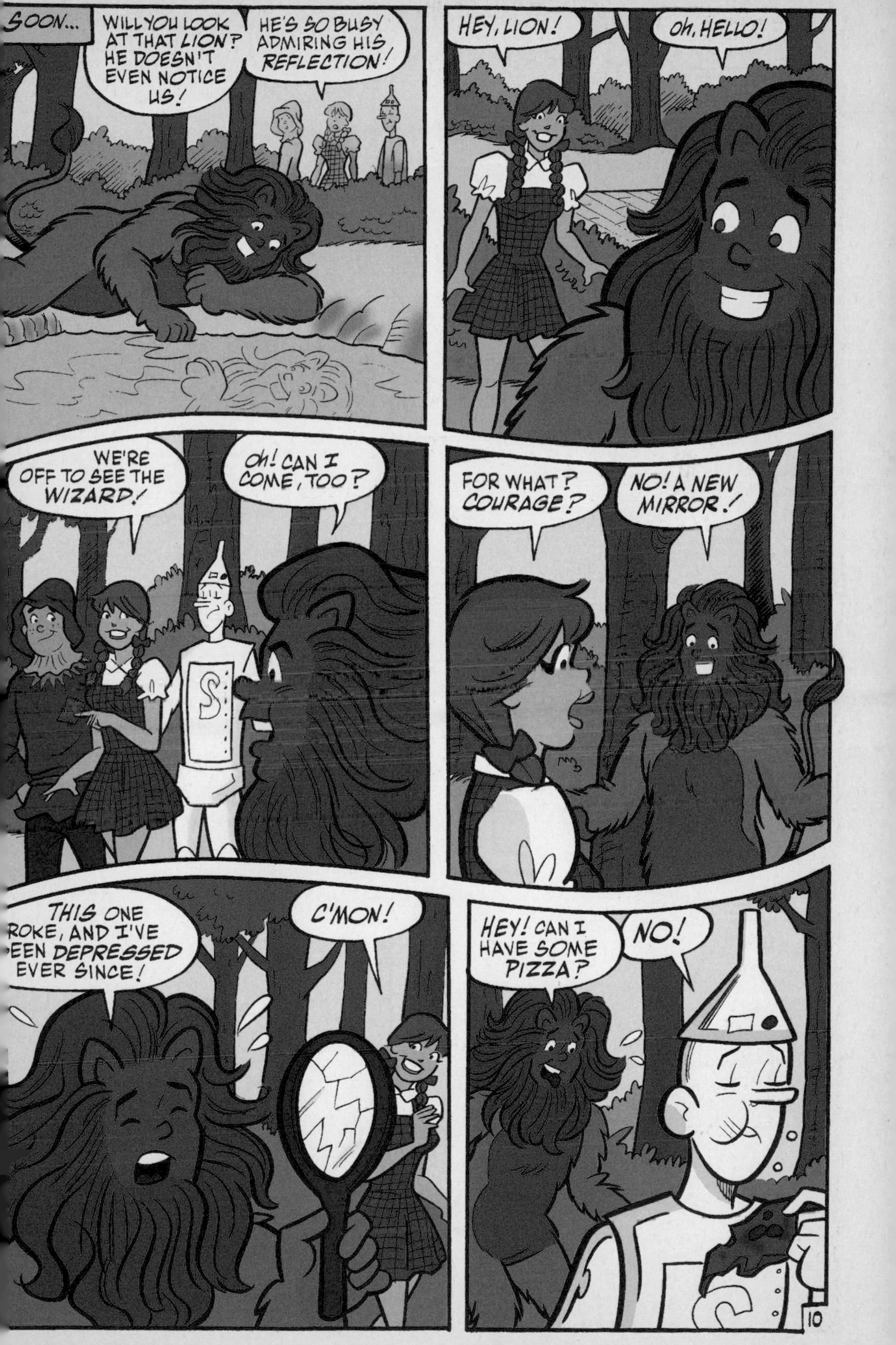
SOON...
WILL YOU LOOK AT THAT LION? HE DOESN'T EVEN NOTICE US!
HE'S SO BUSY ADMIRING HIS REFLECTION!
HEY, LION!
OH, HELLO!
WE'RE OFF TO SEE THE WIZARD!
OH! CAN I COME, TOO?
FOR WHAT? COURAGE?
NO! A NEW MIRROR!
THIS ONE ROKE, AND I'VE EEN DEPRESSED EVER SINCE!
C'MON!
HEY! CAN I HAVE SOME PIZZA?
NO!

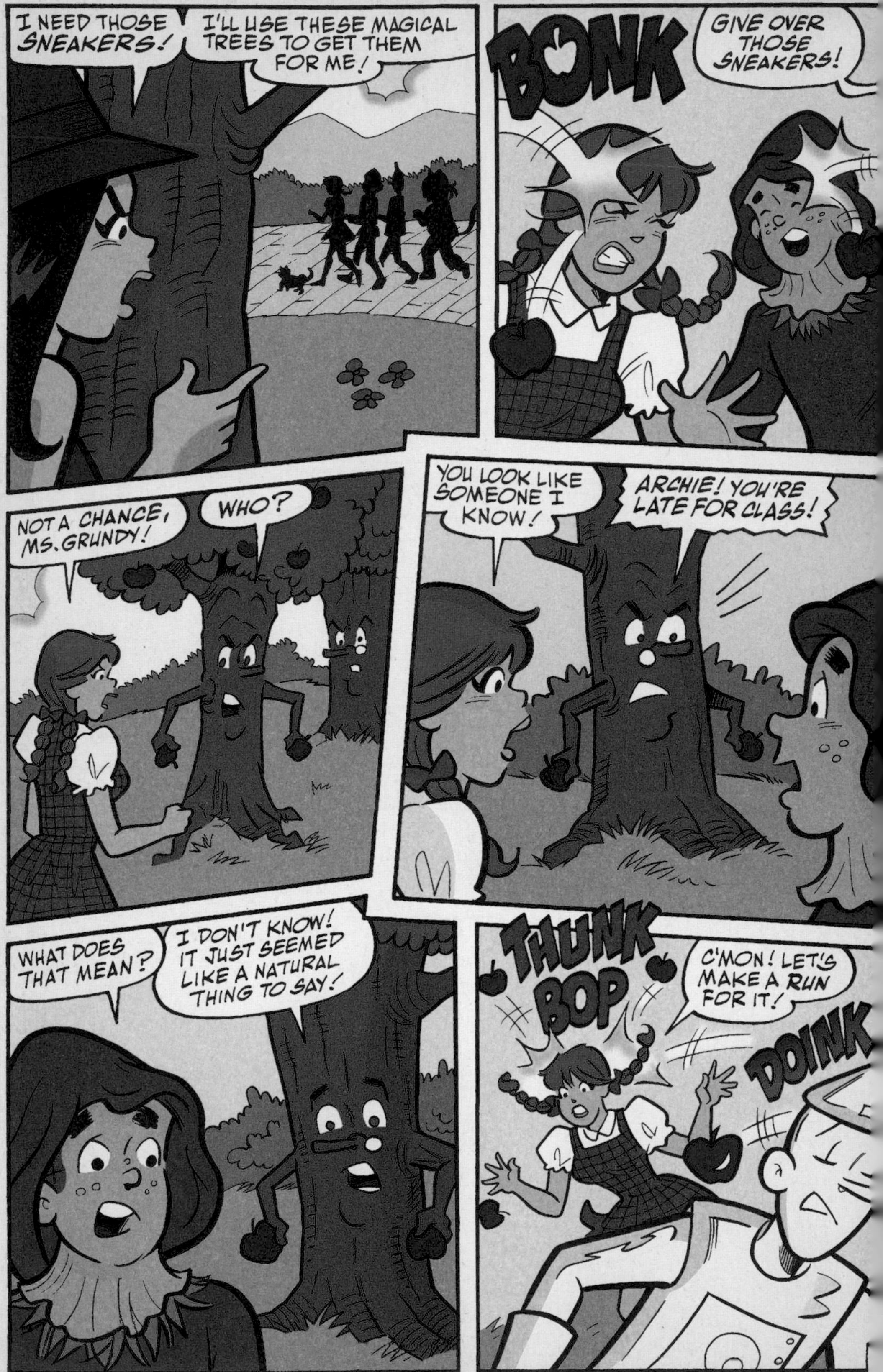

I NEED THOSE SNEAKERS!
I'LL USE THESE MAGICAL TREES TO GET THEM FOR ME!
BONK
GIVE OVER THOSE SNEAKERS!
NOT A CHANCE, MS. GRUNDY!
WHO?
YOU LOOK LIKE SOMEONE I KNOW!
ARCHIE! YOU'RE LATE FOR CLASS!
WHAT DOES THAT MEAN?
I DON'T KNOW! IT JUST SEEMED LIKE A NATURAL THING TO SAY!
THUNK
BOP
C'MON! LET'S MAKE A RUN FOR IT!
DOINK

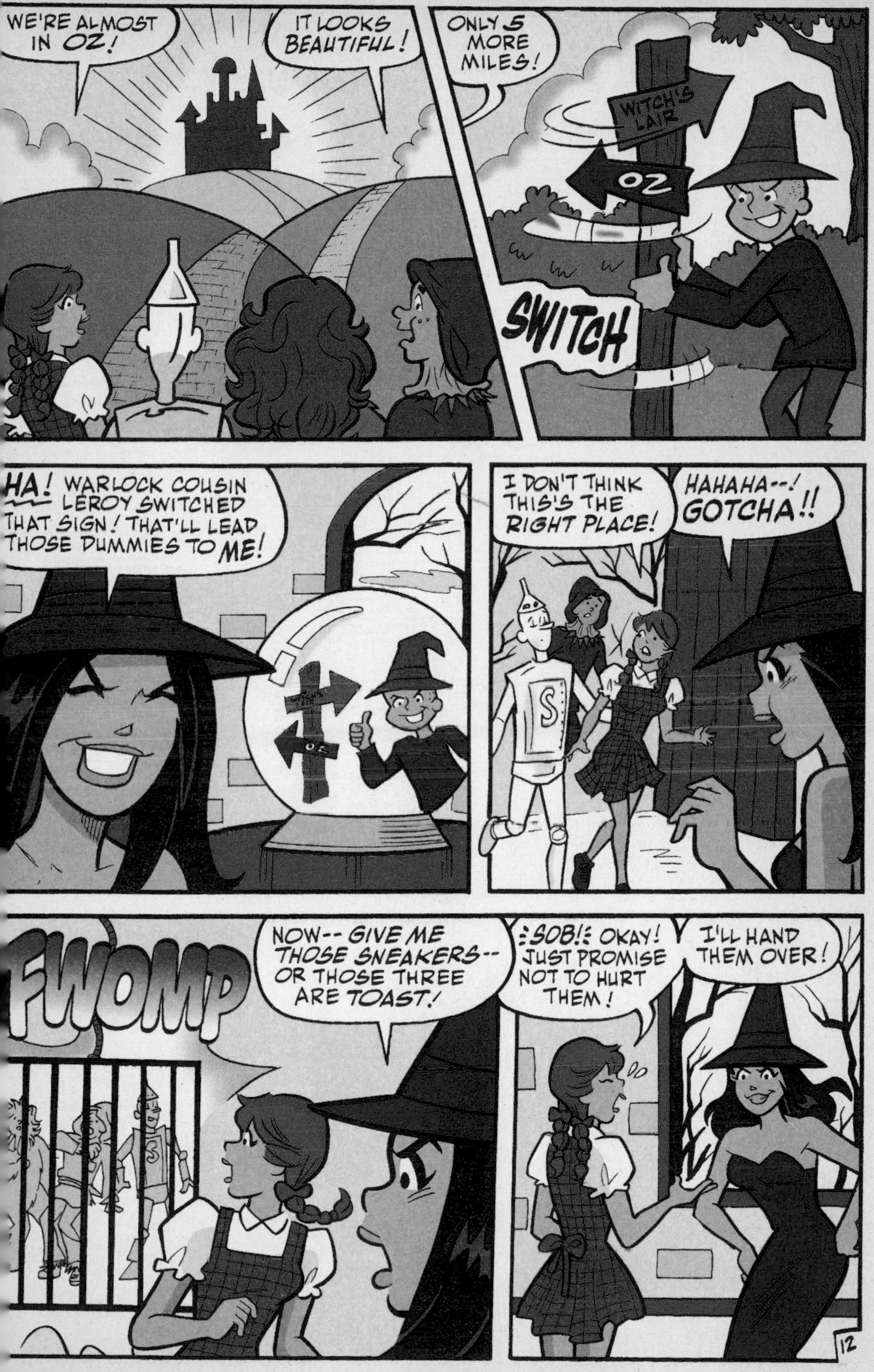
WE'RE ALMOST IN OZ!
IT LOOKS BEAUTIFUL!
ONLY 5 MORE MILES!
WITCH'S LAIR
OZ
SWITCH
HA! WARLOCK COUSIN LEROY SWITCHED THAT SIGN! THAT'LL LEAD THOSE DUMMIES TO ME!
I DON'T THINK THIS'S THE RIGHT PLACE!
HAHAHA--! GOTCHA!!
FWOMP
NOW-- GIVE ME THOSE SNEAKERS-- OR THOSE THREE ARE TOAST!
:SOB!: OKAY! JUST PROMISE NOT TO HURT THEM!
I'LL HAND THEM OVER!
12

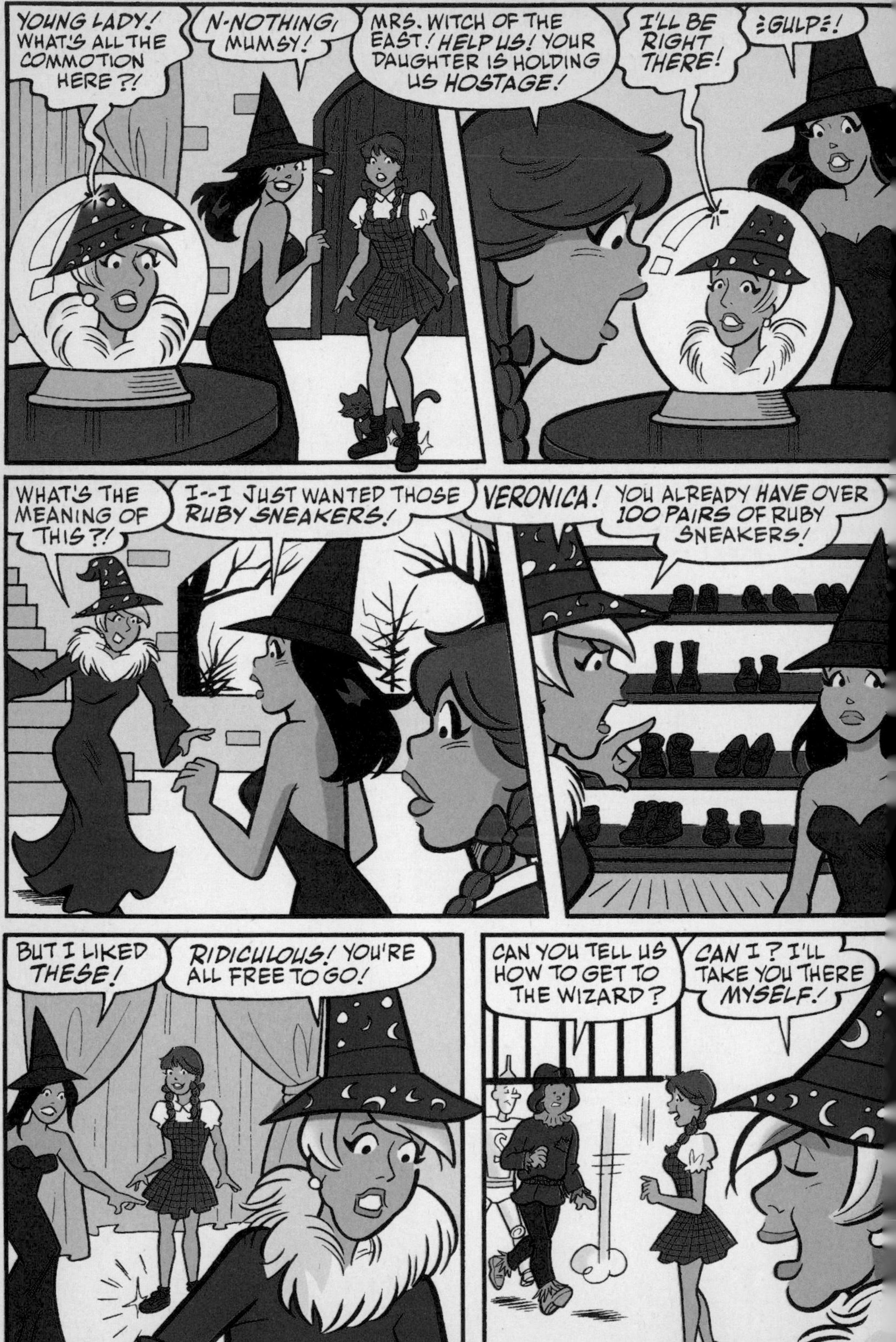
YOUNG LADY! WHAT'S ALL THE COMMOTION HERE?!
N-NOTHING, MUMSY!
MRS. WITCH OF THE EAST! HELP US! YOUR DAUGHTER IS HOLDING US HOSTAGE!
I'LL BE RIGHT THERE!
GULP!
WHAT'S THE MEANING OF THIS?!
I--I JUST WANTED THOSE RUBY SNEAKERS!
VERONICA!
YOU ALREADY HAVE OVER 100 PAIRS OF RUBY SNEAKERS!
BUT I LIKED THESE!
RIDICULOUS! YOU'RE ALL FREE TO GO!
CAN YOU TELL US HOW TO GET TO THE WIZARD?
CAN I? I'LL TAKE YOU THERE MYSELF!

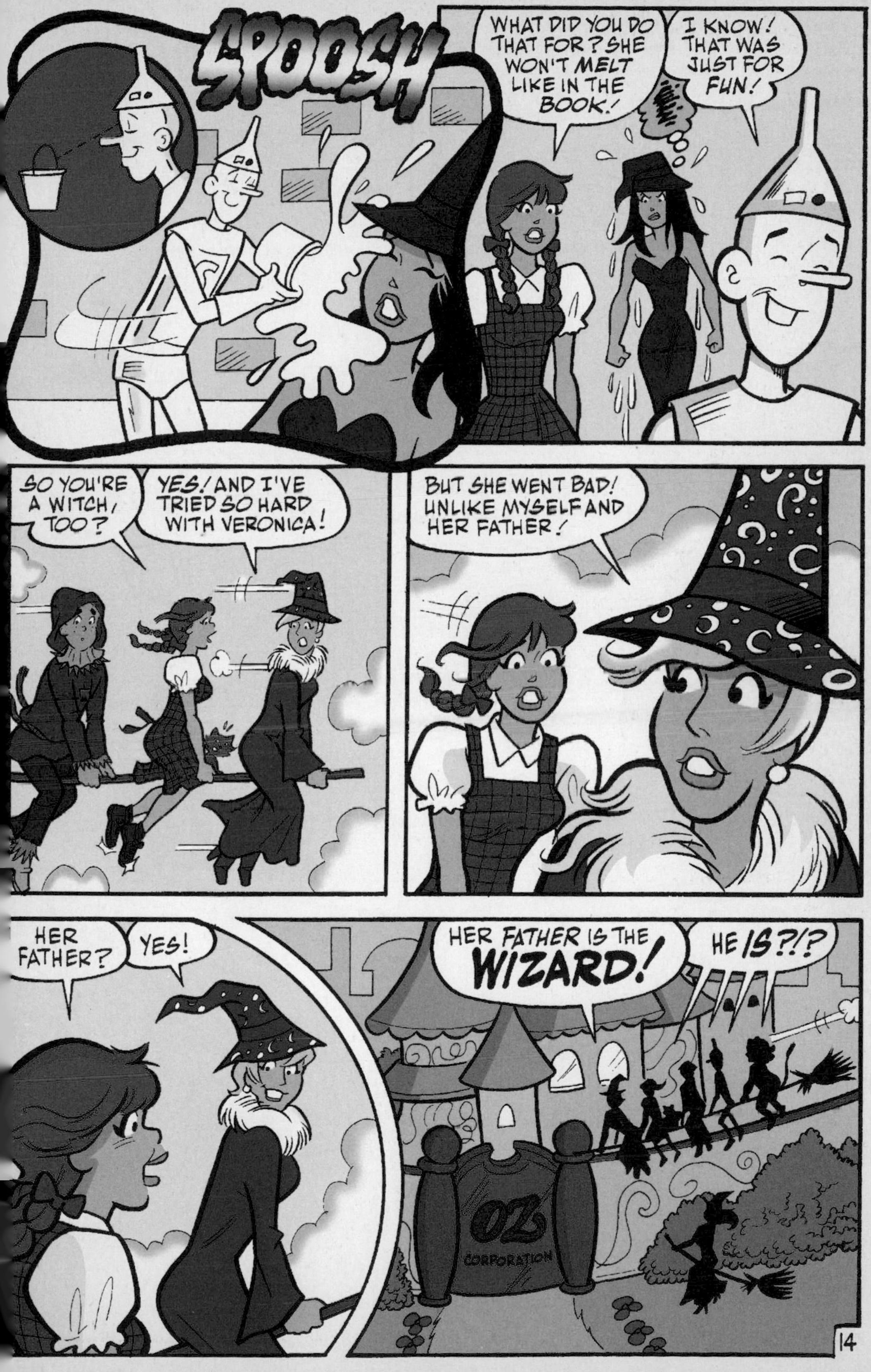
SPOOSH
WHAT DID YOU DO THAT FOR? SHE WON'T MELT LIKE IN THE BOOK!
I KNOW! THAT WAS JUST FOR FUN!
SO YOU'RE A WITCH, TOO?
YES! AND I'VE TRIED SO HARD WITH VERONICA!
BUT SHE WENT BAD! UNLIKE MYSELF AND HER FATHER!
HER FATHER?
YES!
HER FATHER IS THE WIZARD!
HE IS?!?
OZ
CORPORATION

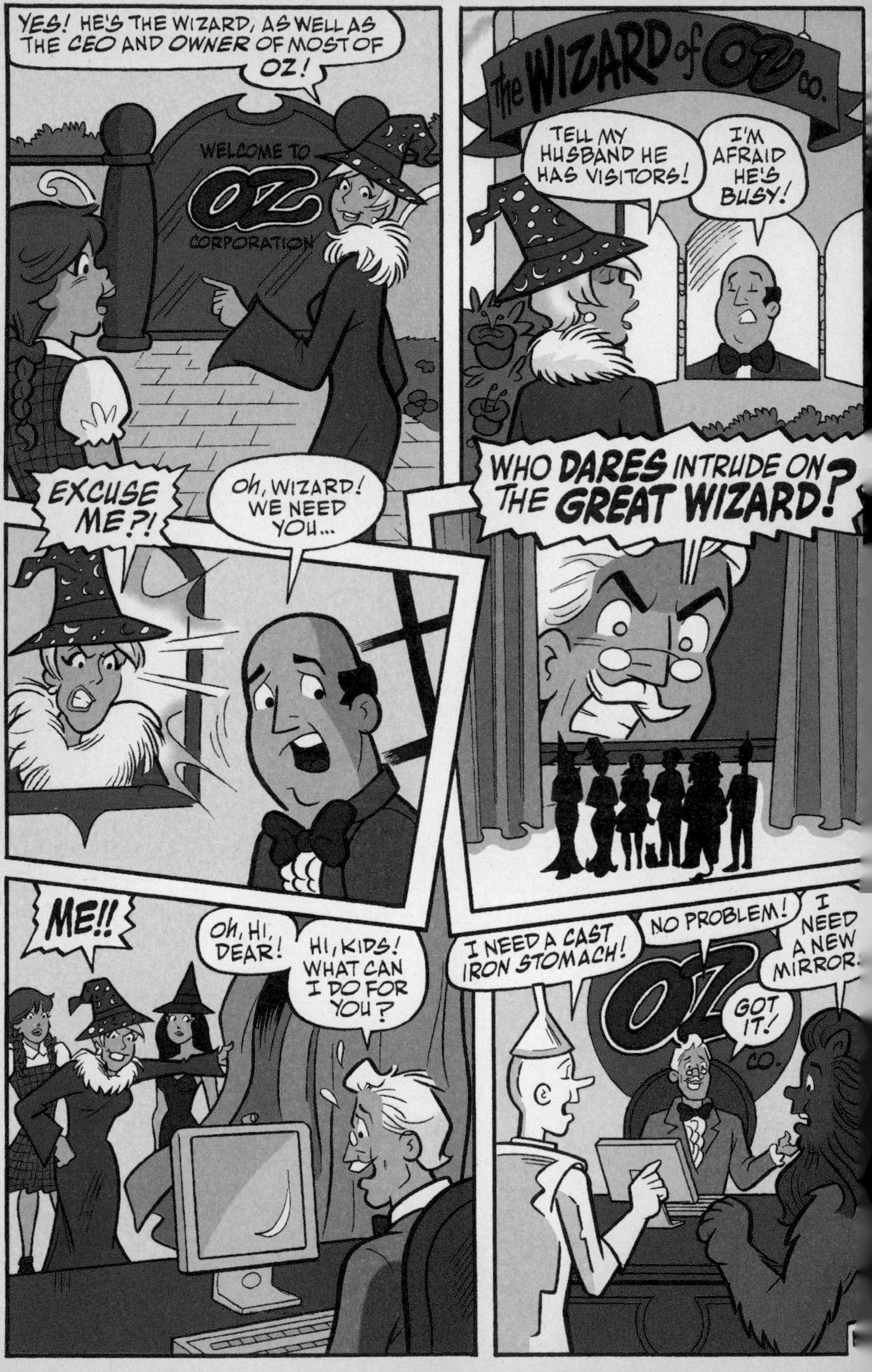

YES! HE'S THE WIZARD, AS WELL AS THE CEO AND OWNER OF MOST OF OZ!
WELCOME TO OZ CORPORATION
The WIZARD of OZ co.
TELL MY HUSBAND HE HAS VISITORS!
I'M AFRAID HE'S BUSY!
EXCUSE ME?!
Oh, WIZARD! WE NEED YOU...
WHO DARES INTRUDE ON THE GREAT WIZARD?
ME!!
Oh, HI, DEAR!
HI, KIDS! WHAT CAN I DO FOR YOU?
I NEED A CAST IRON STOMACH!
NO PROBLEM!
I NEED A NEW MIRROR.
GOT IT!
OZ co.

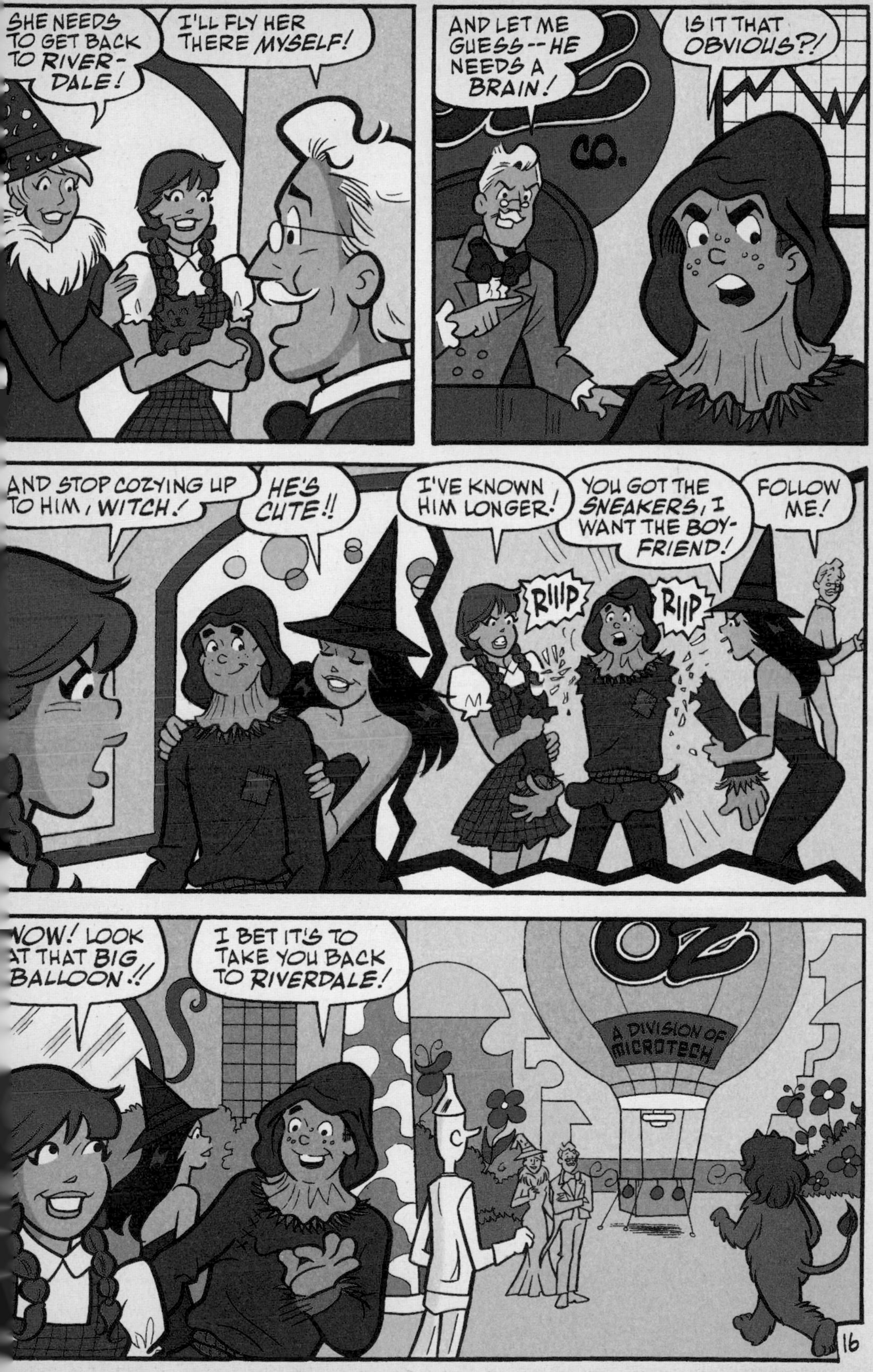
SHE NEEDS TO GET BACK TO RIVER-DALE!
I'LL FLY HER THERE MYSELF!
AND LET ME GUESS--HE NEEDS A BRAIN!
IS IT THAT OBVIOUS?!
CO.
AND STOP COZYING UP TO HIM, WITCH!
HE'S CUTE!!
I'VE KNOWN HIM LONGER!
YOU GOT THE SNEAKERS, I WANT THE BOY-FRIEND!
FOLLOW ME!
RIIIP
RIIP
WOW! LOOK AT THAT BIG BALLOON!!
I BET IT'S TO TAKE YOU BACK TO RIVERDALE!
A DIVISION OF MICROTECH

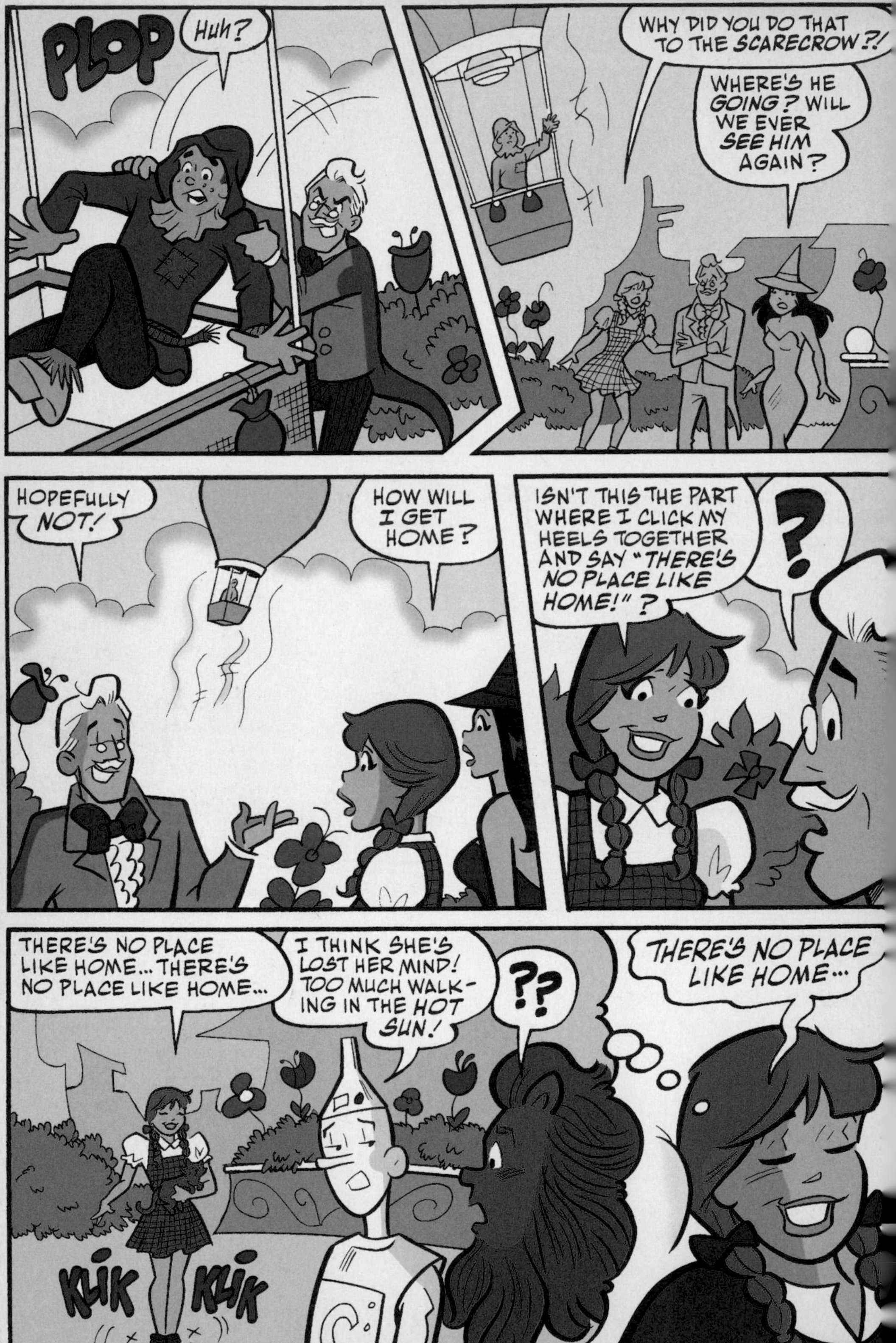
PLOP
HUH?
WHY DID YOU DO THAT TO THE SCARECROW?!
WHERE'S HE GOING? WILL WE EVER SEE HIM AGAIN?
HOPEFULLY NOT!
HOW WILL I GET HOME?
ISN'T THIS THE PART WHERE I CLICK MY HEELS TOGETHER AND SAY "THERE'S NO PLACE LIKE HOME!"?
?
THERE'S NO PLACE LIKE HOME... THERE'S NO PLACE LIKE HOME...
I THINK SHE'S LOST HER MIND! TOO MUCH WALKING IN THE HOT SUN!
??
THERE'S NO PLACE LIKE HOME...
KLIK KLIK

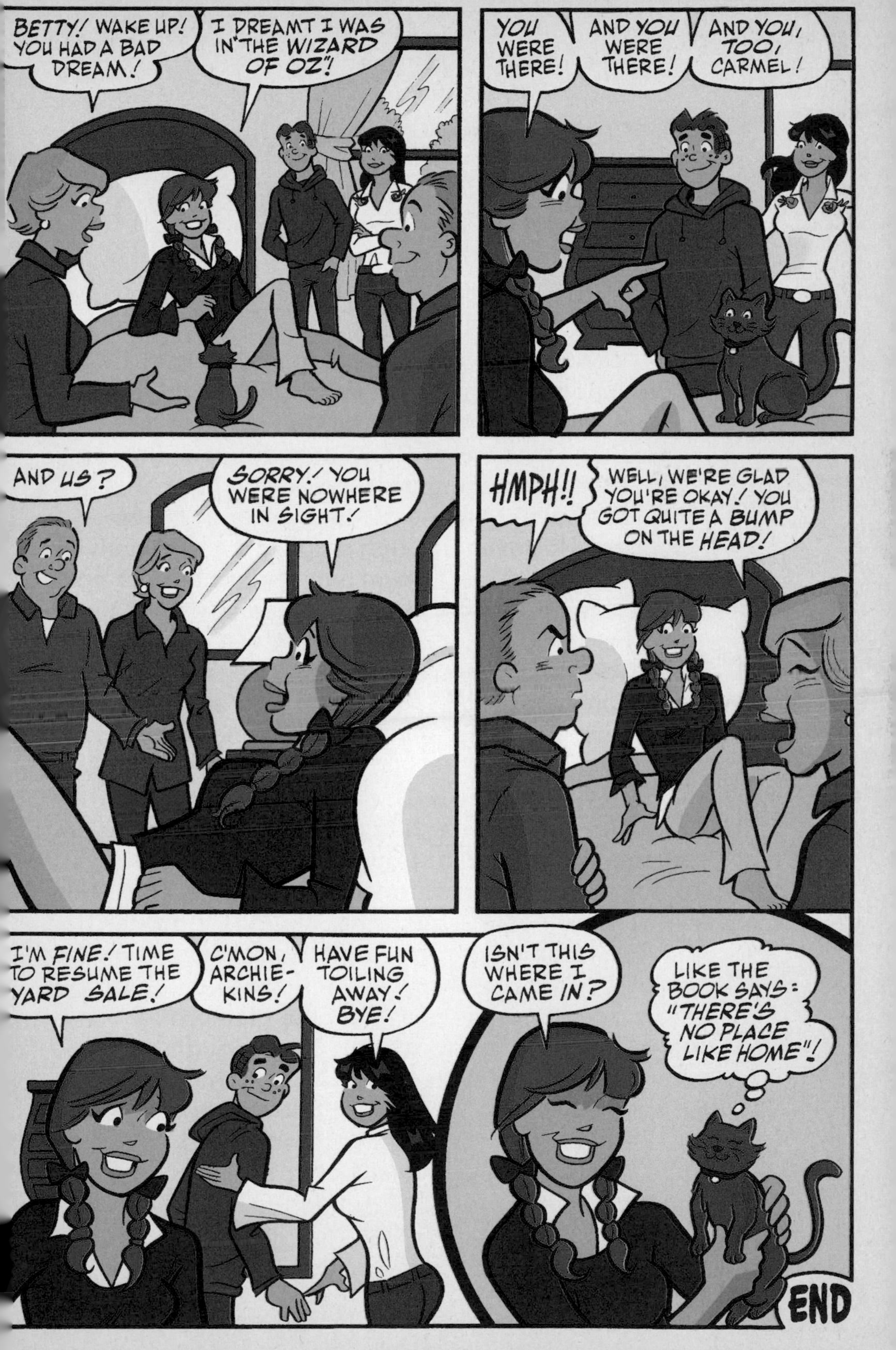
BETTY! WAKE UP! YOU HAD A BAD DREAM!
I DREAMT I WAS IN "THE WIZARD OF OZ"!
YOU WERE THERE!
AND YOU WERE THERE!
AND YOU, TOO, CARMEL!
AND US?
SORRY! YOU WERE NOWHERE IN SIGHT!
HMPH!!
WELL, WE'RE GLAD YOU'RE OKAY! YOU GOT QUITE A BUMP ON THE HEAD!
I'M FINE! TIME TO RESUME THE YARD SALE!
C'MON, ARCHIE-KINS!
HAVE FUN TOILING AWAY! BYE!
ISN'T THIS WHERE I CAME IN?
LIKE THE BOOK SAYS: "THERE'S NO PLACE LIKE HOME"!
END

A Tale of Two Cinderellas

"Cinderella" is a timeless folk story with variations throughout the world, one of the most well-known having been written (as with "Sleeping Beauty") by Charles Perrault. In the tale, Cinderella is a beautiful young girl who is very poor and is mistreated by her evil stepmother and stepsisters. However, through magical events involving a fairy godmother, a royal ball, a glass slipper and a handsome prince, she is rescued and ends up a princess. The story's popularity has even led to the word "cinderella" becoming a general term for someone who achieves sudden success after being unknown and unappreciated for a long time.

In "A Tale of Two Cinderellas," Betty and Veronica pull double-duty as they both take on the role of Cinderella! Locked away and forced to wear terribly unfashionable clothing by their evil stepmother and her annoying stepdaughter, the girls must work together if they ever plan on seeing the outside world. With the help of a hip fairy godmother, the girls become glamorous just in time for the grand ball. Even though they both get to dance with Prince Archie, their evil stepmother will do whatever it takes to ensure that her daughter marries the prince. But the key to his heart lies in a glass slipper.

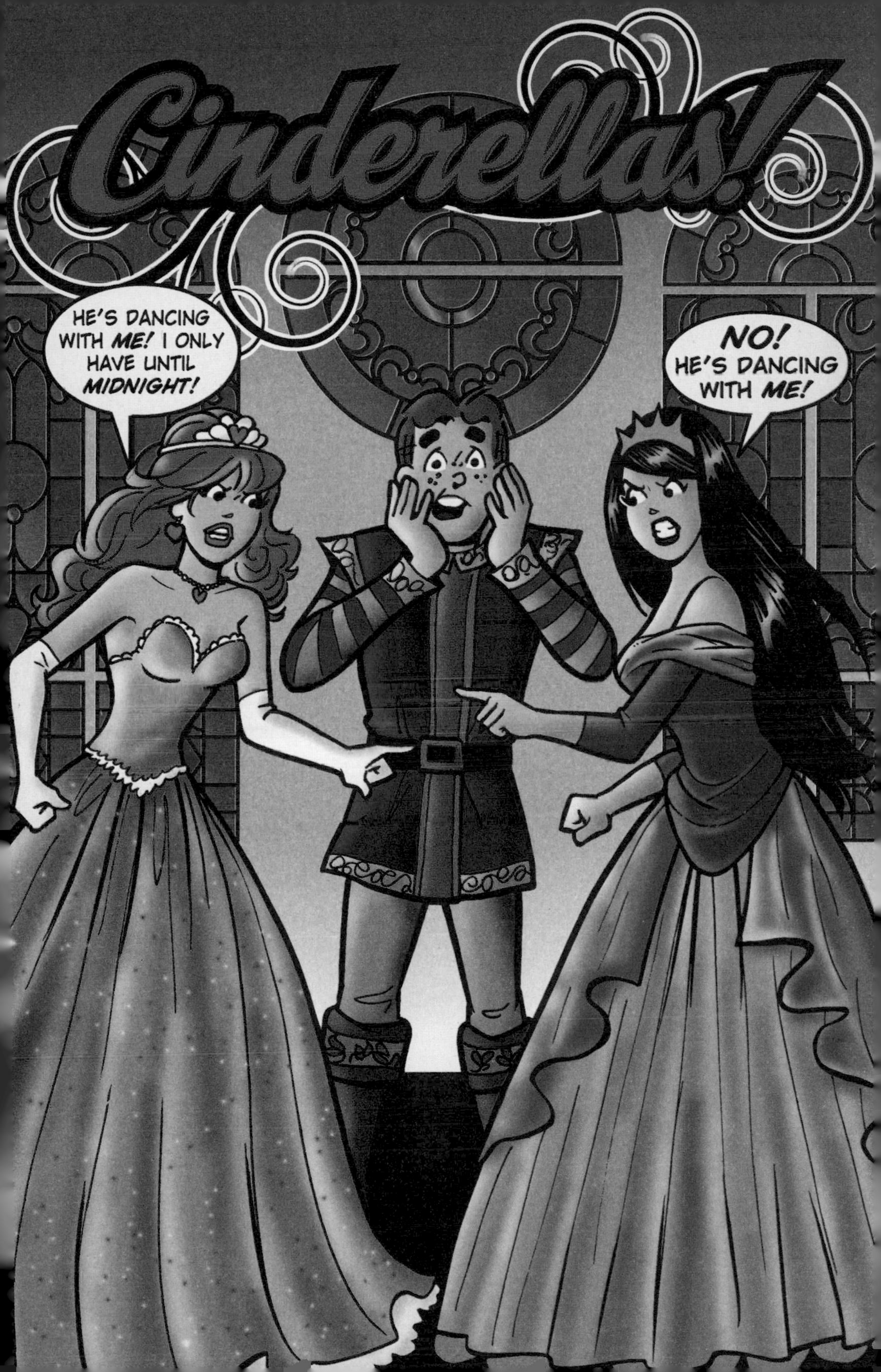
Cinderellas!
HE'S DANCING WITH ME! I ONLY HAVE UNTIL MIDNIGHT!
NO! HE'S DANCING WITH ME!

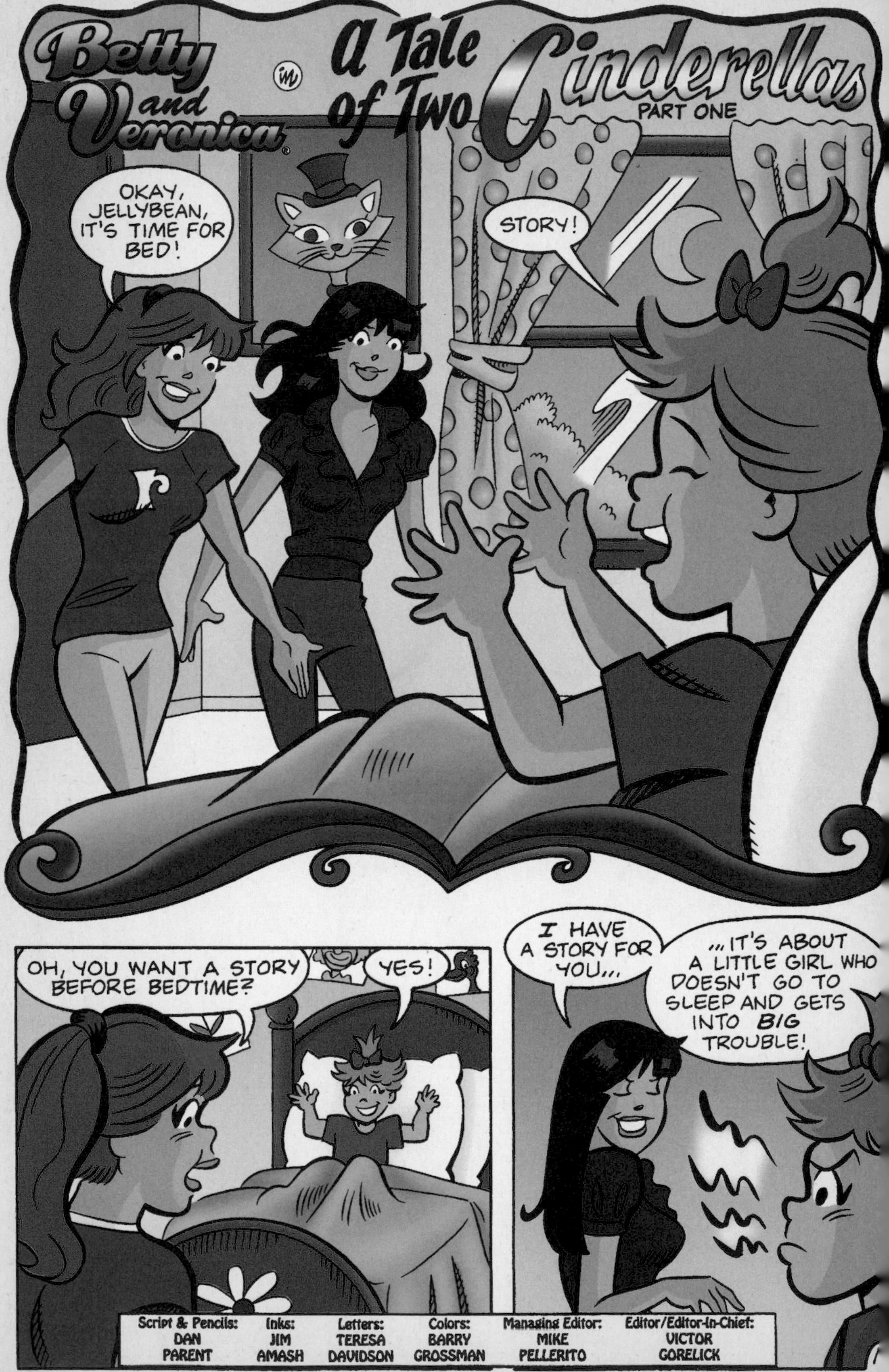

Betty and Veronica in A Tale of Two Cinderellas
PART ONE
OKAY, JELLYBEAN, IT'S TIME FOR BED!
STORY!
OH, YOU WANT A STORY BEFORE BEDTIME?
YES!
I HAVE A STORY FOR YOU...
...IT'S ABOUT A LITTLE GIRL WHO DOESN'T GO TO SLEEP AND GETS INTO BIG TROUBLE!
Script & Pencils: DAN PARENT
Inks: JIM AMASH
Letters: TERESA DAVIDSON
Colors: BARRY GROSSMAN
Managing Editor: MIKE PELLERITO
Editor/Editor-In-Chief: VICTOR GORELICK

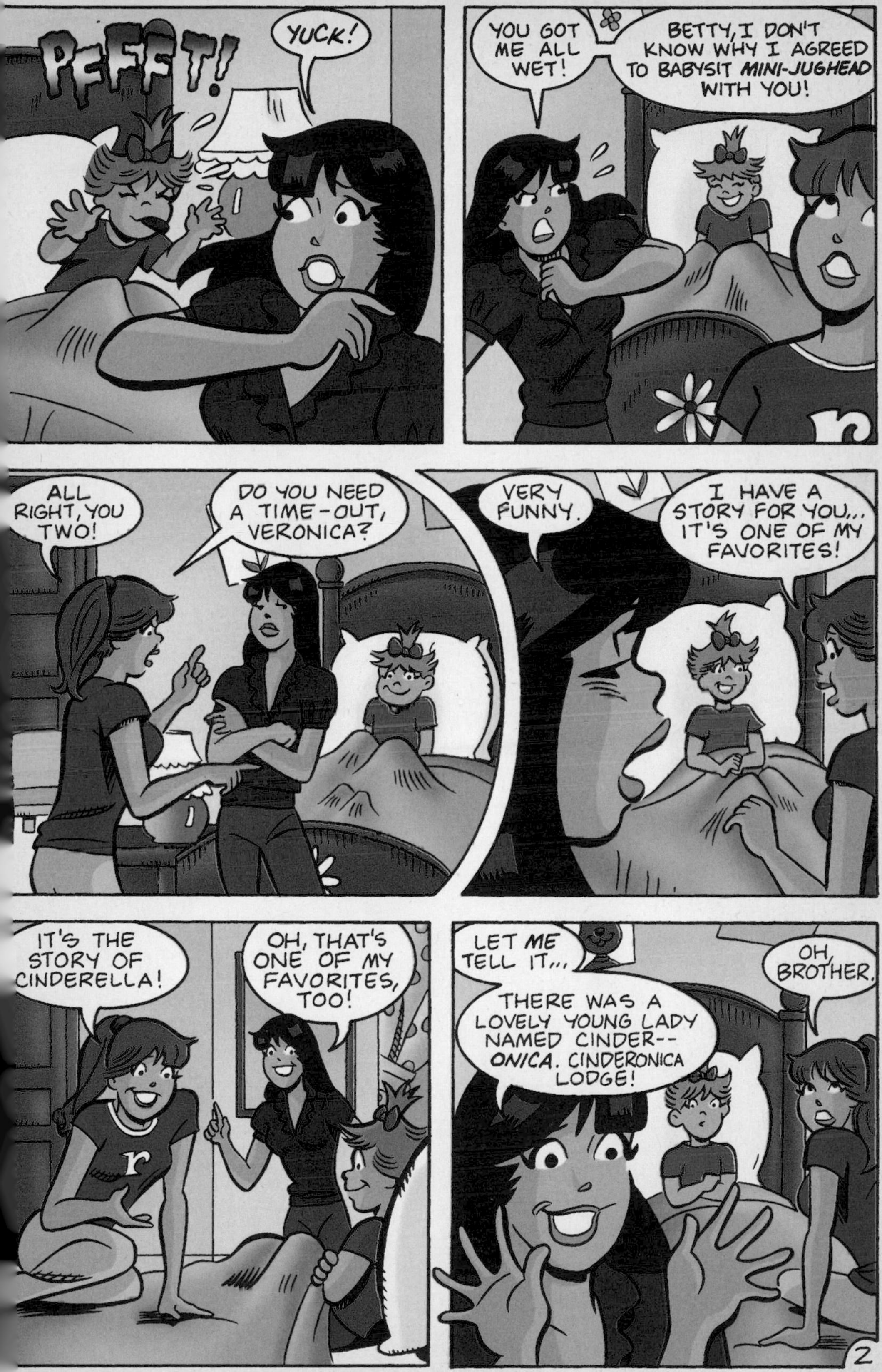
PFFFT!
YUCK!
YOU GOT ME ALL WET!
BETTY, I DON'T KNOW WHY I AGREED TO BABYSIT MINI-JUGHEAD WITH YOU!
ALL RIGHT, YOU TWO!
DO YOU NEED A TIME-OUT, VERONICA?
VERY FUNNY.
I HAVE A STORY FOR YOU... IT'S ONE OF MY FAVORITES!
IT'S THE STORY OF CINDERELLA!
OH, THAT'S ONE OF MY FAVORITES, TOO!
LET ME TELL IT...
THERE WAS A LOVELY YOUNG LADY NAMED CINDER-- ONICA. CINDERONICA LODGE!
OH, BROTHER.
2

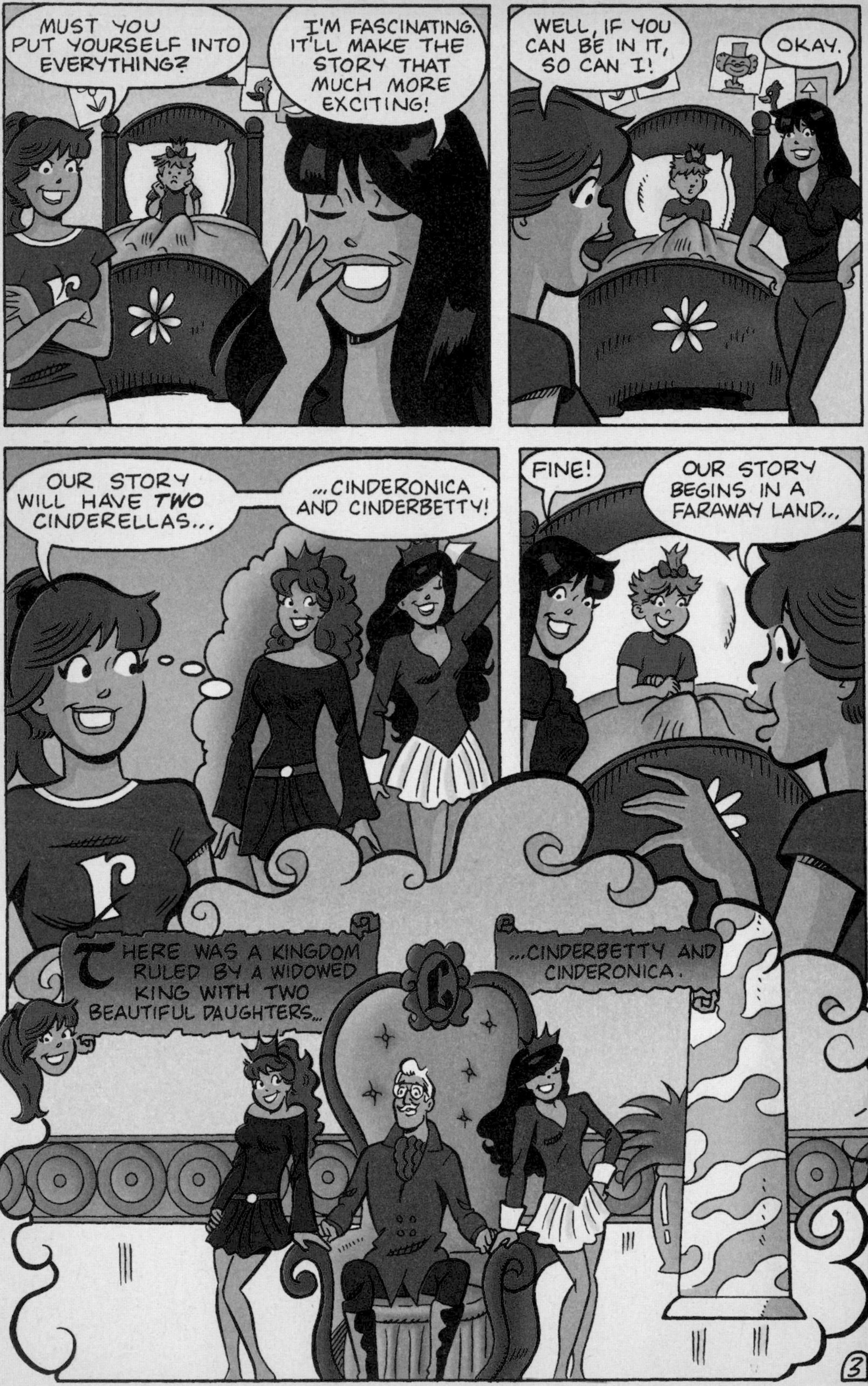

MUST YOU PUT YOURSELF INTO EVERYTHING?
I'M FASCINATING. IT'LL MAKE THE STORY THAT MUCH MORE EXCITING!
WELL, IF YOU CAN BE IN IT, SO CAN I!
OKAY.
OUR STORY WILL HAVE TWO CINDERELLAS...
...CINDERONICA AND CINDERBETTY!
FINE!
OUR STORY BEGINS IN A FARAWAY LAND...
THERE WAS A KINGDOM RULED BY A WIDOWED KING WITH TWO BEAUTIFUL DAUGHTERS...
...CINDERBETTY AND CINDERONICA.
3

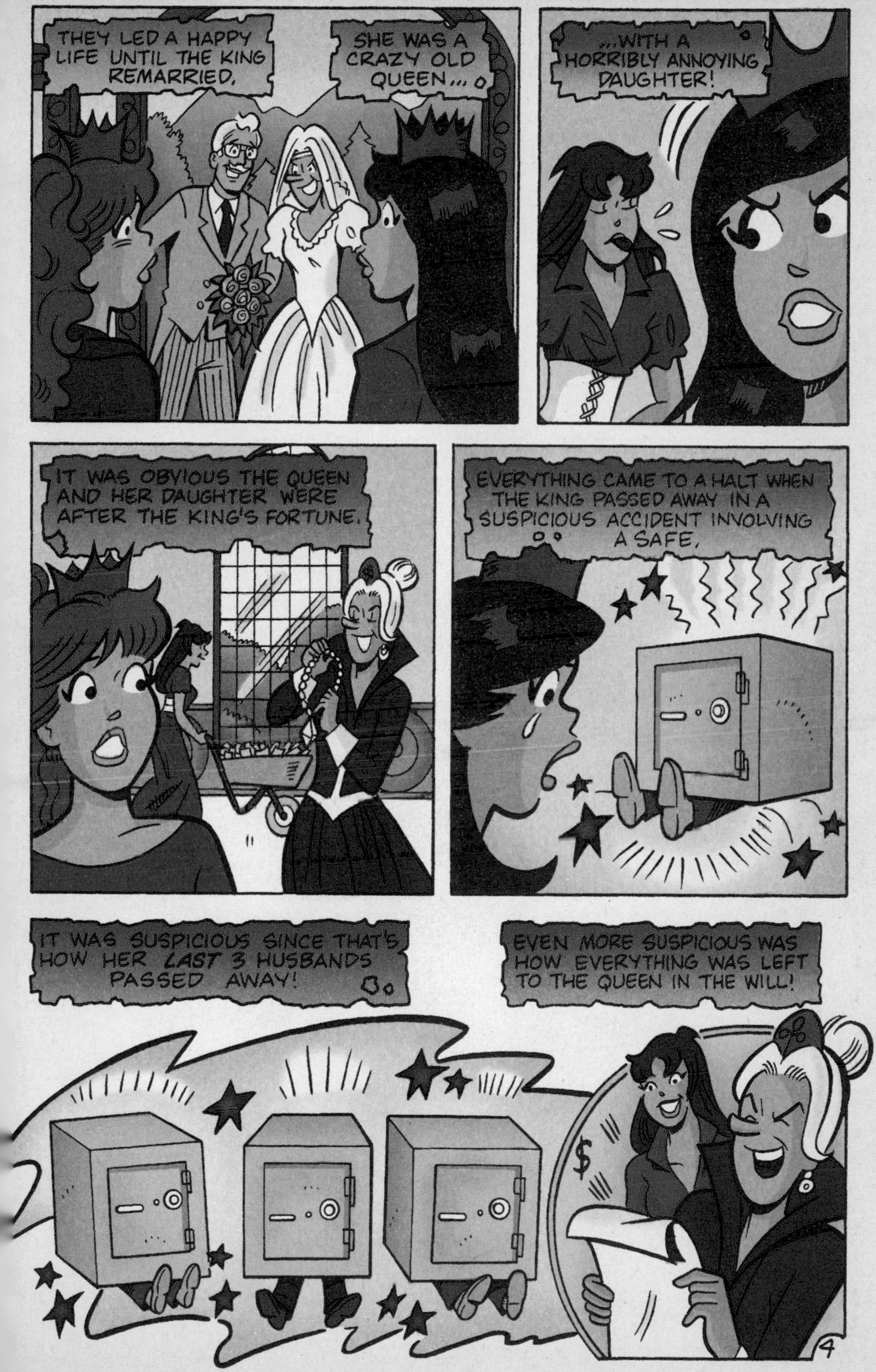

THEY LED A HAPPY LIFE UNTIL THE KING REMARRIED.
SHE WAS A CRAZY OLD QUEEN...
...WITH A HORRIBLY ANNOYING DAUGHTER!
IT WAS OBVIOUS THE QUEEN AND HER DAUGHTER WERE AFTER THE KING'S FORTUNE.
EVERYTHING CAME TO A HALT WHEN THE KING PASSED AWAY IN A SUSPICIOUS ACCIDENT INVOLVING A SAFE.
IT WAS SUSPICIOUS SINCE THAT'S HOW HER LAST 3 HUSBANDS PASSED AWAY!
EVEN MORE SUSPICIOUS WAS HOW EVERYTHING WAS LEFT TO THE QUEEN IN THE WILL!
$

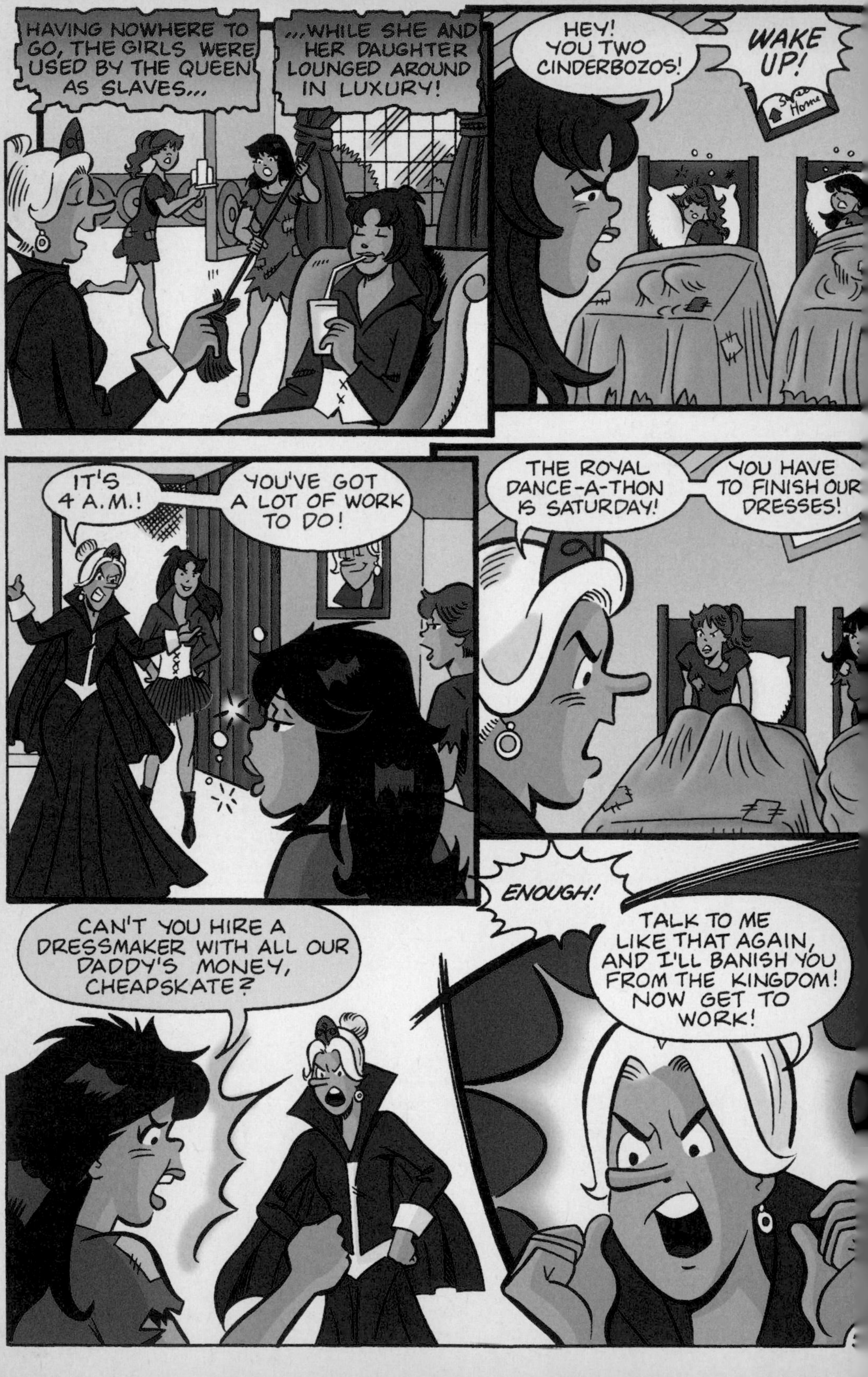
HAVING NOWHERE TO GO, THE GIRLS WERE USED BY THE QUEEN AS SLAVES...
...WHILE SHE AND HER DAUGHTER LOUNGED AROUND IN LUXURY!
HEY! YOU TWO CINDERBOZOS!
WAKE UP!
IT'S 4 A.M.!
YOU'VE GOT A LOT OF WORK TO DO!
THE ROYAL DANCE-A-THON IS SATURDAY!
YOU HAVE TO FINISH OUR DRESSES!
CAN'T YOU HIRE A DRESSMAKER WITH ALL OUR DADDY'S MONEY, CHEAPSKATE?
ENOUGH!
TALK TO ME LIKE THAT AGAIN, AND I'LL BANISH YOU FROM THE KINGDOM! NOW GET TO WORK!

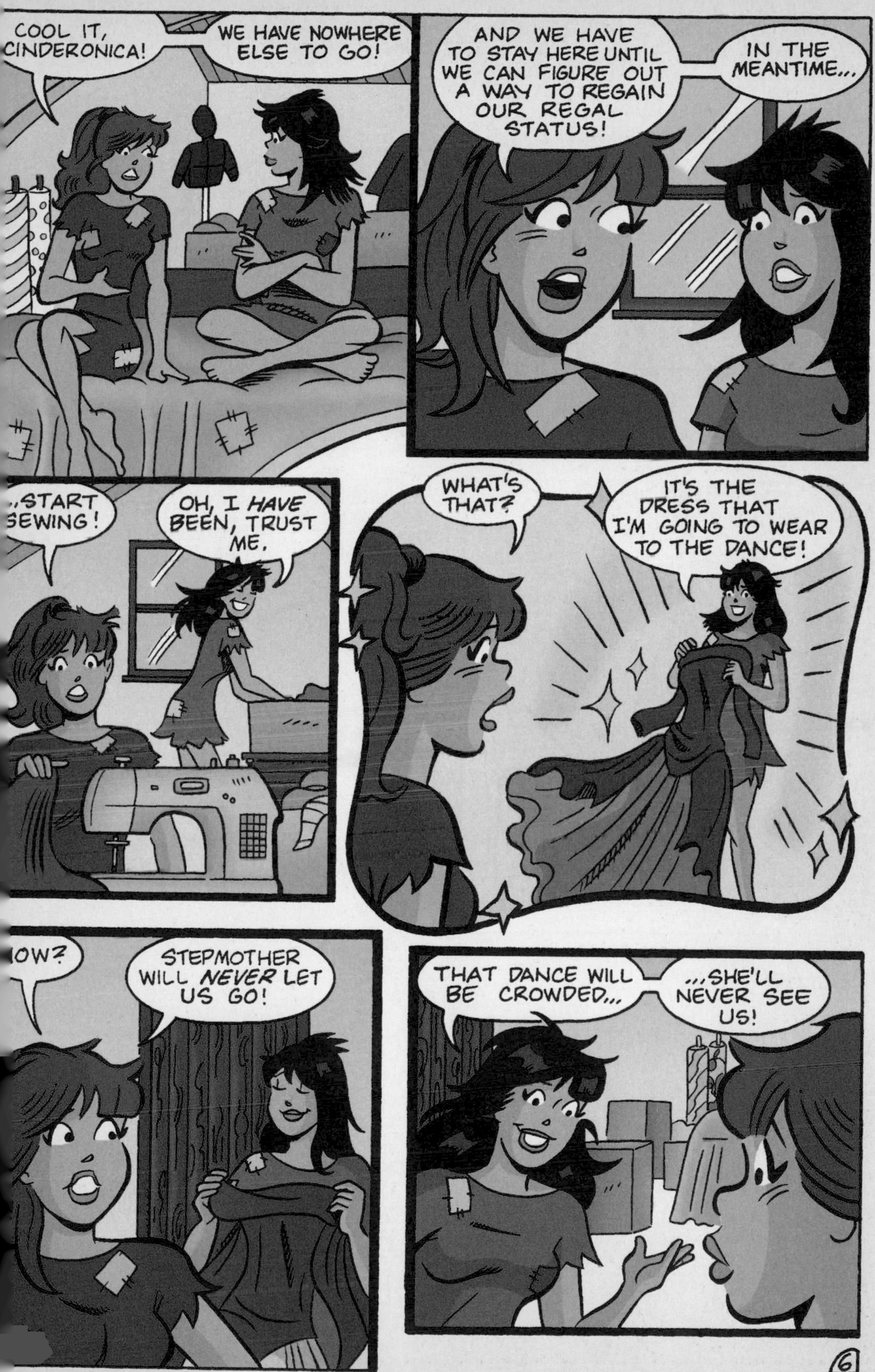
COOL IT, CINDERONICA!
WE HAVE NOWHERE ELSE TO GO!
AND WE HAVE TO STAY HERE UNTIL WE CAN FIGURE OUT A WAY TO REGAIN OUR REGAL STATUS!
IN THE MEANTIME...
...START SEWING!
OH, I HAVE BEEN, TRUST ME.
WHAT'S THAT?
IT'S THE DRESS THAT I'M GOING TO WEAR TO THE DANCE!
OW?
STEPMOTHER WILL NEVER LET US GO!
THAT DANCE WILL BE CROWDED...
...SHE'LL NEVER SEE US!

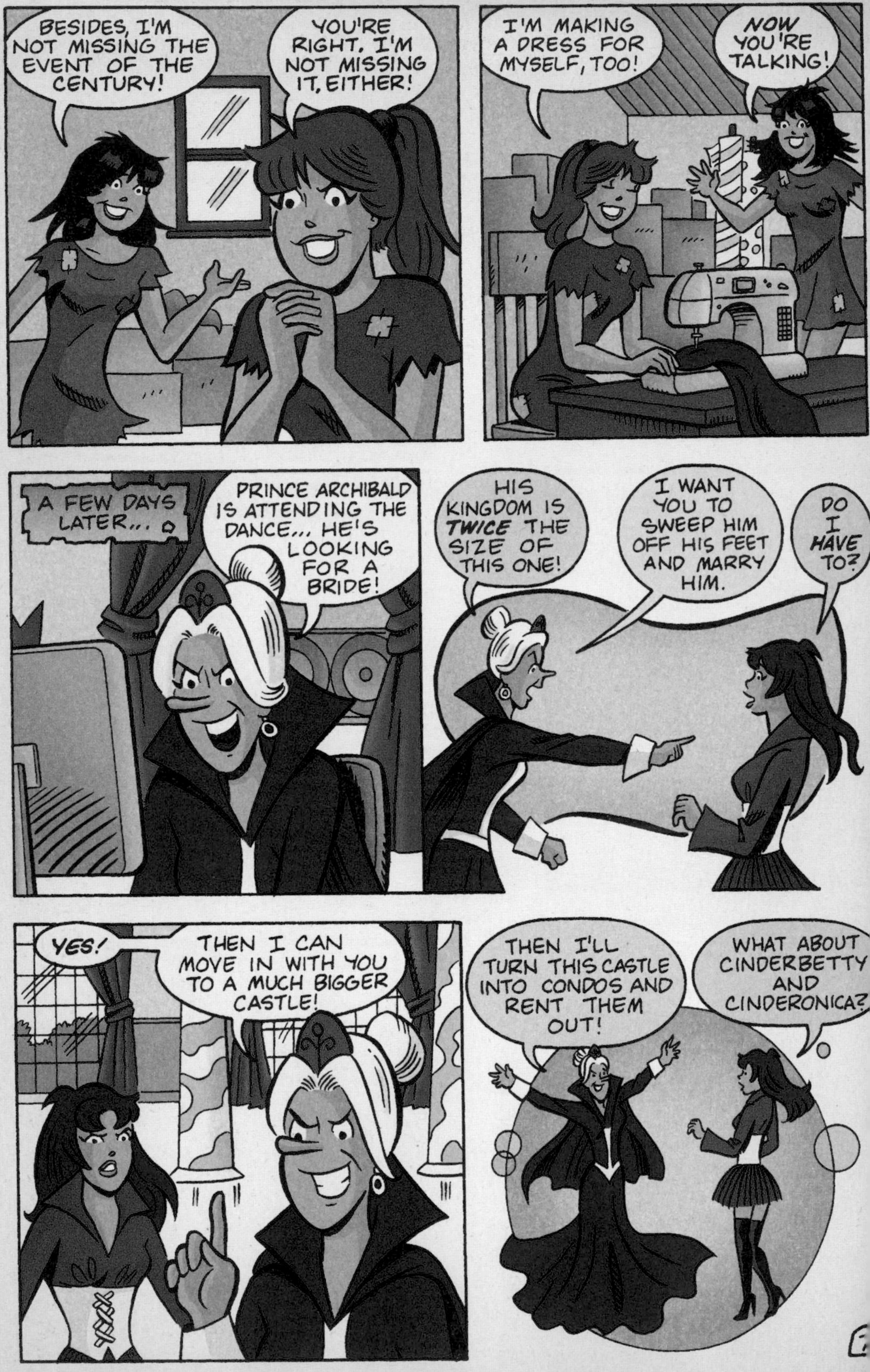
BESIDES, I'M NOT MISSING THE EVENT OF THE CENTURY!
YOU'RE RIGHT. I'M NOT MISSING IT, EITHER!
I'M MAKING A DRESS FOR MYSELF, TOO!
NOW YOU'RE TALKING!
A FEW DAYS LATER...
PRINCE ARCHIBALD IS ATTENDING THE DANCE... HE'S LOOKING FOR A BRIDE!
HIS KINGDOM IS TWICE THE SIZE OF THIS ONE!
I WANT YOU TO SWEEP HIM OFF HIS FEET AND MARRY HIM.
DO I HAVE TO?
YES!
THEN I CAN MOVE IN WITH YOU TO A MUCH BIGGER CASTLE!
THEN I'LL TURN THIS CASTLE INTO CONDOS AND RENT THEM OUT!
WHAT ABOUT CINDERBETTY AND CINDERONICA?

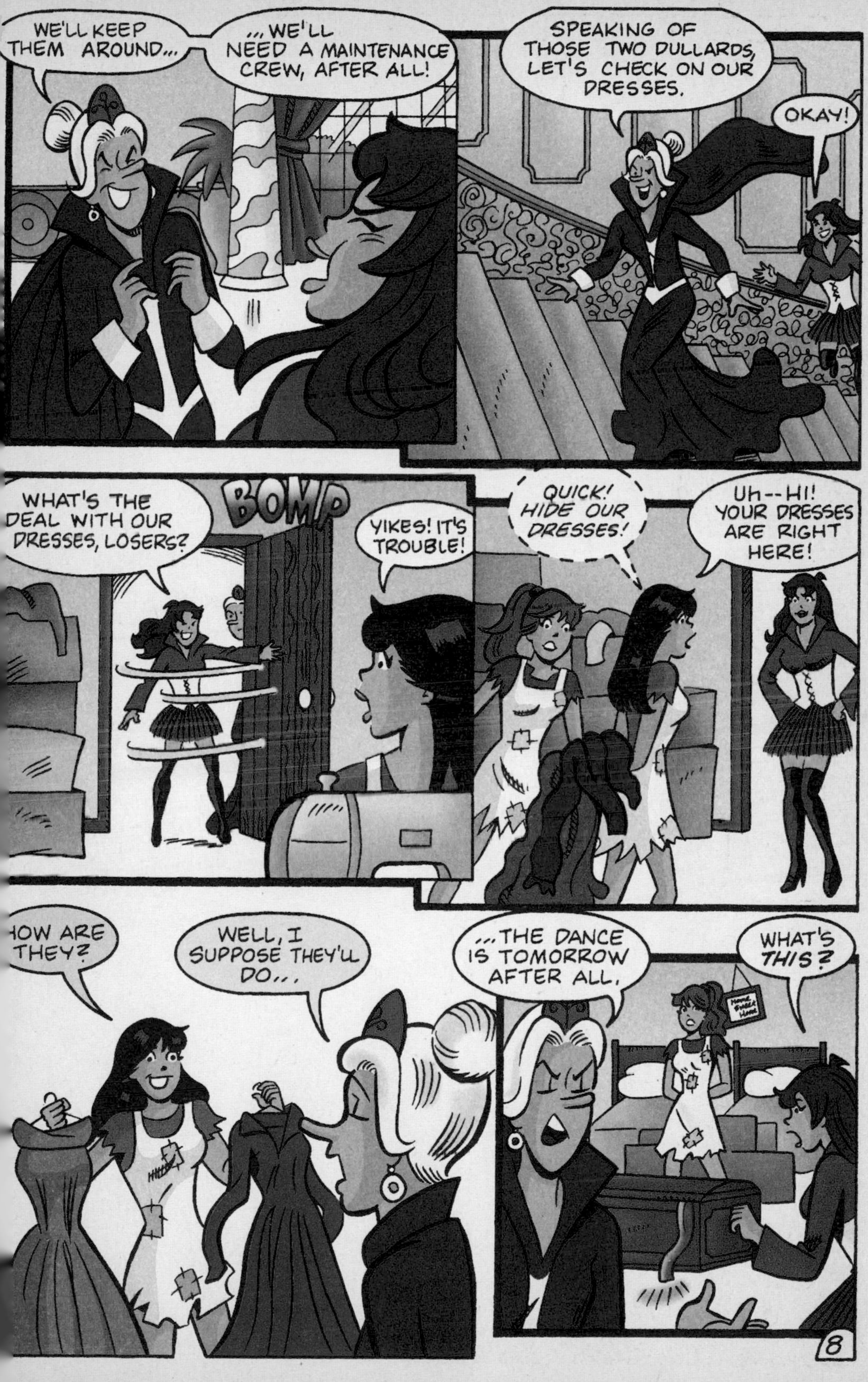
WE'LL KEEP THEM AROUND...
...WE'LL NEED A MAINTENANCE CREW, AFTER ALL!
SPEAKING OF THOSE TWO DULLARDS, LET'S CHECK ON OUR DRESSES.
OKAY!
WHAT'S THE DEAL WITH OUR DRESSES, LOSERS?
BOMP
YIKES! IT'S TROUBLE!
QUICK! HIDE OUR DRESSES!
Uh--HI! YOUR DRESSES ARE RIGHT HERE!
HOW ARE THEY?
WELL, I SUPPOSE THEY'LL DO...
...THE DANCE IS TOMORROW AFTER ALL.
WHAT'S THIS?

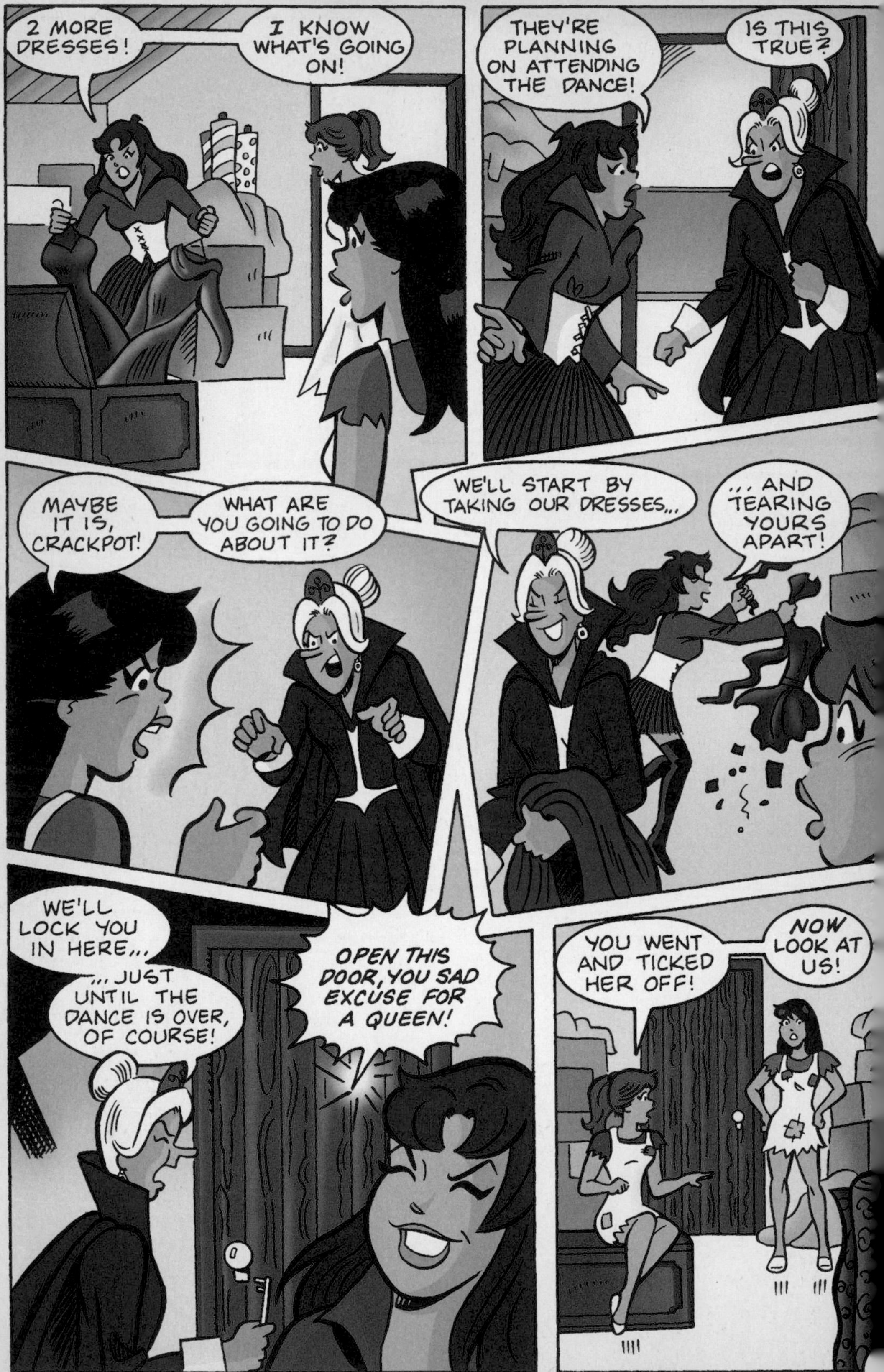

2 MORE DRESSES!
I KNOW WHAT'S GOING ON!
THEY'RE PLANNING ON ATTENDING THE DANCE!
IS THIS TRUE?
MAYBE IT IS, CRACKPOT!
WHAT ARE YOU GOING TO DO ABOUT IT?
WE'LL START BY TAKING OUR DRESSES...
... AND TEARING YOURS APART!
WE'LL LOCK YOU IN HERE...
... JUST UNTIL THE DANCE IS OVER, OF COURSE!
OPEN THIS DOOR, YOU SAD EXCUSE FOR A QUEEN!
YOU WENT AND TICKED HER OFF!
NOW LOOK AT US!

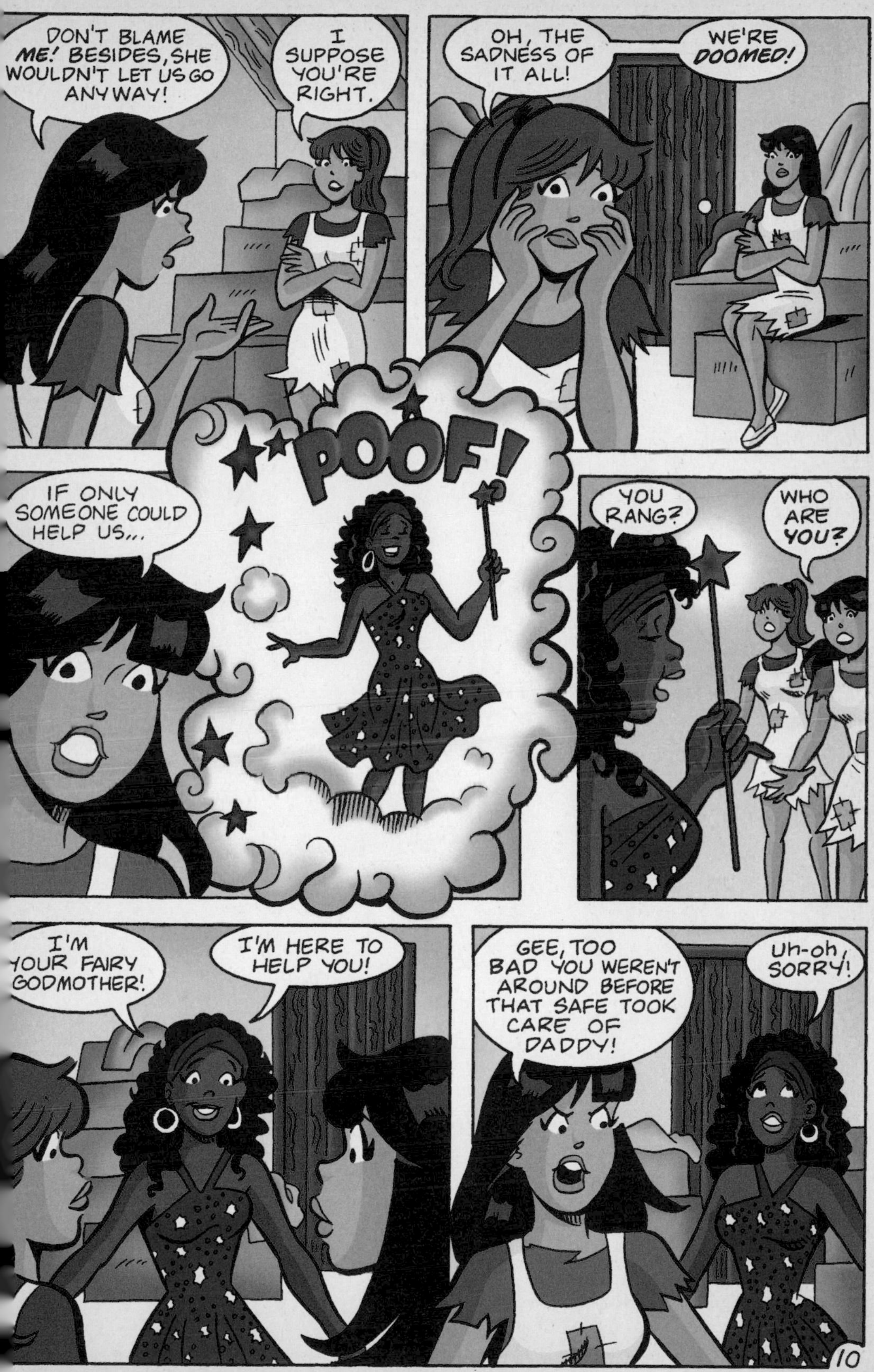
DON'T BLAME ME! BESIDES, SHE WOULDN'T LET US GO ANYWAY!
I SUPPOSE YOU'RE RIGHT.
OH, THE SADNESS OF IT ALL!
WE'RE DOOMED!
IF ONLY SOMEONE COULD HELP US...
POOF!
YOU RANG?
WHO ARE YOU?
I'M YOUR FAIRY GODMOTHER!
I'M HERE TO HELP YOU!
GEE, TOO BAD YOU WEREN'T AROUND BEFORE THAT SAFE TOOK CARE OF DADDY!
Uh-oh, SORRY!

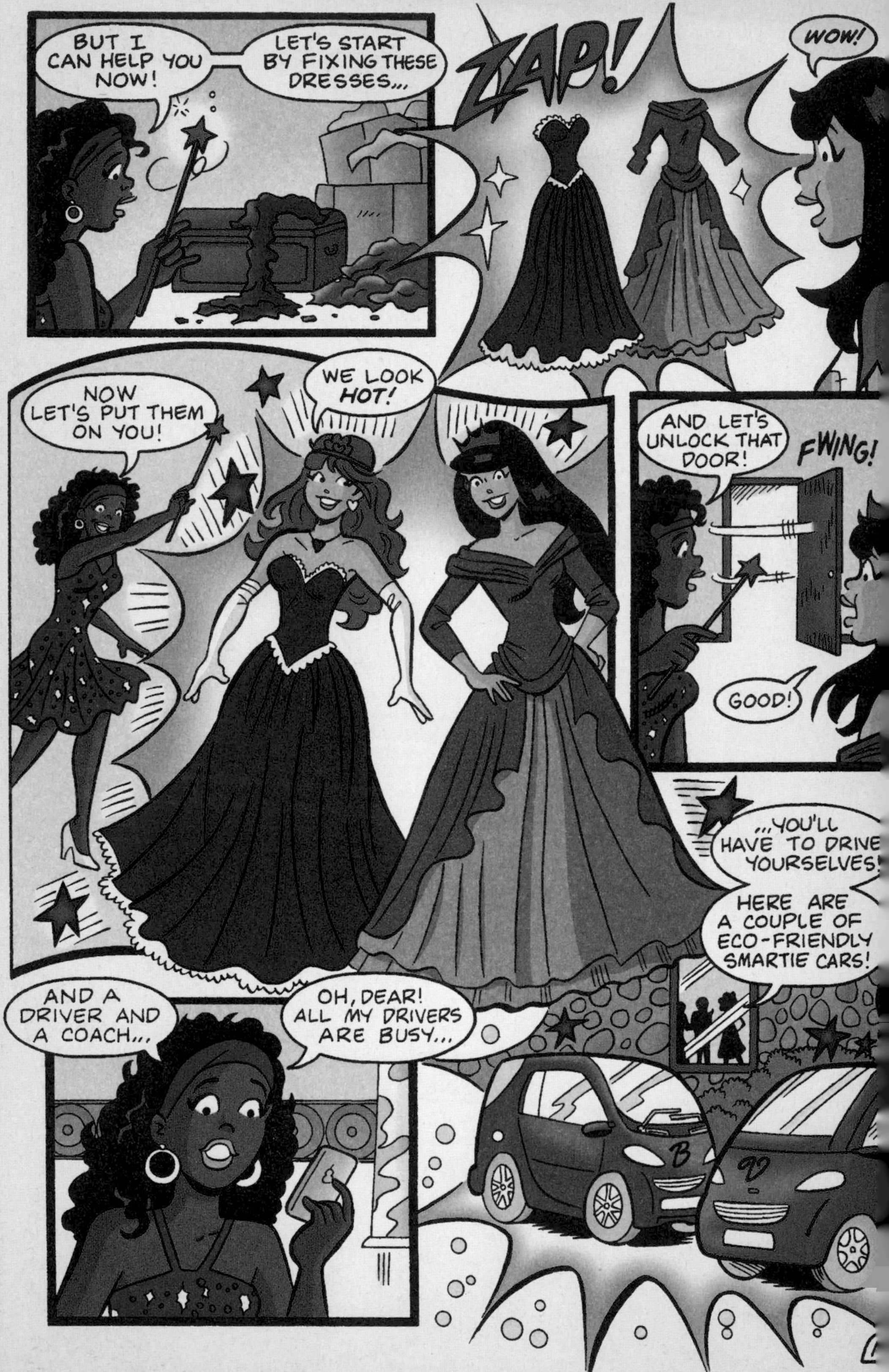
BUT I CAN HELP YOU NOW!
LET'S START BY FIXING THESE DRESSES...
ZAP!
WOW!
NOW LET'S PUT THEM ON YOU!
WE LOOK HOT!
AND LET'S UNLOCK THAT DOOR!
FWING!
GOOD!
AND A DRIVER AND A COACH...
OH, DEAR! ALL MY DRIVERS ARE BUSY...
...YOU'LL HAVE TO DRIVE YOURSELVES!
HERE ARE A COUPLE OF ECO-FRIENDLY SMARTIE CARS!

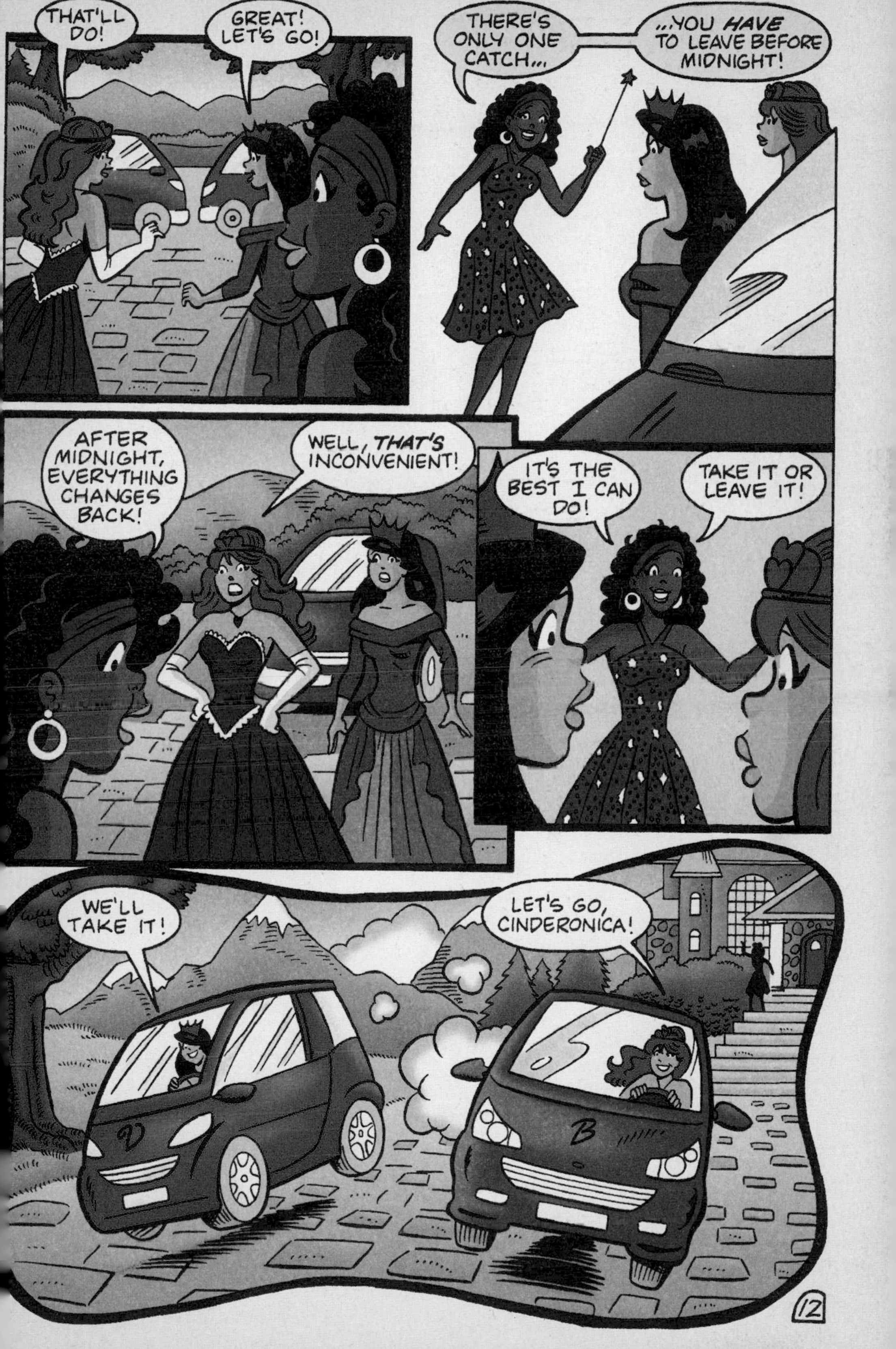
THAT'LL DO!
GREAT! LET'S GO!
THERE'S ONLY ONE CATCH...
...YOU HAVE TO LEAVE BEFORE MIDNIGHT!
AFTER MIDNIGHT, EVERYTHING CHANGES BACK!
WELL, THAT'S INCONVENIENT!
IT'S THE BEST I CAN DO!
TAKE IT OR LEAVE IT!
WE'LL TAKE IT!
LET'S GO, CINDERONICA!
12

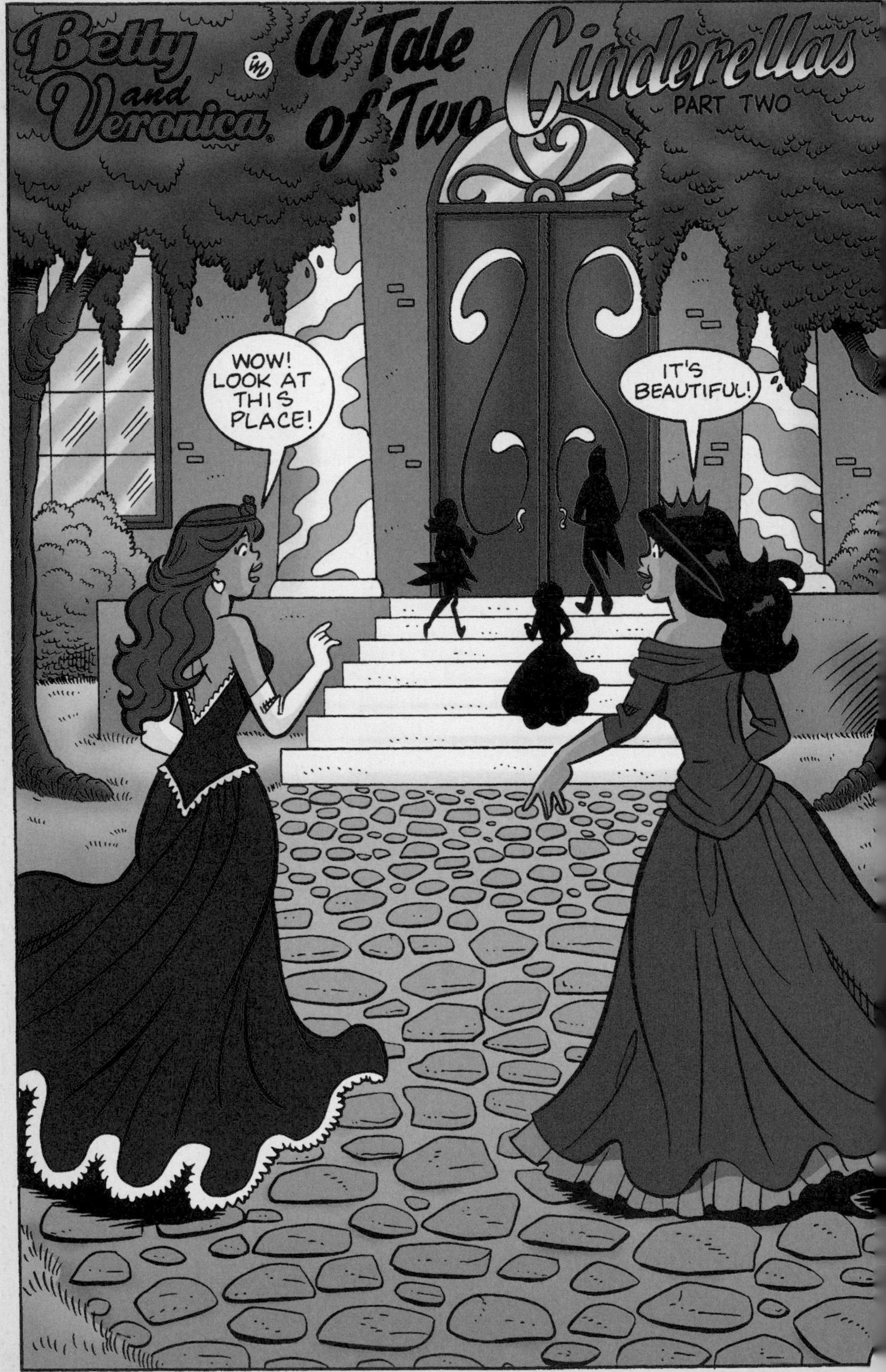
Betty and Veronica in
A Tale of Two Cinderellas
PART TWO
WOW! LOOK AT THIS PLACE!
IT'S BEAUTIFUL!

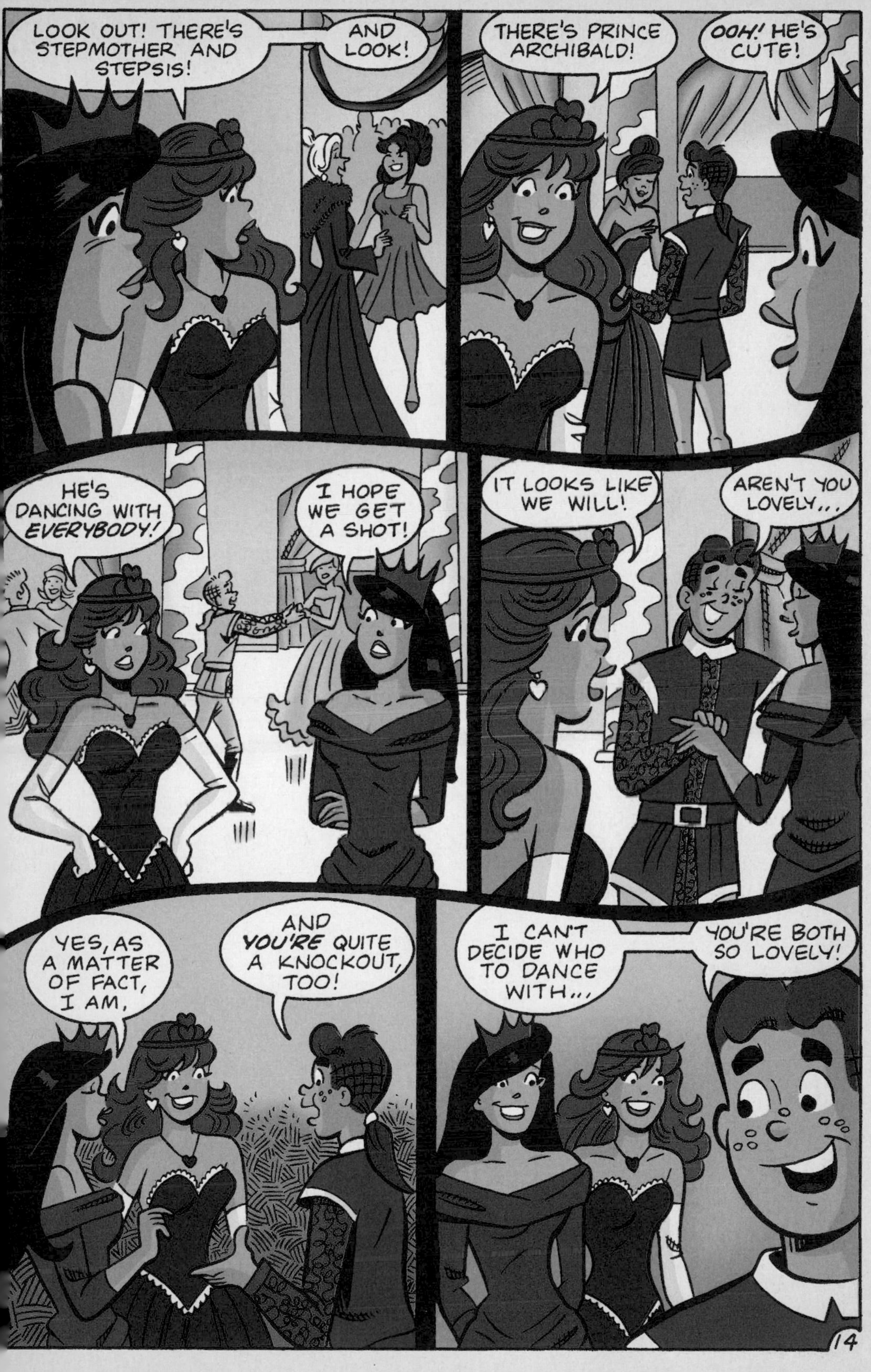
LOOK OUT! THERE'S STEPMOTHER AND STEPSIS!
AND LOOK!
THERE'S PRINCE ARCHIBALD!
OOH! HE'S CUTE!
HE'S DANCING WITH EVERYBODY!
I HOPE WE GET A SHOT!
IT LOOKS LIKE WE WILL!
AREN'T YOU LOVELY...
YES, AS A MATTER OF FACT, I AM.
AND YOU'RE QUITE A KNOCKOUT, TOO!
I CAN'T DECIDE WHO TO DANCE WITH...
YOU'RE BOTH SO LOVELY!

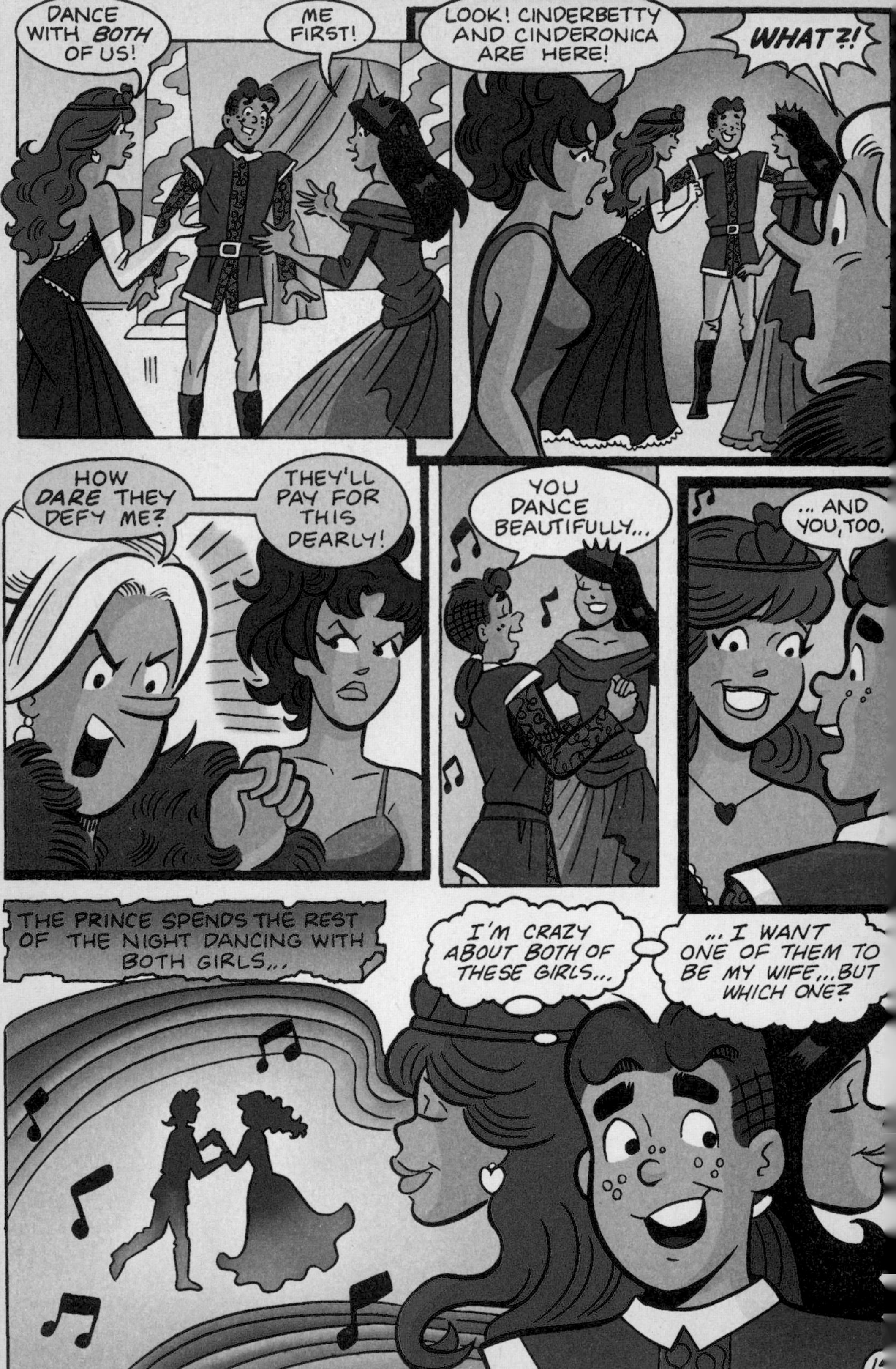

DANCE WITH *BOTH* OF US!
ME FIRST!
LOOK! CINDERBETTY AND CINDERONICA ARE HERE!
WHAT?!
HOW *DARE* THEY DEFY ME?
THEY'LL PAY FOR THIS DEARLY!
YOU DANCE BEAUTIFULLY...
... AND YOU, TOO.
THE PRINCE SPENDS THE REST OF THE NIGHT DANCING WITH BOTH GIRLS...
I'M CRAZY ABOUT BOTH OF THESE GIRLS...
... I WANT ONE OF THEM TO BE MY WIFE... BUT WHICH ONE?

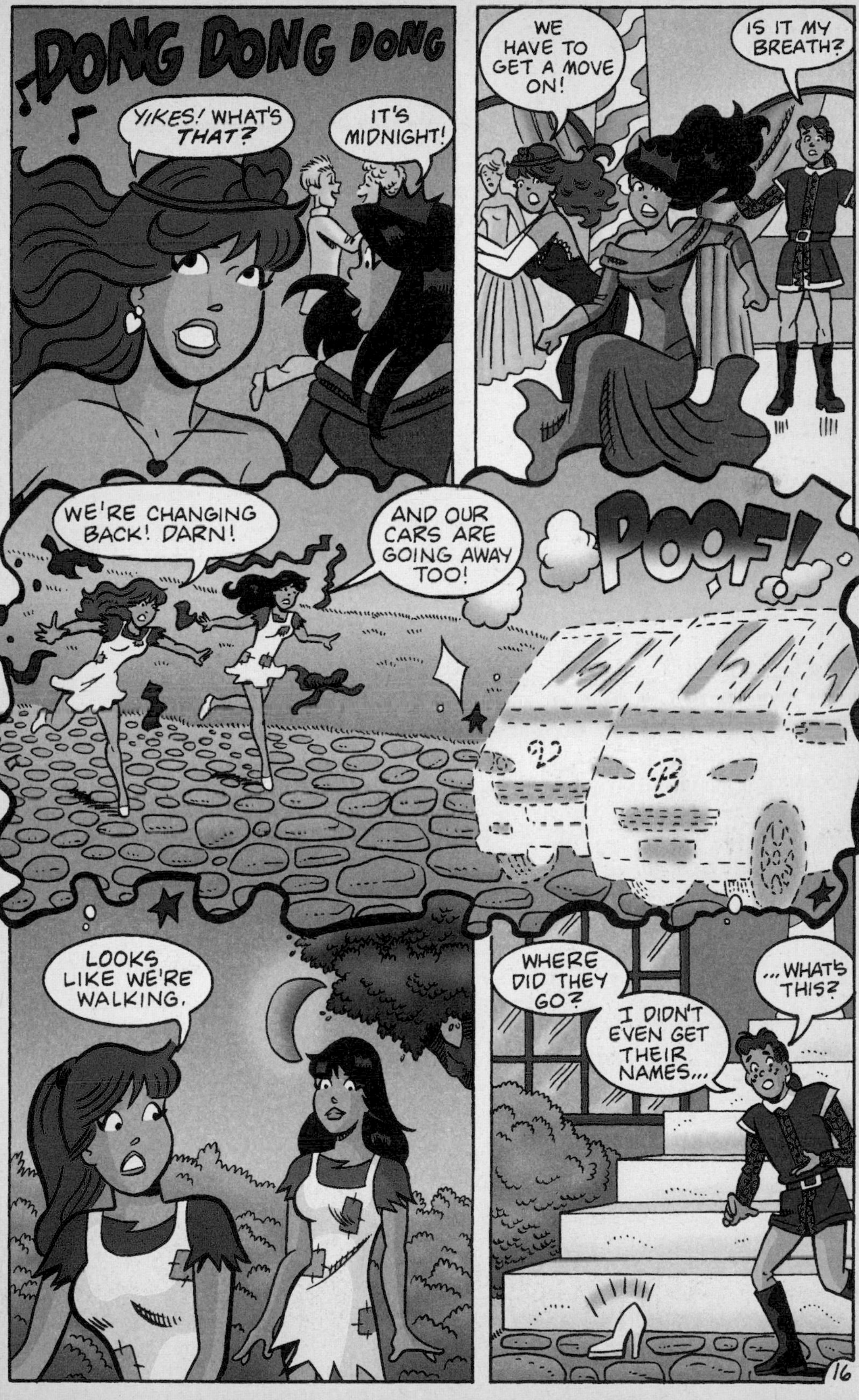
DONG DONG DONG
YIKES! WHAT'S THAT?
IT'S MIDNIGHT!
WE HAVE TO GET A MOVE ON!
IS IT MY BREATH?
WE'RE CHANGING BACK! DARN!
AND OUR CARS ARE GOING AWAY TOO!
POOF!
LOOKS LIKE WE'RE WALKING.
WHERE DID THEY GO?
I DIDN'T EVEN GET THEIR NAMES...
...WHAT'S THIS?

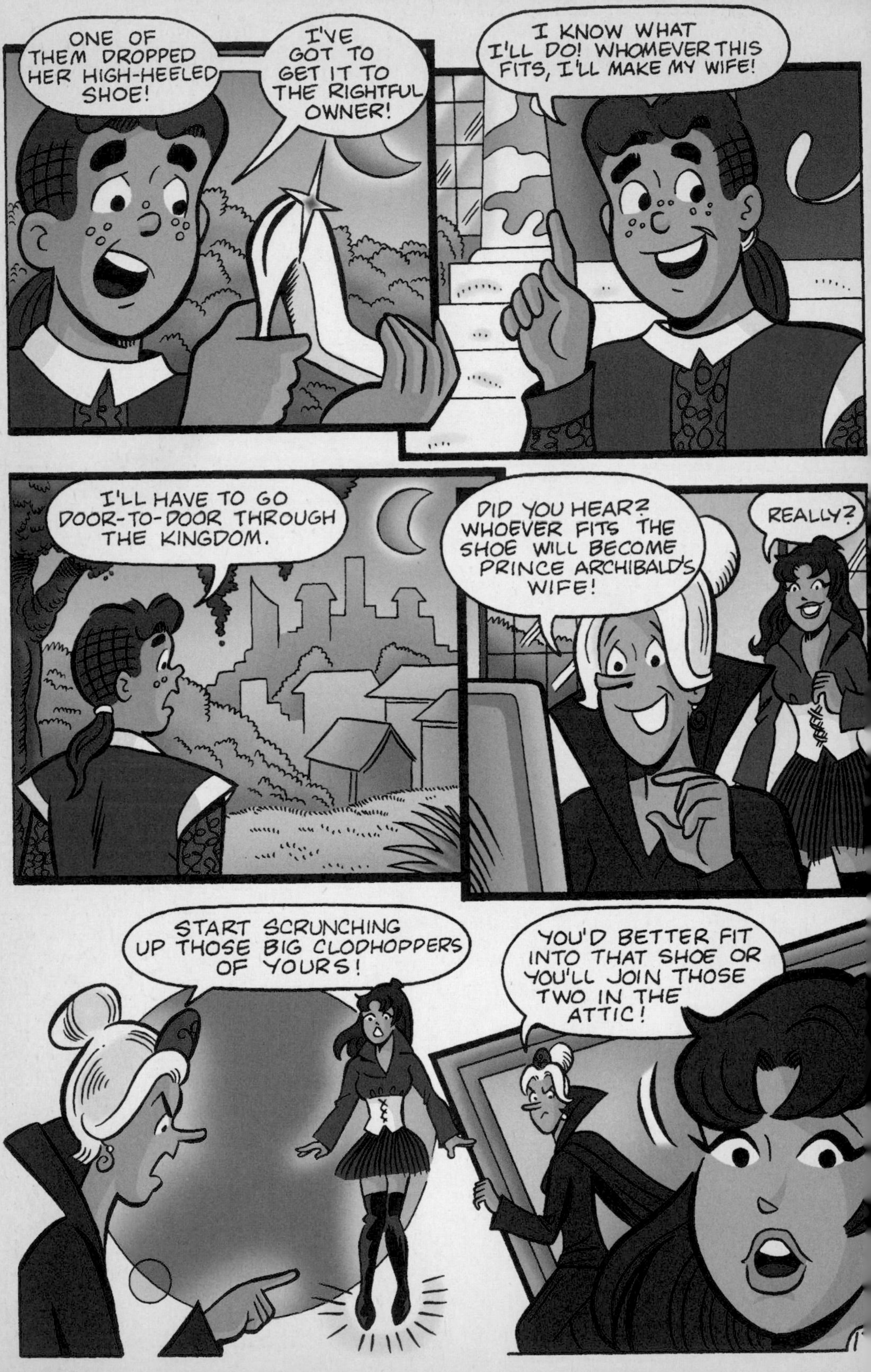
ONE OF THEM DROPPED HER HIGH-HEELED SHOE!
I'VE GOT TO GET IT TO THE RIGHTFUL OWNER!
I KNOW WHAT I'LL DO! WHOMEVER THIS FITS, I'LL MAKE MY WIFE!
I'LL HAVE TO GO DOOR-TO-DOOR THROUGH THE KINGDOM.
DID YOU HEAR? WHOEVER FITS THE SHOE WILL BECOME PRINCE ARCHIBALD'S WIFE!
REALLY?
START SCRUNCHING UP THOSE BIG CLODHOPPERS OF YOURS!
YOU'D BETTER FIT INTO THAT SHOE OR YOU'LL JOIN THOSE TWO IN THE ATTIC!

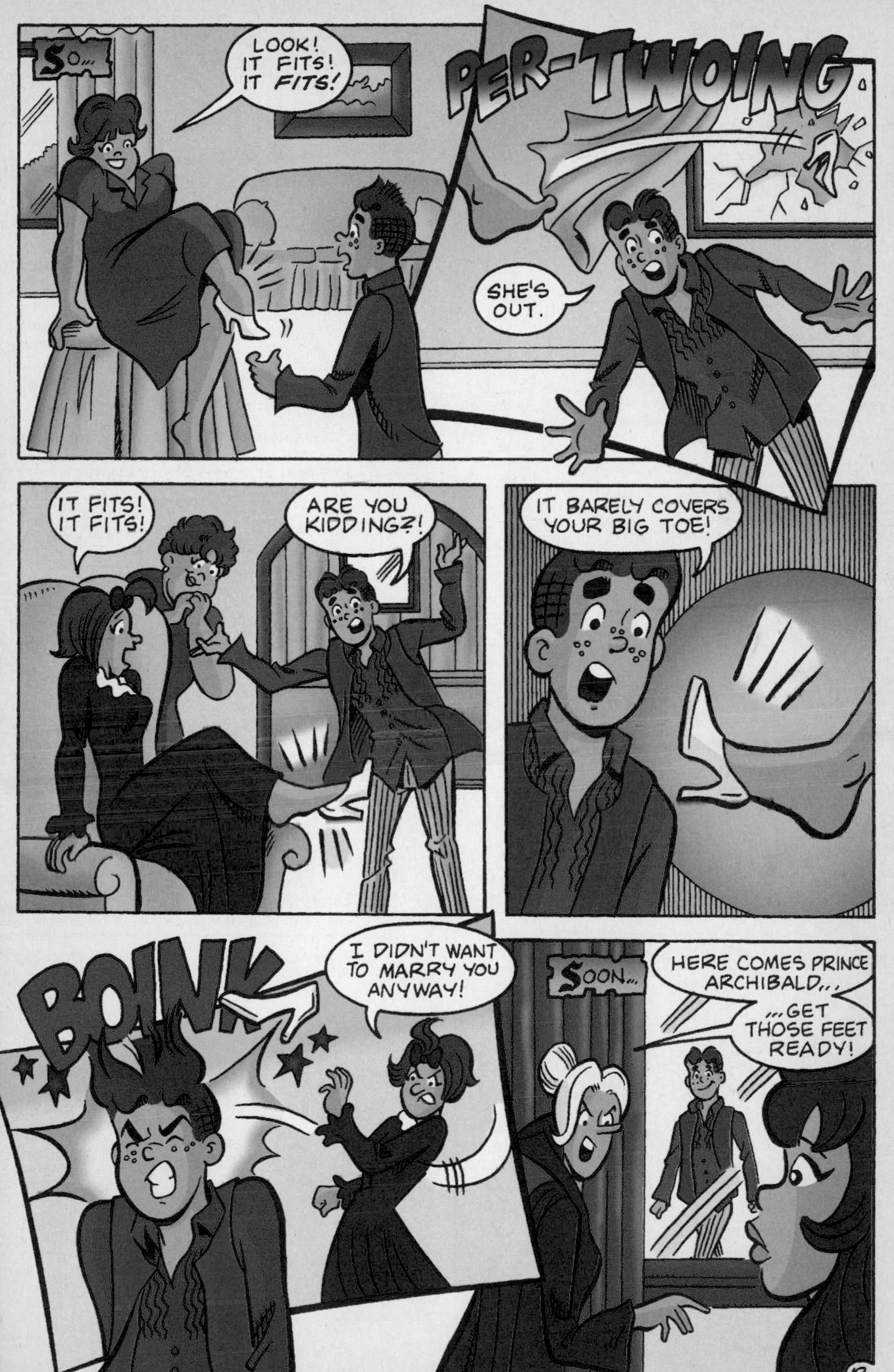

SO...
LOOK! IT FITS! IT *FITS!*
PER-TWOING
SHE'S OUT.
IT FITS! IT FITS!
ARE YOU KIDDING?!
IT BARELY COVERS YOUR BIG TOE!
BOINK
I DIDN'T WANT TO MARRY YOU ANYWAY!
SOON...
HERE COMES PRINCE ARCHIBALD...
...GET THOSE FEET READY!

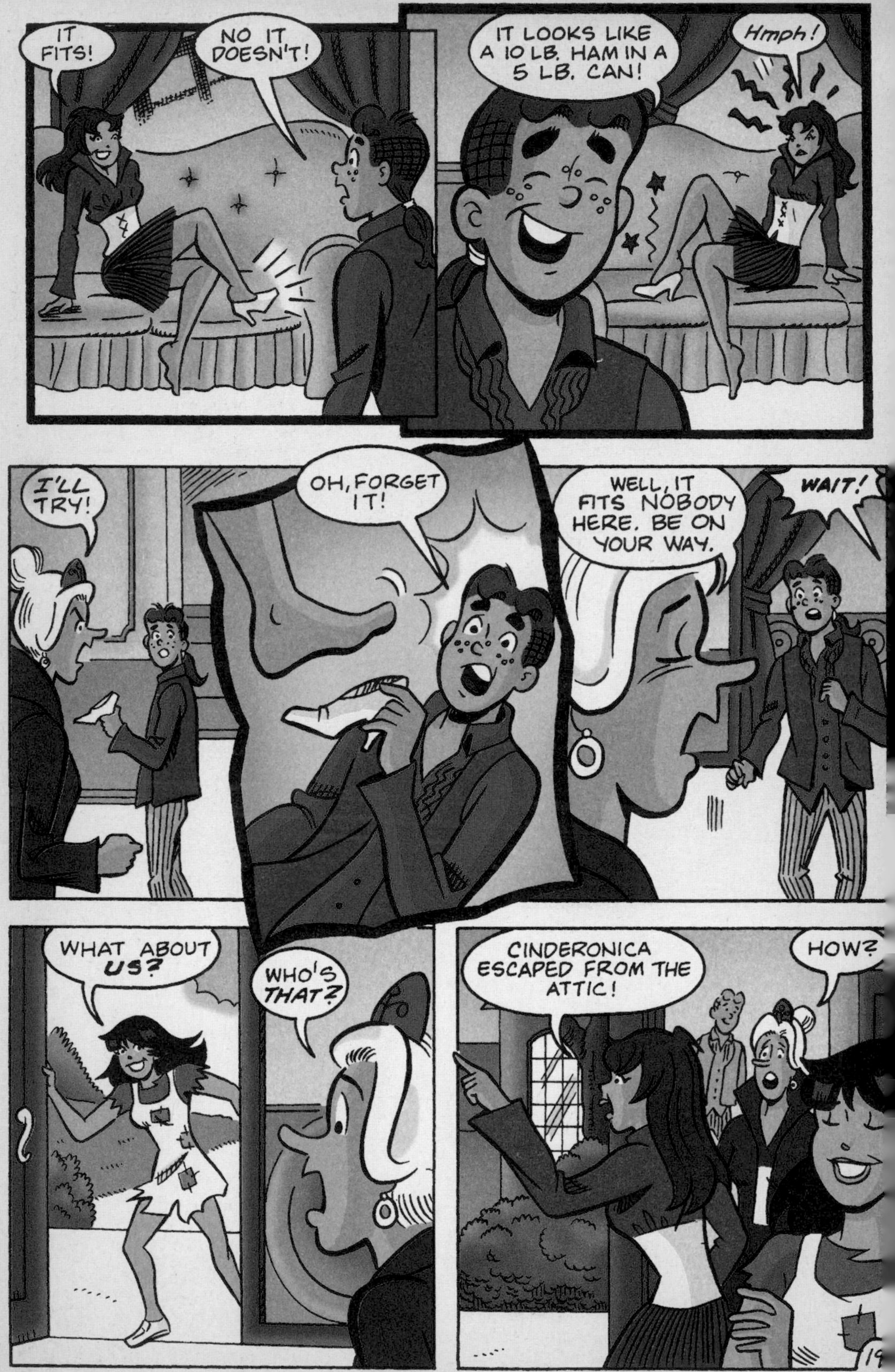
IT FITS!
NO IT DOESN'T!
IT LOOKS LIKE A 10 LB. HAM IN A 5 LB. CAN!
Hmph!
I'LL TRY!
OH, FORGET IT!
WELL, IT FITS NOBODY HERE. BE ON YOUR WAY.
WAIT!
WHAT ABOUT US?
WHO'S THAT?
CINDERONICA ESCAPED FROM THE ATTIC!
HOW?

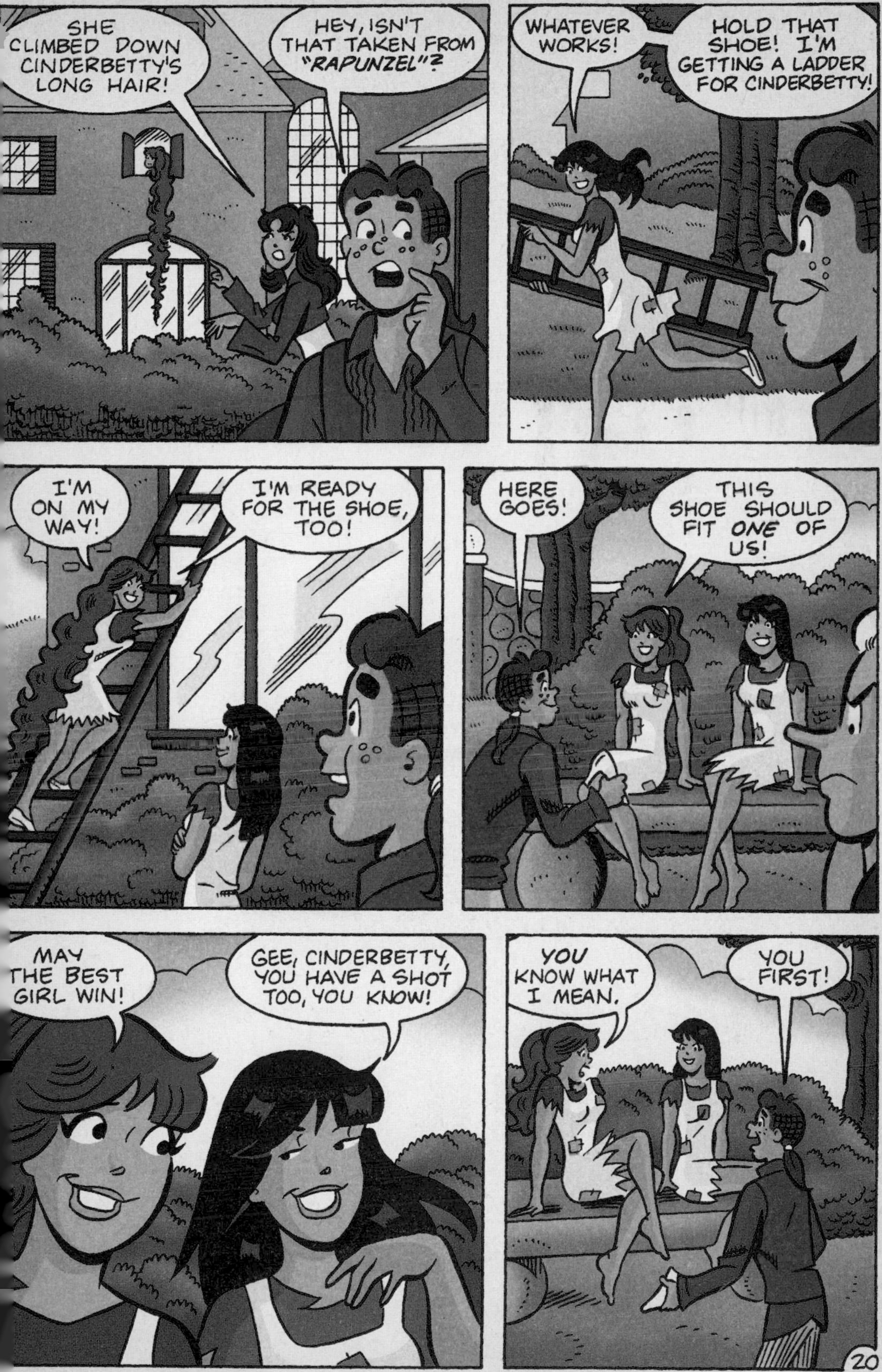
SHE CLIMBED DOWN CINDERBETTY'S LONG HAIR!
HEY, ISN'T THAT TAKEN FROM "RAPUNZEL"?
WHATEVER WORKS!
HOLD THAT SHOE! I'M GETTING A LADDER FOR CINDERBETTY!
I'M ON MY WAY!
I'M READY FOR THE SHOE, TOO!
HERE GOES!
THIS SHOE SHOULD FIT ONE OF US!
MAY THE BEST GIRL WIN!
GEE, CINDERBETTY, YOU HAVE A SHOT TOO, YOU KNOW!
YOU KNOW WHAT I MEAN.
YOU FIRST!

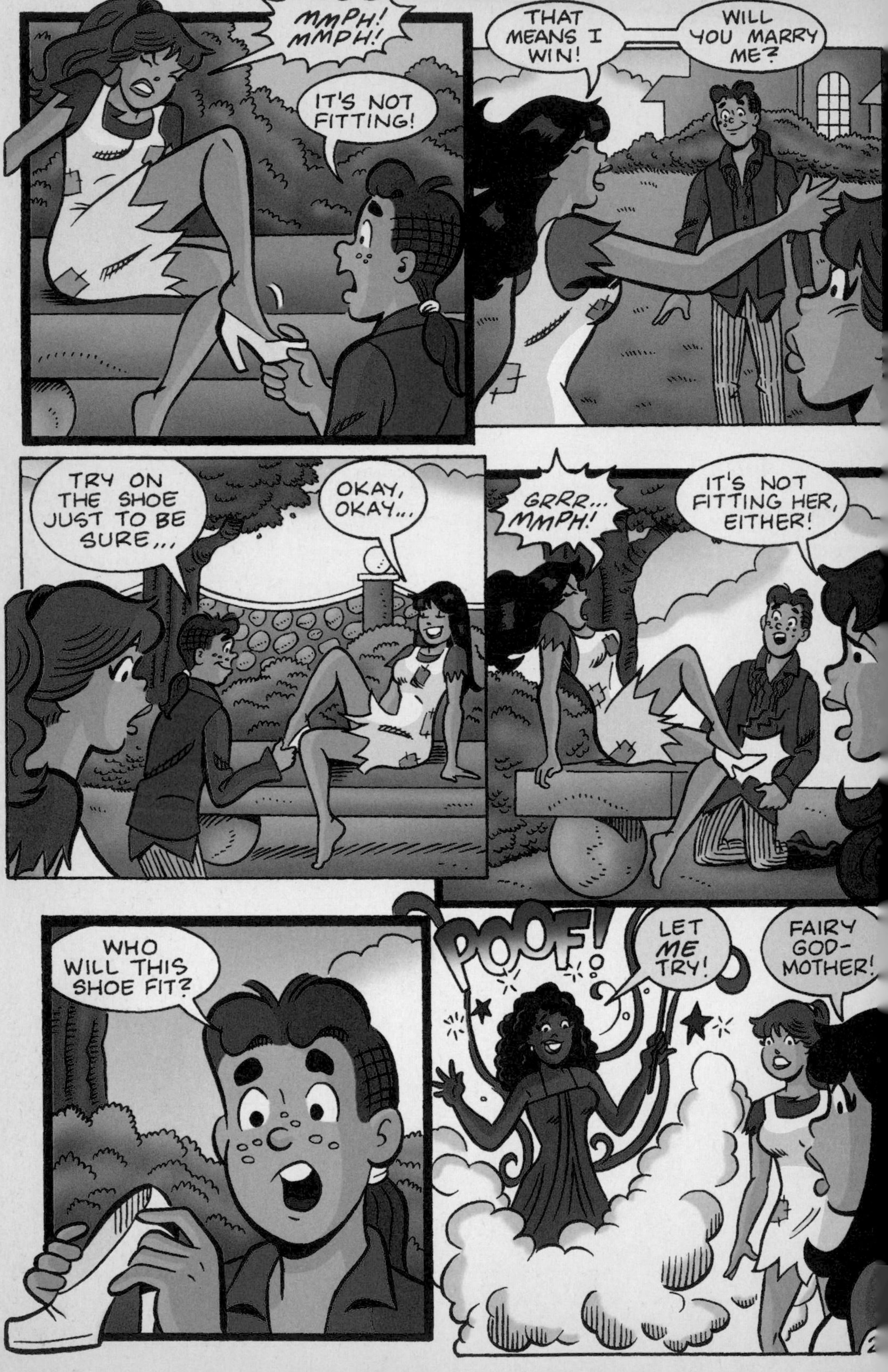
MMPH! MMPH!
IT'S NOT FITTING!
THAT MEANS I WIN!
WILL YOU MARRY ME?
TRY ON THE SHOE JUST TO BE SURE...
OKAY, OKAY...
GRRR... MMPH!
IT'S NOT FITTING HER, EITHER!
WHO WILL THIS SHOE FIT?
POOF!
LET ME TRY!
FAIRY GOD-MOTHER!

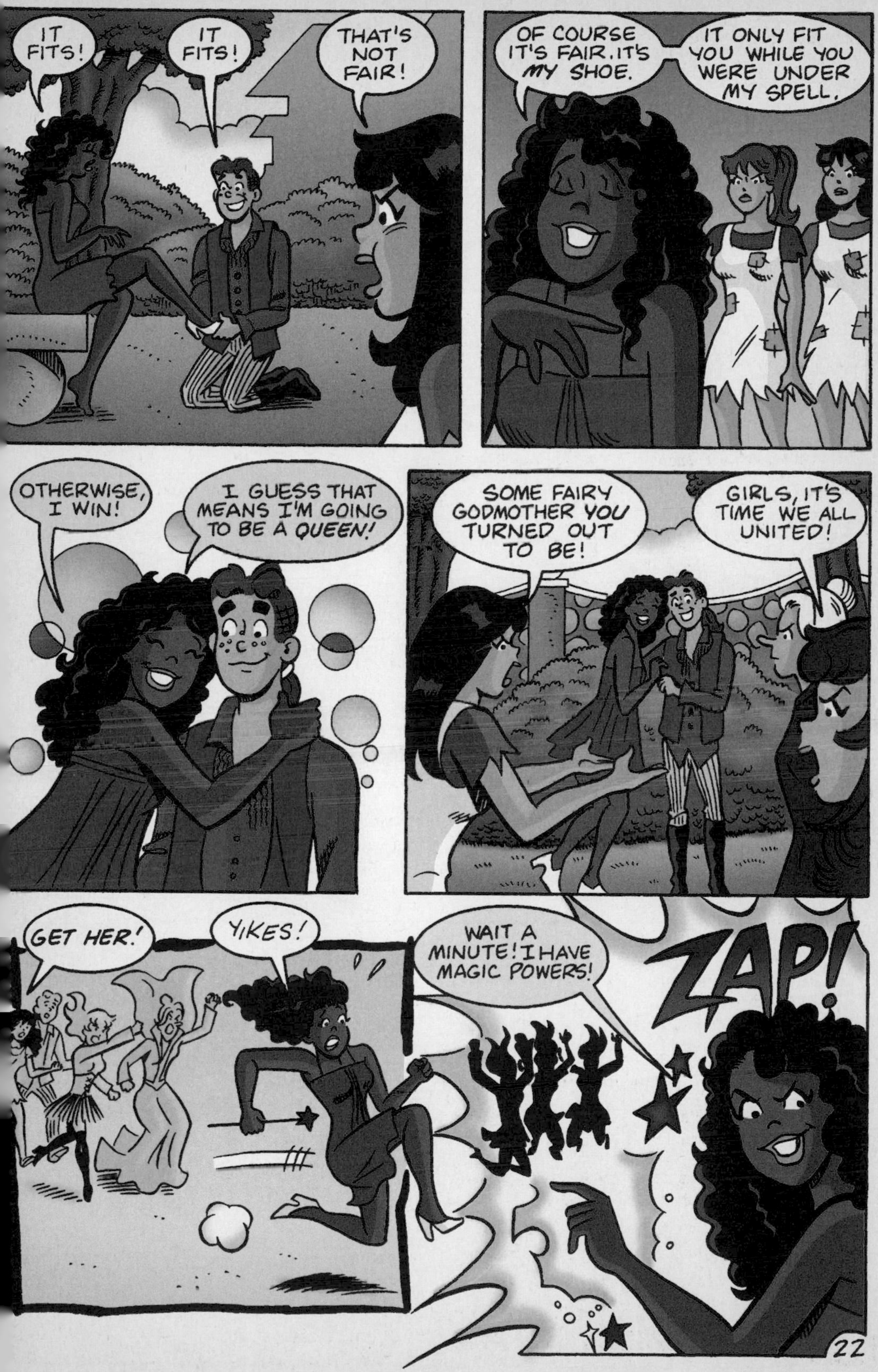
IT FITS!
IT FITS!
THAT'S NOT FAIR!
OF COURSE IT'S FAIR. IT'S MY SHOE.
IT ONLY FIT YOU WHILE YOU WERE UNDER MY SPELL.
OTHERWISE, I WIN!
I GUESS THAT MEANS I'M GOING TO BE A QUEEN!
SOME FAIRY GODMOTHER YOU TURNED OUT TO BE!
GIRLS, IT'S TIME WE ALL UNITED!
GET HER!
YIKES!
WAIT A MINUTE! I HAVE MAGIC POWERS!
ZAP!

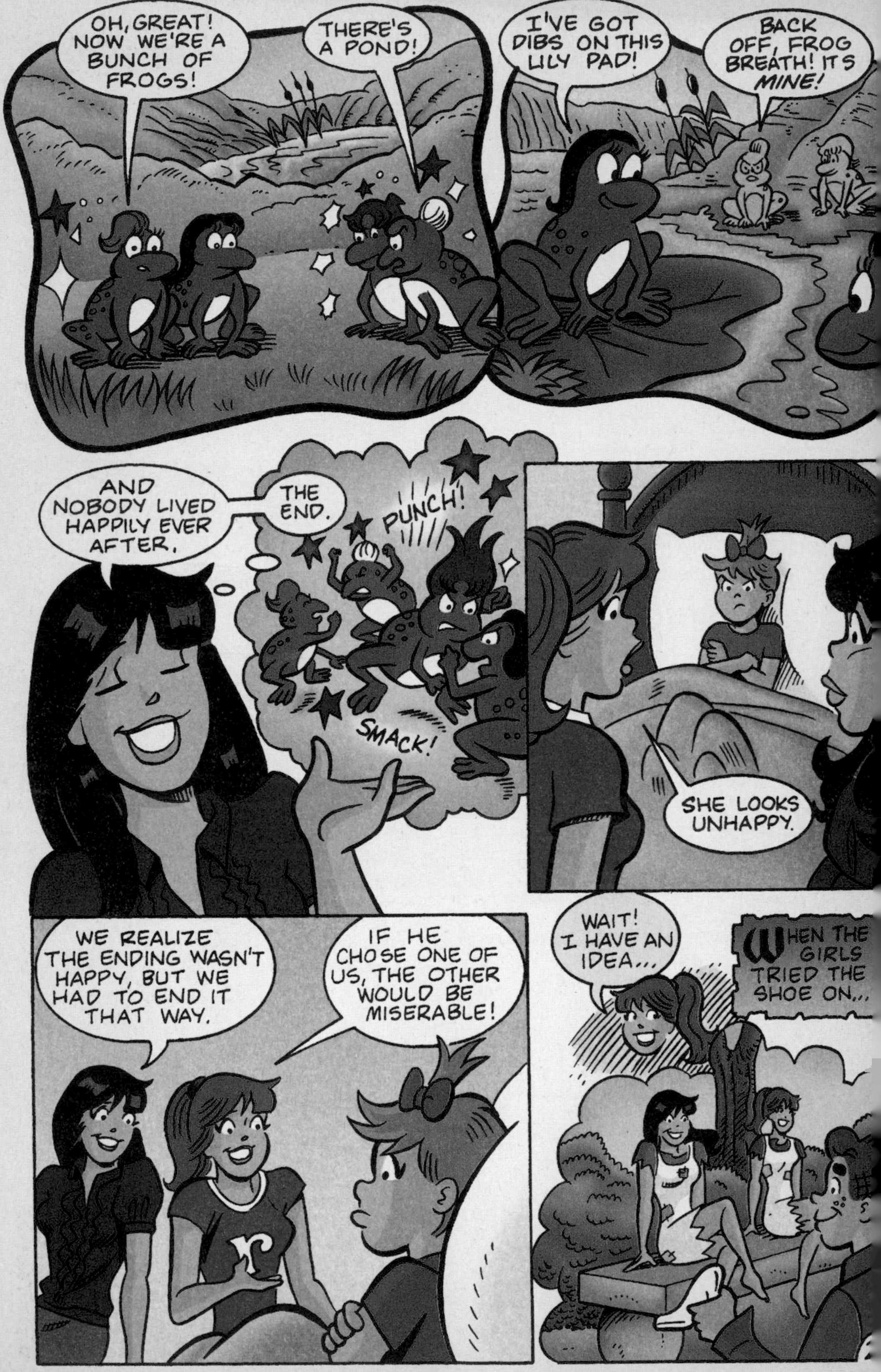
OH, GREAT! NOW WE'RE A BUNCH OF FROGS!
THERE'S A POND!
I'VE GOT DIBS ON THIS LILY PAD!
BACK OFF, FROG BREATH! IT'S *MINE!*
AND NOBODY LIVED HAPPILY EVER AFTER.
THE END.
PUNCH!
SMACK!
SHE LOOKS UNHAPPY.
WE REALIZE THE ENDING WASN'T HAPPY, BUT WE HAD TO END IT THAT WAY.
IF HE CHOSE ONE OF US, THE OTHER WOULD BE MISERABLE!
WAIT! I HAVE AN IDEA...
WHEN THE GIRLS TRIED THE SHOE ON...

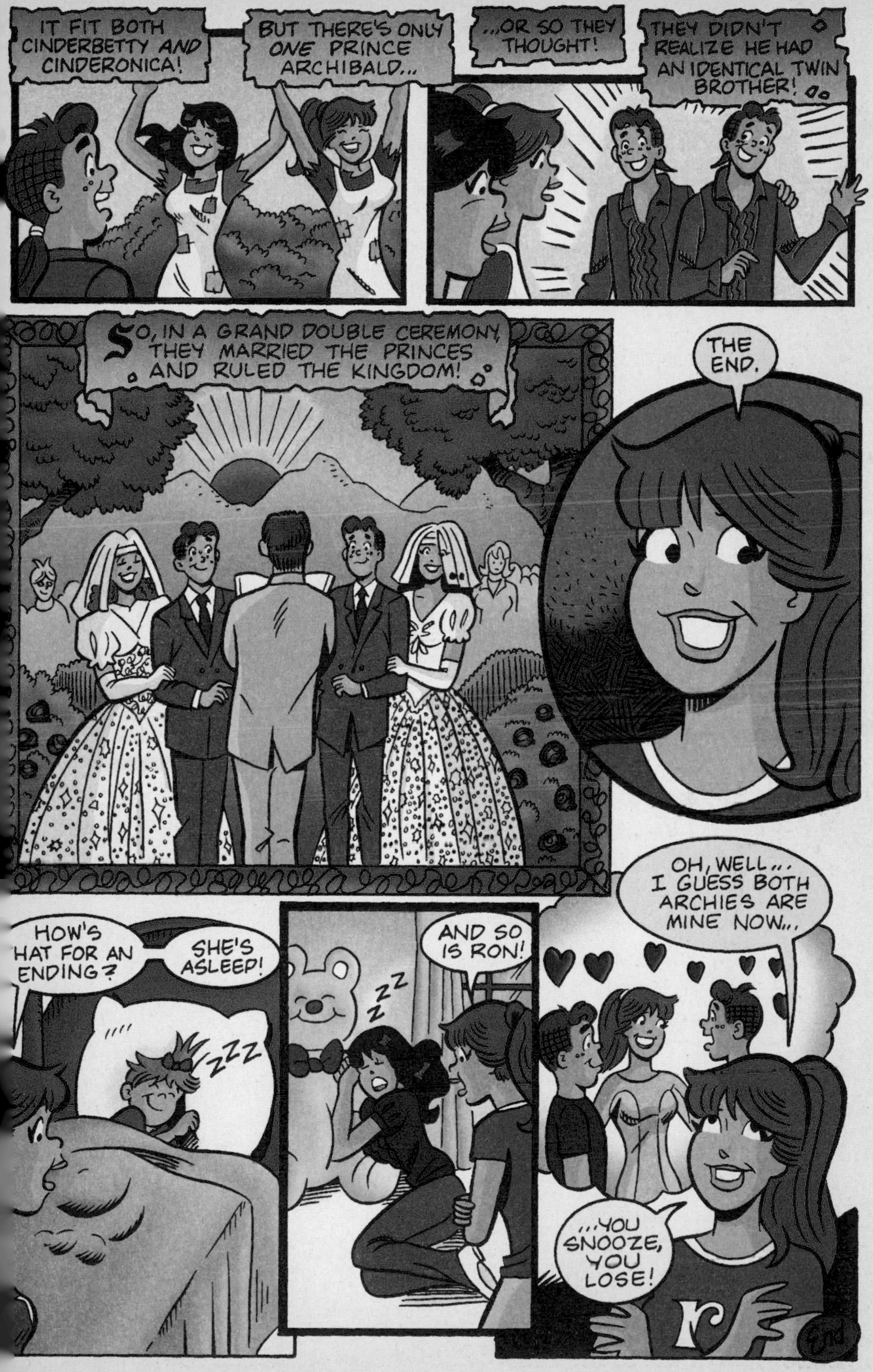
IT FIT BOTH CINDERBETTY AND CINDERONICA!
BUT THERE'S ONLY ONE PRINCE ARCHIBALD...
...OR SO THEY THOUGHT!
THEY DIDN'T REALIZE HE HAD AN IDENTICAL TWIN BROTHER!
SO, IN A GRAND DOUBLE CEREMONY, THEY MARRIED THE PRINCES AND RULED THE KINGDOM!
THE END.
HOW'S THAT FOR AN ENDING?
SHE'S ASLEEP!
ZZZ
AND SO IS RON!
ZZZ
OH, WELL... I GUESS BOTH ARCHIES ARE MINE NOW...
...YOU SNOOZE, YOU LOSE!
End

Afterword

Writer and artist Dan Parent has spent years taking Betty & Veronica on all kinds of wild adventures. Now, in his own words, he'll show you what was happening behind the scenes when he decided to make their fairy tale dreams become a reality.

It's always fun doing parodies of pop culture with the Archie characters, and even more fun taking on classic stories, like the ones in this book. It's a testament to the strength of the Archie characters how well they translate into these old classics. The tough part is picking which classic tales to interpret, since there are so many. I had it narrowed down to about a dozen but picked the following four for no reason other than they grabbed my attention the most.

"The Wizard of Oz" is probably the most well known of all the stories, and I knew that it would make for an eye-grabbing image with the gang as those characters on the cover. Which I think turned out to be true, considering how many of those books I signed when that original B&V Digest came out! You can always tell the popularity of a book by how many people show up at conventions with a copy of a certain book, and that issue was a biggie. The story basically wrote itself. Nobody but Betty could play Dorothy, and with Archie as her closest ally, the Scarecrow was also a natural. Jughead looked like the Tin Man, so that was enough for me. The Cowardly Lion could have been played by someone like Big Moose, but Reggie seemed to fit the bill.

And of course, Veronica as the Wicked Witch, albeit a very stylish and beautiful one, varies from the original story, but hey, that's what artistic license is for!

In choosing another story, "Alice in Wonderland" is my favorite, even if it's not as widely popular as "The Wizard of Oz." Of course, the wildly successful Tim Burton version has somewhat changed that. The great thing about Alice is that it's just plain weird. The story was always bizarre, and still is. Betty of course as the main character, since she personifies that relatable center to this insane world. We had to link the rest of the gang to these bizarre characters which wasn't all that hard once we got started. I try not to stereotype by making Veronica the arch-villain at all times, but who else is best suited to be the Queen of Hearts? Reggie and Jughead as Tweedle Dee and Tweedle Dum weren't much of a stretch. And Archie's always late for everything back in Riverdale, so he works well as the White Rabbit who's always late in Wonderland! I have to say, the Cheshire Cat is disturbing enough as is, but morphing that character with Hot Dog was even weirder!

Next up, it was time to do a classic fairy tale, so "Sleeping Beauty" fit that bill. Betty is once again the heroine, with Veronica as the evil Queen. I thought about having Cheryl Blossom as the Queen and Veronica as one of the good witches who watches over Sleeping Beauty, but that would have put Veronica in a small, supporting role, and we know that wouldn't work at all!

Lastly, I had to come up with a story where Veronica wasn't the evil nemesis, or at least not in the same way as in the other stories. So I changed "Cinderella" into "Cinderellas," so we could have two heroines. Now we can have Cinderbetty and Cinderonica fighting over Prince Archibald. Now there's a change of pace! And Cheryl could play the evil stepsister in all her evil glory. I liked having two Cinderellas battling over that glass slipper, fighting over the prince, yet supporting each other when times got tough. It sort of added a fun angle to the old story.

So, there you have it. My takes on these classic stories. Hopefully I'll do more in the future. Can't you see " Betty and the Beast," "Romeo and B or V," and " Little Red Riding Cooper"? Well, I can!

Dan Parent

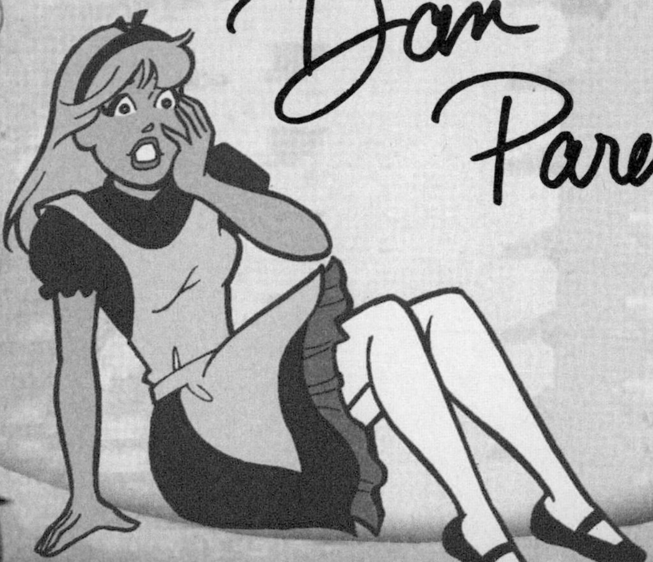

Sketch Book

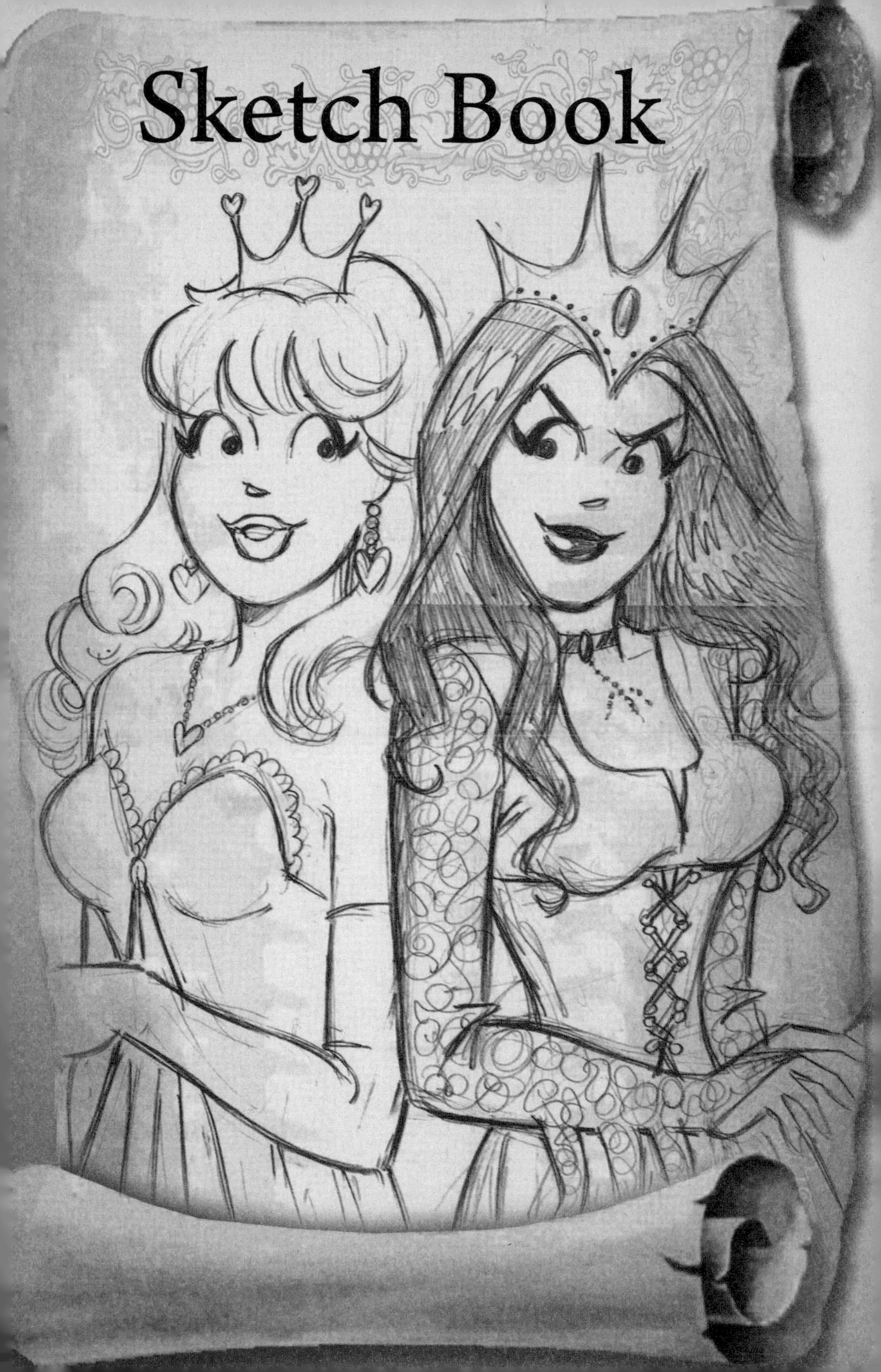

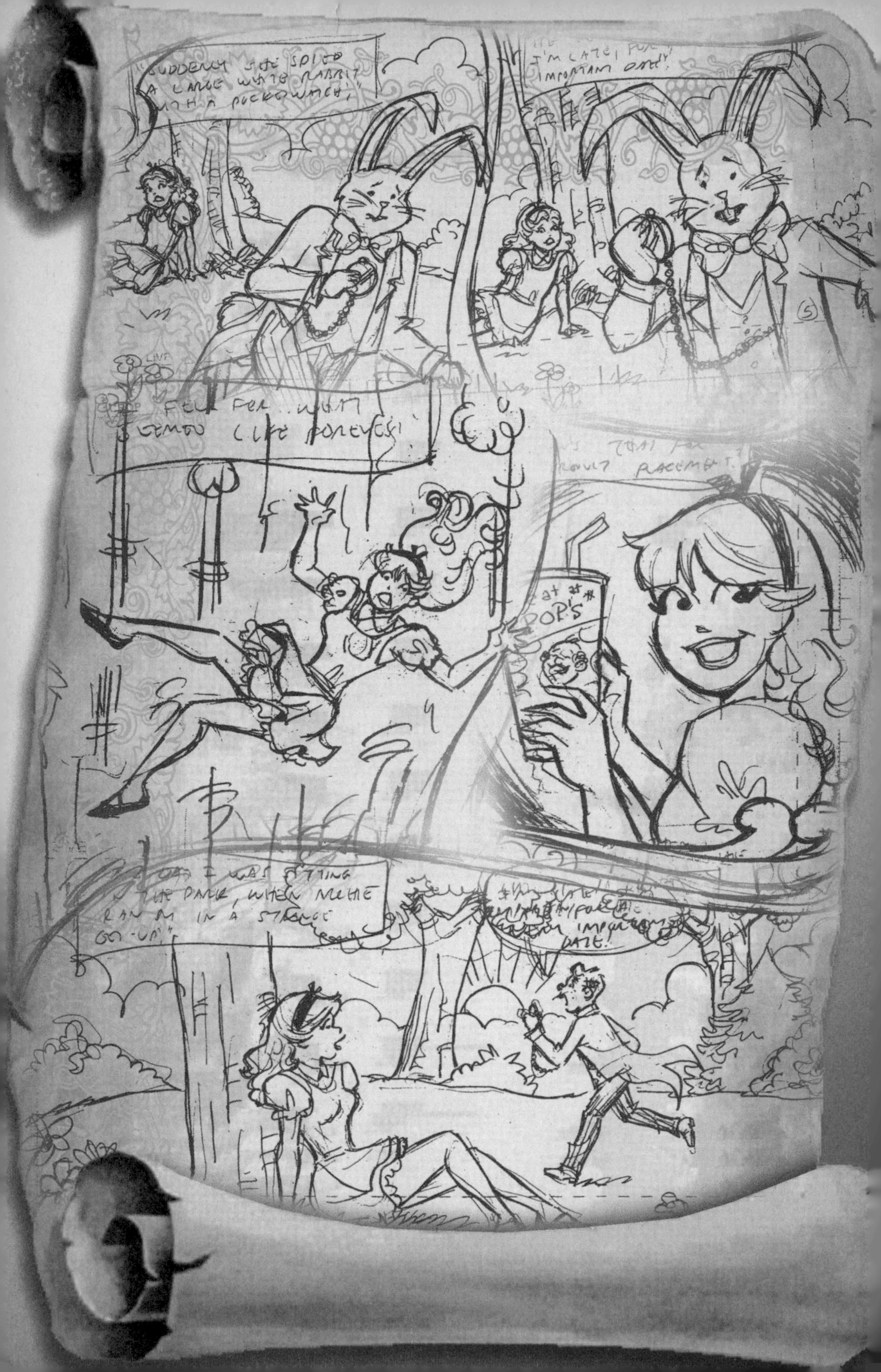
POP'S

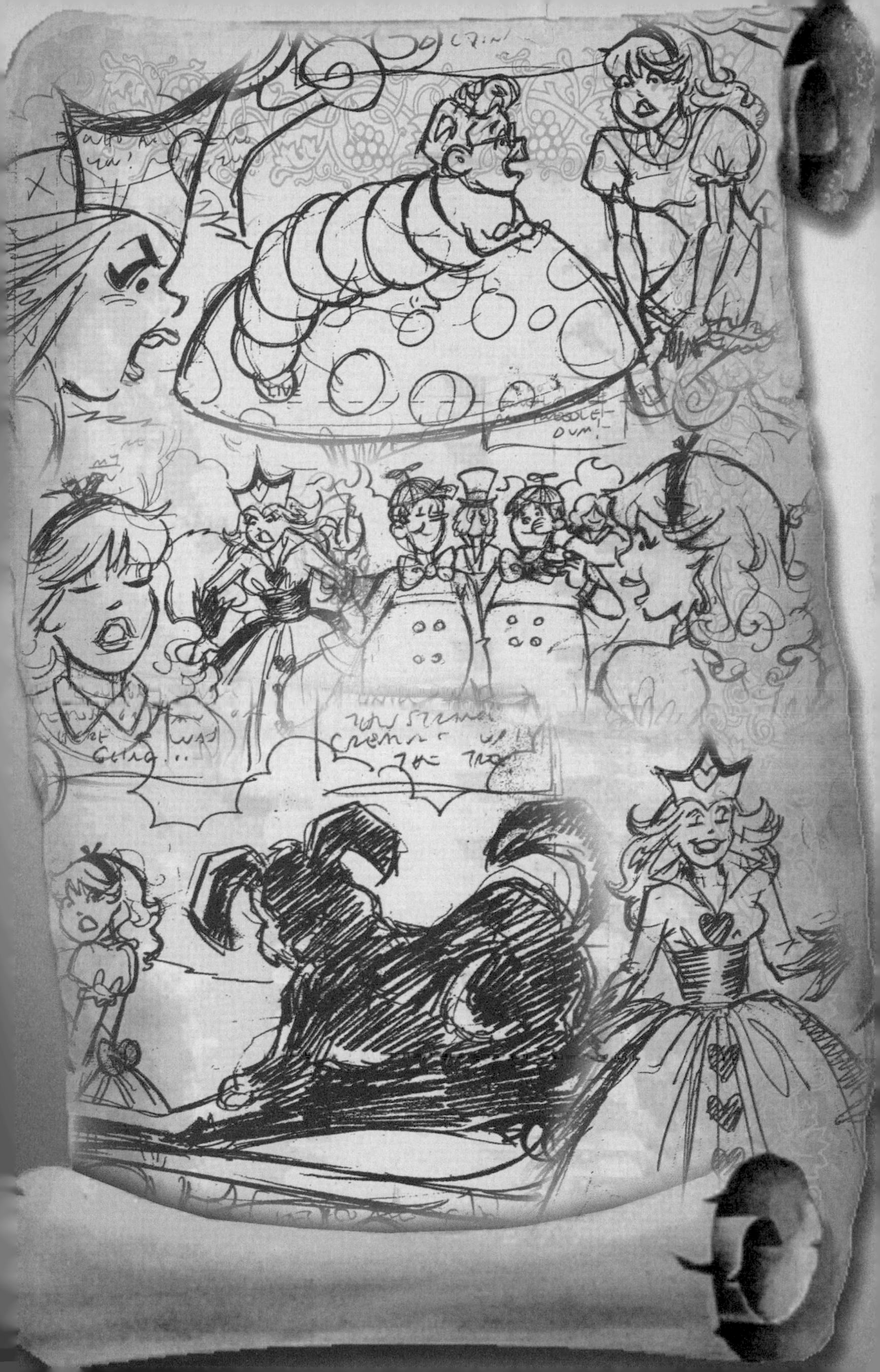
DUM!

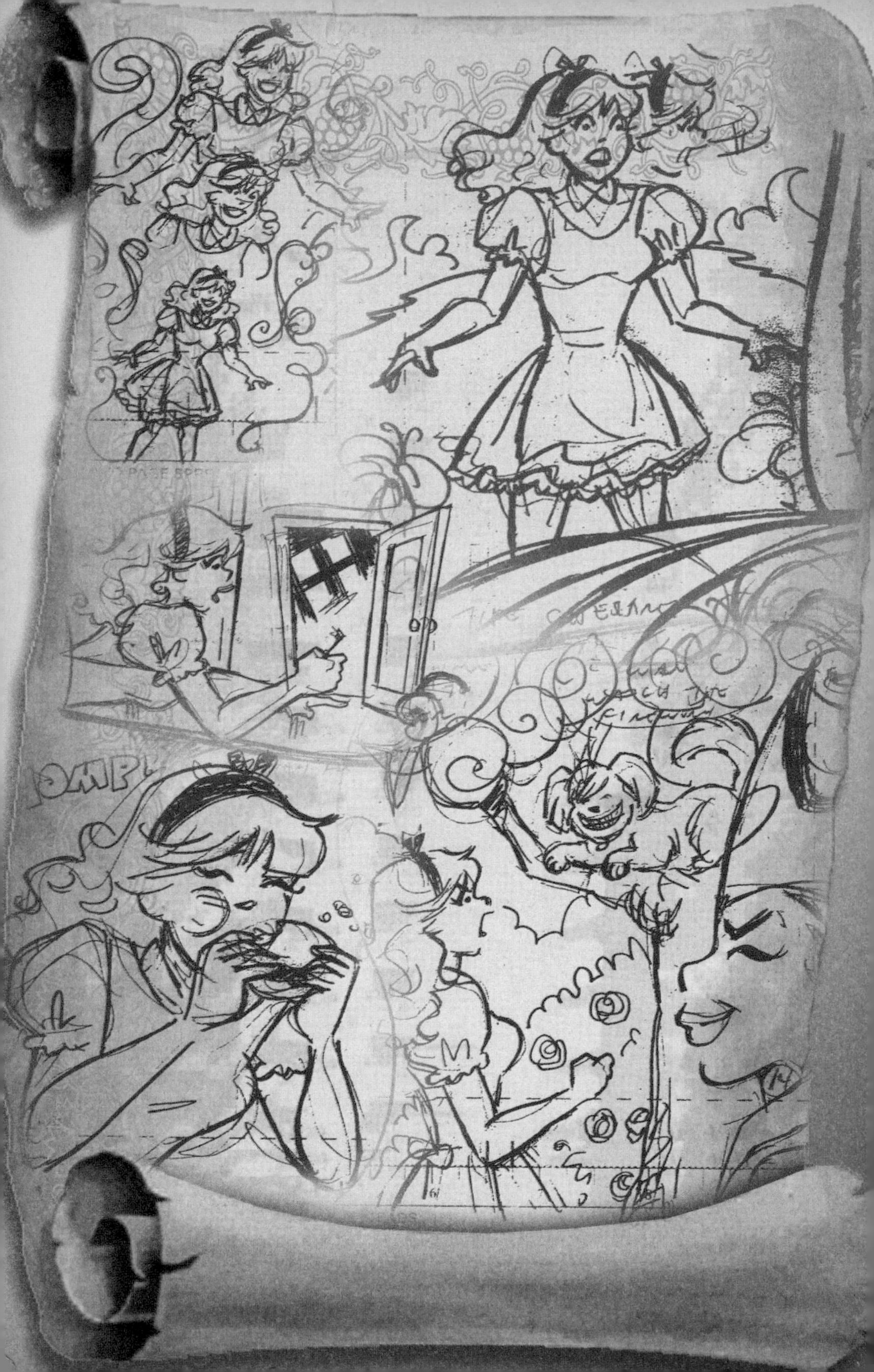

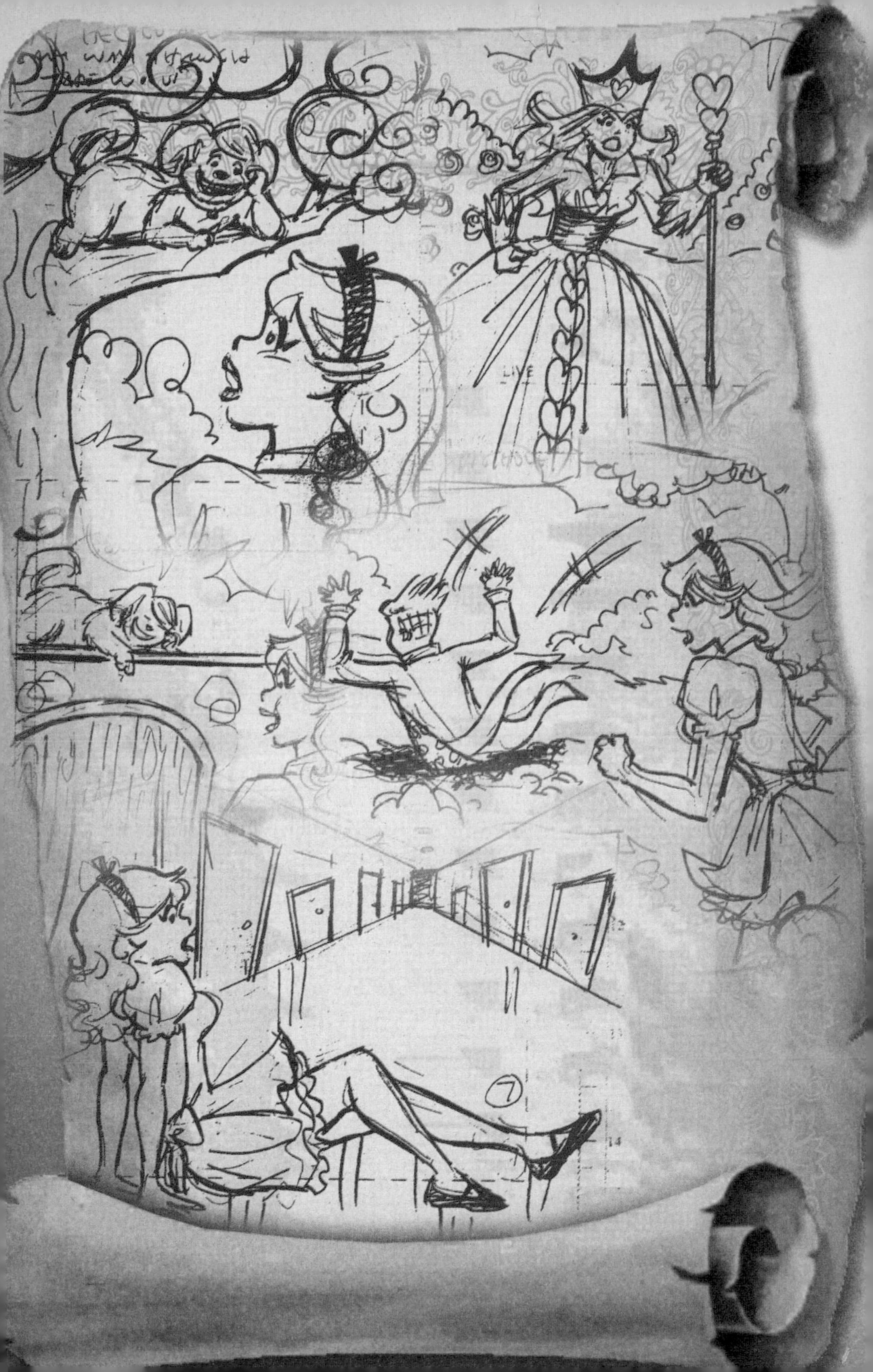

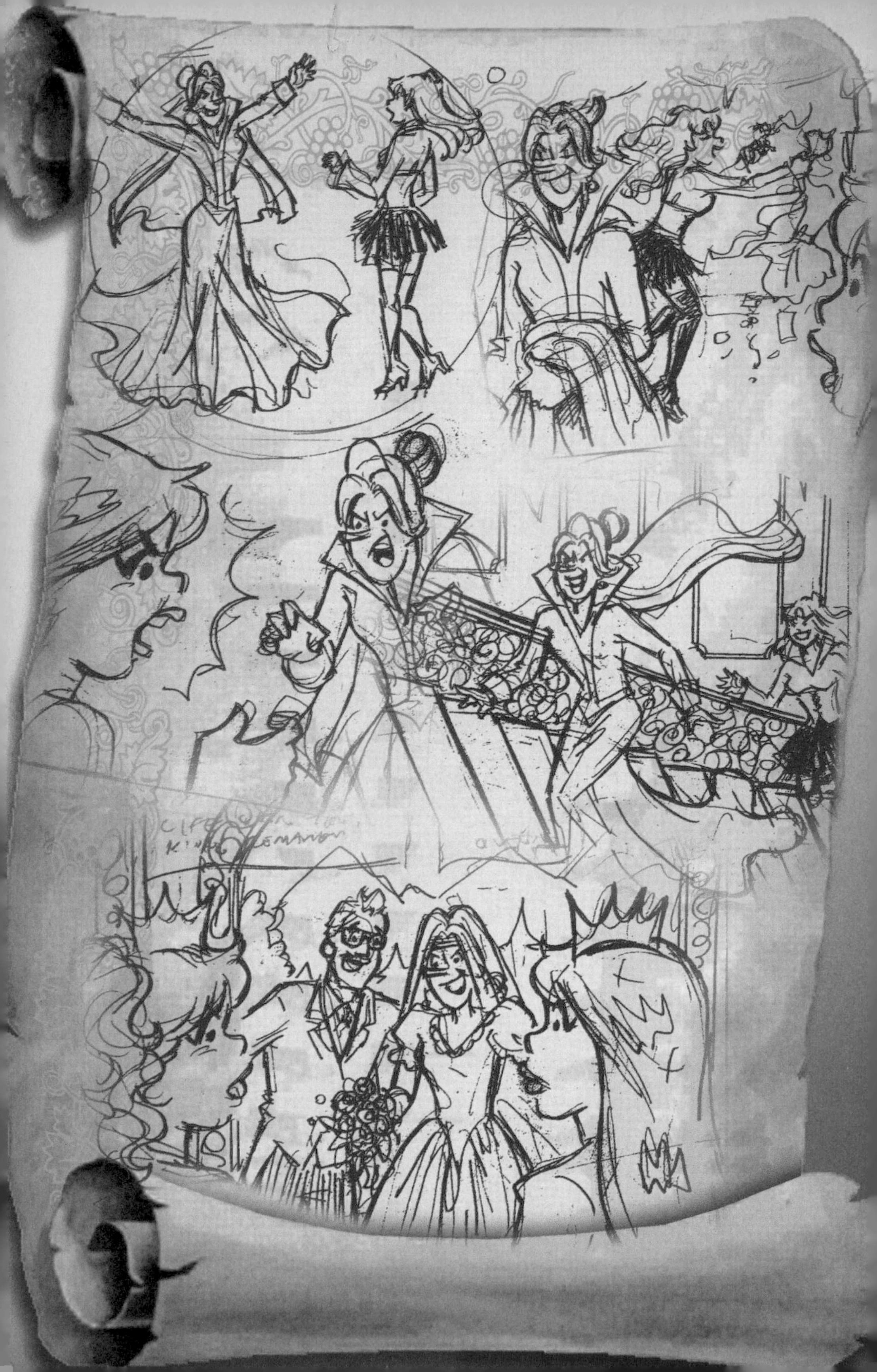

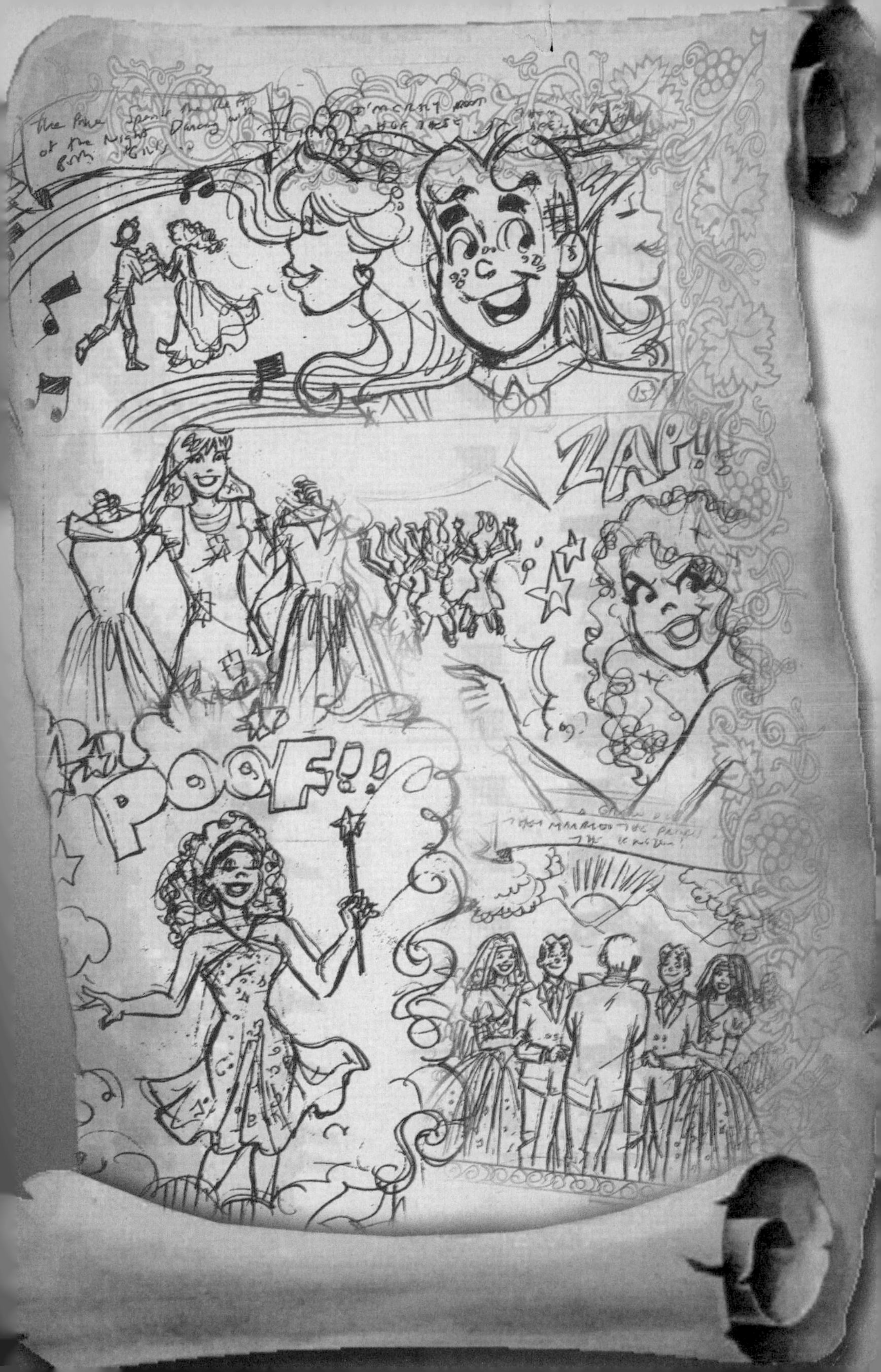
ZAP!!
POOF!!

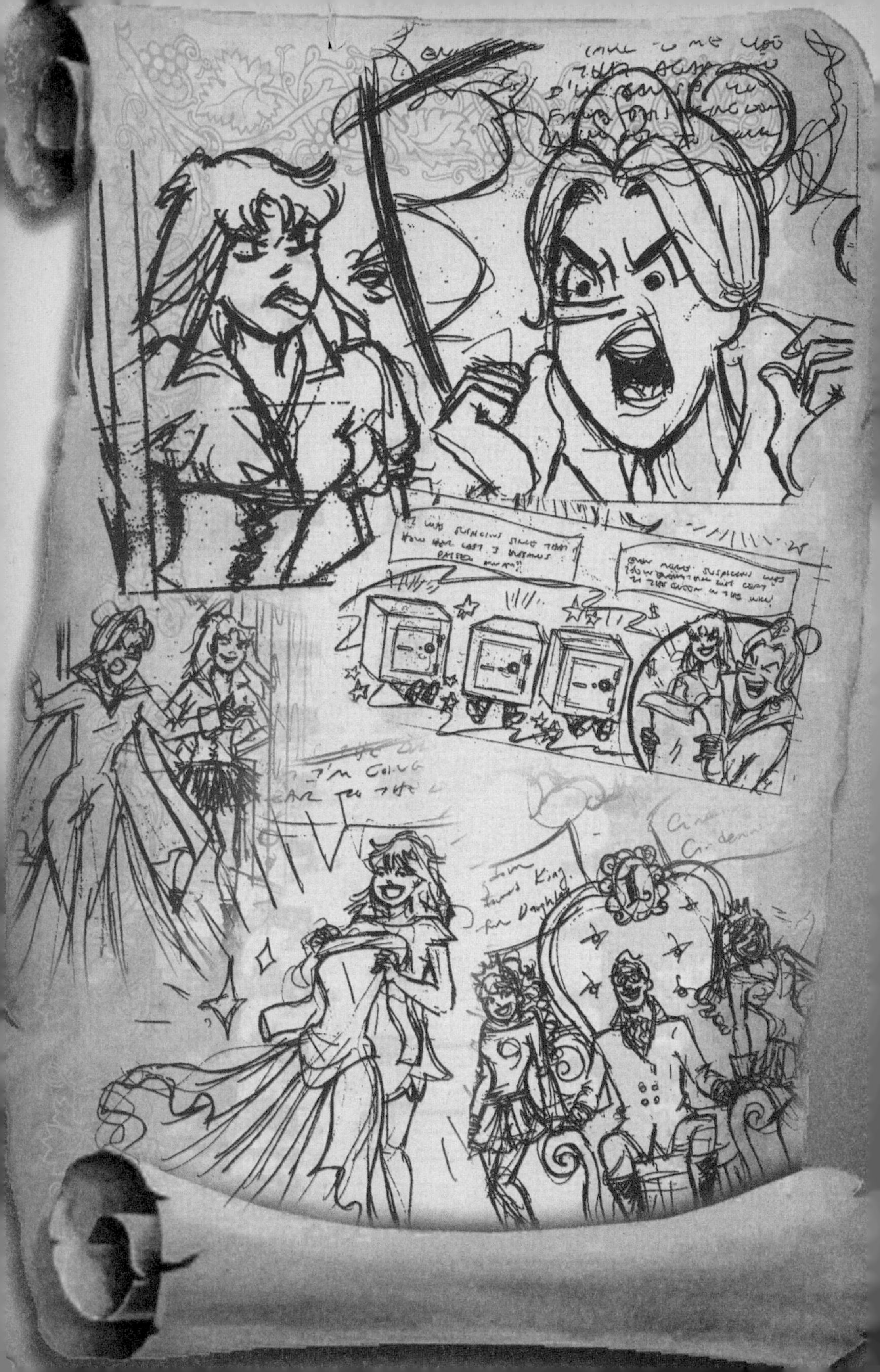

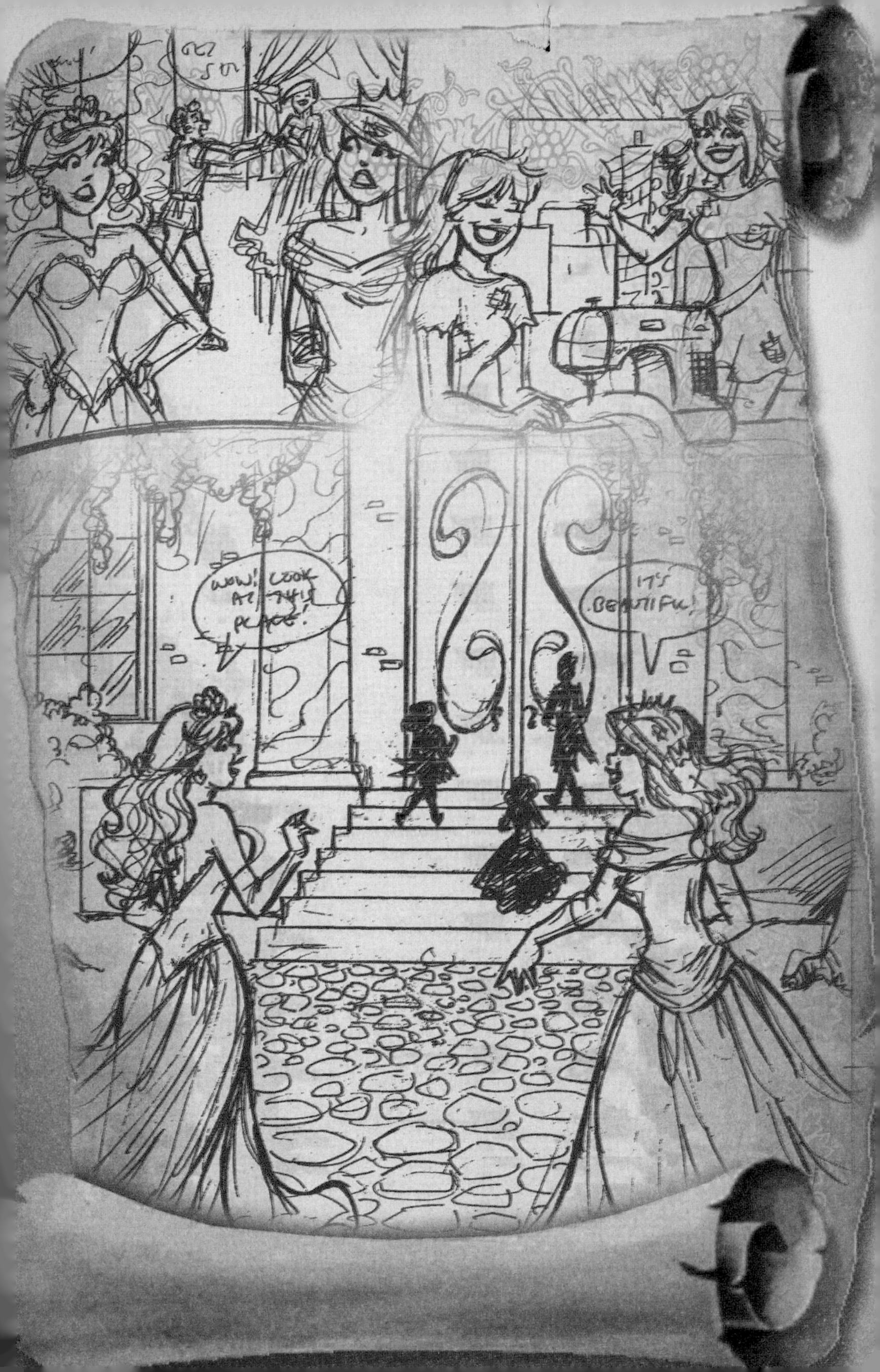
WOW! LOOK AT THIS PLACE!
IT'S BEAUTIFUL!

Archie COMICS

LOOK FOR THESE AND OTHER GRAPHIC NOVELS AT COMIC SHOPS AND BOOKSTORES EVERYWHERE!

AVAILABLE ONLINE AT ARCHIECOMICS.COM

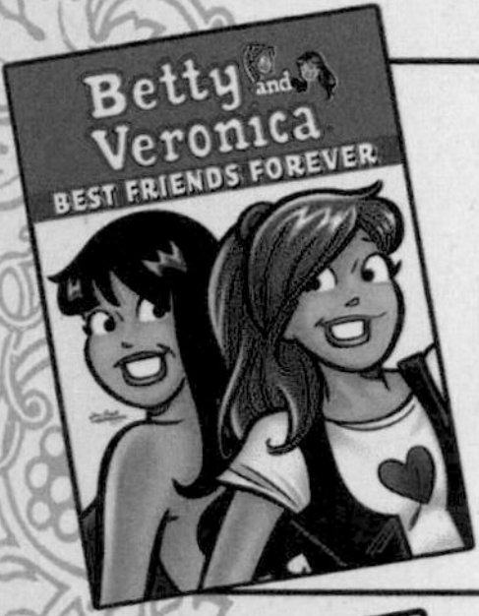
Betty and Veronica
BEST FRIENDS FOREVER

Betty & Veronica: Best Friends Forever

Betty & Veronica prove that when it comes to BFFs they're among the best!

ISBN: 978-1-879794-76-4

Betty & Veronica: Prom Princesses

Dresses, dancing, and plenty of drama - it must be time for the prom!

ISBN: 978-1-936975-30-3

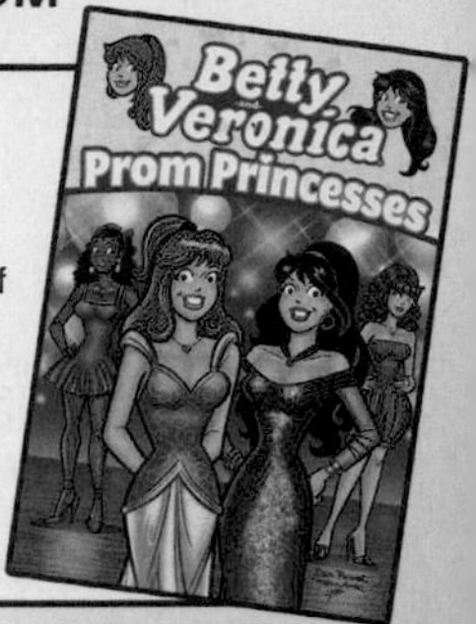
Betty Veronica
Prom Princesses

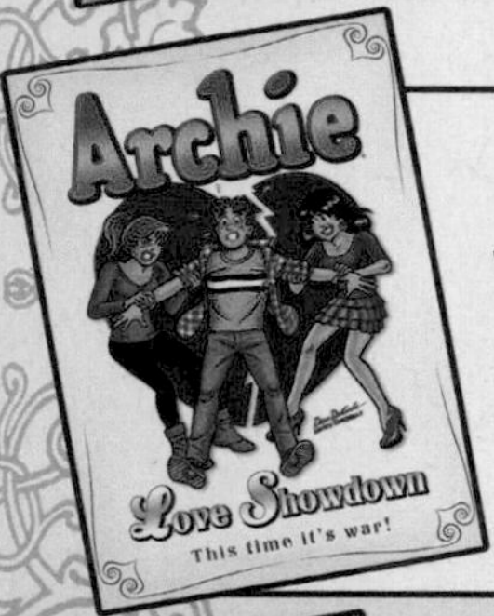
Archie
Love Showdown
This time it's war!

Archie: Love Showdown

Who will it be? Betty? Veronica? The eternal love triangle is torn apart when Cheryl Blossom enters the fray!

ISBN: 978-1-936975-21-1

Jinx

Jinx isn't so Li'l anymore! She's all grown up and off to high school.

Softcover ISBN: 978-1-879794-91-7

Hardcover ISBN: 978-1-936975-00-6

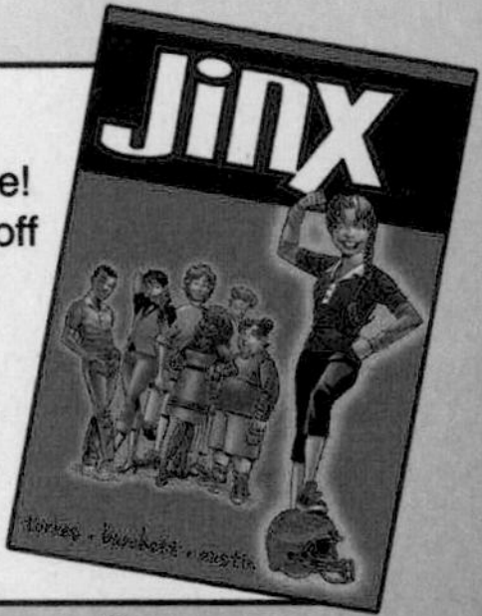
JINX

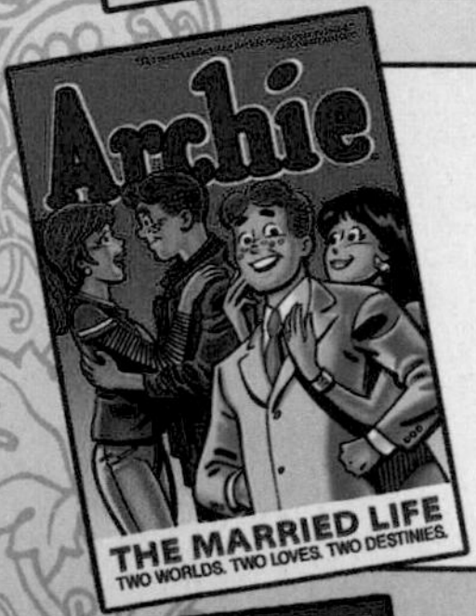
Archie
THE MARRIED LIFE
TWO WORLDS. TWO LOVES. TWO DESTINIES.

Archie: The Married Life Book One

Collecting the first 6 parts of the critically acclaimed Archie Marries Betty and Archie Marries Veronica storylines.

ISBN: 978-1-936975-01-3

Archie: The Married Life Book Two

Collecting parts 7-12 of the critically acclaimed Archie Marries Betty and Archie Marries Veronica storylines.

ISBN: 978-1-879794-99-3

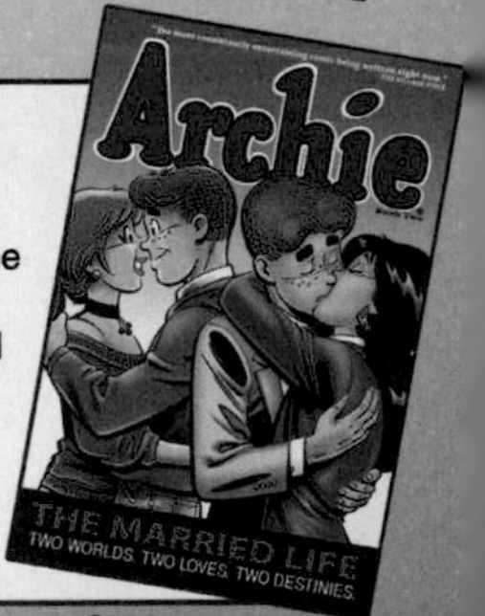
Archie
THE MARRIED LIFE
TWO WORLDS. TWO LOVES. TWO DESTINIES.

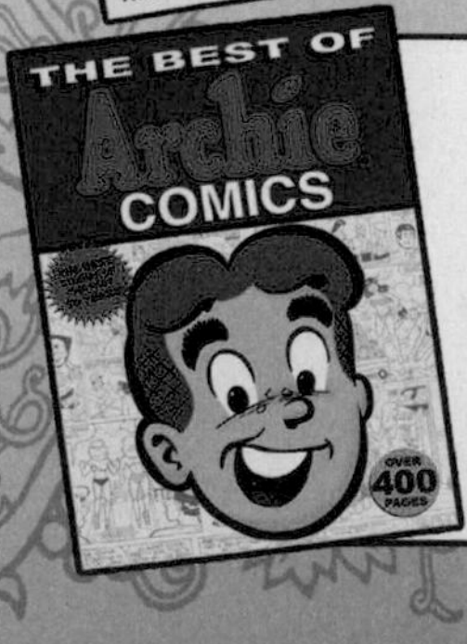
THE BEST OF
Archie
COMICS
OVER 400 PAGES

The Best of Archie Comics Book One & Book Two

Archie, Jughead, Betty & Veronica return with two fantastic volumes of classic comics and stories.

Book One: ISBN: 978-1-879794-84-9

Book Two: ISBN: 978-1-936975-20-4

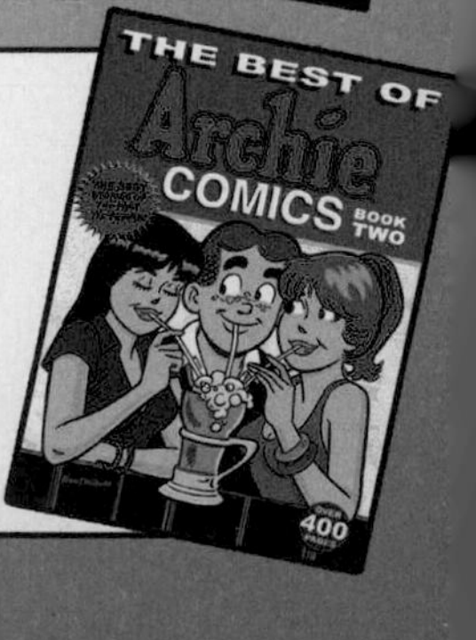
THE BEST OF
Archie
COMICS BOOK TWO
400 PAGES